Emma Hannigan

The Secrets We Share

HACHETTE
BOOKS
IRELAND

First published in Ireland in 2015
by Hachette Book Ireland

First published in paperback in Ireland in 2015
by Hachette Books Ireland

Cataloguing in Publication Data is available from the British Library

ISBN 978 1 4447 5400 1

Typeset in Bembo by Palimpsest Book Production Limited,
Falkirk, Stirlingshire
Printed and bound in Great Britain by Clays Ltd, St Ives plc

MIX
Paper from
responsible sources
FSC
www.fsc.org   FSC® C104740

Hachette Books Ireland's policy is to use papers that are natural, renewable
and recyclable products and made from wood grown in
well-managed forests and other controlled sources. The logging and
manufacturing processes are expected to conform to the environmental
regulations of the country of origin.

Hachette Books Ireland
8 Castlecourt Centre
Castleknock, Dublin 15

An Hachette UK Company
Carmelite House
50 Victoria Embankment
London EC4Y 0DZ

www.hachette.ie
www.hachette.co.uk

In loving memory of my *Oma*, Melanie Fuchs O'Callaghan, who filled my heart with sparkles and shared her amazing story with me.

Also for Tomi Reichental, who I am humbled to know. Thank you for demonstrating the true meaning of forgiveness. Evil will never survive in the world while people like you are alive.

The best and most beautiful things in the world cannot be seen nor even touched, but just felt in the heart.

From *The Story of My Life* by Helen Keller, 1905

Prologue

Dearest Nathalie,
I am not sure how much you know about me . . .

CLARA PAUSED, LAYING DOWN HER PEN ON THE soft cream paper for a moment, unsure of how to go on. She took a long sip of rich, dark coffee, then looked up towards the photograph on her bedside table, as if for guidance.

It was dawn. Her favourite time of day. Only she and the early-morning songbirds seemed enthusiastically compos mentis as she gazed through the partially opened curtains on to the empty street below.

Clara had always imagined she would know the right time to tell her story. For so many years she'd held her silence. But she knew the time had come for her to get her affairs in order.

As a vivacious and sprightly recently-turned-eighty-year-old, she was often jolted by her reflection. Nobody had ever mentioned the fact that her mind and body would somehow disconnect as the years progressed. In her mind's eye she was still a smooth, sallow-skinned, lithe little thing with dancing dark eyes and bouncing brown curls.

Of course she knew that wrinkles and lacklustre locks were inevitable, and being a pragmatic soul, she accepted them with grace. Unlike her daughter Ava, who in her mid-forties was raging a vicious war with Mother Nature. Clara didn't agree with Botox and fillers, but she figured it was her daughter's face and therefore her choice.

The one thing Ava had inherited from her was her love of fabric. As a talented seamstress, Clara had sewn all the soft furnishings in the house herself. From cushion covers to intricate patchwork quilts, she'd carefully designed all her interiors.

Blue was her favourite colour at the moment. She particularly adored the cornflower shading against the crisp white background in the current curtain fabric. It brought back such vivid memories of her early childhood days in Austria. As she tucked her arms behind her head and drank in the pretty floral pattern, she closed her eyes and inhaled deeply through her nose. She could almost smell the delicate scent of the purply-blue Jacob's ladder that dotted the Alpine landscape, interspersed with dainty snow-coloured edelweiss. At that time, with her innocence intact, she had lived a perfect life.

Clara was younger than most when she realised how some people's existence was just a brief passing blessing. The past was so heavily peppered with love and heartache in equal measure, and her story was one that needed to be shared before she closed her eyes in eternal sleep. She had always known that one day she would feel compelled to speak, and when that time came, she would choose the right person to tell.

The one person she longed to tell was currently unobtainable to her, so she'd set the wheels in motion last week.

She'd felt like a real-life version of Miss Marple as she'd sat in Kevin O'Toole's office.

'I need to find someone,' she'd said.

'You've come to the right place,' he said drily, pointing to the *Private Investigator* sign etched in the glass of his office door.

'It's my son.'

'Oh, I see . . .' He coughed awkwardly. 'I didn't mean to be trite, Mrs . . .'

'Clara will do nicely, dear.' She smiled and blinked slowly, holding his gaze. She noticed him relaxing and continued. 'He lives in Los Angeles. That's all I know.'

'Was he adopted as a baby?' Kevin asked, clasping his hands together.

'Oh no . . .'

'Sorry, you have a strong foreign accent, and I just assumed . . .'

'Yes, I grew up in Austria but Max was born here in Ireland. I was married to an Irishman and we raised him here. He left twenty years ago. His anger towards me drove him away, you see. I always figured he would return if I didn't badger him.'

'But obviously he still hasn't?'

'No.'

Clara gave Kevin the details she had.

'Conway is a fairly common name, but we might be pleasantly surprised at how few forty-year-old Max Conways there are living in LA. If he is indeed a doctor as you suspect, that'll make it even simpler.'

Clara had gone away and put the meeting to the back of her mind. She longed to confide in Ava and let her know that she could possibly be reunited with her long-lost brother. But any time she mentioned Max, which was often, Ava's brow furrowed. She had so much pent-up anger towards her younger brother, and Clara wasn't sure that would ever be resolved.

Last night, as she was in the sewing room planning a new patchwork quilt for the guest bedroom, Clara's landline had rung.

'I've found your son,' said a joyous Kevin. 'I thought it was the right man last week, but I needed to be certain.'

Clara thought her heart had actually stopped beating as she grappled for a chair and sat down clumsily.

'Tell me about him, please.'

'He is a doctor, as you suspected. He did indeed transfer his course from Ireland and completed his medical studies. He then went on to train as a surgeon. He works in LA General Hospital and is married to one Amber Conway. They have a seventeen-year-old daughter called Nathalie.'

'Oh my . . .' Clara was reeling. 'I'm an *Oma.*'

'I beg your pardon?'

'*Oma,*' she repeated. 'It's grandmother in German. I had no idea I had a grandchild.'

Kevin promised to send all the details in a letter, but he read out Max's home address.

'Thank you. You have no idea how much I appreciate this.'

'Would you like me to obtain some photographs of the family? For a small extra fee I can have them trailed for a day and send you pictures.'

'Oh no, thank you,' she said. It was one thing having Kevin find Max, but she wasn't going to intrude on his life in a sneaky way.

She'd hung up and sat staring into space until the evening light faded and a chill hung in the air. Not sure of what else to do, she'd climbed into bed and nuzzled down into the duvet. Her dreams had been filled with memories of Max from the moment he was born until the awful day he'd stormed out of her life.

For the first time, she had his address. There was no reason why she couldn't turn up on his doorstep. But Clara knew that would be too big a gamble. She needed to approach this gently in order to maximise her chances of a happy reunion. Finishing her coffee, she concentrated on the job in hand and continued writing.

. . . I am not sure how much you know about me, but I have liter-
ally just found out you exist. I cannot begin to describe the emotions

that are racing through my heart. Suffice it to say that it brings me unspeakable joy to know that I have a granddaughter.

Your father may or may not have told you the reason we became estranged. But I would like to take this opportunity to assure you that I have longed to see him since the day he left Ireland.

Not a day has gone by when I haven't thought of him and wanted to see him again.

I know it's a lot to ask, but I would love it if you would consider getting to know me.

I don't have an email address, which annoys your aunt Ava terribly. So I would be truly honoured if you would consider writing back, or even phoning me.

Of course you would be welcomed with open arms should you ever think of coming to Ireland.

I won't bombard you with a long and tedious letter. Instead I will leave the ball in your court.

A reply would be incredible but I will understand if you would rather not.

Yours faithfully and with untold affection,

Clara Conway (your Oma)

Her hands shook ever so slightly as she sealed the envelope and climbed out of bed. She felt a frisson of anticipation. Change was coming, she could sense it. With one last glance at the photograph next to her bed, she blew it a kiss and hurried downstairs to start her day.

Chapter 1

A SHIVER OF EXCITEMENT SHOT THROUGH Nathalie as she scrutinised her reflection in the full-length mirror. She could barely believe it was finally her prom night.

'Wow,' came a voice behind her.

'Dad!'

'You look stunning,' he said with a smile.

'I saw this gown and thought it would look much better without the straps, so I cut them off. The wrap that was sold with it was just so boring, so I added the cream goose-down one instead! You like?'

She twirled around and did a little curtsey. 'Ooh and I customised my shoes with silk flowers.'

Max stood motionless for a moment. He looked as if he were fighting back tears.

'You OK?' Nathalie asked.

'Sure,' he said, blowing out air loudly. 'You reminded me of somebody just now.' He strode across the room, planted a light kiss on her forehead and pulled a pale blue box from his pocket.

'This is from Mom and me. Congratulations, darling.'

'Oh my gosh, this looks like . . .' She opened the box and screamed. 'It's a Tiffany necklace! Thank you, thank you, thank you!'

'You're welcome, welcome, welcome!' he said, looking vaguely uncomfortable with all the fuss.

As Max fastened the necklace around Nathalie's neck, he reiterated how immensely proud they were of her. Well, to be exact, he regurgitated the speech his wife had just delivered to him. Amber had been responsible for the necklace too. He'd come home from work at the hospital, had the bag thrust at him and was pretty much catapulted into his daughter's room to let her know he loved her.

'She knows,' he'd said in an attempt to avoid the *Brady Bunch* moment.

'Everyone likes to be told they're loved. It can't happen too often,' Amber insisted. 'Now go and do your fatherly duty.'

He was mildly surprised by how thrilled Nathalie was. He made a mental note to let Amber know she'd been right. But then again, he was fairly certain she knew that. Amber was always right. She was always in control and always a step ahead of him with domestic matters.

'Thanks, Dad. You'd better get changed. DJ will be here soon.'

'Right.' His expression darkened.

'How many times have we had this conversation?' Nathalie sighed. 'DJ is a good guy.'

'In your opinion . . .'

'Please, let's not fight tonight. As far as I can tell, any guy I introduce to you wouldn't be good enough. So why can't you let me enjoy my prom?' She rolled her eyes as her father strode off to change out of his operating scrubs.

Max muttered grumpily to himself as he plucked his suit from the bed where Amber had laid it out for him. It was his wife's idea to give up on arguing over this DJ kid. If he had his way that good-for-nothing waste of time would be run off their property never to return. Amber was convinced they should put up and shut up, saying that Nathalie would come to her senses soon enough.

'She's a smart girl, Max. The sheen will wear off with DJ. Allow her to enjoy her prom and let this little flush of love run its course. It's not as if she'll want to marry him, for crying out loud.'

Max wasn't so sure. As he was only too aware, Nathalie came from a long line of incredibly stubborn and strong-willed females. But Amber knew none of that. She knew nothing of his family or what they had done in the past, and he wasn't about to start explaining. Not tonight, or any other night for that matter.

He sighed. Amber was right. It was Nathalie's special night and of course he wanted her to have fun.

Besides, he knew he wasn't great at all the emotional stuff. He tended to leave that to Amber. She was a natural when it came to socializing at hospital fund-raisers. She could sweep into a room and light it up effortlessly. She was brilliant with Nathalie's friends and their air-kissing mothers too. He dreaded all the community schmoozing and found it nigh impossible to stand with a bottle of beer and talk nonsense to men he barely knew. He had enough to occupy his mind between working as a surgeon and being a husband and a father. He kept his cards close to his chest and appreciated it when others did the same. He preferred to concentrate on paying the bills and making sure his girls were well provided for. It was easier to show his love that way. Even though it was twenty years since he'd left Ireland, he still struggled to conform to the American way of conducting himself.

'You don't have to make lifelong pals of all the neighbours, but you do need to be civil,' Amber had scolded him. They'd moved to their current home ten years ago. It was a traditional gated community, where the houses were larger than most, with inhabitants to match.

'I don't have any desire to stand in Chuck's back yard being clapped on the back and referred to as "Doc",' he'd said.

'Well suck it up and get on with it, Max. It's important to Nathalie and me that we fit in around here.'

So Max did the least amount of fitting-in possible. He'd learned to wave automatically and call out mindless greetings like Ned Flanders, and was relieved that it seemed to mollify most of the neighbours. Amber felt he was making an effort too, so it was a win-win situation.

Unlike his wife and daughter, he'd been dreading tonight. Americans took prom night so seriously. It was an industry all of its own. One he most definitely didn't get. But he loved his girls, and if it kept them happy, he'd grin and bear it.

He finished dressing and attached the cufflinks to his shirt. Flicking a comb through his honey-blond hair, he wondered where the creases around his eyes and the dulling of his bronzed skin might end. It was all the rage at the hospital to cruise into the plastics department for a shot of this and a zap of that to freshen one's face. But Max was neither vain nor bothered enough to pitch up. He figured he'd go for the ageing gracefully thing instead. Besides, he had his trump card, which always seemed to please his patients.

'Ooh, you have the most darling Irish accent!'

'I love the way you speak. My grandma was from Ireland too . . .'

He'd just stepped into the living room when Nathalie swept in behind him. Max stood and observed his two favourite girls.

'Wow,' he said, nodding in approval. Once again he was amazed by their closeness and mutual adoration.

'You look so beautiful, Nathalie,' Amber said, grasping both her hands.

'So do you, Mom,' Nathalie said sincerely.

'Ah, once I stick with Ms Coco Chanel, I'm on to a winner,' Amber said with a grin. 'Are you happy with your gown?'

'I love it, thank you, Mom. Most importantly, I've got DJ

taking me, Mackenzie has a date and all our friends will be there. I can't believe I've finally reached this point in my life.'

'Neither can I, baby girl. I still remember how I felt when I discovered I was pregnant. Do you know, I secretly wished for a girl.'

'Why?' Nathalie smiled.

'For moments just like this one . . . For the camaraderie and the frills and spills that only a daughter brings. I'm blessed to have you in my world, darling.'

They hugged, and were both dabbing ever so gently at their expertly made-up eyes as Max cleared his throat.

'OK, you guys. Enough leaky girlie moments. You're both gorgeous and I am unbelievably proud.'

The tender moment was shattered by the arrival of Nathalie's sorry excuse for a boyfriend. Max couldn't abide him. He was everything he *didn't* want to see attached to his precious girl.

'No way!' Nathalie screamed, pointing outside. 'I can't believe he did that.' Flinging the front door open, she rushed down the drive towards the white stretch Hummer with tinted windows.

'So much for her being the belle of the ball,' Max said drily. 'As she charges down the drive looking like she's taking part in a timed sprint.'

'Lighten up, eh, Max,' Amber said dreamily. 'She's young and in love.'

'Just like you were a hundred years ago,' he said, teasing her as he took her in his arms.

'Do you remember my prom?'

'I'll never forget it,' he said. 'I was quaking in my slippery hired shoes, terrified to even open my mouth. Every time I spoke, your father corrected me.'

'He couldn't understand your Irish accent,' she giggled.

'Yeah, that's his version of the story,' Max said. 'I think I can appreciate how he felt now. He told me repeatedly that you were only seventeen and I was far too old for you at twenty.' He leaned against the frame of the door with his arms folded and watched Nathalie as she allowed DJ to place a corsage around her wrist, then pick her up and twirl her around.

'Not so touchy-feely, young man,' Max growled.

'Oh Max, stop it.' Amber swatted him. 'Behave.'

He raised an eyebrow and side-glanced at his wife.

'I've waited a long time to make a guy feel as uncomfortable as I did at your prom. Let me have my moment in the sunshine.' He grinned wickedly.

'You mean thing,' Amber laughed.

'I wish it were simply a joke,' Max said, shaking his head. 'But look at the guy. He's a grease monkey with about as much class as a septic tank—'

'Enough,' Amber said sternly, holding her hand aloft. 'There's plenty of time for meaningful conversations about finding the right life partner. But this isn't one of them. Suck it up and let our daughter enjoy her prom. Besides, she's merely testing the water. If I know Nathalie, she'll be sick to the back teeth of DJ soon enough.'

'As long as she doesn't come home and say she's knocked up and they're off to live in a trailer park.'

'Your imagination runs riot at times, Max,' Amber said. 'Let's just enjoy the moment . . . Please?'

Reluctantly, Max did as he was bid. DJ bounded up the driveway.

'Evenin', Doc.'

Max clenched his jaw and shook the boy's hand before walking silently back into the living room to grab his house keys.

'Doc . . .' he muttered, tutting and grinding his teeth.

The others were waiting in the limo as he dawdled on purpose.

He didn't want to sit in a confined space with this joker. But he knew he couldn't growl at him either, or Amber would be on his case and Nathalie would pout and treat him like a leper for the next week. He sighed and hid his smile, knowing that yet again he was under the thumb of his two women. Eventually he joined them.

'Max,' Amber hissed. 'Turn that frown upside down before I accidentally implant my stiletto in your toe.'

Max fixed a smile on his face.

The journey seemed endless. Amber and Nathalie babbled to one another, while DJ was busy opening all the compartments in the back of the limo, discussing the likely cost of replacing each one. Max tried to zone out and think about something completely different.

Once inside the school gym, Nathalie felt as if she would combust with excitement.

'Mom, look at the balloons and bunting. Isn't it magical?'

The foursome greeted the other kids and parents. The atmosphere was bittersweet, with some parents expressing their dismay at the thought of their children leaving school.

'The years have flown by so quickly,' Amber agreed, as Max stood motionless by her side. 'But I'm happy Nathalie is ready to spread her wings. She's headed for medical school, following in her father's footsteps,' she said proudly.

'There's Mackenzie,' Nathalie said, rushing to hug her best friend. 'You look totally wowzers!'

'So do you!'

'Hey, Jonas,' Nathalie said, kissing her friend's date on the cheek. DJ and Jonas shook hands and banged one another on the back.

Once the speeches and the drinks reception were over, it was time for the parents to leave.

'Enjoy the rest of the evening, and don't forget to have her home by two,' Max said to DJ. 'We'll be at the Four Seasons if you need us before that, darling,' he said, kissing his daughter's cheek.

Nathalie waved her parents off and joined her friends to dance the night away. She grabbed Mackenzie's hand and they rushed to the rest room to touch up their make-up and have a quick chat.

'Did you *see* Jonas?' Mackenzie squealed. 'He's so hot and he brought me this.' She showed Nathalie the exquisite bracelet on her arm.

'Hey, I'm jealous,' Nathalie said. 'That's awesome. He is *so* into you. That must've cost a fortune.'

'I know!' Mackenzie grinned. 'That's what happens when your date is rich!' She bit her lip. 'I've never had anything like this before. My mom nearly choked when I opened it.'

Nathalie beamed back at her friend. Mackenzie had two brothers and a sister, and things at her home weren't easy since her father had lost his job. Nathalie was thrilled to see her enjoying the princess treatment for a change.

'He whispered that I look knock-dead stunning as we were getting into the limo,' Mackenzie said with shining eyes.

'Aw, that's so great, sweetie. For the record, he's right, you look amazing,' Nathalie said. 'He's a good guy. I've got a great feeling about you two.'

'I can't really see why he's chosen me, though. Have you seen how good Whitney looks? She's on fire . . . Every time I look up, she's glaring over at me. If I'd known it was going to upset her this much . . .'

'Huh,' Nathalie scoffed. 'She's pretty, but as the song says, honey, she has an ugly heart. Besides, they split months ago. Jonas made his choice and I happen to agree with him. Besides, what guy wants to sit and listen to her going on and on about her latest photo shoot?'

'I like her, though,' Mackenzie said blinking.

'Yeah, because you're the nicest person I've ever met. I, on the other hand, am not quite as charitable. Where would I be without you? I'd be a total monster.'

'Well, you'll never need to find out.' Mackenzie held up her pinkie and Nathalie linked it with hers.

'So does Jonas know you're planning on going away to college?'

'Yeah, I mentioned it. But he says he'll come and see me,' Mackenzie said, shrugging. 'It's good that DJ and Jonas are buddies. If we stay with them, they'll need to get along, seeing as we'll be buying apartments next door to one another in the future.'

'You said it,' Nathalie answered as she passed her lip gloss to Mackenzie to use. 'Do you reckon we can have a joint wedding? That way we can have babies at the same time . . .'

'. . . and they'll be best friends like us,' Mackenzie finished.

Nathalie hugged her friend and pulled her back out to the dance floor. The music was like a trip down memory lane as the songs that they'd all grown up with pumped from the speakers. Nathalie spotted Jonas watching them. He was eyeing Mackenzie appreciatively.

'Your man is drinking you in,' she said, cupping her friend's ear. She took Mackenzie's hands and moved her into the middle of the floor. She knew from her expression that Mackenzie was dying inside, but she encouraged her to keep going. As Jonas came over and put his arms around her from behind, Nathalie discreetly stepped away, winking at Mackenzie.

The night seemed to pass in an instant. Nathalie was hoarse from shouting and her feet were aching from dancing. Then DJ made the unwelcome announcement that he hadn't paid for the limo to take them home.

'How are we meant to get there?' Nathalie asked. 'It's like twenty minutes away. I'm wearing high shoes in case you hadn't noticed.'

She wasn't about to admit it to anyone, least of all her father, but DJ was swiftly beginning to annoy her.

'Hey,' he said, flinging his hands up. 'I don't earn bags of cash. I paid for the car here. We can call a cab if you don't want to walk.'

'What's up, sweetie?' Mackenzie asked, appearing by Nathalie's side.

'DJ thinks I'm walking home,' she whispered through gritted teeth.

'Come with us, both of you. Jonas has a limo booked.'

'Ah no. Thanks, but I don't want to cramp your style.'

Nathalie grinned as Mackenzie yanked her and DJ to the exit. As they climbed into the long-based black limousine, she was thrilled to see Whitney snarling at their car.

'She's so pissed!' she laughed.

'Aw, you're incorrigible.' Mackenzie swatted her. 'She's not that bad. I'm sure she'll improve as she gets older.'

As they settled in the back of the plush car, Nathalie couldn't have been more delighted. The prom had lived up to their expectations, and she couldn't believe how happy Mackenzie looked as she sat opposite her with Jonas's arm draped around her shoulder.

Chapter 2

'NATHALIE . . . WAKE UP. NATHALIE, PLEASE . . .'

'Uh, stop, Mom.' Nathalie groaned and tried to turn on to her side.

'Nathalie, please.' The loud sobs ripped through her dreams and made her sit bolt upright in the bed.

'Mom?'

Staring at her mother's tear-stained face, Nathalie's head shot towards the door, where her father was standing with his forehead against the frame, openly crying too.

'What's happened?' Nathalie rubbed her eyes. 'Where am I?'

Her prom dress had been replaced by a limp hospital gown and there was a drip attached to her arm.

'What happened?' she repeated. 'Mom? Speak to me.'

Amber's shoulders shook and she looked over to Max. Nathalie gripped her arm and willed her to explain.

'I can't do it, Max . . .' Wriggling free from her daughter's grasp, Amber staggered clumsily backwards and exited the room.

Max edged towards the bed and sat down. Taking Nathalie's hands in his own, he opened his mouth to speak. Nothing came out. Tears coursed down his cheeks.

'I . . .'

'What's going on? Somebody tell me what the hell is happening here!' Nathalie's voice rose higher and higher until she was yelling. 'Hello? Daddy? It seems only five minutes ago that I was dancing with my friends . . .'

'There has been . . .' He gulped and closed his eyes. 'There has been a tragic accident.'

'What?' Nathalie's eyes dashed wildly from side to side as she tried frantically to recall what had happened. 'Who was in the accident?'

'It's Mackenzie . . .'

'Nooo!' Nathalie screamed. 'No. No, don't tell me . . . Is she OK? She's fine, right? Daddy? She's going to be OK, isn't she?'

'She's dead, Nathalie.'

The words hung in the air like slowly dissolving powder. Seconds passed before there was another sound.

'I need to call her. She'll be fine once I speak with her,' Nathalie said, trying to climb out of her bed. 'Find my cell phone.'

'Nathalie.' Max spoke sharply. 'The limousine you were all travelling home in last night crashed. Mackenzie and Jonas were killed. Miraculously, you and DJ survived.'

'Stop it!' Nathalie yelled, covering her ears with her hands. 'Shut up and quit talking. You're giving me a headache. You're lying. You're saying the most offensive and vile stuff. You're making me hate you, Dad . . .'

Nathalie stared at her father's tear-stained face. She'd never seen him cry before. She felt as if she were in a parallel universe. One moment her life was swell, and now all she could feel was this hideous ball of pain inside.

'Why is Mackenzie hurt? Who would want to do that to her? She's my best friend in the whole world.'

'It's the most unthinkable and unbearable tragedy, Nathalie,' Max said. 'A truck skidded and lost control. The back axis swiv-elled around and collided with the back of the limousine, taking it out. It seems Mackenzie and Jonas died instantly, while you and DJ escaped by a hair's breath.'

Nathalie tried to process the information. She could hear the words but none of it made any sense. She closed her eyes and tried to think about the night. She saw Mackenzie dancing with Jonas. She even saw Whitney with one hand on her skinny hip glowering at them. After that it was blank.

This *had* to be a mistake. It couldn't be true. Mackenzie was getting ready for college. They had so much stuff to do. Jonas was going to be there for her, treating her like gold dust and making her feel special.

Nathalie realised her father was still speaking.

'I hate to sound crass or rude, Dad. But I know you've made an awful mistake here. You're wrong. Mackenzie is fine. I know. I was with her.'

The conversation continued. Nathalie wanted to put her hands over her ears. Her father was babbling about internal injuries and how Mackenzie wouldn't have known what had happened, how it was all so quick and she wouldn't have suffered. Suffered! What was he doing here? Trying to break her spirit? This was all insane.

Eventually the talk stopped. When her father left the room, Nathalie lay back against the uncomfortable hospital pillows. She gazed around. She needed to get out of here. That would be a good start. She'd go and find Mackenzie and clear this up. This needed to stop. All the crazy death talk. It was doing her head in.

She groaned as her father and mother returned looking devastated still. She smiled and shook her head slowly.

'It'll be OK, you guys. No need to look so sad. Once I find some clothes, we'll get out of here and I'll find Mackenzie. It's cool, yeah?'

Suddenly Nathalie had an image of Jonas. He was fine too, she assured herself. He wasn't some kid who'd died in a freak accident. Mackenzie wasn't a statistic, yet another horrific road death. She was Nathalie's best friend. She was her other half. She couldn't have died. She wouldn't . . . They had so much to do together . . . It *had* to be a mistake.

'Nathalie, honey,' her father said. 'I've spoken with Mackenzie's parents and some of the staff here at the hospital. We feel it might be beneficial if you see Mackenzie's body.'

Amber held a bunch of scrunched-up tissues to her mouth and nose. A small, miserable sound escaped her lips.

Nathalie sighed heavily. If this would get her parents off her back, she'd go. But she knew in her heart of hearts that Mackenzie wouldn't be there. That it would be someone else. Some poor young girl who probably looked a bit like her. After all, it was prom season. There must've been a pile of proms on last night.

It would be sad and awful and Nathalie would feel for this stranger's family and friends. But it wouldn't be Mackenzie.

'OK, let's do this,' she said as she moved woodenly to the corridor. She shifted her weight from one foot to the other and clicked her fingers. First the left hand, then the right. She repeated it over and over. Her mom came to her side and stroked her matted hair.

'Isn't it odd that I can click really loud with my right hand and barely at all with my left?' Nathalie said to nobody in particular.

Max placed a dressing gown belonging to the hospital around her shoulders. He was babbling again. Only bits of it penetrated her psyche. Her head jerked to the side. He kept mentioning the body . . . That wasn't right. That made no sense.

'Will you stop with the morbid talk,' she said.

Her parents looked at one another in an odd manner and back at her. The pressure of their bewilderment weighed heavily on her. She closed her eyes and thought of the houses she and Mackenzie were going to own some day. Their front yards would be identical. It was all going to work out just the way they'd planned. This was just a big mix-up.

'Nathalie,' Max said gently. 'Honey, you need to prepare yourself for what you're about to see. Mackenzie may not look the way you remember. She will be bereft of colour and life. Are you sure you want this image imprinted on your mind for ever? Because this is something you will never forget, believe me.' He took her in his arms and rocked her from side to side. 'Would it be better for you to remember her the way she was? As the girl you loved?'

Nathalie had had enough of this. She was getting more angry by the minute.

'I want to go in there,' she said through gritted teeth as she pushed him away. Her dad wasn't a huggy, touchy-feely type, and he rarely discussed his emotions. So why now? Why was he trying to crowd her when all she needed was to make sure this wasn't Mackenzie and get the hell out of here? Was it too much to ask? She didn't need any more freaky behaviour. There was enough of a horror show going on.

They walked slowly down one corridor, then another. The light hurt her eyes and her legs were so stiff she felt as if she'd been leaning on them awkwardly and they'd gone to sleep.

When they got there, the morgue was a lot brighter than she'd expected. She realised she'd been visualising a dark, basement-style place with rows of drawers like massive filing cabinets. Like on a TV show. Instead this was more like a regular hospital room. There was a large window overlooking a neat, architect-designed garden with perfect round grassy features and little brick-built paths. Fleetingly Nathalie wondered why the room containing dead people had one of the better views at the hospital.

'Hello, Dr Conway,' the nurse said.

'Hi,' he answered. 'This is my daughter Nathalie. She's having a bit of trouble coming to terms with the news. I know from experience that this can be an effective way of fathoming this kind of trauma.'

The nurse nodded.

'What my dad really means is that I don't believe Mackenzie is dead. She's not. She can't be. You see, we were going home from the prom and we were in a limo. It was all fine . . .'

'Hello, darling,' the nurse said kindly. 'Your friend Mackenzie is right over here.'

'Riiight,' Nathalie said, her voice dripping with sarcasm. 'Come on then, show me the person you think is Mackenzie.'

'Nathalie, you need to listen to the nurse,' Max said. The nurse hesitated for a moment. Max nodded for her to continue.

'Her face and body are covered by a sheet. When you feel you are ready, I will pull the sheet back so you can see her.' The woman's voice was clear and sympathetic. While Nathalie appreciated that she was simply trying to sound kind, she wanted to punch her. Why was everyone treating her like a moron? Mackenzie was OK. She was probably at home in bed resting. Nobody else knew that, clearly. But Nathalie was certain it was all a big mess. The sooner it was sorted, the better.

'Thank you,' she said robotically. Her eyes were drawn to the bed and she stopped in her tracks. Her chest felt as if it had been thumped with a large brick. Beneath the pale sheet she could make out the strong Kelly-green colour of what looked like a prom gown. Scrutinising the form, she decided the girl's feet were bare.

'I'd like to see her now.'

As the nurse gently peeled the sheet back, Nathalie inhaled sharply.

It was Mackenzie all right. She looked so different, though.

'Her cheek is bruised,' Nathalie said as she stared, almost unable to breathe.

'I know, sweetie.' Max placed his hand on Nathalie's shoulder protectively. She shrugged him off. Stepping forward, she tugged at the sheet and brought it down to Mackenzie's waist.

'Your gown is fine, Mackenzie,' she said tenderly. 'You still look beautiful. There's no need to freak out. You're like a pretty mannequin.' She raised her hand; it was shaking violently but she moved it towards Mackenzie's face. It hovered there for the longest time.

Then, taking a deep breath, she lowered it palm first towards the bruise on her friend's cheek. Only her fingertips grazed the waxy skin at first. It was shockingly cold. It was a weird type of cold. Not like holding hands at the indoor ice rink when they were kids. This was different. It was hard, as if Mackenzie had turned to marble.

All at once it was as if the universe had begun to spin in a different direction. The world she'd taken for granted and assumed was filled with nothing but love, life and joy had been wiped out. Instead, she was faced with this new and unknown existence where her best friend since she was three had departed. She'd been hoping with all her heart that she'd see somebody else in this room and that would be that.

Nathalie was certain her friend hadn't wanted to die. She'd liked Jonas for *ever* and they'd only just got together. It made no sense that she was gone. None. A noise that had never emanated from her body before filled the air. Right at that moment, if she'd had the chance, she'd have gone with her.

'Where are you, Mackenzie?' she whispered. 'I want you to come back. I need you here, baby girl.' This was like being in a bad dream, except she wasn't going to wake up.

'We've been best friends since kindergarten,' she told the nurse. 'I met her the morning we started. She was crying for her mamma and I offered her a piece of play dough. We held hands all day long. I even took her to the bathroom when I needed to go. She never said, but I knew she was scared.'

'That's lovely,' the nurse said as tears poured down her face.

'Mackenzie would help me too. I hated math. She was a whizz at numbers. She'd sit and explain how to figure the problems and it would all suddenly seem easier.'

'I'd say she was a very clever young lady,' the nurse said.

'She didn't like science, though. Said it freaked her out when we had to dissect stuff. That's why she was going to do accountancy and I'm doing medicine.'

Max and the nurse nodded, neither of them able to verbalise anything.

'She saw the good parts of everyone. Even when Whitney looked down her nose at her because she didn't have as many clothes as some of the girls . . . Mackenzie would say that it was kind of sad. That Whitney must have some issues and some day she'd be happier.'

Nathalie stared at her friend's frozen face. Why had Mackenzie been ripped away from her? What was the point? She had so much to live for, so much to enjoy. Where was the justice in the world?

'I don't understand where you've gone, sweetie. But please know that I will miss you and love you for every day of my life until we meet again.'

Nathalie stroked her friend's hair for the last time before turning to shuffle from the room. The smell of death was pungent now. All the doubts had been ripped away and there was no pretence remaining. Mackenzie was dead, and Nathalie was afraid of what life looked like without her.

Chapter 3

CLARA HAD ALWAYS ENJOYED WALKING. UP UNTIL recent times she'd been a regular sea swimmer too. The invigorating sensation of the salty water had been one of her favourite things. But lately the cold had become all-encompassing and had a habit of seeping into her bones and making her feel so chilled she'd have to return to bed just to thaw out.

As she posted the letter to Nathalie, she leaned against the post box for a moment. She had no way of knowing whether or not her granddaughter would respond; all she could do was hope.

The warm May air spurred her on as she walked towards the shop that Ava now owned.

Her daughter was proud of telling customers that the shop had been running for sixty-two years and she was the third-generation owner. As Clara walked in the door, she had a clear flashback to the day her mother had started this business.

Clara was eighteen years old at the time and thought it quite normal for her mother to do such a brave and bolshie thing. Her mother had done so many incredibly courageous things that nothing had ever surprised her in the end.

Clara had kept her mother's name above the door, and Ava had chosen to do the same. As the years rolled by, Clara became increasingly grateful for this shop, her mother's legacy.

'Hello, Mama,' Ava said, rushing to hug her. 'What brings you here so early?'

'I was out walking and I have news,' she said gingerly.

'Riight . . .' Ava glanced over her shoulder as she put a dress on to a satin padded hanger.

'Ooh, that's a beauty,' Clara gasped, stepping over to stroke the dark green silk evening gown. 'It reminds me of my graduation gown. The one that set Mama on the path to opening this place.'

'Yes, I know,' Ava grinned. 'I got the inspiration from the photo of you and Dad taken on that night.'

'Mama made me a matching coat. It was the same shade of deep olive green but made from the most exquisite silk velvet I'd ever seen. She hand-stitched tiny seed pearls and sequins down the front panels and attached miniature hooks and eyes so it looked as if it were being held shut by magnets.'

'She was so talented,' Ava said tenderly. 'We both get our artistic eye from her.'

'She would be so proud of you, my dear,' Clara said, for the umpteenth time.

'So,' Ava said, spinning on her kitten heel and marching to the original mahogany desk that was still in use. 'What's your urgent news?'

'I've found Max.'

'I beg your pardon?' Ava spat. Her eyes narrowed as she leaned the heels of her hands on the desk. 'Has he turned up looking for money or something? No, don't tell me, he's realised he has nobody to turn to so he's here cap in hand begging forgiveness?'

'No . . . nothing like that. Ava, please, lovey. I need you to try and forget the bitterness.'

'Huh, well that's asking *way* too much,' Ava scoffed.

Clara lowered herself on to a spoon-backed chair and waited patiently for Ava to stop huffing and puffing.

'OK, go on . . .'

'I used a private investigator to trace your brother. He's a doctor and lives in LA. He's married and has a child . . . a seventeen-year-old . . .'

'Oh . . .'

Clara winced; she could virtually *see* Ava's haughtiness dissolving.

'Is . . . is the child . . . the teenager . . . a boy or a . . . a girl?' Ava swallowed, glassy-eyed.

'A girl,' Clara said quietly. Ava nodded vigorously, and telltale tears seeped down her cheeks.

'I see. And she's seventeen?'

'Yes.'

Just as Clara was about to stand and walk to her daughter and take her in her arms, Ava held her hand up and flicked her head back. 'I don't want to know anything about Max or his family.'

'But Ava—'

'No. Mama, I'm a grown woman and I have the right to make my own decisions. If you want to play happy families with Max after twenty years of silence, that's your lookout. But I don't want any part in it.'

'Ava, this isn't a stranger we're talking about here. It's your brother. My son.'

'If he valued either of us, even a teeny-tiny bit, he wouldn't have left without so much as a backward glance. Too much water has flowed under the bridge for me, Mama. As far as I'm concerned . . . Max is dead.'

Clara had heard Ava say those icy words so many times before. But she'd somehow hoped that the news of her brother's marriage and daughter might change her mind.

A gaggle of excited women arrived in the door of the shop, forcing Clara to move. Ava welcomed them and said she had the bridesmaids' dresses ready for them to try on. Clara smiled to let her know she would man the desk as she led the ladies upstairs.

When Clara and her mother had first opened the shop, they'd only managed to rent a fraction of the space Ava now occupied. The back was a dedicated sewing room where everything from pattern cutting to embellishments was done. Back in the day, the shop part housed two rails and an old-fashioned mannequin.

Clara smiled as she stood at the familiar wooden desk and looked at the refurbished and beautifully lit show rooms that Ava had made her own. Her mama would be thrilled to see just how far they'd come. Clara was certain that her mother had never fully grasped how incredibly ahead of her time she'd been.

The bell above the shop door pinged as Ruth, Ava's assistant, bustled in.

'Oh Clara, thank goodness you're here,' she said, attempting to catch her breath. 'I missed my bus and ended up half running, half walking the entire way.'

'Once you recover, you'll feel all the better for it,' Clara said calmly. 'Nothing like a bit of invigorating exercise to kick-start the day. Now you need a nice cup of coffee and you won't know yourself.'

'Is Ava upstairs with the Parker wedding party?'

'A group of women with hair and skin scarily like a family of orang-utans?' Clara raised an eyebrow.

'Yup, that's them,' Ruth grinned.

'Then yes. She's doing their final fitting.'

Clara waited for Ruth to settle before making her way back out of the shop.

'Tell Ava she knows where to find me, should she want to continue our little chat.'

'OK,' said Ruth.

Clara grinned as she wandered back down Lochlann main street towards her house. She knew Ruth would be busting a gut to find out what they were discussing. She was a curious sort, which Ava found infuriating at times.

'She's interested, that's all,' Clara defended her.

'A nosy little bee, more like it,' Ava huffed. 'She gets full details for people's entire weddings. Right down to the price of the bridesmaids' underwear. I don't need to know the ins and outs of people's bank accounts.'

Ruth was a precise seamstress, however, and Ava knew she wouldn't find her attention to detail elsewhere.

'Nobody's perfect, Ava,' Clara said. 'We all have our little quirks. The trick is to find someone who finds them endearing rather than exasperating. That's when you know you've found your soulmate.'

Clara inhaled the sea air and tried to envisage it cleansing her body and mind. She loved living here in Lochlann and was proud to call it her home since moving here from Austria.

She'd learned to dismiss unimportant things, or as Ava said, to not sweat the small stuff. In fact, she'd lived by that mantra for a long time now. But she wasn't getting any younger and she wanted to have one last-ditch effort at getting her little family back together. She knew it was a long shot, but she didn't want to find herself on her deathbed harbouring major regrets. Turning thirty hadn't bothered her, she'd embraced forty, fifty felt grown-up yet still young, sixty was a sort of proud milestone, seventy was pushing it a bit. But when she'd turned eighty, last month, an odd urgency had engulfed her. She'd had a sudden compulsion to straighten out her affairs. She only hoped she could do it before it was too late.

Ava barely noticed the morning passing. By the time she'd finished fitting the six hyperactive bridesmaids for the Parker wedding, there were two customers waiting to see her on the shop floor.

Neither wanted to deal with anyone else and both were regulars.

Ruth was busy with a ballgown with brain-numbingly intricate detailing on the never-ending yards of hemline, so Ava dealt with her customers alone.

At times like this, she wished Clara were still here. She'd have taken one of the ladies and made her feel as if she were royalty. The first customer was easy enough to organise. She wanted a repeat of a previous dress in a different colour. Then came Mrs Regan. Clara used to be brilliant at handling that woman, Ava mused. She certainly wouldn't have allowed her to order a bright green fishtail-styled evening dress.

Ava knew she was hardly backwards at coming forwards when it came to giving her opinion, but Mrs Regan's mouth was almost as big as her bank balance, and she hadn't the wherewithal to argue just now. She could almost hear her mother in her mind . . .

'Tell her she'll look like a great big snot. She hasn't the belly, bosom or bottom to appear in that design. She looks in the mirror and sees the Little Mermaid; the rest of us see a grassy knoll . . .'

Ava sniggered. Clara never meant to be cutting. Perhaps it was the language barrier, but she had a habit of saying it as it was. Often times, people were shocked and thought she was being offensive. But that couldn't have been further from the truth. Clara was simply honest, and her intention would always be to make a dress that suited her client and made the most of her figure.

'Are you all right there, Ava?' Mrs Regan asked.

'Yes thank you. I was just thinking about my mother. She says the funniest things, you know!'

'Ah, your mother is a character for certain. When I met her at first I wasn't quite sure what way to take her. She has an unusual way of expressing herself at times. I always put it down to the fact that she's foreign.' Mrs Regan sniffed as she said the last word, as if being from overseas were akin to having leprosy. 'But I soon realised she is always right. She has an impeccable eye and I've never left this shop with a dress that doesn't do me justice.'

Ava took a deep breath. 'No, you haven't, Mrs Regan,' she said. 'Which is why I feel I must try and dissuade you from the green you've just ordered.'

She deftly showed the woman a different design, saying it was the next big thing in gowns. Mercifully Mrs Regan went for it and Ava made the necessary adjustments to her order book.

'See you next week, Mrs Regan,' she said in a saccharine-sweet voice, then, grabbing her coat, she took the cash from the safe and let Ruth know she was off to the bank.

Once she'd lodged the takings from the last couple of days, Ava made her way to the park. It was the pride of Lochlann town and many of the residents took turns weeding, adding to the flower beds and ensuring the benches were freshly painted. Clara had brought Ava and Max here as children. They'd thought it was the size of a racetrack as they'd navigated the bends and booted up the straights on their scooters.

So Max was alive and well. Ava had guessed he might be. For months after he left, she'd lain awake at night and worried about where he'd ended up. As time marched on, her tears dried and anger and bitterness hardened her heart towards him. Hearing this news about him was like rekindling a fireball of rage. How could he have stayed away so long? How could he have denied his wife and child the chance to get to know his family? Hadn't he thought of burying the hatchet over the years? For crying out loud, she was an auntie and sister-in-law and had unwittingly shirked both responsibilities over the years.

Sadly, Ava acknowledged that the thing that still hurt most of all was how Max could have allowed his best friend Sean to do what he did to her . . . They'd been extremely close growing up. Surely that counted for something? What about blood being thicker than water?

Knowing she couldn't hold back any longer, Ava stood up and marched from the park. Tears streamed down her cheeks as she tripped along the footpath to the edge of town and turned towards the graveyard. She found her familiar spot instantly. Reading the name on the granite stone over and over again, she sobbed for the love she'd lost and cursed Max for not even knowing about her pain.

Chapter 4

NATHALIE HAD FOUND SILENCE EASIER THAN speaking lately. As far as she was concerned, there was nothing worth saying and nobody worth saying it to. Her parents were tormented and looked at her with an expression of sheer pain each time she walked in the room.

DJ was the only one who didn't annoy her. The beauty of his job at the garage was the fact that his father never noticed if he was there or not. Besides, his folks were ice-box cool. They didn't correct him if he cursed, thought nothing of his drinking and wouldn't dream of asking him where he was going or what time he'd be home. He'd very little ambition, a fact that used to irk her before. But right now, it suited her mood just perfectly.

They'd taken to sitting in places like the water park and drinking beer. Nathalie didn't care for the taste. It was gassy as hell too, but the effects helped to numb the pain.

Of her parents, her mom was being the most annoying. Her father was his usual quiet and brooding self, with fifty per cent extra oddness added for good measure. Thankfully he didn't want her to express her feelings the way her mom did. This morning had started off on the wrong footing. Mom had wanted to discuss her inner thoughts before she'd even had breakfast.

'It's not good to harbour all these emotions, Nathalie. We all miss Mackenzie. She's been a part of our lives for fourteen years. Let me help you.'

'Can you bring Mackenzie back from the dead?' Nathalie asked coldly. 'Can you fly like Superman up to the edge of the earth and reverse time?'

'Nathalie, please . . .'

'Nobody can change a damn thing about what's happened. I don't want to talk about it because it's not going to solve it. So let's drop it, yeah?'

She'd gladly hitched a ride with Max. He was going to work. Well, that wasn't new. He spent most of his time there anyway, but since Mackenzie's accident he was there morning, noon and night.

'Will you be home for dinner?' Amber asked him.

'You go ahead without me. I'll grab something in the canteen. It's really busy right now. There are a few consultants taking summer leave, so I need to be there to fill the gaps.'

Nathalie looked at her mother's desolate face and almost crumbled. She didn't blame Mom for Mackenzie's death, but it was easier to hate her than try to love her. Loving people hurt. They died and then there was a massive gaping hole that would never go away.

'Nathalie, will you be here?'

'Nope. I'm hanging with DJ. See ya.' She quashed the horrible sense of guilt. She didn't enjoy knowing she was hurting her mom. But she couldn't start deep, meaningful conversations. It would tip her over the edge. She couldn't allow herself to think too much about what had happened. She couldn't admit to anyone that she was having vivid flashbacks of the moments leading up to the crash. Nor did she want to relive the intensely loud scraping sound as that massive truck had scooped the limousine on to its side, tossing it as if it were made of paper.

The postman arrived just as they were leaving. Nathalie got into the car and sat waiting for her father to join her.

'Another pile of bills,' he said, throwing them on to the dash-board. 'There's one for you,' he added absent-mindedly. He shot the car into reverse and they made their way on to the main road.

'Who is yours from?' he asked, trying to catch her eye.

'Dunno,' Nathalie answered. 'I'll check later on. Might be another card. The kids from our school year have been super-kind at sending little memories through along with photos.'

'People can be very thoughtful.'

Nathalie didn't answer. She shoved the letter into her bag and closed her eyes, letting her dad know she wasn't prepared to continue talking. As soon as DJ's garage came into view and they stopped in the traffic, she opened the door.

'You can't get out in the middle of the road. Where are you going?'

'I'm calling for DJ,' she said as she leaned into the car. 'See ya.'

Her father had little choice but to drive on as impatient commuters beeped their horns at him.

There was nobody at the garage, so she called DJ's cell. He didn't answer. She perched on the broken wall outside and waited for what seemed like an eternity, but DJ didn't show. After half an hour, she called him again. It went to voicemail once more.

She wandered around aimlessly, not sure of how to pass the time. She made her way to the off licence and waited outside. Nobody she knew came along, so she approached a homeless guy sitting on the sidewalk.

'If I give you money, will you go in and buy me some vodka?'

'What's in it for me?'

'What I get, you get.'

'Sure thing, kiddo.' He stood up, snatched her money and hurried inside. He emerged moments later with a dizzy grin.

'This day's looking up. Nice doin' business with ya, little lady.'

Nathalie found a bench and sat down. Swigging from a brown-paper-wrapped bottle wasn't her usual style, but nothing that was going on right now was exactly as she'd planned it.

By midday, the beating sun was starting to get to her. She'd found a shaded area but she and vodka weren't a great combination, and the spinning in her head wasn't fun. Nathalie knew she needed sleep. Staggering as she went, she made her way towards home. A fifteen-minute drive on the motorway seemed easy, but she found it quite different on foot with over half the bottle of vodka swilling around her insides.

She lost track of time and eventually pitched up at the house.

'Nathalie!' Amber was in the front yard, tending to the neat row of plants. 'What's happened to you?'

'Leave it, Mom. I need my bed.' She tossed her bag on the floor in the hallway and took the bottle wrapped in brown paper with her. Amber shot in after her looking as if she would pass out in shock.

'Have you been drinking?'

'Yup, and as you can see, I still am. It's actually quite good. You should try it more often. Might loosen you up a bit. Make you less uptight. You know, Mom, you need to get a life . . . Dad has his hospital stuff going on. What do you do? Look pretty for a living? Fuck that shit . . .'

'Nathalie!'

Nathalie stared at her mom. Her expression was priceless.

'Mom, you crack me up!' she said, batting her leg with her floppy hand. 'Woo, Nathalie's cursing and drunk. What will the ladies who lunch think of that? This is a scandal! How will we cope? What if one of the rich fat cats on the hospital board hears that Mr Conway's daughter drinks vodka with bums on the sidewalk? Hey, didn't she have like a super-duper education?

What went wrong?' She laughed hysterically as her head rolled heavily.

'Stop it,' Amber said, putting her hand to her mouth in shock. 'You need to sleep it off.'

Before Nathalie could protest, Amber had snatched the bottle away from her.

Nathalie figured it might be a good plan to have a quick snooze. As she lay back against the cool softness of the pillow, voices shot through her head. From Mackenzie to DJ to the homeless guy. They were all mocking her and telling her she was a loser.

Amber phoned Max with shaking hands. His cell went directly to voicemail. She called the hospital and asked his secretary to give him an urgent message to call home.

'Yes, ma'am,' the woman said solemnly. 'He's in surgery for another hour, but I'll make sure he knows you're looking for him.'

Sighing and fighting back tears, Amber plucked Nathalie's bag from the hall floor. The contents spilled out, and she was stuffing them back inside when her hand grazed a letter.

Taking it into the kitchen, she examined the stamp. It was from Ireland. She knew it was wrong to open a letter addressed to someone else, but she couldn't help herself.

Nothing could have prepared her for the shock of what was inside.

Gasping, she tried to maintain control as the reality of what she was reading sank in. Surely this couldn't be true?

Amber tried to take stock of what was happening. How could Max have lied all these years? He'd told her his parents were dead. That his father had died when he was a small child and his mother soon before he came to the States. That was his reason for switching his medical degree from the university in Dublin.

So that meant Sean had lied too? But why?

As she pictured Max's wayward yet oddly charming friend, she saw a slightly naive but kindly guy. Why had they both covered the past so guardedly? What were they hiding?

Her hand hovered over the phone. She longed to call Sean and put him on the spot. He was kind of gormless, or at least she'd thought he was. Would he confess if she confronted him? Why on earth had he and Max fled Ireland? All sorts of dreadful scenarios began to play through her mind. Had they been in trouble of some kind? Had they hurt someone? What could cause a man to turn his back on his family?

Flailing, Amber read the letter twice over.

This woman sounded sincere and genuine. Curiosity began to plague her as she flipped open her laptop. Googling 'Clara Conway', she was disappointed, as very little information popped up. There was a small newspaper article about the reopening of a newly expanded clothing store in a town called Lochlann. But there were no pictures. Clara wasn't on any of the usual social media sites. There seemed to be very little trace of this woman who she'd always thought was dead.

By the time Nathalie emerged with bloodshot eyes and matted hair a couple of hours later, Amber was so fired up she felt she could self-combust.

She'd called the hospital twice more and Max still hadn't answered. So she'd made an executive decision, the result of which she was more than ready to share with her daughter.

'Hello, Nathalie,' she said calmly.

Nathalie screwed up her face and exhaled loudly.

'I feel rough.'

'Why am I not surprised?' Amber said drily. 'So while you were sleeping off the alcohol you illegally consumed in the street with a stranger, I've booked you a trip.'

'Huh?' Nathalie pulled the fridge door open and fished out a large carton of juice. Flipping the lid, she drank thirstily. Ordinarily such slovenly behaviour would irk Amber, but in the scheme of things, this was simply par for the course. She perched on a high stool and folded her arms, waiting for Nathalie to respond.

'My head wrecks. Where's the Tylenol?'

Amber waited silently.

Nathalie rooted in the medicine cupboard and swallowed two pills.

'I'm going back to bed.'

'There's no time for that,' Amber said evenly. 'You need to pack, and I'll help.'

'What are you on about, Mom?' Nathalie asked with immense irritation.

'You're going to Ireland on the early morning flight. You need to pack and then get some sleep. We leave for the airport at five o'clock.'

'What?' Nathalie rounded on her. 'Are you insane? Why are we going to Ireland?'

'*We* aren't going, my dear. You are.'

'On my own?' Nathalie looked slightly less irate.

'You're going to spend some time with your *Oma*.'

'My what?'

'*Oma*. It's Austrian for grandma. She's your father's mother. Her name is Clara and she's invited you to stay. I've spoken to her on the phone and booked your flight. You leave in the morning, as I mentioned.'

'What the *actual* fuck?' Nathalie looked like springs were going to pop out of her ears. 'First of all, Daddy's folks are dead. Secondly, what's the Austria thing? He's totally Irish. He sounds nothing like an Austrian, whatever they sound like. Don't they speak German?'

'Yes they do, but it turns out his mother moved from Austria to Ireland as a child. She still has a strong accent when she speaks English, though . . .' Amber mused.

'What?' Nathalie shook her head. 'You're kidding me, right?'

'No.' Amber stood and walked towards the kitchen door. 'We don't have much time. Let's get packing.'

'I'm not going anywhere!' Nathalie scoffed. 'And you can't make me.'

'Actually, Nathalie, I can and I will. If you think I'm going to sit by and watch you destroy your life, you don't know me very well. I have no idea how to help you. I've felt as if my feet were set in concrete since Mackenzie died. Clara wants to meet you and is happy for you to stay with her for a while. Job done.'

'I'm not some stupid project for you and the other bored housewives at the hospital foundation, Mom. You can't just send me halfway across the world to some stranger who's meant to be dead.'

Nathalie continued to shout as she followed her mother to the bedroom. Amber pulled out a suitcase and was putting clothes inside in spite of the ranting.

The sound of the front door slamming sent Nathalie charging to the hall.

'Tell Mom I'm not going to Ireland,' she yelled. 'You can't make me.'

'I beg your pardon?' Max said. 'Amber?'

'I'm in here in Nathalie's room,' she called back.

Max shot in, looking frantic.

'What's Nathalie saying?'

Amber pulled Clara's letter from the back pocket of her jeans and shoved it at Max.

'Oh sweet Jesus,' he said as he collapsed onto the bed. In silence he read the letter. 'She had no right . . .' His face was florid with rage as he threw the pages on the floor.

'Amazing, isn't it?' Amber said coldly. 'How she managed to come back from the dead and write to her granddaughter.'

'Amber . . .'

'Don't, Max,' she said holding her hand up. 'Right now I can only concentrate on one thing. When our daughter arrived home having consumed most of a bottle of vodka she'd gotten a home-less person to buy her, I figured she needed help. I called your cell and secretary all afternoon, but you didn't see fit to answer. So I took matters into my own hands. As usual I've been left to deal with everything on my own.'

'I was in surgery!' he shouted.

'With no break? And you didn't switch your cell on before you came home?'

'I'm under a lot of pressure, Amber. The hospital is making massive cuts and I've been loaded with extra work . . .'

'You need to get that sorted,' Amber flared. 'The board can't expect you to work non-stop. You're not a machine.'

'I know that, but right now isn't the time to lay down the law. I've seen esteemed colleagues being handed their marching papers. I need to toe the line for a while longer until I know the situation is less volatile.'

'Whatever,' Amber said. 'Meanwhile, I'll deal with our daughter, who is rapidly falling apart, just in case you hadn't time to notice.'

'Amber, please . . . I need you to understand . . .'

'Which bit, Max? The part where you lied about your family? Or the brooding silences that often last for weeks? Where do you want to begin?'

Max stood rigidly and stared at the floor.

'Nathalie leaves on the early flight in the morning.'

'No I don't!' Nathalie shouted. 'I'm *so* not going to some crummy place where I know nobody.'

Amber gave her a steely stare and continued talking to Max. 'I spoke with your mother briefly. I explained that our daughter is in crisis right now and that I fear for her sanity.'

'And after all that she said she'd take her?' Max said with a bitter laugh.

'In a nutshell, yes,' Amber said. 'She sounds like a very clued-in and sweet old lady. I don't know what went on with you guys but I did make a point of letting her know that I'd thought she was dead.'

'Thanks for that!' Max threw his hands in the air. 'Excellent! This day just gets better and better.'

Before she could retort, Amber watched her husband storm out of the room. When the front door slammed, she shuddered. The argument with Max would have to wait. Nathalie was her priority now.

Continuing with the packing, she tried to include all the warm clothes she could find.

'You don't have many sweaters,' she mused. 'I'll give you cash and you can pick some up. European fashions are meant to be stunning.'

'Will you quit acting as if I'm going on some amazing vacation?' Nathalie shouted. 'I'm not going.'

Amber stood up and pushed her shoulders back. Taking a deep breath, she spoke calmly, clearly and with conviction. Nathalie didn't need to know that she was quivering inside and felt as if she would pass out with fear.

'You will do as I say. Nothing is going to get better around here until you stop and take a look at your life and how you want to play it from here on in. You're young, you're terrified, you're grieving and you can't be expected to work this out alone. So I'm helping you. That's my job as your mother. You have a choice. You can go quietly or you can do so with a police escort.'

'You wouldn't,' Nathalie said, looking truly scared for a fleeting moment.

'Watch me,' Amber said. She'd no clue whether the police department would even take her call if she asked them to intervene, but miraculously Nathalie backed down. It was as if she'd run out of steam.

She certainly wasn't helpful with the packing but she stopped yelling and resisting. By the time they fell into bed that night, both women were exhausted.

'I'll sleep here with you,' Amber insisted. 'That way we won't miss your flight.' What she didn't voice was that she wanted to ensure her daughter didn't run away. All she had to do was get her on the flight to Ireland and she was certain things would improve.

As she put her arm around Nathalie, she felt as if her heart would break. How had her sunny-natured girl turned into such a resentful and bitter little terrier in such a short space of time? Not for the first time, Amber wondered why Mackenzie had had to die.

There were too many things broken right now. She couldn't fix them all in one go. Quashing the fear that her marriage was teetering on the edge, she forced herself to concentrate on her daughter. She hoped that this mysterious Austrian woman was the answer to her prayers.

Amber had spent hours on her knees since hearing of Mackenzie's death. Her faith had always been strong, but now, for the first time, she felt certain God had listened. She wasn't in the habit of sending her only child halfway across the world by herself, but drastic situations called for drastic measures. Amber prided herself on being an astute judge of character, and she was crossing her fingers and toes that she was making the right call with Max's mother.

Chapter 5

CLARA STIRRED. THE FORTY-YEAR-OLD WHITE IRON bed creaked in unison with her body as she bunched a pillow behind her head. She smoothed her beloved patchwork quilt back into place. Tracing her fingers over some of the hexagonal shapes, she cast her mind back to her childhood. Sewing these unique bedcovers had been her lifeline at one point.

This particular one had been with her for so long now it was as much a part of her as the liver spots that speckled the backs of her hands, or the creases that surrounded her eyes. Clara still adored the pretty array of fabrics, some floral, others striped, many just blocks of pastel shades. Together they amalgamated to form a complete unit. A little like herself, she mused.

Glancing to the empty space where her darling husband Gus used to lie made her heart lurch, and a deep, dull ache spread through her. She wasn't sure she'd ever get used to living without him.

Still, there was something wonderful on the horizon.

Smiling, she thought of Nathalie. The grandchild she hadn't known she even had until last week. The call from Max's wife had come as a shock. Even though she'd sent the letter in good faith, Clara realised she hadn't actually allowed herself to believe she'd get a response.

Amber sounded like a wonderful woman. There was no doubt they were going through a dreadful time with the death of

Nathalie's friends. But Clara was ecstatic that Amber had decided to allow her the chance to get to know her granddaughter.

'I'm sorry she's hurting,' she'd said. 'This is difficult in so many ways. She didn't even know I was alive so I feel I can take that in one of two ways. I can dwell on it, which will come to no good. Or I can clearly see that this means I have a clean slate with her. Maybe it will help Nathalie to be with someone who won't judge her or compare her mood to before.'

'You're right,' Amber said, as her voice cracked with emotion. 'I'm sorry, ma'am. This is not easy. I'm so confused right now. I don't know whether I'm more embarrassed or angry at Max. Or worried, for that matter . . .' Clara allowed the silence to prevail momentarily. She'd learned over the years that sometimes it was better not to fill those gaps with pointless words.

'I hope you believe I had no idea you were alive and well in Ireland, ma'am.'

'Please, call me Clara, and of course I believe you, dear. Why would you lie? You don't know me, and you owe me nothing.'

'Well that's true, I guess . . .'

'I would be more than delighted if you would accompany Nathalie. Max too, of course.'

'No,' Amber said quite definitely. 'I think she needs to find herself.'

'And I would be honoured to try and help her.'

The conversation didn't carry on much longer after that. Amber promised to call back with flight details, which she duly did. Clara promised to keep in constant contact and let Amber know if Nathalie was unrealistically unhappy.

Before she baked a welcome cake, Clara had two important jobs to do. First she needed to speak to Ava. Secondly to Gus.

She knew Ava often thought her crazy.

'Dad's not actually there. It's his grave . . .'

'I know, dear, but it's my way of feeling as if I'm physically visiting him. It's when I figure he can hear me clearest. I'm sure he's terribly busy in heaven. He can't spend all day every day looking down to know if I need to speak to him. So I go to the grave and do it there.'

So once she'd finished attempting to cajole Ava, she'd go to the grave and tell Gus the good news.

She showered and dressed quickly and called Ava's mobile.

'Mama, what can I do for you?'

'Good morning, dear!' Clara said, ignoring her daughter's brisk tone. Knowing she'd have a limited amount of time before Ava blew her top, Clara spoke swiftly, explaining as best she could, what had happened. How she had found Max and discovered he was married and how she had subsequently sent a letter to America.

'Did you get a response?'

'Yes, as a matter of fact I did. Better than that, my invitation was accepted and I'm getting a visitor.'

'So your darling son is coming home, is that it?'

'Not quite,' Clara hesitated. 'His daughter is coming to visit.'

'Pardon? His what?'

'His daughter,' Clara repeated. 'Ava, she's seventeen and her name is Nathalie.' Clara closed her eyes as she heard the deep gasp coming from Ava. She waited for a moment to allow her daughter to digest the information. When there was no further sound she spoke again. 'Are you still there?'

'Yup.'

'Talk to me, *Liebling*. Tell me what's going through your head. Please.'

'What do you want me to say?' she barked crossly.

'Ah now, Ava. Rudeness doesn't help anyone. I need you to tell me how you're feeling about Nathalie coming.' There was a long pause.

'Her name's Nathalie . . . I see . . .' Ava harrumped loudly. 'This is just fan-tassss-tic,' she seethed.

'Ava, please . . . I know this must be a shock and it's so hard for you especially . . .'

'Hard? Well that's putting it mildly.' There was a loud clunk and Clara feared she'd hung up. 'I dropped the phone,' she said. 'Don't panic, I haven't gone off in a fit of rage or anything,' she said coldly.

'Oh good. I know this is all so much to take on board, but the timing is right, Ava . . . I just know it.'

'How come she suddenly wants to waltz into our lives? Has my darling, precious, non-communicative prodigal brother suddenly decided he wants to speak to us after all these years?'

Clara felt her chest tightening as she willed Ava's anger to cease.

'Sadly this has nothing to do with Max,' she said. 'I wrote to Nathalie not him.'

'Why?'

'Because she's my granddaughter and your niece. Because she should be part of our family.'

'That hasn't concerned her before.'

'She didn't know anything about us,' Clara reasoned.

'And you really believe that?' Ava harrumphed.

'Yes I do, actually. Her mother, Amber, phoned me yesterday.'

'How is this Amber person involved now all of a sudden?'

Clara knew she needed to try and explain things a little more clearly before Ava refused to talk. She'd clammed up about things before and Clara knew she was a hard nut to crack once she closed her mind to someone.

'Amber called as soon as she read my letter. It's a long story but she found the letter and even though it was addressed to Nathalie she opened it. She called the second she read it. Obviously I don't know her, but she sounded so genuine.'

'She did?'

'Yes. Oh Ava, she sounded wonderful. She's so polite and articulate. So American!' Clara giggled. 'Which sounds terribly stupid of me to point out, but I don't suppose I ever imagined anyone connected to Max not sounding the same as us.'

'Well you really are bats now,' Ava said, though her voice softened somewhat.

Clara continued. 'Anyway, we chatted for a short while and Nathalie, it seems, is in the midst of a crisis.'

'I see,' said Ava.

'So, as I said Amber read my letter and clearly saw the invitation I'd issued as an opportunity for Nathalie to try and sort her life out. She asked if I honestly wanted her to come to Ireland. Of course I said yes. Amber set about organising it all and so she's . . .' Clara hesitated. 'She's coming to visit.'

'And that's meant to be normal, is it? After no contact for her entire lifetime, she's going to hop on a plane and drop in for coffee and cake and act as if nothing has happened? When is this emotional reunion taking place?'

'She arrives this evening.'

'Oh,' Ava said, sounding quite winded. 'So soon.'

'Yes, as I said, Amber is at a loss as to what to do with Nathalie. Her best friend was killed in a car accident. Nathalie was in the car at the time and things have gone from bad to worse for the poor mite.'

'Wow, that's rough,' Ava admitted. 'Is Max coming too?' she asked warily.

'No, she's coming on her own.'

'And have you had any contact from Max at all?' Ava demanded.

'No, love. I haven't,' Clara sighed. 'But who knows. Maybe Nathalie will become the glue we all need to bring us back together as a family.'

'I hear what you're saying about Nathalie, she's just a kid, but it will take a lot for me to forgive Max's silence. As the years have clocked up, he's made it crystal clear he wants nothing to do with us. Way back when, I was hurt. Now I feel nothing for him either way. He's dead to me.'

'Ava, please,' Clara said, her voice cracking with emotion. 'Try not to sound so hateful. I'm in the winter of my life, and if there's any chance, no matter how slim, that Max will come back into our lives, I'm going to take it.'

'Let's not talk about him,' Ava said crossly.

'Does that mean you won't come and meet Nathalie?'

'I . . .' Ava hesitated. 'I don't know. It's not just Nathalie . . . There's all the other stuff. Mama, all those things that happened eighteen years ago are part of a time I've buried. I'm not sure I can allow Max to dredge it all up again.'

'I understand, dear,' Clara said with compassion. 'I'll leave you to have a think about it, and if you feel you'd like to meet Nathalie, nobody will be more thrilled than me. Call me any time if you want to discuss it. Maybe you'd come for dinner and bring that nice fellow Michael along.'

'Who?'

'Michael who I met you with last week.'

'Ah, him. Nah, he's toast.'

'Why? He seemed very . . . grounded.'

'Boring, more like it. He was so damn serious. He had to go. I'm going on a date tonight, though. With a guy called Steve. He works at the betting shop in town.'

'I see,' said Clara. She didn't want to sound disapproving. Ava was old enough to make her own choices. But she longed to see her settle with someone decent. She couldn't exactly tell her daughter that serial dating wasn't the way to go. Perhaps it was.

How else would she meet the man of her dreams? All the same, Clara couldn't help worrying.

They finished chatting and Clara placed the phone on the charging cradle. She was always leaving it in odd places and it would take her ages to find it again. And when she did, inevitably it would have run out of battery. Ava got so cross with her when she didn't answer. She'd even closed up the shop and driven over to check on her at one point. Clara knew Ava worried about her, and she was grateful for that. It was part and parcel of being a family.

It was six months since Gus had passed away, yet on autopilot each and every morning her hand reached for two coffee cups from the cupboard. Sadness crept through her for the umpteenth time.

She'd heard great things about the local grief counselling service, so she'd decided to go. It turned out to be a marvellous thing. Her counsellor was called Barbara, and they chatted about all sorts of things: Clara's childhood, Max's departure and the subsequent years of silence.

Apparently the way she was feeling was perfectly normal. Whatever *normal* happened to be! Barbara said it was actually healthy to feel sad. That it was part and parcel of learning to let Gus go.

'But what if I don't want to let him go?' Clara had asked.

'I don't mean you ought to forget him,' Barbara explained. 'There's a difference between remembering and remaining in a state of raw pain.'

'I see,' Clara had said, nodding. She didn't really, though. She couldn't distinguish between the awful hollow aching and simply reminiscing. They seemed to go hand in hand for her so far.

She and Gus had been married for sixty-three years. She was

only seventeen the day she'd said 'I do'. A mere child really. Very few girls got married that young now. That was probably a better idea. Although Clara knew she didn't regret a single day she'd spent with Gus. Her only sorrow was that he wasn't still here to hold her hand.

As she finished filling the cafetière with hot water, Clara thought about Max. Could it really be twenty years since she'd seen her own son? A shiver went down her spine. In many ways the awful argument felt like only yesterday . . .

She had always harboured hope that Max would return and their family could be reunited once more. Sadly, she had under-estimated him when he'd said he never wanted to speak to them again.

It tore at Clara's heart that Gus and Max had never settled their differences. Just before he passed away, Gus had spoken about Max.

'Tell him I never stopped loving him.'

Clara wanted to be able to fulfil that promise, but as far as she was aware, Max didn't even know Gus was dead.

Barbara was constantly advising her to write things down. She said it was a wonderfully cathartic way of baring her soul without having to say it out loud.

'Writing offers such freedom,' she said. 'Especially when you're certain nobody is going to read it.'

Clara's mother had been the best example of that theory. Clara had only discovered all her writing after her father passed away and she had the heartbreaking job of clearing their belongings from the house.

The things her mother had written were so deeply private and Clara knew she hadn't told anyone. It made her desperately sad to think her darling mother had hidden so much of her inner self. But a large part of her could understand it too. She herself wasn't great at imparting her deepest thoughts. In fact, she'd had to stop going to see Barbara because she knew that sooner or later she'd have to talk about her early childhood and the real reason Max had left, never to return.

She wasn't ready to talk. Not quite yet. Not with a veritable stranger and not in a soulless room in the community centre. If and when she decided to speak about her innermost thoughts, Clara knew it needed to be right. The setting, the ears that listened and the timing. As of yet, not all those boxes had been ticked.

Clara smiled as she pulled on a light summer jacket. The morning sun hadn't heated the air yet, as she bustled to the graveyard to spend a few moments with Gus.

'It's happening, darling,' she said a while later, gazing earnestly at his headstone. 'A piece of Max is on the way. His most precious and prized achievement. Nathalie is coming to stay. I hope she'll like me. I hope we'll find a common bond. You'll be there, won't you, dear? You'll help me and guide me? I know you're busy. You're probably fishing and drinking whiskey with Elvis, but maybe you'd look in on me a little more often over the next while? Thank you, darling. I love you.'

Clara felt exhilarated after her chat with Gus. She sped home and put the finishing touches to the spare room. Perhaps it was divine inspiration or maybe it was Gus with his arm firmly around her mother's shoulder as both of them looked down on her, but Clara had a wonderful idea. She would share her mother's letters with young Nathalie. They had so much ground to make up. So many memories had been missed over the years of estrangement. Clara felt giddily confident that her mother's story would help her to bond with her granddaughter. There was a massive gap to fill, and she was certain the precious letters detailing an astonishing story were just what was called for.

Clara loved nothing more than cooking and baking. Since Gus had passed away, she only cooked when she knew Ava was coming. Otherwise things just went to waste. The thought of having someone to fuss over and care for again filled her with excitement.

Fleetingly she hoped Nathalie wasn't one of those girls who didn't like eating. A faddy teen who thought food would poison her and make her fat. According to some magazines Clara had read over the years, lots of people in LA lived on protein shakes while exercising in Lycra to within an inch of their lives.

Darling Gus had adored her cooking and baking.

'I think I fell in love with your mother's food before I even laid eyes on you,' he used to joke. They'd met when he was a boarder at her parents' home many years before. Clara's papa had been a music teacher at St Herbert's school, where Gus was a pupil. Her mama ran an overflow boarding house for ten lucky pupils. There they were fed delicious home-made fare and treated like kings.

As an only child, Clara had rejoiced in having so many other young people to share her home. The fact that they were all boys was a bonus.

Clara tried to picture her granddaughter. Would she look like Max, with his blond hair and aqua eyes? Would she have dark bouncing curls and coffee eyes like her own? Of course Clara had never seen Amber so she had nothing to work with there.

Hope sprang as she drove to the supermarket and glided happily down the aisles filling her trolley with ingredients. She'd make the perfect welcome dinner and bake as many delights as she could today.

For a second, she actually felt like she used to when she and her mama prepared for the boarders so many years ago. She tried to imagine what Nathalie might be feeling right now. No doubt the poor child was still utterly shell-shocked. But Clara felt she was an authority on shock. She'd suffered plenty and borne witness to even more over the years.

Gus had most definitely sent Nathalie to her. She was certain of that.

The renewed sense of purpose mixed with incredible expectation at Nathalie's arrival was wonderful. Excitement sent delicious shivers running through her body. Yet again, she acknowledged what a roller coaster life was. Each time she reached a point when she felt the world was becoming too much, a turn of events would catapult her onwards once more.

Chapter 6

AS MAX LAY IN THE DAY BED IN THE HOSPITAL, THE early-morning light filtered through the blinds. After a long shift in surgery, it had seemed easier to crash at work. Plus it meant he could avoid the mess waiting at home for him a little bit longer. And Max was an expert in avoiding emotional outbursts at home these days.

Suddenly the door shot open and Abe Quigley strode in.

'Max, there you are. I've been looking for you. Come to my boardroom, please. We need to have an important discussion.'

Max clambered out of the bed and pulled his washbag from a locker. Finding a rest room, he brushed his teeth and made an attempt at freshening up. When Abe Quigley, hospital chief and administrator, called for you, it was certain trouble.

Max knocked on Abe's door and walked in, hoping he looked less bedraggled than he felt.

'I'll cut to the chase, Max. The cuts we've begun to make aren't enough. We need to let a bunch more people go or this hospital is going to go under.' Abe smiled briefly as he clasped his hands together. 'I'm not going to allow that on my watch, obviously. Here's the list of people I need you to consider in your department. When I made you head of surgery, you knew matters like this would rest on your shoulders.'

'Yes, sir,' Max said, swallowing hard. As he scanned the list of names, he wanted to cry. Some of these people had been here longer than he had.

'Sir, how are we going to keep the surgical wards open if all these nurses and surgeons go?' he asked incredulously.

'We scale it down. We're only taking on more complex surgeries from here on in. The usual run-of-the-mill stuff like appendix and bypass operations will have to be handed to our sister hospital across town. I've met with their board and they'll pass the more complex ones to us.'

Max's blood went cold. 'When do I need to decide these people's fate?'

'You have until next week. But if you can do it sooner, I'd be obliged.'

Max stood up and took the pages with him. The first person he met as he walked towards his office was Amy Stephenson, a talented surgeon he'd finished his training with. Her name was at the top of Abe's list.

'Hey, Max,' she said, breezing past. She stopped in her tracks and reversed. 'Hey, buddy! You OK?'

'Hey, Amy,' he said, rubbing his face roughly with his hand. 'All good . . . Actually, it's not. But it'll be cool,' he said, forcing a smile.

'How's Nathalie doing?' she asked kindly. 'And Amber?'

'Yeah, fine,' he lied. 'How are your guys?'

'The twins are full of beans. They're so excited. They've been picked to play softball for the county. Means a whole new set of uniforms, which doesn't come cheap, I can tell ya! There goes the planned weekend at Palm Springs for Neil and me. But we can do that any time. The boys come first.'

Max shifted his stance, wishing the ground would swallow him up. Abe emerged from his office and spotted them chatting.

'Not here in the corridor, eh, Max,' he said loudly. 'Take all the meetings in your own office.'

'Of course,' Max hissed. 'I haven't made any decisions,' he added.

Amy looked at him in confusion and her face dropped. Abe slunk away, leaving Max red-faced and flailing.

'Max?'

'I've got to run, Amy,' he managed. 'Catch you around.'

By the time he got to his office and shut the door, Max felt as if the walls were closing in on him. How had his life gone so far down the drain in such a short space of time? The next few weeks were going to bring about a complete change, of that he had no doubt. But right now he had no idea how he would cope with the certain fallout.

The knock on the door made him jump.

'Hello, Mr Conway! I brought you one of the new white chocolate mocha cappuccinos they're doing at the café.'

'Oh thank you, Nancy,' he said, forcing a smile. Nancy was a part-time secretary he'd inherited when his own had gone on maternity leave. She seemed like a nice woman, but he was paranoid that she was sometimes a little *too* nice.

'I hope you enjoy it,' she said as she made a point of leaning forward in her low-cut top.

'Yes, I'm sure I will . . .'

She stared at him, as if waiting for him to say something else.

'That'll be all, thank you, Nancy,' he said.

'Oh . . .' She looked crestfallen. 'I'll be just out here if you need me,' she said, pouting slightly.

Max nodded and swivelled around in his chair so that he was facing the window. Could this day get any worse?

His thoughts returned to the problems waiting at home for him. How had his mother found him after all this time, and why? When he'd first left Ireland, he'd almost expected her to land on his doorstep. But as the months turned to years, he'd become accustomed to not having his parents or his sister in his life.

He'd also met Amber. He'd tapped into her world and that of her parents and sister. They'd gotten together weeks after his arrival in America, signalling the end of his old life and the beginning of a new and better one.

He'd come up against some major resistance from Amber's father at first. He made it very clear that he was not pleased about his precious girl hanging out with a pale, gangly Irish immigrant with no family or money behind him. But Max kept his head down and his focus firmly on his goals. Slowly Amber's father accepted him and realised he was diligent, hard-working and clever.

'You're not the one I'd have chosen,' he said. 'But I gotta hand it to you, Max. You're a grafter and you got brains in that head o' yours. If you keep on minding my girl the way you've done so far, I can't complain.'

They'd never become close. Max was done with the whole happy families notion, so he allowed Amber to do the bulk of that while he only turned up at special occasions. Amber's sister Macy moved to New York and seemed about as keen as Max to stay in contact. Soon afterwards, Amber's folks passed away within months of one another.

Max had finished his training as a doctor and excelled, going on to specialise in heart surgery. Now a renowned and well-respected pillar of the community, he had very successfully rein-vented himself. Even *he* often forgot about his Irish roots, and he was delighted to have a daughter who'd been born and raised in LA. As far as he was concerned, his childhood and the time leading up to his sudden departure from Ireland might as well have happened to somebody else entirely.

His marriage to Amber was serene in many ways. They weren't

fond of open public displays of affection, nor did they make a habit of arguing. They had a healthy respect for one another and their relationship usually worked seamlessly.

So he could safely say he'd never been as angry at Amber as he was at this moment. How could she have gone behind his back and organised to send Nathalie to Ireland? How dare she communicate with his mother like this!

He thumped his desk and tried to imagine what was going on in his parents' house right now. Knowing his mother, she'd be running from Billy to Jack, fussing as his father carried on working . . . With a jolt, he realised that his father must be long retired by now. Was he doddery and stooped, or had he turned into one of those imposing gentlemen who held on to their height despite the passage of time?

Ava, with her fiery temper and throaty laugh, flashed through his mind. He'd always felt most guilty about her. Especially when his best mate Sean had arrived telling him he'd been unfaithful and Ava had called off their wedding.

He'd wanted to pick up the phone so many times over the years. Firstly to tell Ava how sorry he was that her heart had been broken. Because he knew without a shadow of doubt that splitting from Sean would've almost killed her. She'd adored him.

More than that, Max had longed to tell her to give Sean a second chance. To let her know he was a broken man without her. But stubborn pride had always won over, and the longer Max left it, the wider the gap his silence created. His friend's misery was not something he enjoyed witnessing, though. Sean had sobbed on his shoulder in a drunken stupor many times over the years. As time passed, it happened less frequently, but Max knew he had never gotten over Ava.

'Nobody comes close to her. I've tried, and some of the women are a close second, but I can't settle for that. It wouldn't be fair to either of us,' Sean explained. Max had urged him to call Ava. To try and mend the hurt he'd caused.

'Maybe she'll forgive and forget? Time is a great healer, so they say.'

'Said the pot to the kettle,' Sean always answered. 'If you honestly believe that, why aren't you jumping on a plane to the Emerald Isle and mending all your burnt bridges?'

Max had never told Sean the details leading up to his sudden departure, and his friend had always had the courtesy not to ask.

His head throbbed and he felt like crawling into a cave and hiding for a week. Nothing stressed Max as much as thinking about his family. He'd sat and deliberated long and hard at many different points of his life. But no matter how he tried, he absolutely couldn't back down. Even now, after twenty years, his anger and resentment were still stopping him from holding out an olive branch.

He knew Nathalie was in crisis. He didn't need Amber pointing that out. The hollow look on his daughter's face didn't go unnoticed. He hadn't the first clue of how to fix her, however. Besides, that was Amber's forte. She was one of life's fixers. She could look at an issue, no matter how big or small, and come up with a clever and feasible solution.

So after Mackenzie died, he'd done what he always did. He'd buried his head in his work and mentally run away from the problems at home.

Hiding had worked for Max ever since he was a toddler. If his father was cross or he got into trouble at school, he'd shin up a tree or climb into the back of the wardrobe, behind his mother's long coats and dresses, and wait, sometimes for hours, until the dust settled and the thudding of his heart abated.

His greatest feat of all had been the time he'd run here to America. He'd never intended for it to be permanent. But the longer he spent here, the harder it was to return. Once he reached the ten-year threshold, he'd honestly thought there was no going back. He was fine with that. Or so he'd managed to convince himself.

But now that Nathalie was off to Ireland, he'd be connected to his past once again.

Max had never thought he'd live to regret his decision to cut ties with his family. He honestly figured he had it all worked out. He'd even gone over this exact scenario in his head. He'd somehow convinced himself that it wouldn't affect him should Nathalie want to meet them some day.

But now he realised that theories were never truly tested until they came to pass. He hated being exposed as a liar, too. As he knew only too well, lies were the root of so many problems, and he'd just been caught out.

As he went about his rounds, ghosts from the past continued to plague him.

He knew his parents understood why he'd gone. They were well aware of his reasons for hauling his entire life to the other side of the world. But at the time, he couldn't bring himself to tell Ava the truth. He'd tried to make her hate him. But with just a short window of opportunity for that to happen, he'd only managed to confuse and hurt her. The look of sheer bewilderment on her face as he'd walked away that fateful day still haunted his dreams.

He was in a bar on his own, composing a letter to her, the night he met Amber. Perched in a dark corner with a pint of cool beer and a look of utter despair on his face, he'd been pleasantly surprised when a couple of pretty girls asked if they could join him.

Amber had stood out instantly. Dressed in expensive-looking clothes, with flawless skin and perfectly coiffed hair, she oozed sophistication and style. He was drawn to her gorgeous American accent and laughed when she was clearly blown away by his Irishness.

'OMG, you are the cutest guy I've ever set eyes on,' she said giddily. 'And as for that accent . . .'

He was staggered by how much he enjoyed being swooned over. There were no mind games with Amber either. She made it clear she wanted him, and in his vulnerable mental state he was glad to have someone on his side. Her friends were welcoming and he soon slotted into her life. His only hostile moments came from her father, and even he eventually softened.

All thoughts of Ireland were drowned out by the whirlwind that Amber created. He never finished his letter to Ava and only allowed himself to think of her occasionally. He was genuinely happy with Amber, but every now and again he wondered how his family back home were getting on.

Did Ava still live near their parents? He sincerely hoped she was happy now. That she'd found a man worthy of her. Unlike Amber, who was controlled and steady, Ava had been flighty and fun-loving, to say the least. He still winced as he thought of her face the day he'd said he was leaving. She hadn't cried or yelled; instead she'd put her hand on his face, kissed his cheek gently and walked silently away.

It was the most dignified and stoic response imaginable, and he'd felt like a complete shit. When Sean had arrived in America three years after him, Max had been both astonished and delighted. He'd nearly buckled and contacted his sister. But Sean had assured him that Ava was in no mood to have newsy chats.

Max loved Amber wholly and totally. That love had deepened and strengthened over the years, especially after Nathalie had completed their family. He felt it was all so wonderful and perfect that introducing his muck-up of a family would only mar it all. So he'd convinced Sean to go along with his lies.

Fresh anger shot through Max.

Damn his mother for picking this hole in his carefully contrived life. Damn Amber for acting so bloody impulsively for the first time ever. It was just his luck that the one time his wife chose to step out of her comfort zone and do something spontaneous, it had to be *this*.

Chapter 7

CLARA PARKED AT THE AIRPORT. SHE PRIDED herself on her parking. In spite of Ava's protests and constant comments about an eighty-year-old on the loose on the roads, she felt she was still very much in control of her life while she was mobile and independent.

She was far too early. It was incredible to her that Nathalie was in the air, working her way through the clouds to see her.

She wondered what Max was thinking. Had he been tempted to come too? She didn't want to raise her own hopes, but there was a tiny little voice in the back of Clara's head whispering that her son could possibly walk through those doors at arrivals this evening. Imagine what a reunion that would be.

Quashing the thought, and tucking it into the recesses of her mind, she thought of the surprise she had at home, just in case. She'd baked Max's favourite thing in the whole world as a boy . . . The old-fashioned cocoa-scented sponge her own mother used to make, lavished with thick chocolate butter icing, was waiting on a crystal stand in the kitchen.

Clara smiled as she pictured Max as a tiny child and how he used to jump for joy when she announced they'd bake that very cake.

'Can I lick the spoon, Mama?' he'd beg.

Although everyone longed to have the baking spoon, Ava often gave in to his demands. Being the youngest, he probably got away with more than she did. On special occasions, such as birthdays or Christmas, both children would be allowed to eat chocolate cake for breakfast.

'That's so unhealthy,' Gus would grumble.

'Ah, it's a special day, Dr Conway,' Clara would say. 'I don't see anything wrong with it. In fact, this is the kind of thing memories are made of. We don't necessarily recall grand gestures or huge expenditure when we're older. It's the quirky things, like cake for breakfast or spending a cold and wet day in front of the fire instead of going to school, that stay up here,' Clara said, tapping her head. 'The little concessions that make us feel as if we're sidestepping conformity every once in a while!'

This afternoon, as she'd folded the cocoa powder and flour into the rich chocolatey mixture, the delicious fudgy consistency had reminded her of times gone by. Dipping her finger in, she'd savoured the flavour as it evoked memories of better and less complicated times.

'*Köstlich*,' she'd said, in her mother tongue. 'Just delicious,' she'd repeated in English, nodding in approval. It was a long time since she'd spoken German properly but her accent was still unmistakable even after all these years. She wasn't aware of it, of course, but she'd smiled when Amber had pointed it out on the phone.

Sudden nerves washed over Clara as she found the arrivals area of the airport and sat down. She wondered how much Nathalie knew. Had Max told her everything? Had he told her a pack of lies? She'd lain awake the previous night thinking about it all.

The truth of the matter was this. Clara had never told any of her children her entire life story. They knew she'd come from Austria at the end of the war. Of course Ava and Max had known and loved their Austrian grandparents as tots. But they had little or no knowledge of the events that had led the family to settle in Ireland in 1946.

She hoped her granddaughter would like her home. Clara had only lived there for five years. She decided to put Nathalie in the room that offered a view of the sea from one window and the pretty rockery area of the garden from the other.

She'd lovingly placed a small posy of sweet peas from the garden in a miniature vase on the wooden bedside locker. The pinks, whites, and blues picked up the colours of the patchwork quilt on the bed while scenting the room delicately.

Clara would do her best to make her granddaughter feel at home. She had experience of arriving in a strange place with people she didn't know. She'd done the same thing herself many moons ago.

She breathed a sigh of relief when Nathalie's flight number appeared on the arrivals board. She hoped her granddaughter's bags had arrived too. She figured there'd be nothing worse for a teenage girl than losing her belongings in a strange land with the knowledge that the only things she could borrow would come from an old lady! Still, if all else failed, she could always call by Ava's boutique and pick up some clothes. Fleetingly Clara wondered if Ava had cooled down at all. She assumed she would snap out of her current ball of rage at some point soon.

Instinctively she rose from her seat and wandered towards the large sliding doors. A glut of people came first. There were lots of families with cases piled high on difficult-to-manoeuvre trolleys. The joyful scenes as loved ones were reunited made butterflies dance in her tummy.

Momentarily, she wondered if she would spot Nathalie immediately. It would be an awkward start to their time together if they ended up on opposite sides of the arrivals hall not recognising one another.

All worries dissipated as soon as Nathalie strode through the double doors. She was like a carbon copy of Ava at that age. They shared the same slim figure and sapphire-blue eyes, and most of all, Nathalie walked with a sense of self-assurance that Clara instantly identified with. This wasn't a cocky teenage swagger, but more a controlled and confident gait.

'Hello, Nathalie, I'm your *Oma*,' she said simply, holding her arms out.

'Oma,' Nathalie said, forcing a smile, 'it's awesome to meet you.' Her tone didn't match her words. Clutching her shoulder bag and suitcase simultaneously, Nathalie dropped her gaze to the floor.

'I'm overwhelmed to see you, dear,' Clara said. 'You're beautiful.'

'Thanks.'

Clara longed to take her in her arms and hold her for ever. But Nathalie's folded arms and hunched stance didn't invite physical contact. The crowd began to dissolve, so Clara ushered her towards the exit to the car park.

'Let me take your bag,' she said.

'It's cool, I got it.'

Clara wanted to say something witty or cheerful to try and dispel the undoubted awkwardness between them. But nothing was springing to mind.

'I'm so thrilled to meet you, *Liebling*,' she said as they ascended in the elevator to the car.

'*Liebling*?' Nathalie looked puzzled.

'Uh, so it means "darling" in German,' Clara said, grabbing Nathalie's suitcase and tossing it into the boot. 'You'll get used to my little phrases in time.'

'I'd no idea growing up that my dad was half Austrian,' Nathalie said. 'I knew he was from Ireland, but that was all.'

'I take it he didn't talk to you about me, then?'

'No,' Nathalie said. 'He said you were dead. Dad's a good guy, but he's not exactly Mr Emotional.'

'I've only had a couple of conversations with your mother on the phone,' Clara said, 'but she seems very friendly and bubbly. I'm delighted Max found such a wonderful lady.'

As they drove home, Clara did her best to put Nathalie at ease. She didn't want to unnerve her any further, but she was longing to sit opposite her so she could drink in every inch of Max's daughter. She wanted to stroke her skin and examine her eyes and try to absorb all the things she didn't yet know about this beautiful girl.

She had promised herself she wouldn't quiz her granddaughter. She would try and allow information to pass between them organically. If Nathalie felt she was being interviewed, she'd certainly feel uncomfortable.

'Was your father all right with you making this trip?' she ventured.

'He wasn't exactly stoked,' Nathalie replied as she stared out the window.

'I'm sorry to hear that,' Clara said honestly. 'I actually wondered if he might come with you. Silly really, but a tiny part of me hoped he'd be too precious about letting you come alone.'

'My mom didn't give him a whole bunch of choices,' Nathalie said. 'Or me for that matter,' she added, under her breath.

Clara stole a glance at Nathalie. Her pretty face was arranged in a cross pout as she concentrated on the road outside.

'I'm sorry you felt forced to come here, Nathalie. If it helps at all, I won't push you into doing things with me. I'm not about to insist you accompany me to bingo or spend hours weeding my garden. I don't operate that way. I believe we should all make our own choices in life . . . where at all possible, you understand.'

Clara sighed. 'There are so many rules attached to living, aren't there? I often despair at that.'

Nathalie continued to stare out the window, expressionlessly.

'For months after your father first left, I prayed and hoped that he'd come home.' Clara knew she sounded sad. 'But if I've learned anything from life, it's that telling others what to do is a bad idea. It never really works out.'

'Huh, try telling my mom that,' Nathalie spat.

'I'm certain she only wants what's best for you, dear. Most mothers do, you know?'

Nathalie sighed heavily.

'I don't have many regrets in my life,' Clara continued, 'but I am terribly sad that your father didn't ever make it up with his dad. It's too late now and nobody can change that.'

'Why, where is my grandfather?' Nathalie's head shot around.

'He passed away six months ago,' Clara said. She didn't want to cry or seem overly emotional, but tears coursed down her cheeks. 'Oh dear, I am sorry,' she sniffed. 'You don't need to be stuck in a confined space with a howling old woman. I'll stop now. Just ignore me.'

Nathalie glanced over as they stopped at a red light. The compassion in her eyes made Clara gasp.

'My best friend died too,' she said. The harshness in her voice softened somewhat. 'It's cruel when someone you love is ripped away.'

'Yes, it is.'

Clara watched as Nathalie stared unhappily into space.

'Gus was my heartbeat,' she said. 'I'm taking each day without him as it comes. But I won't lie to you. It's not easy picking my way through life alone. I became so used to having him with me. I suppose I never imagined for one second that he'd suddenly go and I'd have to carry on like this. Everything in my life is geared towards catering for two. You know, I've thrown more wasted food in the bin over the last six months than I ever did in my entire previous existence. My brain is programmed to include Gus.'

Nathalie remained silent as they arrived in Lochlann. Clara explained that Lochlann had been her home for a very long time. She said how much she loved it and how she couldn't imagine being any place else. She pointed in the direction of St Herbert's school, where she'd first met Gus and where Max had also attended.

'My father was the music teacher there.'

As they approached Clara's house, Nathalie looked as if she wanted to curl into a ball and hide.

'Are you religious, Nathalie?' She shook her head. 'I can't say I am especially either. Not in the churchgoing sense, at least. I believe in God, though. I think we all go somewhere wonderful when we pass on. I think this life is only the beginning. But I believe things happen for a reason. I suppose I'm more spiritual than religious.' She thought about it as she pulled up at the house and turned the engine off. 'Although sometimes that notion of things happening for a reason can be ever so difficult to accept, *Liebling*.'

'I'll never accept Mackenzie's death,' Nathalie said with conviction. 'It's totally wrong on so many levels.'

'Oh, I agree. It's not fair, nor will it ever seem so. It's such a sad waste when someone young is taken from us. But I do know that the people who pass in and out of our lives all help to shape us. They mould us into the people we eventually end up becoming.'

Nathalie opened the car door in silence and walked around to get her bag from the boot.

Clara wished she knew what her granddaughter was thinking. She ushered her towards the front door.

'Welcome to my home. This isn't where your father grew up. Gus and I moved here in recent years.'

'It's pretty,' Nathalie said hesitantly.

They pulled the suitcase in the door and Clara led the way to Nathalie's bedroom.

'So this will be yours for as long as you wish to stay,' she said proudly.

'Thanks.' Nathalie stood quite still and barely looked around. Clara figured the best policy would be to allow the girl to dictate their relationship.

'I'll leave you to settle in. There's food ready if you're hungry. If not, there's no pressure. I'm sure you're exhausted and probably want to be left alone.' There was no reply, so Clara reluctantly turned to leave the room.

'Did you make the quilt?' Nathalie asked suddenly.

'Yes,' Clara said. 'I hope you like it.'

'It's beautiful.'

'I'm glad you think so.' She smiled.

'How did you make this from scratch?'

'It's not so difficult once somebody has the time and patience to teach you. I could show you how to quilt while you're here, if you wish?'

'Sure,' Nathalie said flatly.

'I'll leave you to it. I'll be downstairs. Join me if you like.'

'Thank you.'

Clara made her way down the stairs slowly. She actually felt like skipping down, taking the steps two at a time and jumping the last three. If she were twenty years younger, she might very well have done so. She wanted to wave her arms about and yell hallelujah that her granddaughter was here. But that wouldn't be correct *Oma* behaviour, and besides, Nathalie was already a little prickly. She didn't want her running away in the middle

geriatrics trundling about with wheelie carts. Rock 'n' roll, Nathalie thought sourly.

Having texted her folks and blocked DJ's friend Garry too, because he had jumped on the bandwagon and was incessantly sending abusive messages about her tossing his buddy aside like waste material, she found herself drawn towards the hallway. The smell of food emanating from downstairs was awesome. She hadn't eaten any of the hideous airline food so she was ravenous. Gingerly she made her way towards the aromas.

'Hey,' she said, feeling suddenly shy. For a split second she wished she'd been a bit less moody in the car.

'Hello, dear, come and sit. I'm about to eat. Will you join me?'

'Sure.'

She perched on a chair and looked around the room. There was an oversized dresser blocking an entire wall, laden down with figurines, trinkets, photographs and pretty boxes. It was the type of place she'd love to root about in for six hours when nobody was looking. There were probably all sorts of hidden things in there.

'I'll dish up. Why don't you look at the old photos on the dresser? There are plenty of your father. He was a gorgeous boy.'

As soon as Clara went into the adjoining kitchen to bash about with saucepans, Nathalie shot over to examine the pictures. She'd never seen any of her dad as a kid. He hadn't changed much.

'Who's in the pictures with Dad?'

'Your aunt Ava.'

'She looks like me.'

'Yes, she does. That was my first thought when you walked into arrivals earlier.'

Nathalie scrutinised the picture. This Ava was so like her it was kind of creepy. She had the same hair, same smile . . . It was totally weird. She really hadn't wanted to talk, but this woman was intriguing her.

'Does she know I'm coming here?'

'Yes, dear. She'll be along to see you at some point. Ava doesn't take kindly to being told what to do. But I expect she'll come when it suits her.'

Nathalie picked up another one of the framed photos. Ava must've been around her own age when it was taken. The hair was a more hickey style and her clothes were God-awful, but the face and bone structure and slender body shape were uncannily like her own. They had the exact same corkscrew curls and round brown eyes. Mackenzie used to tell her she had horse's eyes. She'd meant it as a compliment, but Nathalie had always found it hilarious.

Clara came into the room with two steaming plates. Nathalie sat down and thanked her. She wasn't ready to have a big old warming chat with this person, but she knew she couldn't be too rude either.

'This is traditional goulash. To most people it's casserole, but I prefer to call it goulash. The potatoes were a firm favourite when your father was little. They're sliced and baked in cream and cheese, and of course this is pickled red cabbage.'

'A heart attack on a plate,' Nathalie said drily. 'In LA, everything is fat-free, sugar-free and more often than not dairy-free.' She recoiled from the plate and then gave it a slight nudge away from her.

'I don't go in for that kind of nonsense,' Clara said mildly. 'I've always eaten home-cooked food. In my opinion, moderation is the key. A little of what you like is good for the soul. If you go for all that "free" rubbish, it must become taste-free too.'

Nathalie hesitated. She didn't want to be here, but at the same time, she didn't want to offend this old lady. When she'd shoved the plate, her *Oma* had looked seriously hurt. She could hear her mother scolding her and telling her to mind her manners. Reluctantly she picked up her cutlery and took a small forkful, hoping it wouldn't be awful.

Closing her eyes, she savoured the incredible flavours. The meat melted in her mouth, and as she took some of the potatoes, the creamy comfort they offered was like being hugged from the inside. The pickled red cabbage had a slight sweet-and-sour thing going on, with a hint of spice.

'This is *so* good,' she said, forgetting to be cranky for a moment.

'Glad you like it. I agree.'

Nathalie raised an eyebrow. This old doll was funny. Very direct, and she certainly didn't seem to feel the need to be coy or self-effacing.

Nathalie finished most of the food and thought she couldn't possibly eat another bite, but when Clara placed a slice of chocolate cake with home-made crème anglaise in front of her, she polished off the lot.

'I will be super-sized Nathalie if I stay here too long,' she said, patting her flat stomach as she lounged back in her large spoon-backed dining chair. 'I wouldn't normally eat that amount of calories in the space of a week.'

Clara tutted. 'You're as thin as a stick. You need feeding up if anything.' Nathalie narrowed her eyes, feeling intense irritation once more. Didn't this woman know anything about carbs, fat and sugar? It was a mystery she wasn't in a mobility cart and morbidly obese if this was the kind of stuff she ate on a regular basis.

The house phone rang and Clara rushed to answer it. Her conversation was muffled as she wandered to the other side of the room.

'That was your aunt Ava,' she said with a smile. 'Are you too tired to meet her now?'

'No. I guess not,' Nathalie said, trying to hide her curiosity. She wanted to get a proper look at this woman. She wondered if she was as bubbly and quirky as Oma.

Clara smiled in relief. 'Good, that was the correct answer, because she's on her way over. She won't stay too long if I know Ava. She's always in a hurry, you know?'

Nathalie nodded. This was all quite terrifying. None of these people knew the first thing about her yet they were related. It was all so screwed up. Anger at her father raced through her again. This situation sucked. All she could do was bide her time. Stay here for a couple of weeks and then get the hell home to LA and never come back.

'I am very relieved that Ava is coming over,' Clara said. 'She's feisty, and the fallout between her and your father was most bitter.'

It was on the tip of Nathalie's tongue to ask Clara why they'd fallen out with her dad. But she'd only just arrived and she didn't want to uncover some rank story involving a terrible event. This whole situation was pretty darn awkward as it was without asking leading questions.

It did seem kind of strange all the same. And judging from the smiling faces and happy poses her father was pulling in the photos, he used to be a very cheerful and carefree type of guy. Whatever had gone on seemed to have affected him massively. Maybe, she mused, it explained why he was so uptight and emotionally closed a lot of the time.

One of the photos showed him dumping a bucket of water over his father's head. Max had such a mischievous look on his face as his poor unsuspecting father sat in a blue and white striped deckchair reading his newspaper. The shot had caught the water in mid air. Nathalie smiled. It looked like something she'd have done as a kid.

Her favourite picture by far was one of Max when he must've been around ten years old. His face was covered in chocolate and he was brandishing a wooden spoon. He'd clearly licked the bowl from some baking. He had such vitality and impish glee in his grin, she couldn't help joining in.

As Clara cleared the dinner dishes, Nathalie walked over to the dresser and stared at the photo in more detail.

'That was typical of your father,' Clara said as she looked over her shoulder. 'He was a scamp!'

It was on the tip of Nathalie's tongue to say that he'd turned into a complete control freak who rarely found anything to laugh about and that he'd have had a meltdown if she'd made a mess like that in the house.

But then again, their home wasn't a bit like this one. For a start, Amber wasn't a baker; in fact she rarely cooked from scratch at all. Some of their oven trays were still encased in the factory packaging from ten years ago.

Nathalie wondered what had happened to remove that carefree light from her father's eyes.

They loaded the small dishwasher in Clara's kitchen. Their silence wasn't strained. In fact, Nathalie found Clara's demeanour almost intoxicating. She was naturally laid-back, with no sign of pretence. It was oddly refreshing, and in spite of deciding before she came that she was certain to hate it here, Nathalie was already beginning to feel less tense.

'I remember the first time I got a dishwasher,' Clara said happily as they finished clearing. 'Gus arrived home with it strapped on to the roof of his car. There were no proper delivery trucks at that time. It was almost the size of our kitchen! It was a monstrous machine. Well, I thought it was the most marvellous invention ever!'

Nathalie didn't respond. Instead she walked back over to the table and pushed her chair in, ready to excuse herself and return to the solace of her bedroom.

'Gus was a doctor,' Clara ventured, as if trying to hold on to their time together.

'Seriously?' Nathalie said in astonishment. 'I've applied for med school. But I had no idea that was a family tradition. Dad never mentioned my grandpa was a doctor too.' Sadness replaced her anger momentarily as she wondered yet again why she'd never been introduced to this family. If her dad hated his own father so much, why did he follow in his footsteps? The more she heard, the less any of this made sense.

'Well, you've taken the first step to changing all that,' Clara said, as if reading her mind. 'We'll all get to know one another over the next while, and hopefully lots of questions will be answered.'

Nathalie bit her lip and nodded.

'So,' Clara said brightly, 'your aunt took over my business, which is a clothing boutique.'

'Really?' Nathalie said, unable to hide her curiosity. 'You owned a boutique?'

'Yes, dear. My mother and I set it up many moons ago. She was a talented seamstress and adored fashion. Ava is a fantastic businesswoman and the shop is her life. She's single and doesn't have children.'

'Hang on a minute,' Nathalie said, bowled over. '*Your* mom, as in my great-grandmother, opened a clothing store?'

'Yes,' Clara laughed. 'It's more a boutique than a store. Store sounds like a massive place to me. We both saw a gap in the market, so we went for it.'

'So when was this?' Nathalie asked.

'Oh, now let me think . . . It was the same year I got married, so it was 1953 and I had just turned eighteen.'

'You guys must've been totally ahead of your time! I'd say the locals thought you were from outer space.'

'We were unusual, I suppose,' Clara agreed. 'But neither Mama nor I ever cared much about what other people deemed customary. We were both practical to a fault and realised that many women liked the dresses we'd been making. So a boutique seemed like a very logical step.'

'And Ava took it over from you?' Nathalie asked.

'Yes. I'm delighted really. It's lovely to see it evolving and surviving.' Clara's eyes crinkled as she smiled.

At that moment Ava arrived. Well, shot in the door at high speed in a wave of hair-flicking and hand-on-hip attitude, to be exact. She halted, clearly shocked as she eyeballed Nathalie. In turn, Nathalie stared open-mouthed at Ava.

'Oh sweet Jesus,' Ava said. 'Wow, you look so like . . . me,' she trailed off. 'I . . . I wasn't expecting that.'

'We really do look similar,' Nathalie said. 'Oma told me that was you in the pictures.' She pointed to the dresser. 'I couldn't believe how alike we were as kids. And Dad never thought to mention it. Not surprising,' she said with sarcasm.

Ava rolled her eyes. 'That sounds typical of my darling little brother.'

'Wait a minute, he's not that bad,' Nathalie said, feeling suddenly disloyal. 'He's just not much of a talker, so I guess he chose to keep shtum about this freaky thing.' Her heart began to beat wildly. Ava was looking pretty intimidating.

'Listen,' Ava sighed. 'I know none of this is your fault. I'm not trying to get at you. You're just a kid and your father's behaviour has no bearing on you. But he's an idiot and nothing he says or does surprises me.'

'Hey, he's a good father,' Nathalie said. 'Obviously you just don't know him any more.'

'Yeah, you're right there. And whose fault is that? *We* haven't gone anywhere. It's not as if he didn't know how to get in touch. Listen, I get it that you're going to try and stick up for your old man. But believe me, kiddo, he's a waste of space.'

'For the record, I didn't get a choice about coming here. My mom read Oma's letter and shoved me on the next available flight. It's for my own good apparently. I don't actually want to be here, so you can—'

'Sometimes mothers know best,' Clara said hurriedly. 'I think your mother was aiming to break the ice that has formed over the years.'

'How did your father take the news that you were absconding to the dark side?' Ava asked pointedly.

'Ava!' Clara shot her a stern look.

Nathalie glared back. 'Well, as I said, my mom organised the entire thing. Dad came back from the hospital and had a total freak and acted as if it was all a conspiracy to get to him.'

'Yup.' Ava nodded. 'That'd be Max. Seems the years haven't changed him too much.'

Nathalie knew it was pointless to say anything further.

'Are you sitting down?' Clara asked Ava. 'I have chocolate cake.'

'No thanks, Mama, I'm going on a date. Besides, your chocolate cake is total diet suicide.'

'You know how I feel about diets,' Clara scoffed.

'I do, so don't waste your breath. I'm going. It was . . . surreal to meet you, Nathalie.'

Nathalie swallowed hard, relieved that Ava was leaving. She felt as if she'd been hit by a whirlwind. In fact, she realised, she was totally wiped out. The emotion and the travelling had all caught up with her.

'Why don't you go and get your night things on and I'll bring you a nice cup of cocoa?' Clara suggested.

Nathalie didn't like the idea of cocoa and was so full she felt she could burst, but Clara looked so eager about the whole thing, she agreed. Besides, her *Oma* was genuinely trying to make her feel at ease, unlike her father's sister. They might look alike, but Nathalie knew she never wanted to end up as bitter as Ava.

She climbed the stairs with weary legs and found a nightshirt in her bag. She pulled it on, then made her way to the bathroom and brushed her teeth. Her mom had thoughtfully tucked a packet of wet wipes into her washbag. Sighing with gratitude, she cleansed and returned to her room. Oma was there, sitting on a little wicker chair cradling a mug of hot chocolate. Nathalie climbed into the fresh bed and held her hands out to receive the mug.

It didn't take long for her to totally change her mind about not wanting hot chocolate.

'OMG! What is in this?' she asked, licking her lips.

'It's made with real melted chocolate,' Clara smiled.

'I'm going to be the size of the White House by the time I leave here,' Nathalie said. 'This would probably be illegal in LA!'

Clara laughed and nodded, reiterating that she had no time for faddy diets or the idea of deprivation.

'I cannot express how wonderful it is for me to have you here, Nathalie. I know this is all very difficult for you. But I promise I'll make it as easy as I can. I know what it's like to be in a strange environment with people you don't know. I'll try not to impose on your privacy too much. But please let me know if you need anything.'

'I will, thank you, Oma.' It was kind of cool being able to call her Oma. It was so much less awkward than Grandma.

'Good night, dear. My room is just across the hall. Don't hesitate to come and find me if you need me. Feel free to go to the kitchen or do whatever you like. My home is your home and I'd like you to feel comfortable here.' She blew a kiss before walking out of the room and closing the door gently.

Nathalie was intrigued. What did Clara mean, she knew what it felt like to be in a strange environment with people she didn't know? This woman was different to anyone she'd ever met before. Much as she wanted not to, Nathalie had to admit she liked her *Oma* a whole bunch already. There were so many questions zooming around her head it made her dizzy. Right now, she needed to sleep. But one thing was certain: she wanted to find out what the hell had gone on with Dad.

What didn't fit was why her father seemed to hate Oma so much. She could totally appreciate why he wouldn't want to talk to Ava. If she never met her again, Nathalie felt it would be too soon. But Oma was different. If she absolutely *had* to stay here for a bit, Nathalie figured she might as well try to uncover the secrets of the past.

Ava pulled up at the five-star hotel in central Dublin. She needed a drink. That Nathalie was a right little brat. Ava pitied her mother having to deal with her. Well, she was going to keep a close eye on her. Clara wasn't getting any younger, and the last thing she needed was that little fireball storming in and turning her world upside down. How bloody typical of Max to go AWOL for twenty years and then send his teenage daughter to unhinge them.

Handing the valet her keys, she rushed to the bar. The guy she was meeting was a friend of a friend and she'd been assured he was fun, wealthy and looking for a partner. Ava wasn't in the market for a husband. She'd given up on that notion years ago. But she'd welcome someone who could show her a good time without wrecking her head.

'Ava?' said a slightly balding man in an expensive suit and ridiculously shiny shoes.

'Yes,' she said, groaning inwardly. This was going to be a long night.

'Harry. Pleased to meet you. Can I get you a drink? Champagne, or a cocktail perhaps? I'm having a margarita and it's pretty good.'

She couldn't bear men who drank girlie drinks. 'Sounds good,' she said, smiling falsely.

After the second cocktail, Harry seemed less dweeby and she'd warmed to him somewhat. He was clearly very impressed by her. Ava adored being adored, and the strong cocktails were making her relax.

There was no shortage of conversation as she talked about her clothing designs and he counteracted with anecdotes from the accountancy firm where he worked. While she knew she didn't want to see him again, Ava needed to feel a man's arms around her, just for a few hours.

She took the liberty of ordering a bottle of bubbly while he was in the gents'. An hour and a half later, they were writhing beneath the Egyptian cotton sheets in one of the hotel's executive suites. Harry was eager to please and certainly seemed delighted to have made it into bed with her.

'You're amazing,' he whispered some time later, as she returned from the bathroom and climbed back into bed.

'Hold me,' she said, closing her eyes. Drifting off to sleep, she imagined he was someone else. Someone she had loved once upon a time; someone she'd thought would share her life. Someone who had let her down and broken her heart to such an extent that she'd never been able to settle in a relationship since.

Ava had been quite successful at convincing herself that she didn't need a permanent partner. Most of the time she was fine.

It was only at times like this that she allowed her imagination to wander to the past. While sober, the door to that corridor of her mind stayed firmly shut.

The room was spinning. She'd drunk far too much alcohol. She groaned, disgusted with herself for getting into this state again. It used to only happen from time to time. But lately she'd been hitting the bottle and taking strange men to bed a little too often. Hearing her murmur, Harry held her closer. The drink helped her sleep so she could block out her loneliness and allow her dreams to take over.

As it turned out, she conked out for a couple of hours and woke with a spongy, sour-tasting mouth and a thumping head-ache. Glancing to her right, she stared at the man in the bed.

What the hell had happened? She gazed around the dimly lit room and tried to recall what had gone on.

She thought of Nathalie and her cheeky little stance, and poor Clara running around after her. Irritation stuck in her gullet as she held her breath and slid out of the bed. She was relieved to make it to the privacy of the en suite. Seeing as this debauched behaviour had become a bit of a habit of late, she'd become quite astute at preparing for eventualities: she always had a change of underwear, a rolled-up jersey wrap dress and a basic washbag tucked into her shopper-sized handbag.

Using the hotel shampoo and body wash, she freshened up, then applied her make-up. She'd happily have climbed out the bathroom window and avoided any conversation with that guy. But seeing as they were on a particularly high floor, she resigned herself to an awkward few minutes. Praying he'd be asleep, she cursed silently when she pulled the bathroom door open to find him sitting up in bed, still naked, checking his phone.

'Hi,' he said, smiling widely. 'You're up early. Are you heading off this second?'

'Yeah,' she said, feigning disappointment. 'Much as I'd love to spend the day together, I've got to get to work.'

'But it's the weekend,' he said. 'Come back to bed.' She closed her eyes and racked her brains. What was his name again? John? No. Simon? No.

'Weekends are my busiest time,' she said, swiftly losing patience.

'I thought you were the boss! Call in one of your minions and we can get to know one another a bit better.'

She took a deep breath before speaking. 'It was a lovely evening. I've no doubt you're a great guy, but we don't have a future together. There's no chemistry between us. I don't believe in leading people on for no reason, so I don't see any point in us swapping phone numbers. I've a lot going on in my life at the moment. I don't have room for any more shit.'

'Oh, OK.'

She exited before things could get any trickier. He looked utterly astonished at being left there naked and vulnerable in the bed. By now, Ava was used to that bewildered and dumbstruck look from men. It used to make her feel immeasurably guilty. She'd walk about in a daze for a couple of days feeling like a mean and horrible person. But she'd come to the conclusion over the years that they all moved on seamlessly. None had ever come looking for her again, and she was happier with that.

She'd wanted the marriage-with-kids package when she was younger and more naive. But now that she was in her early forties, she knew it wasn't for her. She liked her apartment, loved her job and embraced the freedom of being single. She never had trouble finding dates, and most men were more than willing to jump into bed with her when the mood took her.

She used protection and was never too inebriated to not ensure she practised safe sex. As far as she was concerned it was a win–win scenario.

That was until last night, however. Last night had been bad. She was blind drunk by the time they fell into bed. Even she could see that things had been on a bit of a downward spiral lately. She needed to get it together a bit more. Her method would only continue to be successful if she didn't mess up royally by getting pregnant or putting herself in danger. Feeling cheap and pretty scuzzy, she asked the valet to find her car and sped off to open the shop.

It was sod's law that the shop was busier than it had been for months. It seemed the entire population of Dublin and their daughters were on the hunt for a dress. She and Ruth were flat out, so it took her until mid morning to phone her mother.

'How is everything going with Little Miss Attitude?'

'Fine. There's no sign of her yet, so I'm leaving her to sleep. She must be exhausted.'

Her mother's ability to ignore a rising argument had always irked Ava. Today wasn't the time to take her to task over it, however.

'OK, let me know if it's brain-wreckingly awkward. I could meet you both for an early bird once the shop closes this evening.'

'Well it might be a nice idea to do that anyway. I don't anticipate any brain damage, mind you.'

'I wouldn't hold your breath on that one. Nathalie is trouble, I'm telling you.'

'How about I bring her over and we'll spend a bit of time together later? Don't make up your mind about her just yet, Ava. Remember, she's only a child. You're the adult here.'

Ava hung up and shook her head with irritation as she dunked two fizzy tablets into a beaker of water. Her mother was always as cool as a cucumber. Not for the first time, she wondered if it was all a front. Did Clara flail horribly internally? Did she put on a poker face and retreat in turmoil to her room, where she gently bashed her head off the wardrobe door?

Thoughts of Max plagued her as she worked. Most of all she wanted to know if he was still in contact with Sean. Were they still friends even? More to the point, did Sean think of her at all, or was she simply a mistake he was glad he hadn't committed to?

A text pinged through on her phone, making her groan. It was from some randomer called Feargall who seemed to think they were meeting for dinner and a movie this evening. She quickly texted back saying a family emergency had come up. He answered saying that he wouldn't bother her again, and that he could take a hint. She rolled her eyes. These bloody men were getting under her skin. Why couldn't they just deal with the fact that she didn't need hangers-on and get over themselves? Why did life have to be so damn complicated?

She was in the back room attempting to fill out a fabric order form when Ruth appeared grinning like a fool.

'Yes, Ruth,' she said, hoping the other woman wasn't looking to have a big long chat.

'Look!' Ruth said, pulling a little basket of exquisite pink flowers from behind her back. 'The florist just delivered these for you.'

'Great!' Ava said, groaning inwardly. She snatched the flowers, then told Ruth she was about to make a private call and ushered her out, closing the door. Plucking the card from the little green plastic stick, she read the message.

Our date meant the world to me. You know where I am. Call me. I'll be waiting. My bed always has space for you. K x

She tossed the card into the waste-paper basket, then squeezed her eyes shut and hoped to God the painkillers she'd just downed would somehow realign her brain and stop her body from feeling diseased. She'd no idea who the hell K was, and cared even less.

She was far too hung-over to deal with all this emotional clap-trap today.

She plopped down heavily on to a chair and bit her lip. There was far too much coming at her at the moment. Men, Max, Nathalie . . . It was enough to drive a girl insane.

The walls were closing in. Much as she hated to admit it, Ava knew it was getting close to the time when she'd have to deal with the past once and for all. If she could ever face it.

Chapter 9

THE SOUND OF RAIN PELTING AGAINST THE
windowpane woke Nathalie. Looking about in disorientation, it
took her a moment to remember where she was. She crept out
of bed and peeped through the curtains. The sky was grey and
woolly and the flowers in Oma's garden seemed to be bowing
in soaked misery.

A delicious smell filled the air as she emerged from her room
and padded down the stairs to the kitchen.

'Hello, dear!' Clara said. 'I hope the rain didn't keep you awake
during the night. It was quite nasty out there. Typical Irish
summer weather, I'm afraid. The forecast says it'll brighten up
later. Fingers crossed.'

'It's so odd to see this kind of weather in summer,' Nathalie
said, shuddering.

'I know, it took me a while to get used to it when I moved
here first.'

Nathalie wanted to ask about a million questions, but she
needed to figure out whether she wanted to get to know Oma
better. It might be easier to be polite, spend a few days here and
call home to say she was fixed, then just split.

'What are you making?' she asked as she crossed the open-
plan room and gazed into an ancient-looking heavy black frying
pan. 'It smells like Dunkin' Donuts.'

'They're buttermilk pancakes. I like them with blueberries

and maple syrup. Will you try some? It's too late for breakfast so I thought these might make a tasty brunch.'

Nathalie's immediate instinct was to say no. She wasn't used to eating all this food. Normally she'd have a smoothie on the way to school – a low-GI version. This stuff looked like a bad breakfast from the before pictures in *The Biggest Loser*. But her stomach, it seemed, had other plans and growled hungrily.

'I'll take that as a yes,' Clara said. 'Sit and I'll bring it to you.'

'Wow!' Nathalie exclaimed involuntarily as Clara put a pretty patterned plate on the table, piled high with perfect round pancakes. The blueberries were like tiny glistening jewels beneath the glossy covering of thick, hot syrup. A generous dusting of something brown intrigued her.

'What's the other topping?'

'Home-made praline. It's toasted nuts in caramelised sugar, ground to a gravelly powder. Trust me, you'll love it.' Clara lifted a dripping pancake on to her plate and spooned extra berries and syrup on top. 'Dig in. If you hate it, you can always have toast, or you can starve.'

Nathalie stared at Clara to see if she was joking. It appeared she wasn't. She was sitting and serving herself as if everything was as it should be. Nathalie cut off a bite and felt her eyes roll.

'This is to die for,' she mumbled.

'Yes, I know,' Clara said happily as she dug into hers. 'I learned all my cookery skills from my mother. My sewing, too. But the big change in our relationship happened when she showed me how to quilt. It was the tool we used to bond.'

'Why did you need to bond? Didn't you guys get along?'

'Not always,' Clara said easily.

'Why not?'

'It's a long story,' Clara said simply. 'I'll tell you sometime.' She picked up the newspaper and began to flick through it. 'I don't know why I bother to read this. It's full of depressing and dreadful stories. Why can't the front page have a great big photo of a kitten or a baby laughing? That'd cheer us all up.'

'I've never thought of it like that,' Nathalie said as she helped herself to another pancake, hoping Oma wasn't going to notice and call her a greedy pig. Mercifully she seemed quite oblivious.

'I could teach you how to quilt if you were interested,' Clara ventured.

Nathalie wanted to shout that she didn't give a fiddler's about the quilt thing. But she guessed she'd better be polite seeing as she was staying at this house and eating so much food.

'Er, yeah. I guess.'

'Excellent,' Clara said happily. If she noticed Nathalie's reluctance, she certainly didn't let it show. 'It's such a murky day out there, it'll be the perfect distraction for us. It'll stop us wanting to murder one another. Nothing worse than sitting in a room with someone you don't know while fishing about in your head for something to talk about. Exhausting and quite unnecessary.'

Nathalie grinned. She was starting to find this woman quite entertaining. She was as crazy as a bees' nest that had been attacked by bears, but her attitude was kind of different.

Once brunch was over, Clara indicated that Nathalie was to help pick up the dishes.

'I never allowed either of my children to be idle. We all helped around the house. I think that's fair.'

Nathalie was mildly taken aback. So was that the reason she was here? To be some sort of a home help? She scowled as they cleaned the kitchen. Clara didn't speak much until she led Nathalie into the room across the hall.

'I present my sewing room,' she said proudly.

It smelled slightly musty but was meticulously organised. Countless rolls of fabric were stacked on top of one another on specially built shelves. The greater part of the room was taken up by a vast table with a brass measuring tape embedded in the end. Scissors ranging from garden shears size right down to tiny mouse-sized ones hung on nails in a row. Once the overhead lights were turned on, the table was brightly illuminated and Nathalie could appreciate how intricate work could be carried out here.

'I'm very finicky about this room,' Clara said. 'I know where every single thing is and I want to keep it this way. You're welcome to make something, but I'll warn you now, it could bring out a hidden violence in me if you mess it up and refuse to clean after yourself.'

'OK, I get it,' Nathalie said, widening her eyes. She half expected Clara to be glowering at her, hands on hips, like one of her teachers. Instead she was over the other side of the room humming in delight. Nathalie was starting to get a handle on this broad. She was direct and to the point, but very mild-mannered with it. It was odd. She'd never met anyone quite like her before. She wasn't sure how to take her at all.

'I listen to classical music while I work,' Clara stated, as she flicked on an ancient-looking CD player. 'The haunting melodies take me to another place, where imagination knows no bounds. Now, take a look at the colours of the materials. Which ones are you most drawn to?'

Nathalie wandered around the room, reaching out on occasion and touching a roll of fabric.

'This place is wonderful,' she breathed, forgetting to be grumpy for a second.

'I think so too,' Clara smiled. 'I'm glad you get it. But why wouldn't you? You have my blood. So would you like to get started?'

'Pardon? With what? What are we doing?' Nathalie asked in mild shock.

'Will we make a quilt together?' Clara asked.

Normally Nathalie would have no qualms about telling someone she didn't have an interest in something. But now she hesitated momentarily.

She hadn't realised there were so many unanswered questions. She'd obviously figured there were all sorts of hassles between her dad and his family, but what had Oma been hinting at earlier? Why had she had problems with her own mother? Did it have anything to do with the reason her father had cut ties with them? Nathalie was guessing the major family feud was somehow all Oma's fault.

'Sure, let's make a quilt,' she agreed. 'I'm quite a dab hand at sewing, as it happens. I like to customise my clothes at home. I often buy things purely so I can alter them or add some sparkles. It's good to own stuff that nobody else has. One-off pieces as such.'

'Yes, I agree,' Clara said.

'I've never done quilting, though. I may not be any good at it.'

'All you need is time and the inclination to create something unique. Do you think you have that?'

'I guess.'

'Americans do a lot of guessing, don't they?' Clara mused. 'When you say that, you really mean yes, don't you?'

'Yes,' Nathalie said firmly.

'OK. Good.'

The other advantage to being in Ireland, Nathalie decided as Clara set about collecting scissors and implements, was that while the pain of losing Mackenzie had been raw and all-consuming back in LA, here she felt slightly freed from the constant ache. In fact her mind was so focused on Oma and keeping up with her that she hadn't much space for feeling wretched.

The phone rang. Clara picked up the extension in the sewing room.

'Hallo, Ava,' she said. 'Oh jeepers, I totally forgot. No, it's done. I have it here. I'll drive by and drop it off. Keep an eye out for me. I'm in my stay-at-home comfortable clothes, so I won't come into the shop and frighten your customers. I'll pull up outside and you can run out to me like a good girl. All right. Yes, dear. See you soon.'

She hung up and grabbed a black suit-hanger from the opposite side of the room.

'I need to drop this gown to Ava. I was putting in the zip. It's a complicated design and I'm the best at it. The fabric is so expensive, Ava couldn't afford for it to be made a muck of. There's no point in dragging yourself out in that rain.'

'I guess. Rain isn't really my thing,' Nathalie said with a shrug.

'So why don't you start choosing some fabrics for your quilt? I presume I can trust you not to pull the place asunder while I'm gone?'

Nathalie was about to either laugh or ask Oma whether she thought she was a wild animal when she realised she'd already run out the door.

'I'll see you shortly then, dear,' Clara called from the hallway, before slamming the front door.

Nathalie was quite surprised by how easily Oma had accepted the fact that she'd prefer to stay here alone. Her mom would've kicked up blue murder and made hurt faces and acted as if Nathalie were betraying her.

As she heard the car starting up and reversing out the driveway, she spied a box in the corner, perched on a side table. The lid was on the floor and she could see a small wad of letters stacked neatly and bound in bunches by elastic bands. Feeling as if she were prying, but unable to stop, Nathalie picked up the top bundle. None of the letters seemed to have envelopes, but all were written to the same person. A man called Master Leibnitz.

Peeling off the band, Nathalie looked at the first letter. It was written in a foreign language. As she scanned it, she realised it was German. Behind each letter it appeared there was a hand-written translation in English. Intrigued, she began to read.

She hadn't gone past the date and greeting when the sound of Clara's car returning out front made her replace the letter, reattach the elastic band and dash back to the table, where she snatched a couple of rolls of material and threw them down.

'Hallo? Nathalie?' Clara called out.

'I'm in here,' Nathalie said, hoping she didn't look quite as freaked as she felt.

'All done. Will we begin some quilting?' Clara walked into the room, explaining how bad the traffic was due to the rain. 'So you've started with some cream fabrics,' she said. 'What colours would you like to introduce? We need to work out a palette before we begin cutting.'

'Sure.'

Nathalie couldn't stop thinking about the letters. She felt insanely curious. There were piles of them in the box and they were really old, dating back to 1930-something. She longed to ask Oma about them, but she didn't think Clara would appreciate knowing she'd looked through her private things.

The phone rang again. This time it was Amber. Clara spoke to her for a moment before passing it to Nathalie.

'Hey Mom,' she said. 'How are you?'

'I'm good,' Amber said. 'How are you getting on?'

'Really well, actually,' Nathalie said, deciding that for now it was easier to play ball. 'You'll be very impressed, Oma and I are embarking on a special project right now.'

They chatted for a while and Clara left the room to give

them privacy. Nathalie said all the things her mom wanted to hear. How lovely Oma was, how beautiful Ava was, and how she was settling in just fine.

'You were right and I was wrong,' she said sweetly. 'It's good to be away from LA. It's totally different here and I think that's a good thing for me right now.'

'Oh darling, I'm so relieved to hear that you're OK,' Amber said. 'Stay in touch, and I'm here for you any time you need me.'

Nathalie forced a smile as Clara reappeared in the room.

'All OK with your mother?' she asked.

'Yes thanks. She's mightily impressed that we're sewing.'

'That's good,' Clara said. 'Now, back to business and enough dilly-dallying.'

For what felt like the hundredth time, Nathalie looked at Clara to see if she was irritated. She wasn't; she clearly just figured it was time to get going. Nathalie raised an eyebrow but did as she was told and began to concentrate on picking out colours.

After a couple of hours, Clara stretched.

'That's more than enough for the moment,' she said. 'Now I will go to the grave. I like to visit Gus there.'

Nathalie baulked. The last thing she wanted was to visit a grave. She'd had enough of the scent of death to last her a lifetime.

'Would you mind if I stay here? I'm kind of jet-lagged and I could use a lie-down.'

'Whatever suits you, dear,' Clara said mildly. 'I won't be too long.'

Nathalie went to her room and watched out the window until she was certain she was alone. Then, gingerly making her way down the stairs to the sewing room, she returned to the pile of letters and picked up the one she'd started earlier. Curling up in a deep armchair, she began to read.

December 1936

Dear Master Leibnitz

Now that the night is drawing in and I am here in my room with only my thoughts for company, I find myself at sixes and sevens. You see, something momentous happened to me today. It was the first time I laid eyes on you. So I am doing what I have always done – committing my thoughts to paper as I dare not utter the things I feel. The things I felt when I looked into your eyes. I would not dare to even address you – you, the master of the house and I a lowly maid – but I am safe here, within these four walls, and this letter is, can only ever be, for my eyes only. Could it be that the whole world turned on its axis today? Or is it simply that I alone am changed for ever by your presence?

Your mother, Frau Leibnitz, seems stern yet fair. Her piercing blue eyes and teased dark hair make her so sleek and exotic in contrast with my unkempt drabness.

I have always been a dreamer, Master Leibnitz. Perhaps it has been my way of surviving. I have the ability to take myself out of a situation and drift away to a more favourable setting.

Using nothing but that same vivid imagination, I have lived through days of pure pleasure. Ones where I am sitting in one of the fine horse-drawn carriages in the park, being waited on hand and foot, while eating warm pastries and drinking rich, sweet hot chocolate.

Today I kept my mind firmly on the task in hand. I was greatly excited when Frau Leibnitz offered me the servant's job and showed me to my quarters.

When I was ordered to clean your music room, I had no idea you were occupying it at the time. The moment you swivelled on the piano stool and met my gaze will stay in my heart for ever.

You are a gentleman in every sense of the word. You seemed genuinely interested when you asked my name. You apologised for frightening me, when it was I who had disturbed you!

As you told me about your arranged marriage to the gentle lady Liza, I was flummoxed. Do you believe in love at first sight? I do. It happened to me today. When you raised your eyes from the ivory keys of the piano and looked into mine, I felt the jolt. Those sky-blue eyes were so filled with angst, I wanted to go to you and wrap you in my embrace and hold you until the pain dissolved.

Why did you ask my advice? What made you think a housemaid such as I would know the answer to any of your questions?

When you started to play, oh, the melody was so moving. Never before have I heard music that was so laden with emotion. The melancholy magic swept me away and made me feel as if I were floating on a fleecy cloud of pure angst. I never meant to cry. I hope you did not notice my tears as they blotted the dark slate of the hearth.

You said the piece was one of your favourites and was composed by Frideric Handel. When you stood and approached me, I was frozen in time. The sounds and smells of the living world faded to oblivion. I felt as if we were cast into an alternative universe. One where only you and I exist . . . Did you feel it too? Do you believe in love at first sight, Master Leibnitz?

Hannah

Nathalie could barely breathe as she finished reading. It was so romantic. She felt as if she were stepping into a scene from an old movie. But who was Hannah, and why were her letters in Clara's sewing room?

She had no idea how long Oma would take at the grave, so she put the letter back in place and rushed from the room to lie on her bed as she'd said she would. As she tucked her arms above her head and relaxed, she closed her eyes and thought about how it must have felt to fall in love at first sight.

Chapter 10

SITTING IN HIS CAR ON THE DRIVEWAY, MAX WAS apprehensive about the welcome that awaited him once he opened the front door. He knew it would be a frosty one and frankly it was the last thing he needed. Today at the hospital had been awful. He'd sat with twenty employees consecutively and told them that they no longer had a job. He'd given most of them the same bullshit speech about the future of the hospital and how there could be a surge in services in eighteen months' time. Some had merely nodded tearfully and left the room carrying the lousy piece of paper detailing their redundancy. Others, like Amy Stephenson, had interrupted him mid sentence.

'Max! Why are you rattling off some half-assed speech to me as if you don't know me? You ate pasta at my house last week. You helped Gerry to put up a bookshelf while refusing to stand too close to the hammer, saying your hands are your livelihood.'

He'd looked at the floor, feeling sick.

'Amy, I'm sorry. I never knew I'd have to do this. I'm clearly not good at it and I don't know how to deliver this blow in a good way.'

'You know why, Max? Because there is no good way to tell a friend that her life is about to enter the toilet. What are you going to do about this? You have sway with the board. They'll listen to you.'

He'd tried to make her understand that Abe wasn't going to

listen to him or anyone else for that matter. She'd left the room and run down the hall, choking on her sobs. Max was about to run after her when Nancy sidled in.

'I'm a good listener,' she said smoothly. 'If you want to, we can close the door and I'll help to ease the pain.' She'd raised one eyebrow, then pointedly smoothed her hand down her too-tight skirt and pouted.

'I need to go home to my wife. Thanks for the offer of help, Nancy, but I'm fine.'

If it were a different time of his life, Max knew he'd be able to tell Sean about saucy Nancy. He knew his long-term buddy would howl with laughter at the comical approaches he was having to deal with. In his right state of mind, he'd be more in a position to deflect her rather clunky advances. But right now, all she was doing was adding to his distress.

Turning his key in the door, Max was unprepared for the ambush of anger that met him.

'How could you, Max?' Amber seethed. He stood still and looked at the floor. 'How could you have told Nathalie and me that your parents were dead? And as for saying that your sister had no interest in keeping contact . . . You sold me a pack of lies when we met. Which parts are real and which did you invent?'

'Amber,' he tried to take her in his arms, 'I've had the day from hell. Can we talk about this later?'

'Don't touch me. I trusted you, Max. From the day we got together, you told me lies. What do you expect me to think? And when I make a monumental decision to try and save our daughter from drowning in a sea of grief, you stride out of here and don't come back for two days.'

'I'm sorry . . .'

'That's not good enough any more, Max. Clearly you've been

running from Lord knows what, for Lord knows how long, but right now, I'm all out of sympathy for you.'

'Amber, you're overreacting. I have very valid reasons for cutting my family from my life. OK, I admit I probably shouldn't have told you they were dead. But believe me, you'd understand if you knew . . .'

'Knew what, Max? I think it's time you started telling the truth.'

'There isn't one single reason why I left Ireland,' he said wearily. 'There are several. But believe me, Amber. None of them has any relevance to us or to how our lives have turned out. Can't you let sleeping dogs lie?'

'Max,' Amber looked truly stricken, 'for years we've both skirted around the fact that you have the ability to sink into bouts of darkness where nobody can reach you. You've always refused help, and as time marched on I tried to accept that this is simply a part of you and a personality trait that you can't avoid.' She took his hand. 'But now I realise that you've been living half a life. Running while looking over your shoulder in case the ghosts of your past come knocking.'

'It's very complicated, Amber,' he said. 'I'll tell you when I'm ready. But for now I need you to know that my love for you and my input into our marriage has never been anything but real. As I said, let's let sleeping dogs lie for now.'

'Sleeping dogs? More like a wild pack of wolves that are currently running at top speed in your direction. If you feel you can't talk to me, I can't force you. But our daughter is over in Ireland bonding with your mother. Her . . . *Oma*,' she said, still tripping on the German word. 'Her *Oma* and by all accounts her aunt, both of whom you've consciously denied her a relationship with. The truth will come out sooner or later, Max. Being your wife, I'd actually prefer to hear it from you.'

He hugged her and closed his eyes. He *did* love her. Amber represented the most perfect aspect of his life. She and Nathalie were his masterpiece. The part that wasn't messed up. The part that wasn't tainted by lies and destruction. He'd never wanted his old world and his new to collide.

He needed to try and fathom the fact that his daughter was now halfway across the world with his mother. What was she hearing? Was his mother unwittingly setting her against him? Would Ava be nasty to her? He knew his parents would treat her with unconditional love and kindness, but his fiery sister was quite another matter. He wondered what Ava was like now. Had she married and gone on to have kids? If so, had Nathalie met her cousins? What would he do if she decided to stay in Ireland and never return? So many questions shot about in the recesses of his mind.

'I spoke to Nathalie,' Amber said, infiltrating his racing thoughts.

'How is she doing?'

'Fine. Just fine.' Amber's eyes filled with tears. 'Honey, there's something you need to know. I didn't have time to tell you the other day, before you hotfooted it out of here.'

'What?'

'Your father passed away six months ago.'

The words hit him like a tidal wave. He walked to the kitchen and perched on a high stool, lost in thought. The sound of his father's voice was lost to him. He strained to try and remember, but nothing came. He had no photographs of any of his family, such was his effort to obliterate them from his life. Guilt washed over him. He'd thought about this very scenario before. He'd convinced himself it would be fine. That he wouldn't be upset and that he could pretend things were just as they had been when he left Dublin. But the reality was quite a different thing. The knowledge that his father had died and they had never been reunited was devastating.

'Is my mother OK?'

'Nathalie says she's "pretty cool".'

'That sounds about right,' he said, in a strangled voice.

'I'm meant to be attending the hospital trust fund-raiser,' Amber said weakly. She looked exhausted and Max wanted to punish himself for being such a shit to her. 'I can cancel,' she suggested.

'No,' he said hastily. 'You can't let them down. The excitement around the hospital today was at fever pitch – excuse the pun. You should go. You've worked so hard on this. I'll see you after.'

'I mightn't be home until late.'

'I'll be here,' he said.

He kissed her and watched her go, leaving a waft of expensive scent in her wake. She was a good woman and didn't deserve to be kept in the dark any longer.

He stood at the front door and waved at her retreating car. He needed to take stock of his life and make some important decisions. He'd run away from one part and now he was in danger of losing the other. If he didn't take care, he'd end up alone.

Pouring a large tumbler of whiskey, he downed it in two burning gulps. He refilled the glass and wandered towards the shower. As the water needled his shoulders, he tried to relax. But deep down he knew the only way to relieve the tension was by telling the truth. By releasing the secrets of his past.

He wished he had a photograph of his father. He needed to see Gus's face and recall properly the sound of his voice. He tried to imagine how his mother had felt these past months, left alone in her home.

He sincerely hoped Ava was still as close to her as ever. Perhaps she had a brood of children who kept Clara's mind off her grief.

How had he managed to convince himself it was acceptable

to abandon his family for so long? It was as if a bubble had burst in his brain and for the first time in twenty years he doubted his own decision. If there was a hole big and deep enough, Max would happily have crawled into it right now.

Chapter 11

NATHALIE HOPED OMA DIDN'T REALISE SHE'D READ one of the letters. She concentrated on avoiding looking at the box containing them.

'So let's get started,' said Clara. 'As I mentioned, I'm a little bit funny about my sewing room. If you mess it up, you'll have to fix it.'

'It's bordering on OCD in here,' Nathalie said. The fabrics were stored in graduating colours, with the darkest ones at the bottom moving all the way to white on top. Pinks occupied one shelf, blues another, then greens and so on. As she turned around and really examined the array of fabrics, Nathalie became sucked in by the mesmerising allure of the patchwork quilt they were about to design.

Clara pulled open the large drawer that ran the length of the massive wooden cutting table to reveal a stack of patterns.

'First you need to decide what shape your patches will be. Square, round, rectangular, hexagonal . . . It's up to you. I'd suggest we do squares, as they're the easiest to work with. For a large bed the best size for each patch is eight by eight, and we'll need a grand total of one hundred and twenty-one.'

Clara pulled out a paper pattern with a maze of squares etched upon it.

'Jeez, this is kind of complex,' Nathalie said, studying the various effects as Clara spread out a choice of patterns. She'd naively thought it would all get started immediately. When she embellished clothes or even altered them at home, there was very little preparation required. This was a whole new ball game.

Now that she could see the number of patches she needed to create this quilt, Nathalie was freshly astounded by the ones Oma had made.

'I had no idea there was so much involved. How long does it take to finish one?'

'That, my dear, is like asking how long a piece of string is. It all depends on how much work you put in, what shape you choose and whether or not you can stick at it. Are you up for it, or would you rather back out now while you still can?'

Nathalie recognised that twinkle in Oma's eyes. She'd seen a similar one many times in the mirror. Nothing grabbed her attention quite like a challenge.

'Bring it on,' she said evenly.

Clara explained the process thoroughly. Once Nathalie was set on her colour scheme, they'd cut the squares and lay them out on the cutting table to give an idea of what the finished quilt would look like. Clara told her she could swap the pieces around until she was happy with the pattern. Next they'd be carefully ironed in preparation for joining.

'I'm a dab hand at that part,' she assured Nathalie as she promised to help. 'I'll certainly assist, but that's all. This has to come from you, and most of all it must come from here,' she said, patting her heart. She explained that people filled their quilts with a whole range of things, from feathers to wool.

'I always use the same wadding. It's just to bulk it up a bit and make it lovely and cosy for the winter. Not that you need to be cosy in LA.'

Nathalie decided on a summery colour scheme to match her bedroom at home. She chose pastel shades of pink, blue, yellow and mauve, and interspersed flowers, checks, spots and stripes to form the pattern.

Once they began cutting, the background music became the only sound apart from the methodical clipping noise of the scissors.

'I can't believe how much I'm *into* this,' Nathalie said. 'I know I'm going to find it difficult to even sleep until it's done.'

'That's exactly how I felt the first time I made one,' Clara smiled. 'Creativity and hunger for design is in your blood, Nathalie. These quilts have served as a therapeutic bonding tool for generations. So I hoped the magic would have an effect on you too.' She watched Nathalie for a while.

'Am I doing it right?' Nathalie asked.

'You certainly are,' Clara said. 'Isn't it amazing that this very activity was just as entrancing to your great-grandmother? It doesn't make any difference that you were kept from me all this time. Blood is thicker than water and we will make up for lost years. I'm very glad.'

Nathalie's expression darkened. She'd almost forgotten why she was here and that she'd been sent here under duress. She didn't answer, instead choosing to continue silently.

After that they barely spoke as they systematically chose fabric and cut it into strips. The idea was that the strips would then be divided to make the squares. All the while, Clara's classical music continued to play in the background. Nathalie hadn't the first idea what any of it was about, but it was surprisingly soothing.

She found herself thinking of Hannah, from the letters, and how she must've felt when Master Leibnitz played the piano for her all those years ago.

When Clara excused herself to prepare a snack Nathalie said she'd be happy to continue with the quilt. She was enjoying the process for many reasons. Firstly it took her mind off missing

Mackenzie, and secondly it was a good excuse to not have to make conversation. This was going to be the easiest way of getting out of here. She'd knuckle down and get this thing done, and that would bring her visit to a natural end. She could take her quilt, skip home and Oma could feel they'd bonded, just the way she had with her own mother, grandma or whoever she'd learned this with. Deal.

'I was hoping we might take a little trip outside after our snack. It looks as if the rain is beginning to clear.'

'Sure,' said Nathalie, assuming they'd be going to the crummy park across the road or some other riveting place.

The second Clara left the room, she glanced over to the box. She was itching to rush over and pull out the next letter along with its translation. But she was afraid of getting caught.

As she ate a tasty snack, Nathalie had to resist blurting out that she'd found the letters and asking Clara to tell her who the mysterious Hannah was. But a sixth sense told her to remain silent for now. She needed to try and build up a bit of trust before she started asking for stuff.

Her silence had clearly made Oma feel she was unhappy.

'Nathalie, I know this isn't easy for you,' she said as they cleared away the lunch things. 'If I might say, you're doing incredibly well. There's a beautiful waterfall a short drive from here. Would you care to go there? It might make you feel less at odds if you had some fresh air.'

'Sure,' Nathalie said. 'I'll freshen up and we can go now if that's cool?'

'I'm ready,' said Clara. 'Though we should take raincoats; as you might have guessed, the weather is a little volatile around these parts.'

Nathalie didn't expect much from their waterfall visit. It didn't exactly sound as if it'd be in competition with Disney. But she felt the least she could do was feign interest. Clara, she figured reluctantly, was doing her best.

They drove out of town, away from the houses and shops. The countryside was like nothing Nathalie had ever seen before. The acid-green leaves on the trees contrasted hugely with the dark green spiky hedges peppered with almost luminous yellow blooms.

'What's that stuff?' she asked in awe.

'Gorse,' Clara said. 'It's prickly and nasty if you need to wade through it but stunningly beautiful at this time of the year. It always makes me think of the sun, even if it's drizzly and grey.'

The hilly landscape looked breathtaking and Nathalie was moved to silence. The patchwork of fields with the backdrop of mauve heather-coated mountains was nothing like LA. Little cream balls of fuzz made her cry out in delight.

'Sheep!' she said, pointing.

'There are tons of woolly jumpers around here,' Clara laughed. 'Don't you just love the ones with the black faces?'

'When I thought of Ireland, this was exactly what I had in mind,' Nathalie admitted. 'It's like the images that are splashed over posters and tourist information back home. All that's missing is the rainbow with the little green leprechaun at the bottom.'

'If you think the scenery is beautiful now, just wait until you experience the waterfall,' Clara said. 'It's a sight I never tire of seeing. The car park is situated behind a grassy incline, so you'll get the most wonderful surprise when we climb to the top of the hill.'

Clara pulled into a parking space. In companionable silence they began to walk. As the waterfall came into view, Nathalie whistled.

'Jeez, Oma! This is like something from a movie scene,' she gasped. 'How high is it?'

'Over one hundred and twenty metres, I think. It's the highest in Ireland. Isn't it spectacular?'

'Totally awesome.'

'I loved bringing your father and Ava here when they were little. We'd take a picnic and they'd paddle for hours in the stream that leads away from the cascading water.'

'I'd say they had hours of fun,' Nathalie said. 'I wish I'd grown up around here.'

'I'm sure you have wonderful memories from your home,' Clara said.

'I guess. The only thing I missed out on was company. I would've loved someone to share all the family memories with. It would've been nice even if there were arguments from time to time.'

'From time to time?' Clara laughed. 'Try *most* of the time! Having said that, this is one of the few places that stood the test of time. Even when they were older and hitting pre-teen stages, when they hated most things in the world,' her eyes crinkled into a smile, 'they still liked it here. I'd pile them into the car, along with friends if they wanted them, and they'd climb on the rocks and dare one another to stand under the flowing water.'

'Sounds great,' Nathalie said.

'If one of them was suffering with rampant hormones, it was a great soul-calmer too. There's no better spot for soothing an addled mind than high up on a giant rock with pure frothy water cascading from the sky! Ever so therapeutic.'

'I guess it's so incredibly enormous that it makes the rest of the world's problems seem insignificant,' Nathalie mused.

They picked their way along the series of boulders close to the foot of the waterfall. Although they were far enough away to avoid being splashed, the proximity meant they could sit and close their eyes and feel as if they were right there in the water.

'Isn't this the most romantic spot imaginable?' Clara asked.

'Yeah, it's pretty darn impressive,' Nathalie admitted.

'Would you bring a dashing young man here?' Clara asked with a grin.

'My folks weren't too sweet on my boyfriend DJ,' Nathalie mused. 'But that's purely down to snob value. Mom wants me to date a guy who'll be a lawyer or a doctor. Someone who'll buy me a large house and take me on vacations to the Hamptons and on cruises around Europe.'

'My parents were different,' Clara said. 'Time marches on, but so many people are still as narrow-minded today as they were a hundred years ago.'

'I'll say,' Nathalie said, widening her eyes and looking peeved.

'Do you love DJ?'

Nathalie thought for a moment. 'Nah. I think I enjoyed annoying my dad. DJ's on a one-way road to nowhere,' she admitted. 'But he was easy to be with. He didn't stretch my brain, he never expected much and was grateful for my company.'

'Is he one of those fellows with blue hair who's covered in body piercings and tattoos and who only speaks in that crazy street rap I hear in the town some days?'

Nathalie grinned. 'Do you listen to rap music much?'

'Sometimes. I like some of the music on other radio stations apart from the usual conversational one I favour. I was raised to listen to music and I love all sorts. But classical is the kind that seeps into my bones and evokes the most emotions in me.'

'You're not the usual grandma type,' Nathalie mused.

'I've always believed in being whoever I want to be. And besides, I haven't had much practice at being an *Oma*.' Clara looked sad. 'It's lovely to have a go at it now. We'll have to wait and see how I get on. Time will tell.'

She looked up at the sky. The sun was about to come out from behind a large cloud.

'Fancy a swim?' she asked.

'What? Here?' Nathalie looked aghast. 'It's kind of freezing, though.'

'The sun is coming out. That's good enough for me.' Before Nathalie could protest, Clara hopped down from the large rock and found a dry pebbly area to drop her clothes. She'd put her swimsuit on underneath in the hope that she might feel like a dip.

She knew it was going to be shockingly cold, icy beyond belief, but she needed to feel exhilarated. As long as there was a bit of heat in the air when she emerged, she'd be just fine.

'Keep watch now, you hear?' she called up to Nathalie. The girl was standing with her hands on her hips and a look of complete awe on her face.

Knowing it wouldn't work to stick her toe in, Clara did what she always did and jumped right in. She surfaced shrieking and flailed for a moment, gulping in air and attempting to allow her body to become accustomed to the biting cold.

'You're crazy!' Nathalie shouted through cupped hands. 'You OK?'

Clara gave her a thumbs-up, bobbled about for a few minutes more and promptly disappeared under the water. Alarmed, Nathalie rushed down off her rock, but the frothing whiteness of the waterfall made it difficult to see anything.

Panic engulfed her. She kicked her shoes off, pulled off her top and jeans and leapt into the water. It was so cold she felt as if a vice was clenching her skull. Getting her bearings, she surfaced, spotted Oma and pelted towards her, scooping her around the underside of her chin and pulling her to the edge of the water.

Before Nathalie could speak, Clara swivelled around in the water and faced her. She was grinning widely.

'Nicely done. You obviously had life-saving lessons.'

Nathalie was astonished.

'You weren't drowning?'

'Dearest, I have been swimming here, often alone, for many years. I knew the water would shock you but leave you feeling exhilarated.'

'Oh my God, you're crazy!' Nathalie looked so furious that Clara burst out laughing.

'I wish I had a camera right now.'

In spite of herself, Nathalie burst out laughing too.

'You're insane!'

Clara nodded. 'A little bit of madness never did anyone any harm,' she said as she stood up out of the chilly water. Putting her hands down, she pulled Nathalie up too.

'What are we going to do now? We're both drenched and we've no towel.'

'Ah, watch and learn,' Clara said, pulling two towelling face cloths from the back pocket of her trousers. She held one aloft for Nathalie to take.

'That's not big enough to dry a mouse!' she said.

'You'd be surprised how effective it is.' Clara smiled back. 'I'm going behind that rock. It'll work but it may not look too pretty! I suggest you go over there,' she pointed, 'and I'll see you back here, dry, in a few moments.'

Nathalie did as she was bid, and was astonished at how well the tiny cloth dried her. Thankful that she'd been swift enough to remove her top and jeans, she pulled them back on, scrunching her sodden underwear into a ball with the flannel. Then with numb fingers she climbed back up to the rock.

'Ah there you are, dear!' Clara said as she appeared with wet hair. 'All dry and ready for home?'

'I cannot believe we dried our entire bodies with a face flannel,' Nathalie said, grinning.

'It's amazing what one can do when circumstances dictate it.'

Nathalie smiled. 'I picked some of the tiny yellow flowers. I don't know what I'll do with them, but I couldn't help myself.'

'I know exactly what we'll do,' Clara said. 'We'll press them and make them into a card. I used to help the children do that when they were little.'

As they drove towards home, Nathalie was quiet once again. She felt sneaky for reading the letter and was trying to decide how she ought to handle the situation.

When they pulled up at the house, Clara announced she was taking a hot bath.

'I'm not as young as I used to be. The cold seems to seep into my bones these days. I love to swim but I need a bit of heat.'

'Take your time,' Nathalie said. As Clara went to walk away, Nathalie stopped her. 'Oma?'

'Yes, dear?'

'Thank you for taking me to the waterfall. It was awesome.'

'You're more than welcome,' she replied, smiling broadly.

As soon as Clara was gone, Nathalie swooped into the sewing room, grabbed the next two letters and sped to her bedroom. Guilt still plagued Nathalie and she couldn't help feeling as if she were violating Oma's privacy by stealing the letters, but the compulsion to read on was her driving force. Pulling her jeans and top off, she found fresh clothes and got dressed. Then, perching on the bed, she spread the first letter out.

The Secrets We Share

December 1936

Dear Lukas

Two weeks have passed and you now consume my every waking thought. When you hushed me and told me that I must address you by your Christian name, I felt as if I'd won a prize.

I am elated and confused in equal measure. Why have you chosen me as your confidante? As you lament the fact that you have no love for Liza, my love for you grows. I wondered until today if you were toying with my emotions. I began to feel as if I were purely a sounding post, an ear to listen to your woes. When you followed me to the basement and turned my face towards yours, my heart stopped, my blood went cold and I didn't know whether to laugh or cry.

I feel as if I'm living in a dream. Did your lips really kiss mine? Did you whisper that you loved me? Surely this cannot be? How could you feel this way? You are destined for so much more. Your breeding dictates that you should be with a woman of class and wealth. There is no place in your world for an orphaned Jewish maid.

The way I feel about you is indescribable. You are the sunshine in my world. You make me feel as if I can accomplish anything. But I know we cannot carry on this way.

I will have to make you hate me. Lukas, you are my first love. But I cannot bear to drag you down. I will have to force you to let me go. My heart aches at the thought of not being with you, but you are not mine to own. For now, however, I am living the dream.

Perhaps I will be punished further along the road of my life for allowing my heart to beat only for you. This feels so good it must be sinful. I am languishing in the delight that is ours at the moment, but I know it cannot and will not continue.

I am floating high above the clouds, yet my feet are firmly on the ground. I had no idea life could be so sweet. I thank God for sending me to you.

Hannah

Nathalie hugged her knees tightly. This was better than any Disney story she'd read as a child. Hannah and Lukas's secret love was so tantalising to read about. She couldn't wait to find out what would happen next.

Chapter 12

CLARA LOWERED HERSELF INTO THE STEAMY HEAT of the bath. Much as she was trying to ignore the passage of time, every now and again she was given a gently nudging reminder.

She didn't feel upset by it any longer, though. Now that she had palpable hope in her heart that she might be able to jigsaw her fragmented family back together again, the urgency she'd been harbouring previously had all but vanished.

The warm water worked magically and she dressed in a soft tracksuit before joining Nathalie downstairs.

When the landline rang, Clara smiled instantly and picked up the phone.

'Your aunt Ava would like to talk to you,' she said, holding it out to Nathalie. Unable to hide her surprise, the girl took it tentatively.

'Hello?' Her eyebrows shot up and she listened carefully. 'Sure . . . OK . . . Thank you. See you then.' She hung up and looked at Clara in shock. 'She wants to take me out and show me her apartment this evening.'

'Yes, so she said. Just the two of you. I think that's a wonderful plan.'

'Wouldn't you like to come too?'

'Oh no, dear. I'd cramp your style. You let your aunt show you a bit of Dublin city without an old dear swinging from your coat tails.'

Clara grinned as Nathalie reluctantly agreed. It made her heart contract that the girl seemed to genuinely want her to join them. No matter what anyone said, Max and his wife had done a fine job of raising Nathalie. Clara knew full well that she was here under duress, but not once had she been rude. She didn't want to count her chickens either, but she sensed a slight thaw in Nathalie's initial frostiness towards her.

'Would an omelette be OK for dinner this evening?' she asked. 'I'm always hungry after swims and I feel I'd like to eat soon.'

'Sounds perfect,' Nathalie said.

'Oh good. Would you be a dear and slip out to the herb garden for me? Take the scissors and snip off as many varieties as you can. We'll do a simple herb and cheese omelette and I'll serve it with my cucumber pickle. It's to die for!'

Nathalie hesitated, and Clara guessed she wasn't familiar with herbs.

'Let me show you,' she said. 'I tend to forget that you probably don't grow these in LA.'

Outside, Nathalie scrunched on to her hunkers and tried to memorise the names of the herbs.

'The thyme has tiny leaves and smells very distinctive,' Clara said, pinching a couple for Nathalie to smell. 'Parsley is the curly one, basil has those dark green leaves and smells like so,' she said, holding up a leaf. 'This is golden marjoram, which I love too, and because it's very strong we'll only take a smidge of rosemary.'

Nathalie looked impressed.

'This is all such an education! I've only ever seen the dried stuff we shake on pizzas back home.'

'Yes,' Clara said. 'I always feel dried herbs are a bit too much like potpourri.'

Nathalie giggled and followed her back inside. As they sat to eat moments later, she was astonished by the delicious tastes.

'How can eggs, cheese and herbs be so darn tasty?' she asked.

'Try the cucumber pickle, it's wonderful.'

'Wow, that's like the pickle from burgers, only sweeter!' Nathalie was smitten.

'Really?' Clara asked. 'I've never had shop-bought burgers, but I'll take your word for it.'

'You've never had McDonald's or Burger King?' Nathalie looked astonished as Clara shook her head. 'Some day I'll bring you.'

'Yes, I'd like that!'

Nathalie noticed Clara wilting slightly as they shared a cup of herb tea and a slice of lemon cake.

'Why don't you have an easy night? Go to bed and read a book or something,' she suggested.

'Would you manage to occupy yourself until Ava calls?' Clara asked.

'Sure. If you feel it's cool, I'd like to go for a walk on the beach. I can see it from my bedroom window. With the bright evenings, I'm sure I'd be safe, right?'

'Oh, completely,' Clara said. 'It's lovely down there at this time of year. Lots going on and plenty of other walkers too. Just don't go in the water while I'm not there.'

'No chance of that,' Nathalie grinned.

She insisted on doing the washing up and posted Clara off to bed.

'Come and tell me all about it when you return.'

Grabbing a sweater and slipping the second letter into her pocket, Nathalie made her way out the gate and towards the beach.

The salty sea air was wonderfully soft as she rounded the corner. Instead of the white powder sand she was used to, this beach was made up of thousands of grey stones and pebbles. A row of pretty little wooden houses, painted in varying candy shades, dotted the landscape. As she neared them, Nathalie realised they were miniature stores, selling everything from drinks and candy to crêpes and ice cream. Cheery bright blue benches framed the promenade that stretched for several miles. The sun was out, and although she guessed after her waterfall dip that the sea was utterly freezing, the water glistened and looked stunning. She walked over to the railings and stared out at the never-ending expanse of the ocean.

'Nice, isn't it?' said a voice from behind her. Turning, she stared at a boy with the palest skin she'd ever seen. 'A whole new meaning for fifty shades of grey,' he deadpanned, nodding at the stones. Nathalie grinned. 'You're not from around here, anyway,' he continued.

'How did you know?' Nathalie asked, suddenly feeling *very* American.

'The girls around here don't have tanned legs like yours. The bottles of fake stuff give an orange glow that doesn't come from the sun.'

Nathalie looked down at her legs and wished she hadn't worn shorts. She felt stupidly self-conscious yet she didn't want this guy to leave. His eyes were so piercingly blue against his ghostly skin and flaming red hair. She'd never seen anyone quite like him before. She couldn't stop staring at his eyelashes and brows. They were the same awesome shade of orange. She'd never seen anyone of his colouring, bar Ed Sheeran perhaps. Whatever about his hair and eyes – he had a body any man would kill for.

'I'm Conor,' he said, holding out his hand. Nathalie gazed down at it; there was an even spattering of caramel-coloured freckles that were so beautifully dotted across his skin they looked as if they'd been drawn on. His arms were taut and his muscles plainly visible. As she tried not to stare, she couldn't help noticing how toned and athletic he looked.

'Nathalie,' she answered.

'Where you from then, Nathalie?' he asked as he walked on and indicated for her to follow. She stumbled on the stones and had to concentrate on not falling. He tripped across them with ease until they reached the shoreline.

'I'm from LA,' she said. 'It's kind of different to here.'

'I'd say it is,' he nodded. 'I'm from Lochlann, born and bred. I've never been on a plane, and do you know, it doesn't bother me one bit.' He held his two pointing fingers to his lips and blew an astonishingly loud whistle. With that a fluffy white dog came bounding up the beach. 'There you are, boy!' he said, bending down to hug the animal. 'This is Herbie,' he said. 'He's a golden doodle, which translates as a cross between a golden retriever and a poodle. Don't you love the word doodle?'

'He's so cute,' she said.

Conor rooted about on the ground until he came up with a large, flat stone, which he proceeded to skim across the top of the water. It bounced three times. He clicked his fingers in annoyance.

'I've been known to do a skim with six bounces.'

'I see,' Nathalie said in confusion.

'Here,' he said, finding another stone. 'Your turn.'

She threw it hoping it would bop across the surface like his had. Instead it dropped in with a plop.

'Ah, better luck next time,' he said. 'Want to go for a walk? I need to let Herbie have a good run or else he'll get bored and eat my mother's shoes. He's gone through so many pairs now we've lost count. He's only a year old, but I fear his days are numbered unless he learns some house rules soon.'

'Oh I'm sure nobody would want to get rid of him. He's like a ball of cuteness,' she said.

'I know. I love him,' Conor said openly. 'Look at his furry legs, they're like massive pipe cleaners, aren't they?' Nathalie laughed. 'So how long are you staying in Lochlann?'

'I'm not sure,' she said. 'I came to visit my grandmother. We'd never met before.'

'Ah, is she afraid of flying like me?'

'It's complicated,' she said.

'I get it,' he said. 'I won't ask.' He walked on in the direction Herbie had just run, and Nathalie followed. His pale skin against his light shorts could have made him look sickly if he weren't so well built. As he walked his calf muscles bulged and his arms swung confidently from his broad shoulders. She had to trot to keep up with his stride. 'You're lucky to have the beach to come to.'

'Yeah, I love it. There's a whole little world down here. The same people tend to come at the same times. But then there's always new and pretty people like your good self.' He stopped and stared at her so intently she felt as if she might melt. Smiling he moved on.

Nathalie smiled back. 'My grandmother is originally Austrian. She lives just up the street,' she said. 'I call her Oma.'

'Ah, that's probably Mrs Conway,' he said.

'Yes, how did you know?'

'My mother used to be friends with her son when they were kids.'

'That's my dad!'

'Small world,' Conor said, nodding. Nathalie was utterly dumbfounded. How on earth could this guy, this random stranger, know Oma and her dad?

'Don't look so shocked,' he said, suddenly realising that she was stunned. 'That's Ireland. Everyone knows everyone else. Especially diehard locals like me! I'll have to tell my mum I met you. That's too funny.'

By the time they'd walked the length of the beach and back, Nathalie was feeling much more relaxed in Conor's company. Most people that passed seemed to know him and said hello. He introduced her to everyone as 'my new friend Nathalie, from LA'. They all seemed delighted with that and greeted her as if this was totally normal.

'I've to fly. I have football training and I'm always late,' he said with an easy shrug as he pulled his fingers through his hair. 'If you're back here tomorrow, I'll see you. Same time, same place.' He went to walk off. 'Or the next day, or indeed the day after that!'

'I get it!' she smiled. 'Lovely to meet you.'

'Believe me, the pleasure is all mine. This beach gets more beautiful every day,' he said with one eyebrow raised. Nathalie giggled and felt her cheeks flush. He blew her a kiss.

'Quick! Jump up and catch it or it'll land on some poor unsuspecting old man by the shore.' She pretended to snatch it in her hand as he placed his clasped hands on his heart. She stood watching as he bounded off with an eager Herbie in his wake.

Nathalie suddenly remembered that she'd brought the letter with her. Looking forward to finding out how the secret romance was developing, she found an empty bench and settled down to read.

January 1937

Dear Lukas

I tried to go. I know it's the best thing for both of us, but you have made it too difficult. I cannot hide my feelings for you and I am being driven by an entity I cannot overcome.

I pulled away first when you kissed me today. It felt so right, but I know in my heart of hearts it's very wrong.

I planned to go this evening. When your gentle knocking sounded on my door I knew I could not do so.

Why did you have to say those things to me, Lukas? Oh, it was music to my ears to hear that you have loved me from the first second you saw me. Yes, of course I felt it too. I can barely dare to believe that you see me as your destiny.

What we did, when our bodies became one . . . it was meant to be.

But I am so scared, Lukas. I do not want to be responsible for ruining your life. You say you will talk your parents round. That you will make them see that what we have is pure and true. You are so certain that they will come to love me the way you do. But I am afraid I do not share your optimism. I know you keep saying this is 1937, but the world still has a long way to go when it comes to poor Jewish girls marrying wealthy Catholic boys. Your papa is head of the Austrian cavalry; mine is an unknown corpse who left my mother to rot on the streets as I was saved by the authorities. I am no scholar, my darling, but I can see that our love will not be allowed to survive.

I wish things could be as simple as you believe. I wish it were true what you say, that love is all we need. That what we have together is enough to overcome the adversities.

For now, I am humbled and delighted to know that you love me and I love you. I will cherish each and every moment we share. I will need to store them in my heart so I remember you for ever.

With all my heart,
Hannah

Nathalie placed the letter carefully back into her pocket and stared out at the ocean. Hannah and Lukas were from such different worlds. She hoped with all her heart that Lukas would decide to fight for his true love in spite of his family. She had a good feeling in her bones that their love would survive.

Suddenly Nathalie realised that she was banking on this love story working out. It was almost as if she'd put her own heart on the line along with that of this girl Hannah. If things worked out well for Hannah, maybe they would work for her in the future too.

❧

There was music coming from Oma's bedroom, so Nathalie put the letter back carefully and made her way upstairs.

'I'm home,' she said from the hallway.

'Come in, dear.'

She walked in and found Clara sitting up doing some sewing.

'What are you making?'

'Ah, it's a tapestry. They tend to drive me bats. I do a bit and put it aside. They're such tedious work, I rarely finish them inside a year. But it's relaxing when accompanied by Chopin! How was the beach?'

'Good. Great, in fact. I made a friend. He's called Conor. Bright orange hair, skin pale as milk and a big fluffy dog.'

'Yes, that's Conor Murphy. His mother was an old flame of your father's, you know. We all thought they'd get married, but it didn't work out. They split up and she was settled with another man in no time.'

'He mentioned they'd been friends. Odd that he knew all about his mother's past.'

'Not really,' Clara said easily. 'Lochlann is one of those places where secrets rarely stay hidden.'

'Conor seems nice,' Nathalie ventured.

'That's one way of putting it,' Clara smiled. 'He has such charm even while speaking to an old dear like me. I've always liked his friendly demeanour, but I still marvel at how handsome he's become. He was a funny-looking little fellow as a child. But I think he's grown into himself now.'

'He's what my father would refer to as an athletic build. He's gorgeous.'

'I agree,' Clara said.

Nathalie offered her a cup of tea; Clara declined, so she excused herself to get ready for her date with Ava.

When she reappeared to say goodbye, Clara did a double-take. With expertly applied make-up, a tight bandeau-style dress and sky-high heels, she looked sophisticated and oozed sex appeal.

'Be still my beating heart!' Clara said. 'You look sensational. I wish I still had a body like that. I did once upon a time, but alas, it was well before Hervé Leger invented that style.'

'You like it?' Nathalie looked pleased and surprised. 'I was expecting disapproval. Dad always has something negative to say when I wear it.'

'He's just worried that all the hormone-driven men will lust after you and the equally driven ladies will hate you.'

Nathalie laughed, then walked over to Clara and hugged her.

'Thank you for being you.'

The sound of a car horn beeping outside flustered her, and she raced to grab a jacket and her bag.

'Take a key. Ava has one and can let you in later, but it's better to have one of your own as well. Enjoy, and I hope you girls have a nice chat.'

'Thank you,' Nathalie said sincerely.

As she rushed out the door, Clara put her hand on her chest. Nathalie's words just now had floored her. *Thank you for being you.*

'Well I'll be damned,' she said out loud. 'Did you hear that, Gus? Mama? Papa?' She looked up at the ceiling and shook her head in awe. 'I think we're getting somewhere. Hallelujah!'

Chapter 13

NATHALIE CLIMBED INTO AVA'S SHINING CHERRY-red sports car.

'This is totally cool,' she said, gazing into the tiny back seat.

'Well I've no husband and no kids, so I figured I only needed two seats,' Ava said as she took off. 'And I decided they may as well be two fabulous seats.'

'Jeez, do you drive at Formula One level in your spare time?' Nathalie asked as she gripped the sides of the seat for dear life.

'No, I guess it's down to being on my own. I don't have anyone else to consider so I put my foot to the floor a lot.'

'Yeah, nobody bar yourself and the other unsuspecting motorists who share the roads. I hate to sound like a grump, but could you slow down a bit? I'm not so great as a passenger in cars. I was in an accident recently.'

'Oh, of course,' Ava said, slowing down hugely. 'My apologies.'

'Hey, it's cool,' Nathalie said, flicking her hair.

Ava smiled. Before long, they pulled into an underground car park.

'I thought I'd take you for a bite to eat at my local Italian. I live in this block of apartments and it's the closest parking space I'll get.'

'Cool,' said Nathalie. She was growing increasingly curious about Ava and her life. 'I had herb omelette earlier, but I walked the prom and I'm hungry again! I'll be huge when I return to LA.'

'Looking at your figure in that dress, I think you'd have to eat several chocolate cakes an hour to look large.'

'Knowing Oma, that's not out of the realms of possibility,' Nathalie laughed.

'What else have you done today?'

'We went to the waterfall,' she said with a smile. 'It was gorgeous.'

'Umph,' said Ava, dismissing it. 'I'm surprised you weren't bored stupid sitting up there.'

'Oh no! It was genuinely awesome. I've never seen a place like it. I swam too.'

'No way! I'm impressed.'

'Well if I'm honest, it wasn't by choice. Your mom pretended to drown, so I jumped in to save her.'

Ava laughed. 'That's one of her favourite tricks.'

'You mean she's done it before?'

'All the time! But even though Max and I got to know it was a trick, we never wanted to take the chance just in case she actually was drowning!'

'That's crazy! *She's* crazy!'

Ava didn't speak, so Nathalie thought she'd better fill the silence. She still felt a little awkward with her aunt.

'I picked some flowers too. Oma promised to show me how to press them and make them into a card.'

Ava's head jerked sideways. 'I'd forgotten how we used to do that,' she said sadly. 'Your father liked it too,' she added. 'Although he began using bees and flies instead of flowers. He thought it was hilarious to send cards with squashed bugs plastered on the front of them.'

'Really? He did that? Wow, that doesn't sound like my always-sensible father,' Nathalie said.

'Yeah, he was a real messer back in the day. He called his cards fly cemeteries!'

Nathalie giggled. 'It's so fabulous to hear things about Dad when he was a child. He never talks about it. The only time he even sounds Irish is when Uncle Sean calls over.'

'Who is Uncle Sean?' Ava asked, narrowing her eyes. 'Your mother's brother?'

'Oh gosh no,' Nathalie said. 'He's not really a blood relation, but he likes me to call him that. He's from Ireland too. Dad and he were friends from way back when. In fact you guys probably know him. His surname is O'Brien.'

Ava inhaled sharply. 'Yes, I knew him,' she said in a strangled voice. 'He and your dad were friends from the time they were little. Sean is six years older than Max, but that never seemed to matter.'

'It never struck me that he's older, I must say,' Nathalie mused.

'That's because he has the brain of a toddler,' Ava said, flicking her hair rather violently.

'I take it you can't stand him, then.'

'After your father left Ireland, Sean followed him a few years later,' Ava said. 'Further proof of what a fool he was. Not that he needed help in that department.'

'I apologise if I've said the wrong thing,' Nathalie ventured uncomfortably. 'Why didn't you get along with Uncle Sean?'

'Oh I got along just fine with Uncle Sean,' Ava spat. 'Until he destroyed our relationship, that is. He left me with no option but to break off our engagement. He turned out to be a weak and selfish creature who I was better off without.'

'Oh Aunt Ava, I'm so sorry.' Nathalie's hand flew to her mouth. 'I had no idea.'

'Of course you didn't,' Ava said, sighing deeply. 'Listen, Nathalie, you don't know the ins and outs of what went on, but take it from me, Sean is an idiot.'

'So things were pretty ugly between you two?'

'Ugly is one way of putting it. I call it shagging some tart, getting caught and running with his sorry tail between his legs to his bosom buddy and fellow muck-up, Max.'

Nathalie looked as if she were about to burst into tears. Ava dropped her gaze and stopped ranting.

'Sorry, Nathalie. None of that is anything to do with you. I shouldn't have bitten your head off.'

'Hey, I'm cool!' Nathalie said, forcing a smile. She was trembling inside. Ava made her seriously nervous. She seemed so bitter and resentful.

'Besides,' Ava said, regaining her composure, 'it's all water under the bridge. It was aeons ago. I'm sure Sean O'Brien doesn't even remember me.'

'I'm sure he does,' Nathalie said. 'Maybe you could get back in contact again? I have his cell number if you want to—'

'No! Thank you. Let's leave sleeping dogs lie.'

'So,' Nathalie said, looking to change the subject rapidly, 'Oma mentioned you have a clothing store. I'd love to come visit some day, if you didn't mind.'

'Do you sew?' Ava asked.

'Sort of,' Nathalie said. 'But my home economics teacher wasn't my biggest fan. I made a miniskirt but she said it was obscenely short and inappropriate. My boyfriend DJ liked it, but he was probably the only one who did.'

'I'm sure he did,' Ava said as a smile crept across her lips.

They made their way out on to the street and walked towards the restaurant.

'My sewing is most certainly better than my cooking, if that helps,' Nathalie said. 'The last thing I baked was apple pie in school. I made it explode!'

'On purpose?' Ava asked.

'Uh-huh,' Nathalie said with a wicked grin. 'It was awesome. I got into so much trouble, though. Dad was called out of surgery and Mom had to attend the principal's office too. Ugh, I'm glad to be out of school. Those people have like zero sense of humour.'

'I like your style,' Ava said, nodding in obvious approval. 'Come to the boutique any time,' she said. 'I've a design workshop upstairs. Mama teaches there sometimes too; she does her quilting thing. It's becoming really trendy around here. But if that's too cruddy for you, maybe you'd enjoy my evening wear workshop? It's not just about sewing from scratch; it's about adjusting or adding to pieces you already own.'

'I would really like that,' Nathalie said. 'Oma is going to do some quilting with me, but I'd love to learn how to make awesome evening bling also. I do my own version back home, but I'm open to learning it properly.'

As they sat at a table and chatted, Nathalie noticed Ava's face and shoulders beginning to relax. She was incredibly pretty when she wasn't scowling. She had amazing style too, Nathalie noticed. If she wasn't mistaken, those were Jimmy Choo shoes she was wearing. She'd paired them with skin-tight dark denim, a beautifully light and wispy white blouse and a cropped leather jacket.

'Wine?' Ava offered.

'Er . . . I'm not really allowed to drink. I'm only seventeen.'

'The legal age here is eighteen. You look at least that. One glass of wine won't kill you.'

'In that case, I'd love one. Don't tell my folks, though.'

'I take it you have actually *had* a drink before?'

Nathalie nodded. 'Some of my friends are like totally anal about not drinking until we're twenty-one. But perhaps it's my European blood, I've been tippling for years. That was the final straw for Mom, actually . . .' She blushed and hesitated.

'Why, what did you do? Guzzle a bottle of wine on your cornflakes and insult the neighbour's dog?'

'Not quite,' Nathalie said, giggling. 'I got a homeless guy to buy me some vodka. Before you think I'm terrible, I bought him some too.' Ava nodded. 'I took mine to a park bench, drank a whole pile and kind of walked home in a bit of a mess. Mom didn't see the fun side, had a total and utter meltdown, like epic style, and promptly sent me here.'

'O-K!' Ava said, widening her eyes. 'It was a nice idea all the same, sharing the vodka with the homeless guy.'

'He had his own bottle,' Nathalie assured her.

'Well of course,' Ava grinned. 'That's a clever way of getting drink too. I like it. You're very resourceful, to say the least. I'm sure your parents were secretly quite impressed.'

'If Mom was even a teeny bit impressed, she was hiding that emotion really well. I've never seen her so pissed. I thought she was going to explode.'

'Yeah,' Ava mused. 'I suppose she was shocked and worried for you. I can't imagine it was ever in her grand designs for you that you'd aspire to hanging out with tramps getting trashed.'

'Probably not.'

'I feel a little hypocritical ordering a bottle of wine now . . .' Ava said, hesitating.

'I won't swig it by the neck, and we're in a restaurant with food too. I think it's a different scene. I won't stagger up a motorway either. I promise.'

'You didn't!' Ava said. Nathalie nodded, wrinkling her nose.

'Sorry, Mom,' she whispered, looking remorseful. 'In my defence, it seemed like a totally cool idea at the time.'

'Oh, don't you worry, I have plenty of those alcohol-fuelled ideas and most of them are fairly disastrous, and I'm meant to be a sensible adult! Maybe being deranged runs in the family and it's totally out of our control?'

'Not our fault . . .'

'Exactly,' Ava said as she flagged a waitress and ordered a bottle of wine. It arrived promptly, and the waitress, making it obvious she wasn't in a chatty mood, glugged it into the glasses, shoved the bottle into an ice bucket and shot off.

'Cheers,' Ava said, taking a large gulp. 'I'm obviously joking when I say it's a good plan to drink and cause trouble. You do know that, right?'

'I get it,' Nathalie grinned. 'So you never married or anything?'

'Nah. The near miss I had with Sean was enough to put me off. I'm not short of men,' she whispered. 'But marriage? Not for me.'

'I'd say you never met the right guy, that's all . . .'

'No,' Ava argued. 'I got my fingers burnt and I wasn't going to stick my hand in the fire again. That's more the reason. Take it from me, kid. Men are rats. All of them. Don't let any of them lull you into a false sense of security.'

'Surely there are some who are good and kind?'

'Maybe there are,' Ava scoffed. 'But they've all kept themselves well hidden from me if that is the case. What use are they at the end of the day?' She sat back. 'Don't answer that, by the way. I'm just mouthing off.'

'Didn't you want kids?' Nathalie asked as they ordered food.

'Jeez, you're definitely related to me. You don't pull any punches, do you?'

'Huh?' Nathalie looked confused.

'You ask a lot of questions.'

'Only sometimes,' she admitted. 'I haven't been doing much talking lately. Lots of shouting and arguing with my folks, but no chats like now.'

'Why not?'

'My best friend and her date died in a car crash a few weeks back. We were on our way home from the prom. Mackenzie was like my other half, you know?' Ava nodded. 'I'm overwhelmed with so many emotions that I can't figure it out in my head. It sucks.' She downed the rest of her wine and Ava refilled her glass.

'Do you feel as if you're on the edge of a cliff and you wouldn't even care if you fell off?'

'Yes!' Nathalie said, leaning forward.

'Do you feel like someone has stuck a massive hand down your throat and ripped part of your soul out and tossed it away?'

'Yes.'

'Do you wonder why the hell most of the world is carrying on as if Mackenzie didn't die?'

Tears began to seep down Nathalie's cheeks as she nodded miserably again.

'Hey, I'm sorry, Nathalie. I didn't mean to make you cry.'

'It's OK,' she said, waving her hand. 'It's actually a relief to find someone who understands how I feel. How do you know all this stuff?'

'I lost someone very precious to me too.'

'You did?'

Ava rarely allowed herself to think back to that time when her life had seemed so easy. She'd had Sean's love and support, the wedding was on the horizon . . . They'd had their whole lives ahead of them. Or so she'd thought.

They ate their meal and finished the wine, both caught up in deep thought.

'Let's get out of here,' Ava eventually suggested.

They meandered across the road and to Ava's apartment.

'This is gorgeous,' Nathalie said. 'It's so chic and European. I love all the white. How do you keep it so clean?'

'I'm kind of a freak. I like order, and because it's only me here, there's no reason for any disarray.'

'You need a serious shake-up. You need to meet someone who'll come in here and spray the walls with colour!'

Ava knew she'd successfully buried the awful sense of loneliness and loss under the surface. She'd gone back to the shop after her split with Sean and reinvented herself. She'd ended up as a different person as a result. One who was a lot harsher and less open than before. It was certainly conducive to running a successful business. But the flip side of it all was that she had denied herself an opportunity to find love again.

'Did it freak you out when we first met? I mean, I could be *your* daughter. I look more like you than my own mom.'

'Honestly, I nearly died when I saw you.'

'I'm sorry.'

'Hey, I'm not telling you this to make you feel bad, Nathalie. I'm saying it because you've actually given me a sense of hope again.'

'I have?'

'I see what an amazing girl you are and it's so incredibly sad that Max is gone from our lives. There's no reason why we can't all try to fix the problems of the past. Death is final, but Max isn't dead. And it's incredible that you exist!'

'Er, thanks, I think . . .'

'Don't mind me,' Ava said. 'I'm having a bit of an epiphany. Being so bitter and angry hasn't helped much over the years.'

'You've done some pretty awesome stuff with your life. You're an amazing businesswoman, you own a super-cool car, this place . . . I think you're great . . . Honestly,' she said as Ava gave her an odd look.

'You know, you're a seriously sensible girl for someone so young.'

'I don't feel that way. Drinking and acting like a lunatic most of the time isn't so great.'

'I know,' Ava said, once again deep in thought. 'Recently I've thought I should have some therapy. I know lots of people who swear by it. I keep ending up doing stuff that's not remotely constructive. I need to learn how not to do that, you know?'

'Without sounding too hallelujah about it, tons of my friends have had counselling and swear by it.'

'That *does* sound *totally* hallelujah,' Ava grinned. 'But right now, I don't feel I've any alternative. If it can help me, I think it's time I tried.'

'Maybe you should pick a male doctor too. Try and find one who's single. You could kill two birds with the one stone. Find some sanity *and* a husband.' Ava burst out laughing. 'Besides, I'm sure it's not that different here to the States: *all* therapists are totally minted. So you could end up really wealthy too. Sounds like a fabulous plan, even if I say so myself.'

'I take it back! You're not sensible but you really are amazing. Now enough of this depressing talk. Suffice it to say I'm delighted to have found you.'

'I love it too,' Nathalie said. 'It's awesome to have another family member that I can relate to.'

'OK,' Ava said with a watery grin. 'I have a new reason to hate Max.'

'What?' Nathalie said in exasperation. 'Why?'

'He's kept us apart.' Ava sighed in mock drama. 'At least things are as they should be once again. I hate Max, but I have you. I've been good at hating your father for this long, it'd almost be a pity to stop.'

She hugged Nathalie as the younger girl began to cry.

'Hey,' Ava said, 'I'm sorry. I don't really hate him as much as I used to.'

'It's not that,' Nathalie said. 'I kind of hate him too. I've never dared to voice that. But it's like having a cardboard cut-out for a father.'

'In what way?'

'He's so emotionally challenged. He's in his own world most of the time. I don't know how my mom sticks him. She's this warm and caring person who would do just about anything for us. But Dad always seems to be slightly removed from us. I could never put my finger on it. But now that I'm learning about his past, it all makes sense. He's damaged by his own actions, Ava. He's missed you guys so badly over the years. It's totally sad: the person he's punished the most is himself.'

Ava found that tragic to hear. It was one thing for her to decide she hated her brother. She was comfortable with that and it was a habit at this point. But it was actually heartbreaking to know that the family split hadn't benefited any one of them. Their father had gone to his grave with unfinished business that could potentially disturb his eternal rest. Their mother was still haunted by the fact that her son didn't want to know her. She herself had lost her only sibling, and for what? There were no winners in this awful situation.

Ava knew she had many years ahead, but Clara wasn't getting any younger. It was time to try and sort this awful situation before it was too late. It was time for Ava to take charge of her life.

Not right this second, though.

Nathalie excused herself and went to the bathroom.

'I'll order a cab,' Ava said, assuming her niece was exhausted. She would deliver Nathalie home and go on into Dublin. Texting Alan, one of her long list of admirers, she was relieved to learn he was in a bar and only too happy to see her.

She grabbed some fresh underwear and a crisp shirt and shoved them in her bag, knowing she wouldn't be home before work tomorrow.

Chapter 14

AMBER COULDN'T PUT UP WITH ANOTHER DAY OF stress. Downing a Xanax, she dressed in one of her classic navy Chanel shifts and slipped her feet into a pair of simple leather sandals. She brushed her hair, which was still in a glossy bob since her blow-dry the day before. She had always been a classical dresser and believed in keeping herself in tip-top shape. She did yoga twice weekly and kept to her gym routine three days a week too. She bought updated make-up each season to stay on top of the latest trends. Max didn't know, but she'd been having Botox for five years and was adamant she would grow old gracefully, with as much unseen help as possible. Unlike some of her friends, she'd resisted going under the knife, but lately she wondered whether it might be a good plan. If she looked more voluptuous and . . . edgy, maybe Max would take more notice of her.

None of that could be achieved in the next few minutes, however, so she'd have to muddle through as she was.

The time had come for her to get some answers. She couldn't dance on eggshells with Max any longer.

She'd always known the day would come, that she would have to confront him, and today was that day.

He'd only spent a few hours in the house since Nathalie left. She knew he was seething with her for sending their daughter to Ireland, but she also knew her husband better than he realised.

Climbing into the car, she steadied herself. She probably

shouldn't drive while on tranquillisers, but there was no other way she'd manage to say what needed saying. She knew she was driving like a snail, but that couldn't be helped. She needed to stay calm and arrive at the hospital feeling as relaxed as possible.

As one of the more senior members of the hospital fund-raising board, she couldn't afford to make a fool of herself. She adored her charity work and would hate to mar that in any way.

Sighing with relief that she hadn't mounted a sidewalk or clipped an oncoming car, she pulled up at the hospital. She spotted Max's car straight away. At least he was actually at work. If he were having an affair, his car might have been parked at some random apartment block instead of where he'd said he would be.

Knowing his schedule, she guessed he'd be in his rooms about now. As she walked down the familiar corridor to his door, she felt as nervous as the day she'd walked up the aisle to marry him. She'd always felt a sense of trepidation with Max. She hated to admit it, but she suspected that their feelings for one another were more than a little imbalanced. She'd always loved him more than he loved her.

It used to scare her and wake her during the night, making her sit bolt upright as she stared over with palpable relief at his sleeping form beside her.

As the years rolled by and Nathalie came along, her edginess mellowed marginally. But she was always relieved as their next wedding anniversary clocked up. Grateful that he hadn't left and thankful that he wasn't flaunting a buxom medical student half her age around town. She didn't bury her head in the sand, but she tried to avoid the more mouthy women in the neighbour-hood. To date she hadn't been approached by any smug-looking gossipy types and informed of an affair.

She was well aware of the notion that the wife was always

the last to know if her husband was straying, but she was certain that any news about Max would travel swiftly. They were one of the only remaining first marriages in their set. They were almost out of vogue at this point. Of the marriages that were still intact, nearly all had experienced some major bumps in the road in the form of affairs. Nobody else knew it, but Amber was under no illusion that she had held on to Max by the skin of her teeth over the years. And she guessed it was largely down to the fact that she'd never questioned him too deeply or made him talk about his emotions.

She managed her own by attending a therapist on a regular basis. During those sessions she cried if she felt the need, giggled uncontrollably if that was appropriate and had deep and meaningful chats when necessary. She kept her calm, swan-like behaviour for her husband, always serene on the surface, and did the paddling underneath at therapy.

The Xanax had kicked in as she wandered down the corridors of the hospital. It didn't make her feel out of control; it simply took the harsh edges off the world. She didn't pop pills that often. Only when she felt as if she might drown in panic, like today.

Max's secretary smiled as she approached.

'Good morning, Mrs Conway,' she said cheerfully. 'Was Mr Conway expecting you?'

'No, Nancy. This is a little surprise visit. I was in the hospital on foundation business and figured I'd drop by. Is he with a patient currently?'

'No, but I'll just let him know you're here.'

'No need, thank you, I'll fly in for a minute. It won't take long.'

Nancy opened her mouth to speak but Amber didn't give her a chance. She was well aware of the fact that Max objected to anyone bursting in his door. But she was his wife, and seeing as he didn't see fit to burst in their front door at home that much right now, she was acting on necessity.

Max's chair was empty, so she turned on her heel.

'Where is he?'

'That's what I was trying to say. He's gone to the cafeteria. Said he'll be back in about a half-hour.'

Amber took a deep breath. The Xanax was marvellous. She should be palpitating right now. Hyperventilating even. Instead she felt inner peace for the first time in ages as she surged forward and took control of her life.

She marched towards the café, going over her speech in her head. She'd tell him how she knew he was furious with her for sending Nathalie to Ireland. But she'd point out that she was the one who really ought to be angry. After all, he'd lied about his family and that raised all sorts of issues. If he could lie about such a monumental thing, what else had he not told her?

She stood for a moment and gathered herself before pulling the cafeteria door open. Satisfied that she could do this, she walked in. At first she couldn't see him. Then she spotted the top of his head. He was at a small table in the far corner of the room. A woman sat opposite him with her back to Amber. She squinted, trying to make her out. She wobbled slightly, cursing the increasing effects of the Xanax. She should've only taken half. She was ready to walk over and ask him to step outside when he pushed his chair back and walked to the end of the table. Holding his arms out, he embraced the other woman. A blonde, shapely woman who seemed to be crying. He took her in his arms and stroked her hair tenderly before kissing her head. The action was so intimate and emotional it made Amber cry out. Rooted to the spot, she willed her legs to move. They moved to the side, just enough for Amber to see who the woman was. At that instant, Max's eyes met hers.

She ran without stopping until she found her car. Wrestling with the jumbled contents of her handbag, she fished out her keys and opened the door before speeding away.

Her cell rang. She rejected Max's call. He called back. On the third attempt she answered.

'Amber! Where did you go? I didn't know you were coming to the hospital.'

'Well that's bloody obvious,' she said. 'I thought I'd surprise you. I hadn't realised you were going to be the one doing the surprising.'

'It looked bad, but it's not what you think,' he said.

'Max,' she laughed drily, 'it's more than bad. But guess what? I can't live in a glass house any longer. I'm on the edge here. I don't know where I stand with you. I guess I never have. I always felt an invisible barrier between us. Something I couldn't quite put my finger on. I learned to live with it. I adapted, compromised and moved forward. But something has shifted now. Your infidelity is the final insult. Whatever skeletons are lurking in your closet, they're clearly only the start of our problems. Judging by the way you were holding that woman, I've been wasting my time.'

'There are no skeletons,' he said, in a slightly patronising tone.

'Oh aren't there? So why did you tell me you had no family, and why have you seamlessly acted as if they're all nothing to do with you? For the record, Max, this isn't normal behaviour. It's not OK and it's not going to continue. I can't live with someone who takes other women in his arms and pretends his family are dead. I thought I knew you, Max. But clearly I don't.'

'Amber, please! I can explain,' he said. 'It's not what you think.'

'Please don't treat me like an idiot for another second. Oh, and for the record, Nathalie sees it too, all this skirting around being a husband and father. She's not stupid. Step up and be the father she needs. I shouldn't have to tell you to do that, but you have zero emotional connection with our beautiful girl. She's missing out as a result. It's time to man up, Max.'

Amber didn't feel a whole lot better as she hung up. She'd imagined a lovely scene where Max broke down and took her in his arms and told her he loved her and that he was sorry he'd shut her out. She'd been ready to support him and tell him it was OK to pour his heart out now.

She hadn't envisaged him taking another woman in his arms and kissing her in public.

She loved Max with every fibre of her being, but she wasn't prepared to remain locked in a one-sided marriage any longer. It would practically kill her to leave him, but she hadn't been raised to act like a victim. More than that, she didn't want Nathalie to see her confidence draining away as she silently taught her daughter to remain in a situation where she wasn't cherished and made to feel wholly loved.

All the way home, Amber sobbed as if her heart would break wondering whether Max had ever loved her at all. Miraculously she made it back safely. She couldn't get out of the car, though, and sat with her head against the steering wheel until a gentle rapping on the window made her look over. Her friend Evie was there, full of concern.

She managed to climb out and Evie helped her into the house. Eventually she calmed enough to tell her friend and neighbour what she'd witnessed.

'I can't believe it,' Evie said. 'Max always seems so smitten with you. Are you sure you didn't get the wrong end of the stick?'

'What would you think if you caught Mike holding a woman's hand and then hugging and kissing her? That she had dust in her eye? Come on, Evie! He's a rat and I'm going to have to deal with it.'

Chapter 15

NATHALIE WAS DELIGHTED WITH HER EVENING. AVA was a pretty darn cool aunt. She was looking forward to getting to know her better. There was something about her that led Nathalie to believe she'd suffered some kind of trauma. She was so reluctant to open up about her true feelings.

She made it to the bedroom, wrangled out of her clothes and grabbed a nightshirt. Tiptoeing to the bathroom, she made a half-hearted attempt at make-up removal and brushed her teeth.

Now that she was back, she knew what she wanted to do. She crept down to the sewing room and swiftly found the next letter. Back in her bedroom, she flicked on her bedside light and settled down to read.

August 1937

My darling Lukas

Our stolen moments shared in my room will be forever imprinted on my heart.

I met with Ava, my dearest friend from the orphanage, today. She had not laid eyes on me for several months. Instead of her usual warm smile, she greeted me with visible shock. Her gaze went directly to my belly, which made her gasp.

Nathalie stopped in shock. She couldn't believe what she was reading. Hannah was pregnant? She read on.

The Secrets We Share

I feel like such a fool. I had no idea that our love would create a child. At seventeen I ought to know these facts, but it seems I have learned the hard way.

Lukas, the very thought of you makes me smile inside and out. You are my angel on earth, my soulmate and best friend. If we lived in a different world, we would be accepted and I know our lives would be filled with laughter.

The Führer is well established here now. His popularity has gone from strength to strength with the authorities in recent times. His police occasionally put into prison those who are so unpatriotic as to ridicule him. Very few are safe from his wrath. I overheard the master, your father, speaking with some men in the drawing room. They say that recently 150 leaders of a Catholic youth organisation have been arrested and accused of treason – for having associated with Marxists.

I'm so scared, Lukas. The government is going along with the Führer's plans by making life harder still for Jews. Our exclusion from both public and private employment has left at least half of my community without a means of livelihood. I visited with my darling friend Frau Schulz at the orphanage and she has advised me not to speak of my Jewish status. She says that in many towns Jews cannot find lodging. Some are finding it difficult or impossible to buy food, including milk for their children, or to get medicine. Over some shops there are signs that read 'Jews Not Admitted'.

The Führer is invading our land and his army is growing in numbers by the day. It is no longer safe for me to be here. I could not have it on my conscience if you were arrested for fraternising with me. I know my time here is running out. I have given myself one more week in your arms. One more week in paradise before I let you go.

Frau Schulz agrees and says she can help me. She has a sister living near the Alps. I will go there and give birth to our child. It will take her a week to organise my transportation.

I know you will survive without me, for you were put on this earth to make a positive difference. You are one in a million and there are great divine plans for you, my love.

My heart is breaking as I try to accept that I have merely seven more days to absorb your being into mine. After that, the love I feel will have to be enough to get me through what lies ahead.

No matter where I go or what I do, I will always treasure the time I have spent with you. You are, and always will be, my heartbeat, my one true love.

Hannah

Nathalie struggled to read the last line. Her vision was blurred by her tears. Anguish ripped through her as she envisaged the poor girl and the heartbreaking decision she'd made.

She turned on her side, still clutching the letter, and cried herself to sleep.

The aroma of fresh bread woke her. Sitting up and rubbing her eyes, she knew she needed to get the letter back to the sewing room before Clara realised it was missing. She was about to get out of bed when she heard footsteps on the stairs. Shoving the letter under her pillow, she called out.

'Hello, dear,' Clara said. 'I didn't mean to wake you. I've baked some soda bread for your breakfast. I've a couple of things to do and was hoping to be back before you woke.'

'You go ahead,' Nathalie said. 'I'll be just fine. I might even go back to the beach for a bit. It was so lovely last night.'

'Good idea. It's sunny, so you should make the most of it. How was Ava last night?'

'Good,' Nathalie said. 'She's so much nicer when you get to know her.'

Clara laughed. 'I'll go now. I need to have a couple of blood tests done. Those sorts of things happen when you're my age. Nothing to worry about, but rather annoying!'

'Oh, would you like me to come with you?'

'Not at all, dear. I'll be back before you know it.'

Nathalie waited until she heard the car pulling out before running downstairs to put the letter away. Feeling scared of what she might read, she picked up the next one in the pile.

September 1937

Dear Lukas

By now you will have realised I am gone. I wish I could have left you a forwarding address, but that would make my actions futile. I need to save you from certain condemnation. You are so blindly in love with me that you think we will be accepted. But I am able to see that this will never come to pass.

I want you to know that I am safe. I went to Frau Schulz at the orphanage and she fulfilled her promise to help. She has sent me to a beautiful little village in the mountains. I took the train to Vienna, then caught a connection to Brixental.

Frau Schulz's sister Alina lives here along with her husband Frank and their three-year-old son Jacob. This little boy is the light of their lives and it's easy to see why. His floppy brown curls, round chocolate-button eyes and peepingly shy demeanour make him most endearing.

Alina is a talented seamstress. She has turned their simple farmhouse into a pretty and comfortable home. I am learning how to knit, sew curtains and bake delicious crunchy bread. Most precious of all, I have begun to make a patchwork quilt. Alina is a wizard at these creations and it's my ambition to be even half as able as she.

Each square has a special meaning. Some are from a ragged sheet I had at the orphanage. Some match the pretty curtains Alina has hung in my bedroom and some will be for you, Liebling. I did a terrible thing when I left you: I stole your blue striped shirt. The one you wore the first day we kissed. When I hold it close, I can inhale your scent and feel like you are still with me. I intend using the material to make a heart shape in the centre of my quilt. That way you will always be in my heart and thoughts and a part of you will still be in my bed.

Not a day passes that I do not think of you. My belly expands at a rapid rate and I feel our child growing inside me. If I didn't have this part of you with me, I know I would cease to be.

Distance will heal your wounds. Some day our time together will seem to you like a passing dream. I have no doubt, nor do I bear you any ill for the fact, that you will forget this girl who once adored you.

I have instructed Frau Schulz to keep my whereabouts a secret. I don't want you to try to find me. No good would ever come of that.

Ava, my dear and loyal friend, is the only other person who knows where I am. At least that way there will be some trace of my whereabouts – a strand of evidence that I once passed your way. A part of my heart wishes I could post this letter to you, my sweetheart, but the sensible part will never allow me to do so.

I love you more than you will ever know. I hope your tears will dry and you can find love once more.

Hannah

Feeling utterly desolate, Nathalie took the key Oma had given her the night before and locked the house. She was filled with a sudden need to breathe fresh air and see normal people living normal lives. To be reassured that life was still going on around her as usual.

The beach was already filling up with delighted children, dogs and walkers. Thinking a rush of sugar would do her good, Nathalie approached one of the pretty wooden kiosks and asked for a whipped ice cream cone.

'Make that two, and I'm paying.'

She spun around to find Conor there.

'Hey!' she said, delighted to see a familiar face. 'I thought you only came here in the evenings.'

'OK, I'll confess,' he said as he handed money to the seller. 'I live over there.' He pointed to one of the grand terraced houses that faced the seafront. 'I have a bird's-eye view of the promenade from my living room window. I spotted you and wanted to chat to you. Do you mind?'

'If you're gonna buy me ice cream, you can spy on me any time,' she laughed. 'Where's Herbie?'

'He's out with my mum. They might trot along in a minute. I doubt they've gone too far. Our lives revolve around this area. A two-mile radius to be exact. My father works in town in an office and my mum helps out at a crèche further along the promenade. Herbie is actually trained to deal with children with special needs. So he often goes to the crèche to visit the kids.'

'That's so cool,' Nathalie said.

They walked to a bench and sat down.

'I just had a call from Darragh. He's my best mate. He emigrated to Australia a couple of weeks ago. His family fell on hard times and had no choice but to join the rest of his extended family down there. I miss him,' he said simply.

'How long were you guys friends?' she asked, enjoying her ice cream.

'Since forever,' he said, nodding.

'I lost my bestie a few weeks ago too,' she said.

'She emigrate too?'

'No, she died,' Nathalie said and promptly burst into tears. She covered her face with her hand, mortified that she'd broken down with this guy. She figured he'd make some lame excuse and run back to his house, never to be seen again. Instead he sat and waited for her to calm before shoving his ice cream in the nearest bin and holding his arms out to her.

'Hug.'

She stood up feeling slightly baffled and embraced him.

'Ah, that feels good, doesn't it?' he said. 'Nothing like hugging it all out.' She stared at him. The feeling of his arms around her just now was wonderful. Her heart was thumping, not because she was sad. She laid her hand on his chest and looked up at him.

'Come on.' He grabbed her hand and pulled her towards a square made from paving stones. 'Let's play hopscotch. The loser gets to decide where we're going on our date tonight.'

'Huh?' She grinned. She knew she should tell him that he was being presumptuous. How did he know she even *wanted* to go on a date with him! He was outrageous. But he was also quite right.

Laughing, she followed and watched with a wide grin as he proceeded to draw a hopscotch grid with a piece of chalk from his shorts pocket.

'Do you carry chalk all the time? Is this part of your master plan, that you stare out your window and spot girls and ensnare them with childhood games?'

'Ah, only the pretty ones,' he said as he poked his tongue out in concentration. 'Now, I should say ladies first, but I've a feeling you're going to be deadly at this. So I'm going first.'

'Hey!' she shouted, shoving him as he threw a stone, aiming for the first square.

'Serves you right,' she laughed as he missed. She grabbed the stone and placed it on the first number, leaping off before he could stop her. She took her time and wasn't remotely put off by his intense stare as she negotiated the entire board seamlessly.

'I'm usually right about people,' he said with a warm smile.

'I knew you'd be brilliant and I was right. So put me out of my misery: where are you taking me tonight?'

'Where am I taking *you*?' she shrieked. 'I won! You're doing the taking out.'

'Superb,' he said. 'I thought you'd never ask. There's a bar at the very end of the promenade where they do traditional Irish music nights. You know the kind? Diddly-aye type of stuff? I play the boudhrán and I'd love a groupie to come and sit beside me.'

'You play the what?' she said, looking confused.

'Come along later and I'll show you,' he said with a cheeky wink. 'I'll meet you right here,' he pointed at the ground, 'at eight o'clock. *Slán.*'

'I beg your pardon?' She blinked, feeling more confused by the minute.

'*Slán,*' he said. 'It means goodbye in Irish.'

'I see,' she said. 'Slan to you too!'

'Not slan . . . The *a* part is a long sound. As if you're saying "lawn". Try it again.'

'Slaaaawn,' she said.

'Now you're talking!'

She smiled the whole way home, wondering how on earth it had come about that she had a date with a guy who wanted to converse in Gaelic and take her to a place to do something she had no clue about.

Chapter 16

AVA WAS AWAKE. AT LEAST SHE THOUGHT SHE WAS. She tried to open her eyes, but her lids were so heavy. She moved her hand and realised that the surface below her was incredibly hard and scratchy. Groaning, she wondered what had happened last night.

She'd met Nathalie. They'd talked. She was going to meet Alan. Lovely, but deadly boring. Great in bed, though.

Images began to flash through her mind. She'd gone to the bar and he wasn't there. She'd met that guy.

He'd been a bit creepy at first. Sat too close to her. Smelled of stale sweat and whiskey. She'd thought of leaving and going home, but knew she didn't want to be in the apartment thinking of all the things she wished hadn't happened to her.

He'd bought her a drink. She strained to remember what it was, and couldn't.

Everything else was a total blur. She pulled her upper body up off the ground and looked around. She'd no idea where she was or what had happened to her. Looking down at her front, she saw patches of blood. She lifted her top to see where the blood was coming from. She'd clearly been kicked or punched in the ribs. She searched the area for her coat and bag. Both were missing. Crawling to the wall, she managed to prop herself up and eventually stand. The pain was excruciating. She staggered to the door. As she made her way outside, she realised she was in a warehouse in the docklands of Dublin.

Mercifully there was plenty of early-morning traffic as commuters made their way to work.

Flagging a taxi, she managed to tell the driver her address. He glanced in the rear-view mirror several times before asking her if she was all right.

'I'm fine,' she said. 'Had a rough night, that's all.'

She kept her cool until they arrived at her apartment. Praying that her car was still there, she was relieved to notice it neatly parked where she always left it. She thanked her lucky stars and pressed the buzzer for the concierge.

'Harold,' she rasped. 'It's Ava Conway. I've lost my wallet. Can you come and pay this taxi and bring my spare apartment key? I'll pay you back as soon as I get inside.'

'Of course, hold tight. I'm coming this minute.'

Ava wanted to bawl. But she knew she needed to hold it together for another few minutes. Harold appeared and paid the driver before leading her to the elevator.

'What happened? Do you need me to call the police?' he asked.

'No,' she said. 'It was my own fault. I was walking home alone. I went to the hospital and they've given me the all-clear.'

Harold opened the door and let her inside. She assured him she had another key, paid him from an emergency fund she kept in her wardrobe and ushered him out. Then, locking the door and bolting it for good measure, she staggered into the bathroom and threw up.

Running the shower, she peeled her clothes off. Her ribs were badly bruised and she had a cut on her elbow, which was where the blood on her clothes appeared to have come from. When it came to removing her underwear, she began to sob. Praying she hadn't been raped, she was relieved to see there were no stains, nor was she cut or bruised down below.

She scrubbed her skin as if the action could wash away the shame.

As she came out of the bathroom, her landline was ringing. She contemplated leaving it but decided she'd better answer. It was Ruth, wondering if she was OK.

'I've had a lady in just now. She found your handbag last night. Your phone is still in there along with your keys. But it seems your wallet is gone.'

'Oh thank God,' Ava said, her voice wobbling. 'I had my bag snatched and I was knocked to the pavement in the process,' she said, the lie tripping off her tongue.

'Poor you,' Ruth said. 'Will I call anyone for you?'

'No. Thanks, though. I'll be there in about an hour. Can you plug my phone into charge?'

Ava knew Ruth was a little bewildered by her reaction, but she couldn't deal with telling her the truth.

She made coffee and set about cancelling her credit cards. As she was making the calls, her landline rang again. This time it was the police. It appeared she had emptied all her accounts the night before. But the fact that she'd used the same ATM machine and each card from her wallet consecutively had raised an alarm.

'We have CCTV footage of you and the man who was forcing you to do this.'

'Oh dear Lord,' she said weakly. 'I can't remember a single thing.' She agreed to speak to the police and said she'd be at the station that afternoon.

As she tried to come to terms with what had happened, Ava knew she'd come to the end of the line with her current life. She needed help, and soon. As soon as she was dressed, she drove to the place she'd secretly frequented for the past seventeen years. To speak to the one person who always understood.

Chapter 17

CLARA MADE A POT OF COFFEE AND SAT WITH Nathalie as she told her about her upcoming date with Conor.

'Ah yes, he's a bit of a character, to say the least. But he's a good boy. I'm glad you're going to hear some traditional music tonight. You'll enjoy that.'

'Am I crazy to say that I find him super-hot too?' Nathalie asked suddenly.

Clara smiled. 'You and the rest of the female population of Lochlann,' she said. 'He's quite a soccer player, you know? Plays for the county and swims at a competitive level too.'

'So that's where the muscles and that divine body come in,' Nathalie mused.

'I'm an old lady, I won't comment,' Clara said with a smirk. 'But suffice it to say I can appreciate why you might find him easy on the eye.'

Once they'd finished their snack, Clara said she was going to do some gardening.

'Would you mind if I go to the sewing room and do a bit of quilting?' Nathalie asked.

'Of course not. I'd be delighted to see you doing that, my dear.'

The box of letters was calling to her. Nathalie peeled the next one from the pile and took it to a part of the room where Oma couldn't spot her if she happened to be passing outside.

The Secrets We Share

Dear Lukas

The most incredible day has come to pass. Our baby is here. She is my reminder that our love wasn't all a dream. She has my soft brown curls and your blazing blue eyes. She is us, my darling. She is the most precious gift imaginable. As soon as I held her, I felt as if some of the fractured pieces of my life have been restored. I wish you could be here to gaze at her rosebud mouth and stroke her soft, peachy skin. You would adore her, Lukas. I know she would sleep even more soundly if you were here playing Handel or Mendelssohn for her.

The labour was difficult and I have never been so terrified. I called out for you and longed to ask Alina to contact you. But I knew that would not be fair. It was, without doubt, the most rewarding sixteen hours of my life. She is healthy, beautiful and completely perfect in every way.

After a night of sleeplessness due to the elation at becoming a mother and constantly staring at her tiny features, I have decided to name her Clara. It means bright and shiny, and she is the product of our love, which was brilliant and vivid. I hope you like this name. It suits her so well.

The snow has silenced the village for over six weeks now. I am cosy and warm here. Alina and Frank have been incredibly kind and I know I shouldn't feel blue. But when I look at Clara, all the love I felt for you comes flooding back. Even though my belly was growing by the week, I used to wonder if I dreamed you in my head. Did I actually imagine our relationship? You see, it is so incredible to me that you would love me back. I will not contact you, however, my darling. That would not be fair. You are my destiny, but I am aware that I am not yours. You are fated for higher things.

I am desperately sorry that you will not see Clara grow up, because she is your masterpiece. Of that I am certain. But this painful choice I am making is for your benefit.

Jacob is the sweetest little boy. He has fallen in love with Clara and I know he will make the most wonderful companion for her. She will never be alone and she will always know love. For that I will be eternally grateful.

I miss you every day, Lukas. I hope you are moving on with your life and that you have found love once more. Perhaps you have taken Liza's hand in marriage and you are planning a life together. I wish you love. I wish you happiness.

I love you as much as I did the day we met.

Hannah

'So it was you, Oma,' Nathalie whispered. It all started to make sense. The frightened girl was her great-grandmother.

Her mind whirred as she tried to take it all in. In the letters, Hannah had been the same age as Nathalie was now. She looked around the increasingly familiar sewing room. This house and this place were so welcoming, yet she'd found it kind of scary to come here. How terrified poor Hannah must've been. She had Alina and Frank, who were clearly being awesome. But she had no parents and no Lukas.

So far the story of Hannah and Lukas was the most incredible story she'd ever read, but to know they were actually related to her made it all so much more meaningful.

She knew Oma could walk in at any moment, but now that she knew who Hannah was, Nathalie *had* to read one more letter. Placing the one she had just read carefully back in the box, she plucked out the next one, together with its translation. For the first time, she looked properly at the English writing. It matched Oma's writing, she realised as she glanced at her sewing notes. So Oma had translated all this precious correspondence.

The Secrets We Share

Dear Lukas

I have made a heartbreaking decision. Our beautiful Clara is seven months old. She is sitting steadily and has a smile as big as the moon. I want to give her the world. I want her to have a better life than I can provide with my limited resources.

Alina and Frank have been endlessly kind and generous with both time and funds. But they too are struggling to put food on the table. I have tried to no avail to find cleaning work locally. The village of Brixental is too small to offer much employment. Also, Herr Hitler is taking over. Since February he has occupied Austria and is determined to cleanse the country. He is ordering his Nazi party to exterminate all Jews. My presence in Alina and Frank's Catholic home is a danger. I cannot ignore the fact that I could cause their demise. If they are found harbouring me, they are certain to be punished.

As per Herr Hitler's rules, I, along with all other Jews over the age of fifteen, must register and take an identity card. This card will tell soldiers of my Jewish status. In turn I will be forbidden to work.

Alina and Frank have offered to take care of Clara. I am going to the city to take a post. This job is with some people who are distant relatives of Frank. He has not told them I am a Jew and they have not asked. When I have the price of our fare accumulated, I will return for Clara and take her to America. There are opportunities there and we may start a new life, away from the horror that is unfolding here.

Jacob is besotted with Clara. It is the sweetest thing I have ever encountered. He plays with her and teaches her non-stop. I know it will tear at my heart to walk away from here and leave our daughter behind. But I have no choice.

It comforts me somewhat to realise that Alina, Frank and Jacob adore Clara so.

I hope that it will not be long before I return.

You are still in my heart, where you will always remain as my one true love.

Hannah

Tears rolled down Nathalie's cheeks as she read the words. Hannah had had to leave her baby behind? The sense of anguish in her great-grandmother's letter weighed heavily on her heart. She couldn't read any more today.

Replacing the letter, she returned to her quilt and worked on autopilot, grateful that she had something to do with her hands to help occupy her mind. This story was becoming more and more painful, and now it was personal too. How would it all end?

Ava kept her head down as she walked out of the police station. She hoped no one she knew was around to see her. She felt so sordid. As it turned out, the man who had robbed and beaten her was known to the police and had been convicted previously for causing grievous bodily harm. He was on parole and the police assured her he'd soon be right back behind bars.

Knowing she'd had a lucky escape, Ava shuddered as she tried not to let her imagination run wild. One thing was for sure: she wasn't going to allow a situation like last night to arise again. She had to sort herself out.

She made her way to the shop and collected her phone before walking towards her mother's house. The police had given her the number of a counsellor in case she felt traumatised by her ordeal. What she didn't want to point out was that there was a whole host of demons that she needed to exorcise too.

Dialling the number, she was surprised when the secretary told her there was an appointment available the following day.

'Really?' she said.

'We try to fit trauma cases in immediately,' the woman explained. Ava booked the session and hung up, wondering how it might all pan out. Knowing that her mother would worry, if she didn't hear from her she called the house to let her know she was up to her tonsils at the shop.

'Hello?' Nathalie's voice came on the line.

'Hi,' Ava said, wincing. She would hate her niece to know what had happened after they'd parted company last night.

'Aunt Ava,' Nathalie said, sounding delighted. 'Are you OK?'

'I'm fine,' she lied. 'I was just calling to say that I think I have some sort of bug. You weren't sick, were you?'

'No,' Nathalie said.

'Oh good, just a bug in that case, I suspect. Would you mind letting Mama know that I've gone home to bed and not to worry. I'll probably be off air for the rest of the day.'

'Sure,' Nathalie agreed. 'But call if you need anything, won't you?'

'I will.'

Nathalie walked out to the garden to let Clara know Ava's news.

'Oh, that's not nice. Did she say if she needed me to go to the shop for a while? I'm sure Ruth needs a bit of a break.'

'Sorry, she didn't say,' Nathalie said.

'Not to worry, I'm sure Ruth will call if she needs me. She usually does,' Clara said. 'I'm going to continue with weeding this bed if you're all right inside?'

Nathalie said she needed to wash her hair for her date with Conor that night. She was relieved when Clara didn't question her too much. Yet again she marvelled at how different Oma was to her mom. Amber would need to know every minute detail of what Nathalie was doing and when she wanted to do it.

Oma, on the other hand, was so cool about it all. You never knew what she was really thinking.

Chapter 18

AS SOON AS CLARA WAS ENGROSSED IN HER gardening once more, Nathalie found the next letter and braced herself for news of Hannah.

March 1943

Dear Lukas

As you will know, the Nazi party is continuing to brainwash, ransack and murder Jewish communities. I have fled several places of work in terror as my employers discovered I am a Jew and threatened to turn me over to the authorities.

Long gone are my girlish plans to travel to America. I am no longer looking for a place to earn money but rather one that will allow me to work in exchange for being permitted to live.

I am expected to wear a star on my clothing, and Hitler has insisted that all Jewish women be addressed as Sarah and all men as Israel. I do not attempt to make friends any longer. It is far too dangerous, as I am not certain who I can trust. This world I am living in is beyond terrifying. I have seen things I wish I could wipe from my psyche. The atrocities that are being reported are entirely heartbreaking. I have witnessed Jews being dragged from houses to be beaten and even raped on the streets.

There are many ghettos and underground areas where entire families huddle like starved and frightened rats. I am not willing to join them just yet. Those places are the most volatile and suffer the most attacks from soldiers. The people who live there are mostly educated and once wealthy folk who have had their homes and businesses destroyed. This is the cruellest outcome I could ever imagine for any human being. How can people become so animalistic, Lukas?

I have only stayed for single nights in these ghetto communities. I feel that movement offers me the most safety. It is all about survival now. I have managed to go from job to job by hiding my star in my coat and pretending to be Catholic. I learned enough from Alina and Frank about their customs to bluff my way through. The last house I fled was the closest I have come to being captured. The soldiers associated with Dachau concentration camp seized my fellow worker and captured her. In terror she called out to me that she hoped I would escape. After that, the master of the house guessed that I was a Jew.

I have seen newspaper articles detailing the torture that continues at Sachsenhausen and Buchenwald. Thousands of innocent people are being obliterated. Since Anschluss Österreichs, the annexation of Austria into Greater Germany, the Nazi regime has taken hold. I know this evil man Hitler is unstoppable. I fear it is only a matter of time before I am captured or murdered.

The only thing that keeps me going is the memory of your face. The feeling of your arms around me and the knowledge that our baby girl is safe with Alina and Frank. I have not been in a position to contact them to let them know that I am still alive. But even if I had the chance, I would not take it. They can pass Clara off as their own, and that way she will be safe. Any contact I make could endanger our daughter. I will not allow that to happen.

For today, I am safe. I found new lodgings only yesterday in a large house where there are many staff.

Wherever you may be, Lukas, I hope you are happy. As I stare at the sky, it is a comfort to know that you are at least beneath the same stars as me.

I am living in fear, my darling. But I am trying to concentrate on filling my heart with love, just the way it was when we were together. If this is the last time I write to you, which I sense it may be, I hope you know that the memories we share have shown me that there is love and happiness deep in my core in spite of the ugly war that is raging in our world.

You and Clara are the sparkle in my eye and the warmth in my heart. No matter what becomes of me, I will always know what it feels like to love and be loved.

For that I thank you from the bottom of my heart. Hitler and his evil army can destroy many things, but not the love I hold for you and our daughter. I will own that until the day I die.

Hannah

Panic crept through Nathalie as she wiped her tears with her sleeve and grabbed the pile of letters. She knew she was risking discovery by Clara, but she needed to know if Hannah had survived.

Relief flooded her senses momentarily as she saw that the next letter was in Hannah's handwriting too. But this letter was different to the others. Firstly it was written on several types of paper. And the writing on the translation was incredibly shaky, leading her to believe that whoever had done all this work was unbelievably upset by what they had read.

April 1943

Dear Lukas

My fears have become a reality. I know I will not be writing to you much more. Even if I survive, which is hugely doubtful, I have very few supplies with which to continue my letters. I tucked some pages into my clothes along with a pencil.

I am in Bergen-Belsen concentration camp. The master at the house I was at last gave me up to the soldiers. As an incentive for people to hand over Jews, Hitler's men were offering monetary rewards in exchange for prisoners. The temptation was too great and I was sold.

In the murky darkness and the lashing freezing rain we were herded together. I was kicked and beaten, but unlike some of the other girls, I was not raped, due to the fact that I was vomiting so frequently. I think my ribs are broken, as I am struggling to stand up straight, and there are boot marks on my ribcage.

The soldiers yelled, 'Schnell!' as they forced us to hurry into the unknown blackness. As the other women and I neared the railway, I could see the wooden-slatted train carriages, and hear the panicked wailing of the passengers inside.

As they flung open one of the large wooden doors at the back of the train, I was met by a stench of urine, sweat and human waste. People were huddled together, trying to shield themselves and stay warm. Many were stripped naked, and those who were clothed were disgustingly soiled and soaked. Although I did not relish the thought of being made to get into the carriage and join them in their nightmare, I was relieved at the notion of being allowed to sit.

Due to the fear, the cold and the searing pain in my ribs, I struggled to climb inside. I heard the noise of the soldier's baton swooshing through the air before I felt the pain as it cracked across the back of my skull. Two hands reached out from the darkness and, like an angel carrying me on its wings, I was pulled aboard. As I reeled from the blow, I was met by a pair of soft brown eyes. Stella introduced herself and tugged me over to the side of the carriage from where she'd scurried. I know she saved me.

We huddled together and sat rocking back and forth. The shutters were slammed down and the noise of the steam engine shuddering to a crawl made some of the prisoners cry out in fear. Nobody knew where we were being taken or what would become of us.

As the hours passed, the inky night was diluted by strands of light shining through the slits of wood on the sides of the carriage. At last the train ground to a halt.

The Secrets We Share

There was no food given and no water offered. Two buckets were placed at the end of the space, for use as a toilet. We remained there for hours. I huddled into Stella's embrace for warmth and comfort, and prayed.

By the time night fell again, those buckets were overflowing and many of the smaller children were vomiting uncontrollably. A stench of desolation and degradation filled the air.

The darkness brought more movement, as the sound of the steam engine roared forth once again. This routine continued for four nights. All the while, I remained huddled with my new-found friend. I thanked God for sending her to me.

In faltering whispers she told me how she'd been captured. She was living near Vienna in a tiny apartment with her family. When the soldiers arrived, her mother and younger sister managed to slip away through a trapdoor in the kitchen floor to the cellar of the building. As the soldiers ransacked the place, throwing all their belongings on to the floor, they unwittingly hid the trapdoor, ensuring their safety.

Stella was grateful they had escaped but was traumatised by witnessing her dear brother being shot in cold blood. Alone and terrified, she was taken to the train. She'd been as glad to meet me as I was to find her.

I told her all about you, Lukas. She knows about our darling Clara too. Speaking about you both has renewed my faith in love. As I told Stella how you both make my heart sing, I am once again reminded that I am never truly alone. You are not here with me physically, but you will live on in my heart alongside Clara.

As we contemplated what would become of us, the train shuddered to a halt for the last time. The doors were forced open from the outside, and flashlights were shone around the cabin. We were all ordered out. The snow was falling thick and fast. The soldiers pointed towards a large open field. Dressed in full uniforms along with boots, fur-lined *hats and gloves, they were better equipped to cope with the weather. I, like most of the others, was wearing a blouse, woollen skirt and flimsy boots. Without a coat, all I had to shield me from the elements was my own determination.*

As we trekked across the endless fields of sludge, my boots became clogged with mud and grass. The sheer numbers of people tramping the same ground meant that the mud became churned up and coated our legs, making it difficult to walk. My muscles burned so badly that I considered lying down and giving up. But the image of your face and Clara's dancing smile spurred me on.

For what seemed like hours we followed the guards, each step bringing us closer to what I feared could be death.

I stayed in close proximity to Stella, hoping to God we wouldn't be separated. As the barbed-wire fencing and searchlights came into view, the sounds of gasping, gulping crying spread through the crowd like a contagious disease.

By the time all the prisoners had managed to stagger to the edge of the camp, the sun was about to rise. Using a megaphone, one of the guards stood on a large metal box and ordered us into two groups. Half of us staggered to the left and the others to the right. We were very much to the outside of the extreme left, so it was an easy choice. But we could hear panic from the people closer to the centre, confused about which way to go.

With irritation and impatience, two guards with batons shoved their way through the middle to indicate where each person should stand.

My group was ordered to follow a guard.

We walked towards the open gateway that led into the camp. As we reached the centre of the compound, all hell broke loose behind us. Several soldiers opened fire at the remaining civilians and did not stop until the crowd was silent.

I felt my legs giving way as I took in the carnage. Silence has never sounded so scary, Lukas.

The Secrets We Share

As the sun rose, I began to notice the meek peeking eyes of the prisoners who were already at the camp. They were sheltering in tunnel-style brick-built chambers.

Nathalie placed the letter down with shaking hands and picked up the next one, which had been scrawled on a scrap of paper that appeared to be the label from some sort of dried bouillon.

June 1943

Dear Lukas

I have been at Bergen-Belsen for two months now. I managed to steal this broth label so I can write to you. My life has become a game of survival. The horrors I have witnessed are unbearable and I will most certainly die here. Stella is very low. She is sweet-natured and has little to hope for.

I consider myself one of the lucky ones. When reality becomes too much, I can dream. I can force my mind to think of an imaginary house where you and I are happily raising Clara. At our home I can block out the horror of the present. The morning is the worst time here. The moaning and wailing increases as the barrow women approach. They come to remove the dead, you see.

The lifeless bodies are swung by the arms and legs into great wheelbarrows and taken to the crematorium. There are no gas chambers here at Bergen-Belsen. I read about some of the other camps before I was taken here. I know that many of them round up prisoners and gas them in great numbers. So I thank God for small mercies. I have learned that being quiet is my safest course of action. The soldiers are easily angered and will shoot on sight should a prisoner cause them bother. They are merciless with people who attempt to escape also.

There are many people here, but I cannot say there is much laughter or fun, ever.

We have a little routine going, though. In a way, we have formed our own community and know we must make the best of this horrid situation. We cook over campfires in large cauldrons. The food is mostly soup, consisting of water and a tiny amount of potato or other vegetable. It is nothing short of a miracle when a slice of sausage appears in my cup. Black bread is also seen as a treat and is rationed sparsely.

I am eternally grateful that I left our baby where I did. I could not live with myself if I thought she was being subjected to this torture. I would take this punishment a thousand times over to protect her.

Stella is ill and I can literally see the life draining from her eyes. I fear she is giving up. I do not blame her. There are days when I wish I did not harbour this strong urge to live. It would be so much easier if I could simply lie down on the dusty earth and pass on to the next world. There has to be something better than this.

Where are you, Lukas darling? Are you sitting at your piano mesmer-ising some pretty girl with your brilliance? I hope you are living a life less dire than mine. My suspicions are that this is the case. This, my Liebling, is hell personified, led by and organised by the purest form of evil imaginable.

I love you with my all of my heart. You are in my dreams and you pull me through the moments when I fear the shadows will win the battle I am waging.

Nathalie sat barely breathing as she tried to fathom the fact that the piece of paper she was holding had actually come from a concentration camp. She'd heard of them, of course she had; at school she had learned about the dreadful atrocities that had been committed by Hitler and his government. But never in a million years had she ever thought she would come so close to witnessing the true horror of what had unfolded at that time.

She hesitated before picking up the next letter, not sure she could actually stomach it. Her heart stopped as she realised this was the last one. She peered into the box, hoping she'd been mistaken. But nothing else was left.

This time the note had been written on a piece of brown paper bag. She left the original scrap on her lap as she frantically read the translated document.

1944

Dear Lukas

I know not what month we are in. I presume winter is nigh as the nights are becoming colder and the light is fading earlier.

Life at Bergen-Belsen is more of a struggle with each passing day. My dear friend Stella lost her fight to live some months back. Her emaciated body had become too weak to go on. Like many others, she looked like a balloon pulled over a skeleton. Her eyes had lost their light and she was too exhausted to continue. I hid her body for two days. I could not bear the thought of my sweet and gorgeous girl being tossed into a barrow and treated like she was nothing. She was everything to me. She was my only confidante in here.

I stowed her at the very back of the shelter we have occupied since getting here. There are only a few ragged blankets remaining and some of the other prisoners became fractious. She was using up precious blanketing and they are all terrified of infectious disease. They took her body and left it for the barrow women. I could not fight them. I felt like I'd failed Stella. I let them kill her and obliterate her body. I hope she is at rest now. I hope she has found paradise. But I miss her so badly it churns me up inside.

Now I have nobody to tell about our love. I cannot trust others to keep Clara's whereabouts a secret, so I have chosen to remain silent.

I still go to you and Clara in my imagination, though. You are in our home still. We have a fire with plush spinach-green chairs and thick velvet drapes that pool on the floor in luxurious style.

Sometimes I become so confused that I am not certain of who I am or where I belong. You are so real to me, Lukas. I can smell your scent and feel the coarse bristles of your whiskers as you lean down to kiss me.

I can hear Clara's voice as she calls to you and beckons me to join in.

My hands are shaky now, Lukas. I find it increasingly difficult to write and focus on the words. I think the angels are calling me. I did not want to go with them before. I had an incredible urge to live. But now I feel my time is coming to a close. No matter what happens, I will wait for you, my darling Lukas. I will watch over you and Clara and I will protect you with my love.

Hannah

Nathalie put her head in her hands. A noise behind her made her jump up in fright. She turned and came face to face with her grandmother.

'Oma! It's you. It's so terrible . . .'

'I know, dear, I know,' Clara soothed, enfolding Nathalie in her arms.

'I'm sorry . . . I shouldn't have looked . . .' she sobbed.

'Yes you should,' she said. 'I wanted you to see.'

Nathalie stepped back. 'You mean, you left them there so I would find them?'

Clara nodded. 'There are so many strands to your family, Nathalie. I didn't know how else to tell you. You come from generations of strong women who knew what pain was and somehow managed to overcome it.'

'Are there any more letters, Oma?' she asked, beseeching her to say yes. 'Please, I have to know what happened to Hannah.'

Clara held her tightly and stroked her hair.

'All in good time, *Liebling*, all in good time.'

Chapter 19

CLARA HAD KNOWN SHE WAS TAKING A GAMBLE leaving those letters on view in the sewing room. She was banking on Nathalie being as curious as she herself would have been in the same circumstances.

The anger and bitterness that had flooded the air as Nathalie stepped into the arrivals area of Dublin airport had been the final push she required.

Clara knew she could easily sit and *tell* Nathalie her parents' story, but it wouldn't come close to reading about it first hand. She was sorry the poor girl was so traumatised by the brutal reality of what had happened to Hannah, but she knew that her incredible example would teach Nathalie more about life than any other means.

As they began to sew Nathalie's quilt, Clara could already see a change in her granddaughter.

'Do you think suffering is passed on in a silent genetic thread, Oma?'

'Ooh, how do you mean, dear?' Clara asked.

'Well, Hannah went through hell. I'm guessing you did too . . . Ava has faced her fair share of heartache and now I'm here attempting to pick up the pieces of my life . . .'

'I don't think that's genetic, my dear. I think that's just life. The grass isn't greener on the other side. Nobody lives a perfect existence without so much as a shred of sadness.'

'I guess not.'

Clara put on a classical CD and turned the music up. Words were not necessary at times and she knew this was one such occasion. Methodically they placed the cut-out squares in a pattern, swapping and changing them until Nathalie was pleased with the result. Shyly she pulled a vest from beneath a pile of fabric.

'This was Mackenzie's. Could we incorporate it somewhere?'

'Sure,' Clara said happily. 'The best quilts have pieces that remind the owner of someone special, or indeed a time that means a lot.'

They cut the vest material and added it to the quilt.

'By the way,' Clara said through pursed lips, dotted with pins, 'the quilt need never be totally finished. There's always room to add more. So any time you find something pretty, or a scrap that has meaning, add it in. Make a new row and broaden the beauty.'

Nathalie watched like a hawk as Clara showed her the best stitch for linking the squares. The sewing machine was very different to the one she used at home and so it felt alien to her at first, but once she got the hang of how to manoeuvre the fabric, it was deeply satisfying. Lost in her own world, she was thoroughly enjoying the process of quilting.

'I'm going to take a little trip to Gus's grave,' Clara said. 'I go quite often and it gives me a sense of peace. Would you care to join me?'

'Er . . . where is it?' Nathalie asked.

'Not far. Out the gate and left, walk for approximately ten minutes and it's there, overlooking the sea. It's rather beautiful really. I often wonder why graveyards are built in such wonderful locations. It's hardly for the occupiers. It must be to keep the minds of the visitors sane.'

Nathalie smiled, enjoying Oma's left-of-centre musings.

'You're right, graveyards are often housed in beautiful settings. I guess we deserve to rest someplace pretty when we've finished our work on earth.'

'So would you like to come, or are you happy here?'

'I might stay here and carry on with this if you don't mind too much?'

'Of course.' Clara hugged her. 'I'm delighted you've been bitten by the quilting bug!'

Left alone, Nathalie began to wonder what had happened to Hannah in her latter years. She knew she could ask Oma outright, but she didn't want to rake up dreadful memories for her. It was probably best to wait and bide her time.

She finished another couple of rows of her quilt before stretching. She was looking forward to her date with Conor. The thought of him made her smile. He was a rare character and she knew full well that he was a bit of a rogue, but she was grateful to have met him all the same.

She was about to leave the room when she noticed something tucked into the side of the cardboard box. It was a small bundle of letters. This must be the final batch. With a beating heart, she took them carefully out and sat down.

25 April 1945

Dear Lukas

I am free! Just over two weeks ago, the most incredible miracle occurred.

It was early morning, and as the sun rose, I heard a siren sounding. Fearing the worst, I joined the others at the edge of the compound. Officials and men in uniforms I didn't recognise, along with reporters with large cameras, had gathered on the other side of the barbed wire.

Some announcements were made, which were not altogether clear at first. We all assumed we were going to be exterminated. It was of course the natural conclusion for us. We had been treated like beasts for so long, we thought we were being rounded up and shot in one swoop. Panic set in and there were cries from some of the more vocal prisoners that we should stampede. That maybe we should crush the fencing and make a dash for it. That perhaps some people might survive if we did this.

The shouting and pushing came to a stop as a man climbed on to a box and shouted into a megaphone that Bergen-Belsen was to be disbanded and we would all be free to go.

A feeling of euphoria and disbelief spread through the rippling crowd of starved and bewildered prisoners.

Lukas, I did not dare believe that this was actually happening. I pinched my leg to ensure I was not dreaming.

Over the course of the next few days, the wire fencing was torn down. Trucks took groups of people away, a few at a time. I did not rush forward to be taken first. I had no idea if we were going to a better or a worse place. My trust in human kindness had worn thin. By that point I did not know how it felt to be treated with anything but disdain. Still, I figured that anywhere had to be an improvement on what I had endured. My energy was all but spent and I knew that one way or another, the ordeal of Bergen-Belsen was behind me. If my life was over too, I was not in a position to fight.

We arrived at a great grey hospital where we were taken one by one to a room. The nurse spoke gently and slowly, asking questions. It became clear that she was trying to determine what diseases I might have.

My self-esteem was at an all-time low. I felt ugly and dirty, and knew I must look like a terrified rat.

I could not fathom whether I was simply overcome or gravely ill, but I felt the room spin. Sounds droned in a slurred manner and I blacked out.

The Secrets We Share

When I came to, a man with dark heavy shoes and grey trousers came into my vision. I could only see his feet. The pain in my head was so severe that I couldn't bring myself to sit up and regard him.

He crouched down and introduced himself as Dr Schmitt. I guessed he was in his fifties, with greying hair and a rather bushy handlebar moustache. His eyes were filled with concern and I instantly knew he would look after me. Unlike the soldiers, who had only ever looked at me with scorn and disgust, this man was treating me like a human being for the first time in so long.

He examined me carefully and said he would work with the nurses to make me better. He helped me stand and led me to the bathroom, where one of the nurses had drawn me a bath.

I saw my reflection in the mirror. Oh Lukas, I could barely believe I have become this poor creature with thinning matted hair, ghostly pale skin and protruding cheekbones so sharp they looked like they could pierce right through my pinched face. My piteously pointed chin made me resemble a tiny elf. At the age of twenty-four, I looked like a mere child.

I cried as the doctor left the room and the nurse lifted my dress over my head. There was barely enough skin to cover my skeletal frame.

The water was divine. I thought I had died and gone to heaven as the cleansing soapy water lapped over my emaciated body, making me feel for the first time as if I could possibly come through this atrocity.

The nurse helped me out and dried me tenderly, offering me a clean soft nightshirt. The feel of the freshly laundered snow-white sheets against my skin was akin to being wrapped in angels' wings.

I woke to find Dr Schmitt sitting by my side. He was smiling and so was the lady beside him. He introduced her as his wife, Giselle. They explained that they were taking part in a programme that helped concentration camp survivors to restart their lives. They offered me free board and lodgings at their home.

I'm here now, Lukas, and it is far more wonderful than any words can convey.

I have a cosy converted attic space, with exposed beams and a painted iron bed. For the first couple of days after I arrived here, I simply gazed around the house in awe. By anyone's standards, Dr Schmitt and his wife live in a beautiful house, but in comparison to Bergen-Belsen this place is more wonderful than I could have ever imagined.

Giselle and I are making quilts. I knew a little of what to do, having spent that spell at Alina's home. But Giselle is patient, kind and so incredibly enthusiastic that I am finding myself swept away on the cloud of positivity she creates.

I told her last night about Clara. She was amazing, Lukas. She thinks I should go back and find her. I am going to continue making quilts, and I hope to sell them and use the proceeds to buy a ticket to America. Giselle occupies a stall at a nearby market. She sells many hand-made goods along with her own wonderful patchwork quilts. She has generously told me I am welcome to sell whatever I complete and keep the profits. At long last I will be able to take our baby girl to a better life. I have learned a skill that I am certain will be of use to me in America. Perhaps I can find a job as a seamstress. A world that was so incredibly hostile has been turned around. I am slowly regaining my faith in humanity. Giselle and Dr Schmitt are showing me that the evil I experienced is not universal.

I still long for you, my Liebling. *I think of you all the time and I know I will never love another man the way I loved you. I sometimes wonder where you are and who you are holding in your arms. But my greatest fear is that you are unhappy.*

I still love you as much as I did the day I first found you.

Hannah

Tears soaked Nathalie's cheeks as she learned of Hannah's release. Obviously she knew Hannah hadn't died, but the emotions that engulfed her as she tried to imagine the intense relief her great-grandmother must've felt was awesome. She rocked back and forth as she realised just how precious this quilt-making was for her family. Feeling a wave of fresh love for Oma, she shook her head and thanked her silently for showing her how to do this wonderful craft. How precious that Clara had accepted her with open arms and instantly striven to engrain in her an activity that had linked the women of her ancestry. Nathalie had never felt so special or included.

It was a joy to her to see that the letter, no longer written on dirty scraps, but on pretty cream embossed paper, was adorned with much steadier handwriting. The joy Nathalie experienced at knowing that Hannah was safe and well was like a balm to her soul.

There weren't many letters remaining in the final bundle, so Nathalie forged onwards, picking out the next one. She was so grateful to Oma for writing these out in English so she could understand what was being said, yet she was still able to hold the original documents.

December 1945

Dear Lukas

I am dumbstruck. I am sitting in my room, where I am supposed to be fetching my coat and hat. Dr Schmitt is downstairs in the kitchen waiting for me.

He returned from the hospital just now and asked me if the name Lukas Leibnitz means anything to me.

I barely had a chance to answer when he informed me that you were brought into the hospital this morning. It seems you were struck by a car while wandering from the train station.

He says you have been searching for me ceaselessly for the past eight years.

Lukas, I do not know how to entertain these thoughts in my mind. Is it really true that your heart has sought mine with the same yearning all this time?

I want with all my being to go in Dr Schmitt's car to the hospital and see you. But my original reservations remain. I believe I am not your destiny. I wanted to protect you from a relationship that you should not be a part of.

Dr Schmitt is adamant that you want to find me, however. He has begged me to come with him and see you at once.

My heart is singing. I feel as if I must be the luckiest girl in the world to have you waiting for me. But I am more terrified than I have ever been in my life.

Fresh guilt has washed over me. Have I caused you years of torment where you have been desperately unhappy too? My heart is breaking all over again. I hope you will forgive me.

Dr Schmitt is calling me from the kitchen, urging me to come now. He is reiterating that you are a broken man, not from the collision with the car but from your exhaustive search for me these past years.

Oh Lukas, I need to see you. Against my better judgement, I will see if we can truly be reunited.

My heart is lifting almost out of my chest. The butterflies in my belly are alive and fluttering, letting me know I am about to redeem the greatest prize of all. Love.

Hannah

Nathalie felt as if her own heart would burst right out of her chest as she imagined what must have been going through her great-grandmother's head right at that moment. The man she'd loved in her dreams for so long had come to find her.

Squealing in delight, she reached for the next letter. It was the last one. This one was in an envelope. She almost wished she could savour the moment and keep hold of it until tomorrow.

But she'd never been good at waiting, so she pulled it free from the envelope and read eagerly.

My darling Lukas

Today has been wondrous. I cannot believe you have found me and I have found you. By the time I reached the hospital earlier, I was having serious doubts. What if you saw me and decided you did not love me any more? I feared I would be a disappointment to you after all this time. I am not the same carefree girl you once knew. The froth and joy that I once owned has been obliterated.

I am terrified that I may be too damaged for you to love. As I walked the shiny hospital floor towards your ward, my hands were shaking and my legs felt as if they were made of jelly.

I stood for the longest time outside the door. I had to steel myself to go to you.

There were eight beds in the room, but I saw you immediately, Lukas. All my nerves and previous worries melted away as our eyes met. All I could do was run to you.

The other patients in the ward must have thought we were insane. The sound of sobbing and crooning as we were finally reunited must have been quite a spectacle.

I know so much time has passed, but you felt instantly familiar to me. As your gentle hands closed around my face, I looked into your eyes and recognised what I saw. The look of pain mixed with love that poured from your very soul made me quiver. It mirrored exactly what I felt too.

Lukas, I felt so ashamed as you asked me why I left you. You seemed so traumatised and troubled. Not for one minute did I believe you felt the same way I did. I honestly thought I was doing you a service by going. I'm sorry, Lukas, I had no idea I was leaving you so devastated. It nearly killed me too, but I suppose I never truly dared to believe that you loved me as much as I loved you. There was nothing in it for you. I'm a Jew, a servant girl; you had every-thing going for you.

Oh Lukas, when you said that all the titles, money and big houses in the world meant nothing without me . . . All I could do was stare at you, too frozen in the moment to even cry. That was when I realised that something had changed inside. For the first time in my life, I felt inner peace. All the fear and torture evaporated at that moment when you said you loved me.

I am beside myself with joy. I can scarcely believe that you want the same things I do. You want us to go back to Brixental and find Clara. We leave tomorrow. As I write this letter, you are with Dr Schmitt organising papers so we can leave Austria. You fear that the political situation is still quite volatile and you want us to flee to safety. I would go to the ends of the earth if it means being with you, my love. I can't express the relief I feel at knowing that you want to be with me and Clara. I have been accustomed to looking after myself, and the thought that you want to mind me is such a comfort.

I know I should give you my letters now. After all, they are all addressed to you. I will show them to you in due course. That way you will know that I never forgot you or stopped loving you. Finding you once more has renewed my faith in humanity. Coupled with the incredible kind-heartedness of Dr and Frau Schmitt, I know that goodness is alive and well in this world. I will strive to look to the future, to move onwards and upwards and to put the images of suffering and hatred to one side. If you are by my side, I know I can achieve anything.

I thank God for reuniting us and I look forward to the amazing times we are about to share.

I have never stopped loving you in my dreams and now I will have the opportunity to show you just that. The exhilaration and delight that is flooding me now is so intense that I almost understand why I had to suffer so greatly these past eight years. Perhaps it was God's

way of ensuring that I appreciate all the wonder I know He will create
in our new life together.

The future has never looked so bright.

Hannah

Nathalie put the letter down and sighed. She couldn't help smiling through her tears. How incredible that Lukas had been searching for Hannah all those years. She was sure that what they had had was true love in its purest form. It made her desperately sad that the two hearts could have been together all along and that perhaps Hannah might have avoided being taken to Bergen-Belsen. How would their story have panned out then?

The tragedy of it choked her. Her emotions were spilling over, and all of a sudden she wanted to know so many things. How Oma had felt when her parents came to collect her . . . what she'd thought when they said they wanted to take her away. Had she known they were coming? Was she terrified?

Nathalie paced up and down the room, willing Oma to return. She gazed out of the window, then opened it, straining her neck so she could see as far up the road as possible. There was no sign of her grandmother, so she grabbed her keys, locked the door and followed the directions Oma had given her to the graveyard.

With each quickening step she thought of more questions that needed answers. She hoped Oma would be open to talking, that she was comfortable about baring her soul and explaining what had gone on at that time.

As she jogged along the path that led to the grave, she felt such a rush of love for her grandmother. She'd been through a massive upheaval. How had she managed to bounce back and go on to live a normal life?

As she entered the sprawling graveyard, Nathalie looked out

for Clara. Not sure which way she ought to go, she ran to the left, her eyes scanning row after row of gravestones. There was no sign of Clara. Rushing back to the gate where she'd entered, she ran the opposite way. Her throat was dry, and she was ready to give up and go home when she spotted Clara in a far corner. She was about to call out to her, such was her excitement, when she was reminded by a passing lady with her head bowed solemnly that she was in a place of rest. Instead she rushed over. Clara was crouched at the grave, chatting as if she were sitting with someone living. Nathalie halted, not wanting to interrupt. Oma had her back to her. She moved her hands as she talked.

'So I don't know what to do, Gus,' she was saying. 'I know Nathalie will understand much of my story now. She knows about Mama and Papa and how they came together. But how do I break the news about Max?'

Nathalie held her breath. She was about to step forward and tell Clara she was listening, but curiosity got the better of her. Without moving a muscle, she waited.

'Max is still so angry. He hasn't come over nor has he phoned me. If you could forgive me for having that affair, it would make sense that he could too. You were the most amazing father to him, Gus. He couldn't say you weren't. The fact that you weren't his biological father meant nothing. You were the one who loved him, who taught him everything from riding a bike to knotting a tie. I still feel the weight of my guilt. You shouldn't have died without seeing him. It's all my fault . . .'

Nathalie thought she was going to faint. An affair? Her grandmother had cheated on Gus, the supposed great love of her life? How could that be? Turning on her heel, she ran from the graveyard and back along the road. Her chest began to ache as she struggled to breathe. Bursting into the house, she bundled a few possessions into her rucksack, threw her key on to the table and pulled the door shut. She didn't want to be here when Clara returned.

Chapter 20

AVA HAD TAKEN SOME PAINKILLERS, WHICH HAD helped massively with the physical pain. But nothing seemed to help with the whirring that was going on inside her head.

Knowing she didn't have to go near the shop, or anybody else for that matter, she opened a bottle of white wine. She hadn't eaten anything, but she convinced herself that was actually a good thing in the circumstances.

After the first glass, she felt a whole lot better. She flicked on the television and sat staring numbly at a chat show where people were shouting and condemning one another. She was pretty screwed up, and so were her family, but thankfully even they weren't as bad as the crew on screen.

She was halfway through her third glass when her landline rang. She winced. Very few people had that number. She leaned over and saw that it was Clara. Guessing that she was simply checking up on her, she let it go to voicemail.

'Hi, Ava, it's me.' Clara sounded frantic. 'I know you're not well and you're probably asleep, but you need to call me urgently. As soon as you get this message, please call me back—'

'Mama?' Ava snatched up the phone. 'What's wrong?'

'Ava,' Clara was breathing heavily, 'is Nathalie with you?'

'No . . . What's going on?'

'I think she's gone. I've just returned from visiting your father's grave and she's not here. It looks like she left in an awful hurry.

The drawers in her room are all pulled out and it looks as if she was acting frantically. I can't think why. Unless she overheard . . . Oh my God, Ava, we have to find her.'

'Why?' Ava was confused. 'What's happened?'

'I'll explain later. We simply must find her.'

'I have her mobile number. Let me call her and I'll buzz you back,' Ava said.

Clara hung up and Ava dialled Nathalie's cell. It went straight to voicemail. She hung up and tried again, to no avail, so she called her mother back.

'There's no answer. I've left her a message, so hopefully she'll call me back. What makes you think she's run off?'

Clara dropped her head into her hands. 'I was at the grave and chatting to your father just now,' she said. 'I think she may have followed me. If she did, she would have overheard me talking . . .'

'About what?'

'The reason Max left.'

'What do you mean, the *real* reason . . .' Ava sounded strained.

'Now isn't the time to discuss this,' Clara said sounding panicked. 'Ava, I have a horrid feeling at the pit of my stomach. If anything happens to that beautiful child, I'll never forgive myself.'

'What do you think we should do, then?' Ava's voice sounded pained.

'I think we need to call the police, and then we should contact Max.'

'No,' Ava said loudly. 'Whatever about the police, but don't call Max yet.'

'But—'

'No,' Ava said again. 'He has a low enough opinion of us all. Let's try and find her first. We don't need him freaking out. Besides, what can he do from over there? Nothing. He'd just be in a state.'

'All right, we'll wait,' Clara said.

'Why don't you call the police and I'll have a quick shower and come over? I bet Nathalie will be back in no time.'

Ava put the phone down and stood up. Her head was spinning and she wished she hadn't drunk so much wine. Flailing towards the kitchen, she shoved two pieces of sliced bread into the toaster. She prayed that a hot shower and some soakage would sober her up. The thought of Nathalie out there alone, with nobody to turn to, scared the living daylights out of her.

She thought back to how she herself might have coped in a strange land aged seventeen while dealing with a crisis. Her blood ran cold. Look at her now, and she was in her forties. She was still a bloody mess. What hope had Nathalie?

Clara was speaking to a kind but firm man at Lochlann police station.

'But she's only seventeen and she really doesn't know the area,' she argued. 'And I fear she's distressed.'

The policeman was patient and said they would absolutely alert the guards on duty, but that they couldn't treat Nathalie as a missing person until she'd been gone a full twenty-four hours.

'I've made a note of her details in the book and I promise we'll call you should she present.'

Clara hung up feeling desolate.

By six o'clock that evening, the rain was pelting down outside. Clara had got Nathalie's cell number from Ava and left several messages begging her to get in touch.

By eight o'clock, she was frantic. Ava looked equally worried. Gone were the soothing scenarios of Nathalie blowing off steam. By now, both women were worried sick.

'What exactly did you say that might have driven her away?'

'Lots of things,' Clara said as tears slid down her cheeks. 'Oh Ava, my past is never going to stop haunting me, is it? I've carried a secret in my heart for years. Your brother found out . . . That's why he left . . . I know I sound like I'm talking in riddles right now. But I promise I'll explain things once I know where Nathalie is and that she's safe.'

'OK,' Ava said tightly.

'I thought that by hiding things I'd make it all easier on all of us,' Clara said mournfully. 'But I was wrong, Ava.'

'Secrets have a way of coming back to bite you, no matter how many years go by.'

'Should we call the police again?' Clara said.

A knock at the door sent them both running.

'Hi,' said a tall, broad-shouldered guy. 'I'm Conor Murphy, I was meant to meet Nathalie earlier but she didn't show. I know I'm probably making a fool of myself, but could I see her for a minute?'

'Ah, hello, Conor, you're Brea's boy,' Clara said.

'Yeah, the very one,' he confessed, grinning.

'I haven't seen you for quite a while. You've turned into a wonderful young man.'

'Thanks, Mrs Conway. I know I'm probably going to feel like a total eejit in a minute, but I was wondering why Nathalie didn't show up for the gig tonight. I thought she wanted to come.'

Clara brought him in and introduced him to Ava, then explained the situation.

'Wow,' said Conor. 'So you haven't seen her since lunch time.'

The two women looked at one another, shaking their heads miserably.

'I'll go back down the seafront and have a look in the bar. She may turn up there.'

They swapped phone numbers and promised to keep in touch.

'I'll call if I see or hear anything,' Conor said. 'I'm sure she'll turn up, Mrs Conway. If it helps at all, she told me how cool you both were. She seemed really pleased about being here and getting to know you all.'

'Thanks, Conor,' Ava said. 'That helps a lot. Let's hope she turns up safely soon.'

'Yes, and I know she was thrilled about meeting you too, Conor,' Clara assured him. 'So please know that the reason she didn't show up this evening has nothing to do with how she feels about you.'

'Thanks, Mrs Conway. Catch you later,' he said moving off.

By midnight, both women were beside themselves. Conor had texted twice to say she hadn't appeared.

'What do you think we should do now?' Ava asked.

'I think you should go home to your apartment. If young Nathalie decides to go anywhere, I'm guessing it'll be to you. You understand her and you're closer to her age. Besides, you're a neutral party in this family war. You've done nothing to hurt her and you most certainly haven't lied to her.'

Ava agreed to do as her mother wished. Not only had she sobered up, she had a thumping headache. She walked as far as the town and got a cab the rest of the way. Knowing she wasn't going to sleep a wink, she pulled on a comfy tracksuit and lay in bed with both her landline and her mobile phone poised at her side.

Clara made a pot of coffee. She knew she ought to go to bed and try to rest. But until Nathalie turned up safely, she wasn't going to so much as lie down.

Years of being brave and attempting to make the best of things seemed to have taken their toll. Tears soaked her face as she prayed that tragedy wasn't going to strike her family yet again.

'Generations have endured pain. If you can hear me, Gus, please help. Bring Nathalie home safely. For the first time in my life, I don't think I can do this any more.'

Chapter 21

NATHALIE HAD HAD NO IDEA OF WHERE TO GO. She'd contemplated walking along the seafront and dancing about waving her arms in the hope that Conor would spot her from his living room window and come out. But she knew that his family had connections with the Conways and she didn't want to leave a trail to her whereabouts. Coming to Ireland had been a mistake. Her father was right. This place was cursed. It hadn't helped with her issues; it had added to them.

The only places she'd been were the waterfall and the Italian restaurant with Ava. If the waterfall wasn't so far away, she'd gladly go there and jump in. She could picture the newspapers' glee at the thought of publishing photos of the suicide spot. But there'd probably be a ton of tourists hanging out there, watching the cascading water mixing with the rain. It was so damn cold in this country when it rained. All she had on was a long-sleeved T-shirt and jeans, and she was shivering. She needed to be someplace with privacy so she could lock herself away and try to get her head around this complete disaster that was her family.

Her mother had drilled into her head from a young age that she was to approach a police officer if she found herself alone or in trouble. But she guessed that didn't cover asking for help because her family had turned out to be like some crazy screwed-up version of a daytime talk show.

Shell-shocked, she checked into a hotel. She'd taken money from an ATM as she hadn't wanted her father to trace her credit card transactions. It would be just his style to get on to Amex and have them find her that way. The anger she felt towards him and Oma was almost choking her. Let them worry themselves sick. They deserved it.

Why hadn't Oma told her the moment she'd landed why the family had become estranged? It was all so messed up. No wonder her dad wanted nothing to do with Ireland. Momentarily her heart went out to him as she thought of how betrayed he must've felt all those years ago.

But anger soon took over again. He should have told her the truth. How had he allowed her to come here knowing what he did? How had he let her live with Oma while realising the truth would come out and break her heart?

Nathalie longed to know the answers to the countless questions that were zooming about in her brain right now. The small voice of reason that was lurking in the back of her mind was whispering that there must be a rational explanation for what had gone on. But she was too hurt and confused to make sense of it.

She needed to reach a point where she was prepared to listen and find the whole truth for once and for all.

That time certainly wasn't right now.

She knew she was probably causing widespread panic, and a part of her was pleased that they would all be looking for her and wondering where she had gone. It would teach them a lesson, she thought bitterly.

Her thoughts were so mixed up. Her allegiance flew from her father to Oma. She liked Oma. In spite of what she'd heard her saying this morning, she'd fallen in love with her. She was quirky, cool and so intriguing. A part of Nathalie felt that by running away today and hurting her father, she would give him a taste of his own medicine. Oma must've been totally freaked when he took off all those years ago.

Once she'd checked into the hotel and ordered two bottles of wine, she wasn't sure what she should do. She drank one of the bottles and realised it made her feel worse. So she filled the bath with the intention of relaxing.

The voice of reason was almost winning over the anger and resentment when a thought struck her. She grabbed her washbag and rustled around. The sound of the painkillers rattling inside the plastic bottle pleased her. The hospital had given them to her after the crash. She hadn't bothered taking them. She'd been so numbed by losing Mackenzie, she wouldn't have noticed if someone had cut her legs off.

Now, however, she needed all the relief she could find.

Stepping out of her clothes, she balanced the wine glass on the side of the tub and climbed in. Lowering herself into the steaming hot water, she relished the burning sensation as her skin turned red and prickly.

'Liars . . .' she said as she swallowed the painkillers with four large gulps of wine. She knew she'd probably vomit, but right at that moment she didn't care. If she slid into the bath and drowned she wouldn't care either. All she wanted was for the pain to stop.

The heat along with the sudden rush of alcohol and drugs made her woozy. The feeling was wonderful. All her troubles melted like lemon drops. Just like Dorothy from *The Wizard of Oz*, she was floating and zooming to a beautiful place.

Faces, names and scenes zoomed in and out of her focus, a mixture of emotions trying to take centre stage in her mind. First she was relaxed and happy. Then a feeling of terror would engulf her and she'd cry out. Next she'd hear her father, then

Oma; all they were saying was 'blah, blah, blah' but she knew it was lies all the same. Then the images stopped and peace engulfed her.

Max heard the phone ringing in his dreams. Used to being woken by his bleeper, he sat up instantly and looked around. The rock-hard doctor-on-call beds at the hospital were fine for the odd hour of sleep, but this was his second full night here.

Amber had made it very clear that she needed time and wasn't ready to enter into any conversations with him. She'd called him a liar and a cheat and refused to allow him to speak.

'You've done enough lying and I can't cope with any more.'

So Max did what he was best at and ran away from it all.

The phone rang a second time. He picked it up and looked at the number. It was an Irish one, and not the one Nathalie had called him from before.

'Hello?'

'Is that Mr Conway?' a strange woman's voice asked.

'Yes,' he said, sitting up. 'This is Max Conway.'

'Hello, sorry to disturb you, I'm not sure what time it is there, but this is Lochlann Hospital calling. I believe we have your daughter Nathalie with us.'

'Pardon? Why? What's going on?'

'Mr Conway, your daughter was pulled from a full bath by a hotel chambermaid several hours ago. She'd consumed a large quantity of alcohol along with a substantial number of painkillers. She's lucky to be alive.'

Stunned, Max took the details and said he'd be on the next available flight to Ireland. Then he grabbed his clothes and ran to his car, calling Amber as he went.

'What do you mean, the hospital called?' she shrieked, bursting into tears. 'Max, if anything happens to her . . .'

'I know,' he said. 'We need to get to Ireland. I'm on my way home. Can you call the airport and book flights?'

Amber had already hung up.

As Max pulled into the driveway, he had never been as scared in his entire life. Nathalie was his world. She was the one perfect thing he'd created. He couldn't carry on if she died.

He found a white-faced Amber throwing things into a suitcase. Without looking round, she told him she'd booked flights and they needed to leave for the airport immediately if they were going to make it.

'I've notified the airline desk that our daughter is in hospital fighting for her life and they've assured me we'll be escorted to the plane with minimal delay.'

'Well done,' he said, grabbing a few extra bits and zipping the case shut.

'Anything we've forgotten can be bought,' she said. 'Let's go.'

'Amber, I—'

'Not now, Max,' she said wearily. 'Everything else can wait. Nathalie needs us.'

Max drove as fast as he could, praying that this was going to have a happy outcome. From the moment he'd heard Mackenzie had died, he'd been so aware of how lucky they'd been that Nathalie had survived. It would be cruel of fate to snatch her away after all. Surely that couldn't possibly happen . . .

Chapter 22

MERCIFULLY THE FLIGHT LANDED ON TIME. WITH the eight-hour time difference between Dublin and Los Angeles, it meant they were hitting the Emerald Isle at midday.

On the way to the hospital, Max called Sean.

'Hey, buddy.'

'Max! How are you?'

'I've been better. I'm in Ireland.'

'What? Are you serious?'

'Nathalie is here. Amber and my mother arranged a trip and now she's in hospital. It seems she tried to take her own life. We don't know if she's going to survive.'

'Jeez, Max, I don't know what to say.'

'There's nothing you can say. I just thought I'd keep you in the loop.'

'Cheers. I'll be thinking of you all. Oh, and Max?'

'Yeah.'

'Sorry . . . Nothing. I was going to say something but it's hardly appropriate right now . . . Good luck . . .'

'Spit it out, Sean,' Max said.

'If you see Ava . . . would you tell her I asked after her?'

'Yeah, that'll go down well after twenty years. But I'll tell her.'

'Sorry, mate, you have more than enough stuff wrecking your head.'

'Hey, no worries. You've always said the wrong things at the wrong time. Why stop now,' Max said.

'Sorry,' Sean said. 'Stay safe, and I hope Nathalie is gonna be OK.'

'Me too. Catch you soon, buddy.'

Max hung up and shook his head. Between him and Sean, they'd made a right cock-up of things. He didn't feel angry with him for asking him to send his regards to Ava, however. He was hardly in a position to take a higher stance on behaviour towards his family. People in glass houses and all that, Max mused.

Clara was making a chocolate cake when Ava arrived.

'It's hardly the time to start baking.'

'Ava, I haven't slept and there's nothing else I can do. I couldn't have idle hands.'

'I know, I'm sorry.' Ava hugged her. 'We need to find Nathalie,' she whispered.

'I know. How about I phone the hospital? If I ask for that nice Dr Francis, he might have a look at the records for me. Your father was very good to him when he was an intern.'

Clara found it odd dialling the hospital number once more. She was relieved when Dr Francis came on the line a short time later, but when he told her gently that Nathalie had been admitted the previous night, tears ran down her cheeks.

'Thank you, dear. You've been very helpful,' she managed before hanging up.

'What is it?' Ava asked.

'She's there. It seems she was taken in last night. He said he can't divulge the details but that her parents have just arrived from Los Angeles.'

'What? Max is here?' Clara nodded.

'Ava, what will we do? Should we go to the hospital and see them?'

'Absolutely,' Ava said. 'Turn the oven off and leave the baking. I'll drive.'

Just as they were about to leave, however, the landline rang.

'Hello?' Clara said frantically.

'Oma?'

'Nathalie.' Clara burst into tears. '*Liebling*, are you all right?'

'I've been better,' she said weakly. 'But I'm gonna be fine. Mom and Dad are here and I want to get out of this place. Can I come home?'

'Of course you can, my darling sweet child. I'm so relieved. Will I send Ava to collect you?'

'No, Dad has a cab.'

'OK, *Liebling*. See you shortly.'

Clara hung up. 'She's on her way home.'

'Thank God.'

'With Max and Amber . . .'

'What?' The colour drained from Ava's face. 'Max is here? He's coming to this house right now?' Clara nodded. 'Holy shit.'

'Um, precisely,' Clara said, sitting down. She stood up again abruptly. 'The cake. It's Max's favourite. I'll finish it.'

'Mama, nobody gives a fiddler's about cakes right now.'

'I do.' Clara's face was stern as she whipped the ingredients into a creamy batter and scraped it into a tin.

As she wiped her hands, a taxi drew up outside.

'They're here,' Ava shouted, running to open the front door.

Clara peered out the window and saw a glamorous woman with chestnut hair climb out of the cab. She was helping a very wobbly-looking Nathalie. Then Max came into view. Her Max. Her son and the light of her life for so long. A sob escaped

Clara's lips as he turned around. Age suited him. He was so like his father it was almost scary.

Taking a deep breath and squaring her shoulders, she followed Ava.

Outside, Ava was hugging Nathalie and telling her how much she loved her. She led her inside and Clara hugged her on the way past. Amber held her hand out and shook Clara's.

'It's lovely to meet you, Mrs Conway.'

'It's wonderful to meet you too, dear. I wish it could be under less stressful circumstances, but you are most welcome. Please come inside.'

Amber nodded and followed Ava and Nathalie, leaving Max to face Clara. He looked directly into her eyes before dropping his gaze.

'Hello, Max.'

He kept looking at the ground as a sob escaped his lips. Clara walked slowly towards him. She lifted one hand and placed it gently on his shoulder. He didn't flinch or move backwards. Raising the other hand, she pulled him into her arms and rocked him from side to side, feeling as if she could die of heartache.

'Welcome home, my son.'

'Thanks, Mama.'

They stayed there for what felt like an age, before Clara coughed and took his hand, leading him inside wordlessly.

Nathalie was sitting on the edge of a chair in the kitchen. Her frail body shivered as she wrapped her thin arms around herself.

Clara approached and knelt down in front of her. 'We're all so glad you're safe, *Liebling*. We love you so much.'

Sobbing, Nathalie threw her arms around her neck.

'It's OK, child.'

'I need to lie down,' Nathalie said, looking from one face to another. Her haunted eyes made each one of them nod in agreement.

'I'll help you,' Amber said.

After they'd left the room, Clara did what she always did in a crisis and made coffee.

The atmosphere was incredibly tense as Ava and Max eyeballed one another.

'I wish this could've all happened at a better time,' Clara said.

'I don't know if there ever would have been a better time,' Max said. He closed his eyes for a moment. 'I'm sorry I didn't know about Dad's death,' he said. 'I . . . I wish I'd been here.'

'So do I,' Clara said, without condemnation. 'I know he did too. He never gave up hope that you'd come home some day.' Max nodded.

'Is that it?' Ava said, pulling her fingers through her hair. With wild eyes she turned on Max. 'You bugger off for twenty years with not so much as a glance backwards. You fail to even realise our father has died and now you pitch up acting as if it was a bit of a shame but we'll all move on?'

'I didn't say that,' Max said sadly.

'So why did you go, Max? What was so bloody awful that you felt you had to turn your back on all of us?'

Max looked to Clara, who was hovering by the sideboard. She picked up an old photograph of the four of them smiling at the beach.

'We had some wonderful times,' she said. 'It wasn't all awful, you know.'

Ava threw her hands in the air.

'I'm out of here. I'll come back later when he's gone. I want to see Nathalie, but this,' she waved her arm, 'is a crock of shit.'

'Ava!' Clara said, trying to catch her hand.

'Leave it, Mama.'

'Don't go,' Clara pleaded. 'Sit down. We need to talk. It's time.'

Ava looked from her mother to Max. He nodded ever so slightly and pulled out a chair.

Clara sat at the head of the table, where Gus used to sit. Silently she begged him to help her.

'I need to take you back in time, so you can fully appreciate my actions,' she began.

'I'm listening,' Ava said.

'I was born in January 1938, in Austria . . .'

Ava was mesmerised as Clara told them all about the picturesque little village where she lived with her parents and older brother Jacob.

'Jacob? We have an uncle and we've never met him?'

'Not quite,' Max scoffed before holding his hands up. 'Sorry, continue.'

Clara went on to tell them that her mama was a seamstress and adored turning lengths of plain fabric into anything from curtains and cushion covers to beautifully embroidered dresses . . . How she had the most exquisite traditional Austrian dirndl dresses with matching coats. They'd lived on a farm, and although theirs was a simple life, she'd been blissfully happy.

'Jacob and I would climb trees, race through the fields and help Papa with the animals.'

Ava had an image of a gorgeous little girl skipping like Heidi through meadows with the backdrop of the Alps to make it all look perfect.

'In the winter of 1945, my entire world was turned upside down. I remember that day as if it were yesterday. Jacob and I were attempting to build a tree house in one of the larger trees out the front when a car pulled up.'

Ava listened agog as Clara explained that neither of them recognised the car or the people who climbed out. Jacob was incredibly protective of Clara and gathered her to him. They both stayed in the safety of the boughs of the tree and waited for their parents to appear from the house. All these years later, Clara could almost hear the dog barking without stopping. Jacob was four years her senior, and although Clara had a vague knowledge of the dangers of Hitler's men, her brother was far more informed. He instructed her to remain silent in case they were bad men coming to take them away.

'My parents didn't rush out of the house as we'd imagined they would. Instead they walked ever so slowly and my mother appeared to be crying. My father had his arm around her shoulder and seemed to be supporting her as she struggled to walk.'

'Who were the people?' Ava asked.

Clara closed her eyes for a moment. Ava gave her time to gather herself.

'They were Dr Axel Schmitt, along with Lukas and Hannah.'

'As in Oma and Opa?' Ava said, looking even more confused. Clara nodded.

'I don't understand. If you say Lukas and Hannah were your parents – and they're the only grandparents *I* ever knew growing up – who were you living with?'

'As it transpired, I had been born at the house I'd grown up in, but Jacob was not my brother. Alina and Frank, the couple I'd been living with, were not my biological parents either. Hannah and Lukas were. I had been fostered.'

'How come nobody ever told you?' Ava looked angry.

'It wasn't quite as simple as that,' Clara explained. 'You see, my biological parents were from different worlds. My father, your *Opa*, was the son of a cavalry officer from the salubrious first quarter of Vienna. His family were wealthy and held in high social esteem.'

'And who was Oma?'

'An orphaned Jewish housemaid.'

'No way . . .' Ava looked utterly stunned. Max remained tight-lipped.

Clara's voice faltered as she told Ava what her mother's letters had eventually divulged.

'So Alina and Frank knew your mother could possibly return for you some day?'

'Yes, but I'm certain they assumed Hannah had been captured and murdered. She was gone eight years, so as you can imagine, the odds of her returning were almost nil.'

'So how did Lukas eventually find her?'

'Before she left to live with Alina and Frank, Hannah wrote a letter to her best friend in the world, a girl who had grown up with Hannah at the orphanage and was working as a house-maid in Vienna. When she was eventually captured and taken away, her employers found the letter under the mattress and brought it to Lukas.'

'How did they know who she was talking about?' Ava asked.

'The letter was fairly self-explanatory. Would you like to read it?'

'What? You have the letter?' Max asked in shock.

Clara struggled to her feet and made her way across the room to the kitchen dresser. Within seconds she had found a large photograph album bound in leather.

'How come we've never seen this before? It's not exactly small,' Ava asked.

'It's been here ever since Oma and Opa died. I suppose you never went rooting and I didn't draw your attention to it either.'

Clara spread the album out on the table. Behind the first clear plastic page was a yellowed yet still perfectly legible letter written in black ink.

'It's in German,' Max said, searching Clara's face for answers.

'I've translated it,' she smiled. 'If you turn the page, you can read the English version.'

Clara's heart thumped loudly and her throat tightened as she fumbled in her haste to turn the page. As soon as her children read the first line of the letter, they both looked up at her.

'It's addressed to someone called Ava,' said Ava.

Clara nodded.

'Am I named after this woman?'

Clara nodded again. 'When you were born, Mama asked if she could name you. I agreed, and so you became Ava.'

Silence prevailed as Max and Ava read the letter.

September 1937

Dear Ava

I am writing this letter to say farewell. As you know, I am expecting Lukas's baby. My belly is growing bigger now, so I have decided to run away. I understand that you want me to tell Lukas about this child, but I will not be the cause of his demise.

His family will shun us both if they find out. He stands to lose everything. I love him too much to allow that to happen. I have seen Liza, the girl he is to marry. She is beautiful and refined and acts like a princess. This is the type of woman Lukas deserves.

Don't worry about me, Ava. I know I will be just fine. Frau Schulz at the orphanage has made arrangements for me to stay with her sister Alina in the west. I will go by train tomorrow to Brixental. There I will be safe and Lukas can continue with his life as planned.

I know I will never meet another man like him. But I understand that he was never mine to love in the first place. Destiny does not place people like me with people like Lukas Leibnitz.

I will have our baby to keep my heart from breaking and most of all I will always know what it means to find true love. When I feel as if I cannot go on, I will close my eyes and remember how I felt when

Lukas held me in his arms. I will recite over and over again all the wonderful things he whispered in my ear when nobody else could hear. The scars on my heart will remind me that I was loved once.

Thank you, dear Ava, for believing me when I told you that Lukas loves me. I know I did not imagine what I saw in his eyes. So no matter what becomes of me, it is enough to know that he loved me unconditionally, even if it was only momentarily.

When we were alone, religion, status and social expectations disappeared. For those precious stolen moments everything was perfect. I wish with all my heart that our love were enough to bridge the gaps. But I know that is an impossible ask.

The world we live in would never accept us.

In time I am certain Lukas will forget the little servant girl who passed through his house and touched his heart.

I am sorry to go without seeing you, Ava, but I cannot bear the pain of saying goodbye. You are the closest to a sister that I have ever had. I will remember your smile for ever. I know I am burdening you with my awful secret and for that I am truly sorry.

I am sure you despair of me. But I have caused enough trouble in Vienna and a fresh start in a new place is the best thing for me.

I hope you are settling into your new home and that the people there are being kind to you. I will be in touch once I am settled. If your employers offer you a summer holiday, perhaps you might come on the train and spend it with me?

In the meantime, I beg you not to tell Lukas where I am. Stay safe and know that I will keep you in my heart and my prayers. Until we meet again, my lovely friend. I bid you auf Wiedersehen.

Hannah

'Oh Mama, I can't even begin to imagine how Hannah must've felt writing that letter.'

'Isn't it heartbreaking? She was so astonishingly brave.'

'What became of Ava, though? Did the girls ever get to meet up again?'

'No, *Liebling*. As I said, she was captured by the Nazis and executed. My father was shocked to receive the letter. He said that the boy who delivered it was devastated and insisted that his mother had done everything in her power to protect Ava.'

'Gosh, that makes me shudder. But I am honoured to be named after Oma's best friend.'

'Ah, you gave your *Oma* such joy, Ava. Both of you did.' Clara looked at Max.

'So how does all of this fit in with Max leaving?' Ava asked.

'After you were born,' Clara said, 'I was very ill. So your father took it upon himself to have a vasectomy operation without telling me. The hospital had informed him that it would be detrimental to my health to have another baby.'

Ava looked at Max in confusion.

'A couple of years passed and I often wondered why I'd never become pregnant again. I longed for another baby and was terribly upset by the fact that I hadn't conceived.'

'Dad never confessed?' Ava asked. Clara shook her head.

'One day, out of the blue, there was a knock on the door. As soon as I opened it, I recognised Jacob. He'd been travelling around Europe demonstrating a new method of brain surgery.'

'It must've been overwhelming to see him again,' Ava said.

'It was, dear. He and Gus hit it off instantly,' Clara recalled. 'They'd sit and talk shop for hours on end. Many bottles of whiskey were consumed during Jacob's five-week stay.'

'He stayed for five weeks?' Ava said. 'Wasn't that a tad long?'

'It didn't seem that way,' Clara admitted. 'He slotted in so well. As his time in Ireland was coming to a close, I found myself slipping into a decline. I'd said goodbye to him once before and I was dreading having to do it again. I knew it was totally different because we were adults, and of course we'd exchanged phone numbers and addresses. But Jacob was headed for America. In those days it wasn't quite as easy to get there, and with a small child to consider, I knew I wouldn't see him for a long time.

'Before he left, Jacob asked us to dinner in the local hotel. He was staying there overnight as he'd hosted a medical conference the evening before and hadn't wanted to disturb us by landing in at all hours of the night. We were so excited about dining at the hotel. We rarely ate out and it was a big deal.'

As they arrived, Clara explained, Gus's pager went off, indicating that he was needed for an emergency at the hospital. Apologising to Jacob, he fled, promising to return when he could.

'We were both sad for Gus to miss out on a special dinner, but a part of me was secretly glad to have Jacob to myself for his last few hours.'

Clara told them about the bottle of champagne that arrived at the table. She had never been much of a drinker.

'The bubbles dancing on my tongue tasted delicious. I drank it as if it were lemonade. Wine followed, and with it came a round of reminiscing about the days when we had run freely through the fields and climbed hills and trees in Austria.'

'It must've been amazing to have that conversation with someone who'd been there with you,' Ava said.

'It was, *Liebling*,' Clara said. 'I hadn't spoken of those times since leaving. I longed to many times, but I never wanted to upset my parents. So it was truly cathartic to finally revisit those happy days.'

She explained that Jacob had been painfully shy as a boy, intensely sensitive, while she had always been the more adventurous and mischievous one.

'It was never his idea to climb trees, or capture bees and keep them in jars under our beds,' she said with a smile. 'Jacob said it was all down to me that he'd become a surgeon. You see, he'd locked himself away for years after I left.'

Jacob had explained that the years of solitude had afforded him the time to study. Medicine had always intrigued him and he excelled at his exams. A dogged sense of determination spurred him on and made him into one of the finest brain surgeons in the world.

'He attended a medical conference near Vienna. There he met Dr Axel Schmitt, the wonderful man who had saved Mama after the concentration camp. The last time he'd seen Jacob was that fateful day he'd brought my parents to collect me in Brixental. Dr Schmitt was the one who drove us to Vienna. From there we took a train to catch a ship that would take us away from Austria to our new lives as a family in Ireland.'

'What a small world,' Ava said. Max remained silent.

'Indeed,' Clara smiled. 'He recognised Jacob's name, and during the course of their conversation he told him how we had settled in Lochlann. When Jacob arrived in Ireland, he went to the post office in Lochlann and found us instantly.'

Clara smiled and looked down at her hands as she steered the conversation back to Jacob's final night in Ireland.

'Emotions ran high that evening. I became overwhelmed by the alcohol and Jacob carried me to his hotel room.'

There was a pause as everyone stared at her.

'I'm not proud of what I did, but I never regretted it.' She looked directly at her son. 'That night I became pregnant with Max. After we made love, Jacob begged me to leave Gus. He said he'd never loved anyone else and that meeting again as adults had taken that affection to another level. He vowed to be a father to Ava, and said that he was sorry for hurting Gus but he couldn't bear the thought of being without me.'

Ava sat shaking her head in disbelief.

'I knew the following morning that I'd made a grave mistake.'

Max guffawed. 'And you wonder why I left twenty years ago . . .'

'I didn't mean *you* were a mistake, Max,' Clara said with such sadness. 'You were never anything other than a miracle in my life.'

'Go on, Mama,' Ava encouraged gently.

'I told Jacob that I loved Gus. Always had. That he was the only man for me and that my emotions had got the better of me the night before. That I should never have made love with him as I didn't love him in that way. I was very clear with Jacob that I would never leave my husband.'

'How did he take that?' Ava asked.

'He was devastated. He honestly thought he'd won me over and I would leave with him. He went through all the conversations we'd had during his stay. He had interpreted things completely wrongly and honestly thought I was in love with him. Whereas all that time I had been viewing him as a brother, not a lover.'

'Messy,' Ava said.

'It was awful. I had nobody to blame but myself. I had betrayed the man I loved most in the world while destroying my relationship with a man who could have been my friend.'

'I understand why you acted the way you did,' Ava said, sighing. 'Memories are such intense things. It's difficult to control yourself when emotions take over.'

Clara smiled at Ava, grateful for her daughter's empathy.

'I hid my pregnancy from Gus for a couple of months. I knew that Jacob had to be the baby's father,' she said. 'I contemplated not telling Gus, but I knew I couldn't live a lie.'

'So you told Dad the truth?' Ava asked, aghast.

Clara nodded. 'I know this might sound contradictory considering what I did . . . But I loved your father so much. I felt I owed it to him to be truthful. I knew I was taking a massive gamble and that Gus would be well within his rights to walk away from me.' Clara sighed and fought back tears. 'He was devastated. Naturally he was also furious. But he chose to stay.'

Clara explained that she wanted to be honest with everyone involved in the pregnancy, so she wrote to Jacob and told him the news.

'Jacob phoned and begged me to leave Ireland and go to him. He wanted to look after me and the baby and offered to become your father,' she said looking at Ava.

'Did you consider going?' Ava asked.

'No,' Clara shook her head. 'I hated myself for giving Jacob hope. He loved me in a way I didn't love him. The man I'd given my heart to was Gus. I told Jacob so. He sounded so desolate and heartbroken and I wished with all my heart that I could take away his pain.'

'So you successfully destroyed two men who loved you,' Max said harshly. 'Until many years later when you continued your little reign of destruction and added me to the list. Bravo, Mama.'

Clara looked at Max and over at Ava. The pain in her eyes was almost unbearable.

'That's enough, Max,' Ava said coldly. 'Comments like that aren't going to help anyone. Let's try and refrain from adding to the hurt.'

'Easy for you to say, Ava. Nice for you when you're nothing to do with any of it.'

'It *is* to do with me,' she spat back. 'I'm in this family too. I was left to carry the can when you left. I was the one who had to hold the fort when you careered off. I had to stroke Dad's brow as he died and called out *your* name. Don't you dare insult me by saying your behaviour hasn't affected me.'

Max dropped his gaze and gestured with his hand for Clara to continue. She went on to explain that three months after Jacob had left, a letter arrived. It was from a Dr Walter Brandt, a fellow Austrian who shared accommodation with Jacob.

'He was writing to inform me of Jacob's death. He'd skidded on a corner in the wet, lost control of his car and died instantly. Amongst the few possessions Dr Brandt found in Jacob's room was a sealed letter with my name and address on the front, which he kindly posted to me.'

Clara stood up shakily from her chair and made her way to the dresser. Opening the drawer, she found the letter instantly. Silently she peeled the envelope open and placed the letter on the table for all to see. Once again, she'd translated it from German to English.

My darling Clara

My earliest and happiest memories involved you. The day you were taken from me was branded on my heart.

I tried to learn to live without you, but never quite managed to make it work.

I thought that healing people and saving lives would help ease the hollow feelings inside. But alas that didn't work either. I thought I was happy enough until we were reunited. But I realised as soon as I met you that I'd been merely existing, not living, while without you.

The five weeks we spent together were the best of my life. I felt whole again and more animated than I ever thought possible.

I cherish each and every moment we shared. I've recalled each conversation and banked each smile in my heart.

The night we finally joined as one meant the world to me. I know I wasn't imagining the love I saw reciprocated in your eyes. Perhaps if we'd met at a different stage in time, we could have been together for ever . . .

I accept that you love Gus. Why wouldn't you? He's a wonderful man. I wish I could change your mind and convince you to leave Ireland and begin a new life with me. But I've come to realise over the years that many wishes simply don't come true.

I hope Gus can forgive my intrusion in your marriage. I didn't mean to hurt him, but most of all I never intended to cause you a moment of heartache.

Thank you for telling me about our baby growing inside you. If there was any way I could have you both with me, you know I'd do it. I would sweep you away and hold you close to me until my dying day.

But as you rightly pointed out, you've already moved your entire life once before. I appreciate the offer of being involved in our unborn child's life. But I am an all-or-nothing type of person.

I also believe in the saying that if you love someone, you should set them free . . . And that is exactly what I intend doing.

You see, I've tasted sweet fruit and nothing else will ever compare.

I love you with my heart and soul. I never stopped loving you.

I need you to know that you were my inspiration and my driving force to succeed in life. I never gave up hope of finding you and spending the rest of my days with you. Perhaps I pinned my hopes on history repeating itself. After all, it worked so beautifully for your parents. Alas, it seems miracles don't happen twice.

I am comfortable in the knowledge that you were mine even if it was only for a few short hours.

I wish you joy and untold happiness. I hope you will raise our child to be just like you. When you think of me, I hope you can smile.

I promise not to invade your life again. You have made your decision and I respect that. If it's OK with you, I will hold our night together as my most cherished. But I know when I am beaten and I know when to step aside. It will be better for you and the baby this way. He or she will have a wonderful father in Gus. My presence would only cause confusion and inevitable hurt. You are and always will be my one true love. Thank you for filling my dreams.

Jacob

'I found the letters – from Jacob and from Dr Brandt,' Max said. 'I didn't tell a soul for months. But a blazing row with Dad prompted me to spill it all out . . .' His head drooped. 'The truth came out in the most ugly and insulting way,' he said. 'I'm still so ashamed by what I said to him. Clearly Dad had no idea I knew anything and I should have talked to him, man to man instead of behaving like a nasty brute and yelling at him.' His face crumpled as tears of guilt and frustration poured down his cheeks.

'What did you say?' Ava asked.

'I'd crashed his car and he was understandably furious. He yelled at me for taking the keys without his permission. I retaliated by saying that he wouldn't have minded if I was his real son. And that he probably wished I'd died in a crash, just like my real father.'

Clara stood up and walked over to Max, placing her hands on his shoulders.

'Gus *was* your father, Max. Maybe not biologically, but he loved and adored you from the second you were born. I was terrified he would leave me once he heard what I'd done. I'll never forgive myself for the hurt I inflicted upon him at that time. He didn't deserve it.'

'So that is why you turned your back on your family?' Ava asked.

'I felt like an outsider,' Max said sadly. 'No matter how much Gus tried to convince me he loved me as much as you,' he gestured to his sister, 'I didn't believe it. I couldn't fathom how he could possibly accept a baby created by a sordid affair.'

'That's such an ugly way of putting it,' Ava snapped. 'Besides, he'd raised you and shown without doubt how he felt. I don't get you, Max.'

Clara turned to her daughter. 'Ava, we all make choices. They shape our lives. Who's to say if they're right or wrong? Too many years have been wasted. Too much hurt and anger has got in the way of what's important here. I've waited such a long time to have you two together again. My only regret is that darling Gus isn't here to see it. I propose we wipe the slate clean and start again.'

Nobody said a word for a very long time, until Amber reappeared.

'Nathalie is sleeping,' she said.

'We'll go to a hotel and get freshened up,' Max told Clara. 'We'll be in touch.'

As he went to stand up, he remembered something.

'Oh, for what it's worth, Ava, Sean said to say hello.'

'Are you still in contact with him?' she asked.

'Yeah, all the time.'

'Would you give him my number?' Ava handed him a business card. 'There's something he needs to know.'

Chapter 23

AVA STAYED WITH CLARA FOR A SHORT WHILE longer. They chatted about Jacob, and although she admitted to being shocked, Ava assured Clara that she loved her.

Feeling exhausted, she promised to return and see Nathalie later on, once she'd checked in with Ruth at the shop. She had just pulled out of the drive when her mobile rang. She answered without looking at the name on her caller ID.

'Hello.'

There was silence, but she knew the other caller was connected.

'Hello?'

'Is that Ava?'

Her heart stopped and she almost stalled the car. Surely that wasn't who she thought? Swallowing hard, she tried to sound nonchalant.

'Yes, this is Ava. Who am I speaking to?'

'It's Sean.'

She bit the inside of her cheek. Her hands were shaking and the hairs on the back of her neck were standing on end.

'Hi.'

'I got your number from Max,' he said hurriedly.

'Yeah.' She hesitated. 'I didn't think he'd give it to you straight away.'

'I called as soon as I got his text.'

'Yeah, so I noticed.'

'So how are you?'

Ava pulled the car to the hard shoulder. 'Sean, I need to tell you something. Can I call you back when I get in?'

'Yeah. I'm at home, so call when you can.'

She drove straight to her apartment, abandoning all ideas of going to work. She texted Ruth, then made her way to her living room. The smell of stale wine was awful. Lighting a scented candle, she grabbed the landline and transcribed Sean's number from her mobile phone.

Before she could dial, memories of the awful events that had shattered her heart crowded in on her. She thought back to that fateful morning eighteen years ago when she'd rushed out of the house to greet him. It still broke her heart when she thought of how excited she'd been . . .

'Sean! I was just about to call you. Guess what . . .'

His expression had made her stop in her tracks. They only locked eyes for a second, but that had been enough.

'What?' she asked, swallowing hard. 'What's wrong?'

'Ava . . .'

'What?'

'I'm sorry. I never meant it to happen . . . I don't love her . . . I love you . . .' He looked like he hadn't slept in a week. His hair was matted, his skin grey, and the guilt was written all over his face.

'No,' she whispered.

'Ava, you've got to listen. We can work it all out. It's so stupid really. I wasn't even going to tell you because I knew it would upset you needlessly. She means nothing to me. I was drunk, she was drunk, one thing led to another. You know how it is . . .' He looked desperate. But more than that, he looked pathetic. Ava didn't *do* pathetic. Nor was she about to sign up for a lifetime with some dweeb who couldn't even manage to remain faithful *before* they got married.

'I don't know how it is,' she said. 'And what bothers me even more than the fact that you've been unfaithful is the thought that you considered not telling me! What kind of person are you?' Her voice was like steel. She wasn't going to let him know how she was feeling inside. Inside she was screaming. She wanted to thump him. She'd never hit another person in her entire life, but my God, she wanted to box him.

'Here's your ring. You make me sick. I cannot believe I was actually planning on spending the rest of my life with a double-crossing weasel like you. Don't contact me and don't come near me again. We're over. I won't change my mind and I won't forgive and forget.' The words tripped off her tongue like bullets from a machine gun, and even though she knew she'd long to have him back, she couldn't allow herself to be compromised.

'But Ava,' he threw his hands up in the air, 'we can't let a tiny thing like this come between us. We have our whole lives planned.'

'No, Sean. We *had*. But you've ruined it and there's no going back. You might think dishonesty and being unfaithful are tiny things. I don't. You made a choice to sleep with another woman. That's your prerogative but I am allowed to make a choice too. I am choosing to not be with you any more.'

When she walked back into her house and shut the door, Ava knew that was it for her. She wouldn't be able to trust him and that was final.

The news that he'd gone to America had shocked her. She never admitted it to anyone, but she'd been stunned, especially when word came through the grapevine of mutual friends that he'd taken the fiancé-stealing slut with him.

'At least you know it wasn't a flash in the pan,' her friend

Sarah had said tentatively. 'He must love her if they've gone all that way to America together.'

'How lovely for them,' Ava said.

Her parents had been amazing. Ava shied away from mutual friends to such an extent that she lost touch with most of them. It was easier than the prospect of having to avoid all conversations about Sean and how he might be getting on with his new lady in the States. She wasn't able to pretend she was fine when she wasn't.

The shop was the next problem. Normally Ava loved the interaction with customers. Especially as most of their pieces were custom-made so she got to know the clients quite well. At that time she hadn't the heart to look enthusiastically at women coming in for a special dress for a wedding or ball. Fun and socialising just wasn't on her agenda and she wasn't even able to do it on other people's behalf. She knew that it wouldn't be good for business to greet people with a face that would stop a clock, and besides, she wasn't of the opinion that others should be made to suffer alongside her. It was her shit and she'd have to deal with it.

'If you don't mind, I'll concentrate on buying and designing our off-the-peg collection for the moment,' she said to Clara. 'I don't think I have it in me to tell ladies they'd be better off with a dress two sizes bigger and four inches longer. I fear I may be offensive.'

'That's all right, dear,' Clara said cheerfully. 'You'll be as right as rain before long. You'll bounce back. Women do. It's in our nature. Try to fathom in your head that Sean is only a man.'

Ava had thought long and hard about that statement. Her mother had said it matter-of-factly, with no malice intended, nor did she mean for there to be a discussion on the subject. As far as she was concerned, men were very different to women and had limitations that nobody could do anything about. Full stop.

Ava did bounce back, but not for quite a while. The next few months were harder than she'd ever imagined possible.

She kept her pregnancy a secret for months. She was quite astonished at how easy it was to lie once she started.

'I've been comfort-eating,' she said to Clara one afternoon when her mother questioned her expanding waistline.

'Ah, it's better than hitting the bottle or starving yourself,' Clara said. 'You look amazing. In fact, you may not want to hear it, but you look better with a few extra pounds. You have the ability to look gaunt at times.'

Ava knew her mama meant it and was genuinely trying to be kind. But she hated her new shape and most of all she despised lying to everyone.

But once she started fibbing, it seemed to snowball. Each time she attempted to tell Ruth in the shop, or her parents, she chickened out. Winter brought chunky knits and large coats, all ideal for hiding her expanding belly.

Six weeks before her due date, Ava knew she had to come clean. But she simply couldn't figure out how she'd tell her family at that late stage.

The dilemma was solved when she went into premature labour at the back of the shop.

'Mama,' she called out, grimacing. 'I . . .' Pains gripped her and she staggered sideways, knocking everything off her desk. The loud clatter sent Clara running.

'What's happened?'

Ava stooped and went down on all fours, rocking back and forth.

'Ava! What's wrong, lovey?'

'I'm in labour,' she managed. 'Call an ambulance. I'm too early. The baby isn't due for another six weeks.'

If Clara was shocked, she didn't show it. Jumping into action, she dialled for an ambulance and gave clear and concise instructions.

'They're on the way. Just try and breathe through the pains,' she said.

Ava closed her eyes and wished the ground could swallow her up. Fear and shame washed over her.

'I'm so sorry . . . I should have told you before this . . .'

'Let's not worry about that at the moment. You have more pressing things on the agenda,' Clara said firmly. 'We'll have plenty of time for talking later. Right now, put your energy into delivering this child.'

The ambulance arrived. Clara shut the shop and accompanied her. She'd already called Gus.

'She's what?' Gus shouted. 'Are you sure?'

'Yes, dear, quite sure. Now, can you meet us at the maternity hospital?' Clara said, hanging up.

Ava, in spite of her terror and pain, began to laugh.

'What's so funny?' Clara asked with a wry smile.

'You!' Ava giggled. 'This is totally bananas. I'm certain I've freaked the living hell out of you and yet you're as cool as a cucumber and acting as if Dad is from outer space because he's yelling.'

'Hm,' Clara said calmly. 'I suppose I could go ballistic right now, but that's not going to help matters, is it? Things happen in life. Most of the time they're unexpected. We humans don't run to a perfect schedule, so there's no point in losing the plot, as you would say!'

The ride in the back of the ambulance was noisy, bumpy and horribly uncomfortable. The contractions became more frequent and painful.

Once they reached the hospital, the horror began to truly unfold.

The nurses rushed Ava to a delivery suite, where a monitor was wrapped around her tummy. It all happened so quickly after that. Even now, as she thought back to that day, Ava found it difficult to properly remember the exact details.

'The baby is in distress,' a nurse said. Buzzers went off, doctors rushed in, and before she knew it, Ava was whisked to an operating theatre.

'Who is your doctor and which obstetrician did you attend during your pregnancy?' a gowned and masked surgeon asked.

'I didn't go to any,' Ava said and burst into tears. 'My fiancé left and I concealed the pregnancy.'

'It's OK. You need to remain calm,' the nurse said, stroking her hair.

'We don't have time to wait for an epidural to take effect,' the doctor said. 'We'll have to knock you out. Can you sign this consent form, please?' He handed her a pen and clipboard. Ava managed to scribble some sort of comprehensible name and waited to be put to sleep.

The next thing she remembered was waking to see her parents sitting in chairs at her bedside. Her mouth was dry and her tongue felt thick and carpet-like in her mouth. She wanted to speak but couldn't.

'Hello, lovey,' Clara said, kissing her forehead.

'The baby . . .' she managed.

Clara pulled her chair closer and leaned in.

'The baby is tiny and very beautiful,' she said evenly. 'But she's very sick, Ava.'

'Wh . . . How? Oh no.' She wanted to scream and cry, but she was so weak and dehydrated, the only sound that came from her was a long, low crooning noise.

Gus notified the nurse that Ava was awake. Within minutes the small hospital room was swarming with medical staff.

'I'm Dr Roberts,' said a kindly-looking woman. 'I'm in charge of the neonatal intensive care unit here at the hospital.'

'Hello,' Ava said weakly. 'Can you tell me what's happening with my baby?'

'Your little girl has been born with something called spina bifida. Do you know anything about this?'

'No,' Ava said, looking terrified.

'Well, the name means split spine,' said Dr Roberts. 'There are many different types of spina bifida. The type your daughter has is called anencephaly. This occurs approximately twenty to twenty-eight days after conception, possibly before you even realised you were pregnant.'

'What does it all mean?' Ava asked, panic-stricken.

'When a baby develops normally,' Dr Roberts explained, 'the neural tube folds and closes to form the brain and spinal cord. In your baby's case, the neural tube was unable to close completely. Anencephaly basically means an absence of the major portion of the brain, skull and scalp.'

'Oh sweet Jesus, no!' Ava burst into tears.

'Your baby looks perfect facially, but there is a portion of her skull to the rear that has not been covered by skin or tissue.'

'Is she in pain?' Ava asked.

'No,' said Dr Roberts. 'We have made certain that she's comfortable.'

'What's her prognosis?' Gus asked hurriedly.

Dr Roberts took a deep breath and sighed.

'The longest a baby with similar anencephaly has survived to date is ten days.'

Ava knew there were still people in the room. Somewhere in the background of the spinning horror that had become her reality, she could hear her parents crying. Suddenly all she wanted was to hold her daughter.

'Can you take me to her?' she asked.

'How about we bring her in here?' the doctor suggested. 'In the circumstances we feel it would be advisable for you to hold her and perhaps take some photographs. I have to be frank with you, Ava. We reckon you are looking at hours rather than days.'

Ava nodded silently. As the medical team shuffled out of the room, she struggled to sit up. Wincing in pain, she realised she couldn't move on her own.

'Take it easy, sweetheart,' Gus said.

'Yes, let us help.' Clara circled the bed and nodded to Gus to take the opposite side. They cranked her up to a more comfortable position as the tiny baby was wheeled in. She was in a see-through cot and was swaddled in a pink blanket. The nurses had placed a little pink cotton bonnet on her head.

'Oh look at her!' Ava wailed. 'Oh Mama, look!'

All that could be heard in the room were sobs as Ava held her arms out to the delicate little mite. The baby's eyes remained shut and she was struggling to breathe.

'Ava,' Dr Roberts said, 'I hate to be the bearer of further bad news, but your baby is extremely weak. We feel it's a matter of minutes. We'll be outside the door.'

Ava's vision blurred as she held her precious little daughter in her arms.

'How can she look so very beautiful and yet she's got such an ugly malfunction draining the life out of her?' she sobbed.

'Because she's an angel, that's why,' Clara said firmly.

'Here, Mama,' Ava said, holding the child up.

'Oh no, pet, you keep her for the small amount of time you have.'

'I want you all to hold her. Just kiss her and pass her back,' Ava pleaded. 'I want her to be remembered. If you hold her, you'll never forget her.'

Clara took the tiny bundle and momentarily cradled her, then kissed her repeatedly before handing her to Gus. Tears ran shamelessly down his face as he too kissed the little mite. In utter anguish he handed her back to her mummy.

Ava held her daughter against her skin. As she kissed her and crooned that she loved her, she looked up at her parents.

'I'm going to call her Angelina, because she's my little angel.'

'That's wonderful, *Liebling*,' Clara said.

As she stroked Angelina's soft, velvety cheek, Ava felt as if there was nobody else in the world outside the two of them.

'Will we leave you?' Gus whispered.

'No, Daddy,' she said. 'Stay and let her know we love her. She needs to know we're her family.' He nodded.

An atmosphere that Ava had never experienced came over the room. It was serene, yet markedly different to normal. As if the world was actually on pause.

As soon as Angelina took her final shuddering breath, Ava could almost see her soul and short-lived spirit rising and leaving the room. The exact details of everything else that had gone on were blurred in emotion, but that moment was emblazoned in her mind for ever.

'Sleep well, my darling Angelina. Thank you for showing me love. I will never forget you and I hope you will look down on me and forgive me for doing this to you. I'm so sorry, baby girl.'

As Ava kissed her daughter and continued to stroke her cheek, Clara crouched down.

'You didn't do anything wrong, Ava,' she whispered. 'It's not your fault. You didn't know Angelina was sick.'

'No,' she said in a daze, 'but I knew I was pregnant and I hid it. I didn't go to the doctor and I didn't ask for the care I needed. I was so angry with Sean for leaving me. I found out I was pregnant the day we split up. I allowed my own selfishness to override the importance of medical intervention.'

'Ava, there's no cure for anencephaly,' Gus assured her. 'All the doctors could have done was warn you about what's just happened. Nothing could've changed this tragic outcome, darling.'

Although the medical team told Ava exactly the same thing, she felt deep down that she'd failed her child. More than that, she thought God had punished her for being so weak after Sean's departure.

Her parents were sworn to secrecy and Ava made it crystal clear that Sean was never to find out. The funeral was a simple service conducted quietly at the graveside, with only Ava, Gus and Clara present. Afterwards, Ava drove away in her car alone.

Since then, she'd never really allowed any man into her heart.

Now, shaking with nerves, she dialled Sean's number. He answered on the first ring.

'Hi, Ava.'

'Hello, Sean.'

'How's it going?'

She smiled. 'How come you haven't lost your Irish accent?'

'I pride myself on holding on to it,' he said. 'I think I rebelled against turning into an American. Maybe it's denial.'

'I need to tell you something,' she said. 'I hope you can forgive me for keeping this from you. In my defence, I figured I was doing the right thing, and I'm ashamed to say that I wanted to punish you.'

'OK,' he said sounding intrigued. 'Go on.'

Ava proceeded to tell Sean all about Angelina.

'I was running out to the car to tell you I was pregnant that day . . . when you told me you'd slept with someone else.'

There was silence on the line.

'Sean?'

All she could hear was his soft sobs; he was clearly struggling to take the information on board.

'Ava, I'm so sorry. I can't actually put how I'm feeling right now into words . . .'

'I'm sorry too, Sean.' Her voice cracked, and although they were thousands of miles apart, for the first time in twenty years they were truly united.

Sean bombarded her with questions about their daughter. He wanted to know every last detail. At first Ava found the questions heartbreakingly difficult to answer. But she forged on, knowing he deserved to be told the facts.

'My mobile phone feels like it's cooking the side of my face,' he said. 'Can I call you back on a landline?'

'Sure,' she said.

They talked for a further two hours. Not just about Angelina either. Sean told Ava how lost and destroyed he'd felt after they split. How he'd tried to make a go of it with other women since, but nothing had ever worked out.

'So you're not married or attached right now?' she asked.

'Nope. As I said, I've come to the conclusion that I'm meant to be alone. Even the girl I came here with turned out to be wrong. I made a total hash of my life and I guess I've gotten what I deserve . . . Nobody.'

'Don't say that,' she said softly. 'The guy I knew and loved was one in a million. I think that's why I've never managed to replace you . . . It's not from the want of trying,' she added drily. 'I've been a serial dater for the past twenty years.'

'Good for you,' he laughed.

'It's not really,' she said as fresh tears began to fall. 'Oh, sorry,' she said. 'This has to go down in history as the most leaky phone call ever!'

'It's probably the longest too,' he pointed out. 'Including the call on the mobiles, we've been talking for hours.'

They both fell silent.

'I don't want to hang up, though,' he said honestly.

'Me neither,' she admitted.

'It's just a crazy idea . . .' he said. 'But how would you feel about going to dinner with me some night?'

'Ha,' she laughed. 'I'd love that, but I don't think either of us can afford the taxi bill!'

'I'll fly home if you'll see me.'

Ava sat up. Her eyes were burning from crying and lack of sleep, but she suddenly felt more awake and alive than she had in a long, long time.

'Would you really?'

'Yes, really.'

'I'll book a table,' she said evenly. 'The restaurant at the Shelbourne Hotel in Dublin.'

'Give me three days and I'll organise stuff with work.'

'Are you totally serious?' she giggled.

'I'll be there. I should've been there eighteen years ago. This is my second chance, Ava.'

'Now I feel as if I can put the phone down.'

'I know,' he laughed. 'So it's not goodbye, just adieu.'

'Just adieu,' she repeated as she hung up.

Cradling the phone to her chest, she lay back against the cushions. A silly smile spread across her lips. She felt sixteen again. She felt fluttery. She felt insanely happy.

Chapter 24

BACK AT THE HOTEL, MAX WALKED AHEAD OF AMBER and headed directly for the bar, where he asked for a double whiskey on the rocks. Amber traipsed after him. When she heard what he was ordering, she raised an eyebrow.

'Won't that make you jumpy and freaked?' she asked. 'We both know the effect whiskey has on you.'

'I reckon I passed the freaked stage several hours ago. Besides, this is strictly medicinal. If I were that way inclined, I'd be popping Valium like candy by now.' He rubbed his face with his hand.

'I understand,' Amber said, guiding the suitcase to the side so that she could sit in a soft wing-backed armchair. There were so many things she wanted to say. Questions she longed to ask him. But she could see he was already stretched to breaking point.

He downed the whiskey and she ordered some sandwiches and two glasses of wine.

Knowing he needed to keep Amber in the loop, Max filled her in on the conversation he'd had with Ava and Clara.

'So, the big white elephant that has shadowed our marriage has finally been outed,' Amber said. 'I had my theories all along, of course. All of them were wrong, though. I suspected you'd been adopted and had been treated differently to the rest of the family.'

He shook his head.

She'd most definitely assumed his extended family hadn't wanted anything to do with him. Now she felt immensely guilty. Should she have encouraged him to get in touch with his sister? Who knew, she could possibly have gotten through to him and resolved this sad mess a long time ago.

Amber found Max's family fascinating. It was amazing to see where her husband had hailed from and who he was like. Max had met her folks, of course. He knew who her people were. Whether or not he gelled with them was irrelevant. That wasn't the point. He had a handle on her background.

They were both exhausted emotionally and physically, but Amber knew they had to sort things out.

'So would you like to explain why you were kissing Amy in the middle of the hospital canteen the other day?' she said, looking at him with steel in her eyes. 'I know this is probably not a great time to discuss this. But as far as I'm concerned, we may as well deal with everything here and now.'

'Are you ready to listen?' he asked, looking furious.

'Don't take that attitude with me, Max. I've done nothing wrong here.'

'Neither have I,' he hissed.

He pulled his fingers through his hair and looked at her.

'I've been having a nightmare at the hospital. Abe has instructed me to let people go. I've had to give most of my staff their marching orders, including Amy. I'd just confirmed with her that she'd be leaving and she was crying. I hugged her and tried to comfort her. You walked in.'

Amber felt such relief, she thought she might cry.

'I was certain you were having an affair,' she said.

'Why?' He looked pained. 'What have I ever done to make you believe I don't love you, Amber?'

'There have been so many gaps in your life. I always worried that you weren't entirely happy.'

'I haven't been entirely happy, but never because of you.'

As she sat opposite her husband, Amber wondered how she'd gotten to a point in her life where she'd become so mistrusting. But there had always been a sense that Max was slightly pushing her away.

She told him so.

'Amber, I've struggled for so long to come to terms with the fact that I am not the man I thought I was.'

'How do you mean?'

'When I realised I wasn't Gus's son, but instead the son of a man who was tortured and crazy, it scared the hell out of me. So I felt I needed to control myself at all times.'

'Oh Max,' she said. 'That's not possible. You've got to realise that you're an amazing man. Look at the folks you heal, your staff. They all adore you.'

He looked so beaten by life at that moment that Amber wanted to take him in her arms and never let go.

'You're more than I deserve, Amber,' he said. 'You can walk into a room and light it up. When you take control of a fund-raiser, it gets done and you raise more money than the other members put together. Women envy you, men adore you. I guess I've always felt I'm not truly worthy of you.'

They ignored their wine and sandwiches. Amber took his hand and led him upstairs, and showed him just how much he deserved.

❧

As Amber lay sleeping a while later, Max was deep in thought. The reason he'd run from Ireland and never wanted to return was simple. Being a doctor, he had quite a bit of knowledge about genetics. His father, Jacob, had been a weak and self-centred excuse of a man. It frightened the living shit out of him. He had recurring images of ending up like him.

Obviously he hadn't been raised by Jacob. Gus was his role model, his mentor and his father in every other sense of the word. But he couldn't assume he wouldn't end up like Jacob. He'd seen it happen. He knew of couples who adopted children, and no matter what traits they attempted to bestow on their kids, they still ended up behaving in a way that was totally alien to the parents.

Look at Nathalie, he mused. She'd only met Ava recently, and yet from the moment she was born he'd seen resemblances between the two. She looked like Ava, had a temper like Ava and for all the world could easily be mistaken for her daughter. Genetics were powerful, and there was no getting away from them, no matter where he ran.

The other reason he hadn't come home was because he'd lost all respect for his mother and Gus. More than that, he despised them both for living a lie and for pulling the wool over his eyes. He hated them for acting as if they had the perfect marriage and an idyllic life when underneath the surface they were damaged and messed up. He'd needed a fresh start in a place where nobody knew about the deceit and he didn't have to pretend.

The most ironic part of all this mess was that he'd ended up being the biggest liar of them all. He'd run away and continued the lies while dragging poor Amber and Nathalie into his despicable web.

He'd been so certain he was doing the right thing all those years ago. Lochlann was a small village back then. Everyone knew what everyone else was doing. As a family they were watched all the more because his mother was foreign. The fact that she had her own business and thought nothing of juggling that along with raising her family wasn't the norm back in the 1970s. But Clara hadn't worried about what other people thought. He'd hated that about her. He often wished she'd stay at home and act like all the other kids' mothers. She'd wear clothes that were like something from the cover of *Vogue* instead of the housecoats most other women favoured. She loved lipstick, the brighter the better, and wouldn't be seen dead without it.

All his life, Max had longed to be the same as everyone else.

Now, as he lay in the hotel bed, he knew he'd been incredibly deluded.

He wanted to ask forgiveness from his mother and Ava. He needed to speak to Nathalie and apologise for denying her contact with her family. And most of all he needed to prove to Amber that he loved her beyond reason.

He had so much to be thankful for. He sincerely hoped he hadn't left it too late. He wasn't good at eating humble pie, but tomorrow was going to be a feast.

Chapter 25

THE EARLY-MORNING LIGHT SEEPED THROUGH THE curtains and nudged Nathalie into the day. As her eyes fluttered open, her slumber was replaced by a nagging feeling that something was hanging over her. The events of the previous couple of days came back to her, and she groaned. What had she been thinking? Imagine if that chambermaid hadn't found her at the hotel.

She climbed out of bed and looked out the window. It was early, before five, and she didn't want to wake Oma. Pulling on a tracksuit, she picked up a key, crept out the door and clicked it gently shut behind her.

As she made her way to the beach, she heard someone calling her name, and turned to find Conor jogging towards her.

'Hi,' she said, feeling incredibly glad to see him. 'What are you doing out here so early?'

'Herbie is an early riser,' he said, nodding towards the pale, curly ball of fur bounding about in delight. 'Where did you get to?'

Nathalie explained what had happened, feeling more stupid by the second.

'Heavy,' he said.

'Is that it?' she grinned.

'What do you think I should say?' he asked. 'That it was a bad plan? That I don't want you to do it again? That I'd be raging if you died before I had a chance to kiss you?'

She looked up at him. 'Do you want to kiss me?'

'Uh, yeah!' he said. 'Of course I do. Why wouldn't I? A stunner like you, with your all-American accent and your beautiful brown skin. Even though you make me look like a corpse beside you, it's worth the risk.'

She laughed as he stepped closer. She didn't realise quite how much she fancied him until his lips met hers.

'You're not my usual type,' she murmured.

'Why, because I sound like a leprechaun and look like a ghost?'

'No,' she said, growing serious, 'because you're a really decent guy. I usually go for total zeros. Besides, you're totally gorgeous. I also see the way the other girls look at you. You could charm the birds off the trees, Conor.'

In true Conor style, he didn't answer. Instead he grabbed her hand, whistled to Herbie and charged towards the ocean.

'No way!' she shrieked as he picked her up and strode into the sea.

'This is the best hangover cure,' he assured her as they bobbed about gasping for breath. 'Everyone needs to swim at sunrise.'

They turned to watch the sun, which looked as if it was being pulled right out of the water and into the sky like a great big glowing puppet.

'What do we do now?' Nathalie was shivering. 'I'm freezing! This tracksuit wasn't meant for swimming.'

They agreed to meet for breakfast as soon as they were changed and dry. Nathalie traipsed home, giggling at the squelching noises coming from her shoes. Clara was still asleep, so she changed swiftly and ran back to meet Conor.

He'd brought a flask of tea and some toast that he'd wrapped in a napkin. They perched in a sheltered part of the cove and looked out to sea. Conor wrapped a warm blanket around her and handed her a mug.

'You're the sweetest guy I've ever met,' she said sincerely.

'Apart from your daddy, I assume. I've a sister and nobody comes near Dad with her.'

'Sadly, my dad isn't like yours, by the sound of it.'

'Really?'

Nathalie recalled her seventh birthday party. She remembered that day as clearly as if it were yesterday.

'Is Daddy coming home before the other kids get here?' she'd asked her mom.

'He promised and he'll be here,' Amber assured her.

All her friends arrived, the bouncy castle was inflated and a real-life princess had even come. She was busy doing face painting and sprinkling fairy dust around the garden, much to the delight of the children. But Nathalie couldn't relax. She kept running inside to the kitchen to check if her daddy was home yet.

'Can you call him again please, Mommy?'

Amber had gone so far as to hand her the phone and allow her to leave a voicemail on his cell.

'Daddy, please hurry home. I need you to meet the real princess. Mackenzie wants us to cut the cake. Come on, Daddy!'

The cake was finished, the princess had returned to her castle and the balloons were all burst by the time Max arrived. Nathalie had fallen asleep in her party dress, refusing to remove it until Daddy saw her.

'Otherwise he won't know I'm pretty,' she'd explained to Amber.

'Oh, he knows that every time he looks at you, sweetie.'

Next morning Nathalie thought he would take her in his arms and apologise for missing the day. She figured some poor person had been in an accident and required his help. That happened when your daddy was a surgeon. She knew it because he told her often enough. She needed to learn to share him when he was helping to make sick people better. But that break-fast after her birthday party was just the same as any other. He'd slurped his coffee while leaning against the kitchen counter and necking a slice of toast with his phone held aloft as he checked his messages. Not once did he try to make amends. That was the moment she gave up expecting her father to act like a daddy. She began to call him Dad and never relied on him after that.

That morning was all the more memorable too because it was one of the only times she'd heard her mom cursing. Amber had followed him out the front door at speed and yanked his arm back as he was about to leave.

'Is that it?' she had yelled. 'You miss her birthday party and leave her to cry herself to sleep and you think it's OK to just drive out of here as if you're the king of the castle?'

'Stop shouting, Amber, you're embarrassing yourself.'

'I don't give a shit about who I embarrass. You broke your daughter's heart yesterday and I hope you're proud. I can make excuses for your coldness towards me. Believe me, I have dozens of them stored up in my head. But I will never understand how you can disappoint an innocent little girl who thinks the world of you. Shame on you, Max. This is a new low. You want to hear me embarrassing you? Well you're a heartless bollox and I hope you are fabulously fucking happy with yourself.'

Once the door-slamming was over and Amber had showered and washed her hair, the day improved dramatically. Nathalie skipped school so they could go to the mall. They bought clothes and toys and had cheesecake for lunch. Her mom sat opposite her as they shovelled in cake and took her hand. With tears in her eyes she apologised for her dreadful behaviour that morning.

'It's never OK to speak like that, but your father drove me over the line.'

'It's OK, Mommy, I understand. I won't call people that name unless they really and truly deserve it.' Amber had gone from looking stricken to roaring with laughter. The same day Nathalie put her father in one box, her mom was elevated to quite a height.

'Well it's good that you have that relationship with your mother,' Conor said. 'But maybe after all the hassle you've caused recently, you've shocked your poor father into submission.'

Nathalie stared at him. She had never met anyone so direct.

'You know,' she mused, 'you could be right. I think I freaked the shit out of him.'

'Not always a bad thing. Although next time try not to have a near-death experience while you're at it.'

She spent the next hour cuddled into Conor as they chatted about life and what a weird world it was. They swapped phone numbers and then she reluctantly stood up.

'I'd best be getting back. I don't want them to think I'm trying to do myself in again.'

'Ah no, one suicide attempt is enough for the moment,' he grinned.

'See you later?'

'Not if I see you first,' he said, waving and calling to Herbie.

By the time she got back, Clara was up and about. She was in the sewing room, ironing part of the quilt.

'Hi, Oma,' Nathalie said. 'Sorry if you were worried.'

'I heard you coming in and leaving again. I guessed from the pile of soaked clothes that you'd been swimming with your young man.'

'You're a regular Ms CSI,' Nathalie said. She hesitated, before apologising for all the worry she'd caused.

Clara sighed and beckoned for her to come over. As they sat side by side, she explained what had happened to make Max leave.

'Wow,' was all Nathalie could say. 'I'd never have guessed. When I overheard you at the grave talking about your affair, I felt shocked and betrayed – on my dad's behalf as much as anything. But now that you've explained it was Jacob you slept with, it becomes a bit easier to understand.'

'I'm not proud of what happened,' Clara said. 'But I cannot change the past.'

'None of us can,' Nathalie said sensibly. 'But what about Hannah? What became of her, Oma?'

'Well, my parents became involved with St Herbert's school, where your father and Ava went eventually. It started out as a boys only school, but in later years they took girls also. But back in the day, Hannah housed boarders and my father taught music. Seeing as we were settled, Lukas made the decision to write to his parents and tell them where he was and with whom.'

'Didn't they know about you or Hannah at that point?'

'They knew about Hannah, but not about me,' Clara answered. 'A month later, Lukas received a letter from his mother. His father had passed away as the result of a riding accident, and she was gravely ill. She asked him to return to Vienna. She said she wanted to make things right before she died.'

'Gosh, he must've been so upset.'

'He was tortured by guilt and wanted to bid his mother fare-well, but he was adamant that Mama and I went too.'

'You must've been buzzed about going back to Austria,' Nathalie said. 'Did you get to see Alina, Frank and Jacob?'

'Sadly not,' Clara said. 'I asked to see them, naturally. But as it turned out, Madeline Leibnitz, my *Oma*, was literally waiting to see her son before she passed away.'

'Oh no, what was wrong with her?'

'She had cancer,' Clara said. 'And by the time we met, she'd wasted away to a tiny slip of a thing. But even in that dreadful stage of decline I could tell she'd been very beautiful.'

Clara told Nathalie she could distinctly remember the look of terror on Hannah's face as they returned to the house and the mistress from whom she'd fled.

'She was petrified of upsetting Oma Leibnitz and was certain she'd be greeted with scorn.'

'And was she?'

'You bet,' Clara said, shaking her head. 'Poor Mama had to listen to an outpouring of anger and bile like I'd never imagined another human being could utter.'

'How awful,' Nathalie said, shuddering.

'Well I guess that as far as Madeline Leibnitz was concerned, Mama was responsible for stealing her only son and ruining his life.'

'How was Madeline towards you?'

'The moment I walked into her bedroom, I knew she and I would be just fine,' Clara said. 'It was dark, the heavy maroon and gold drapes pulled tightly shut. Oma Madeline said the light hurt her eyes. Her voice was strong and commanding even then. She shouted at me to come closer.'

'Jeez, I think I'd have run away as fast as I could,' Nathalie said.

Clara threw her head back and laughed. 'Oddly enough, I didn't even consider that,' she said. 'I was only ten years old at that point. I suppose youth and naivety were on my side. I'd never experienced cruelty or nastiness, so I didn't expect it from my Oma.'

'What did you do?'

'She patted the side of the bed and asked me to sit. I did as I was bid, out of nosiness more than anything else! But as I looked into her eyes, something changed in her expression. The steely stare seemed to fade, only to be replaced by heartbreaking sadness. She told me I was beautiful and held her hand up for me to hold.'

'Wow,' Nathalie said. 'I feel like all I keep saying to you is wow,' she added. 'Go on, please.'

'Oma Madeline stroked my hand and told me that she would die happy knowing Lukas had found me. She promised to watch over us all and said she would change her will to ensure that her fortune was left to me.'

'Who was she leaving it to before?'

'Who knows?' Clara smiled sadly at the memory. 'Maybe we deprived the cats of Vienna of a small fortune.

'Oma Madeline died the following morning. Her funeral was terribly grand and full of smart, beautiful people. My father took Mama and me into one of the expensive clothing shops in the first quarter. I will never forget the look on Mama's face as she stroked and stared at the wonderful clothes. It had been her dream since she was a tiny girl to own outfits like that.'

'A bucket-list moment?' Nathalie asked.

'Yes,' Clara grinned.

'The day Madeline Leibnitz was laid to rest, so too were many of my mother's fears of inadequacy. Once we returned to Ireland, things became so much better for all of us.'

'Did you get a whole pile of cash from Oma Madeline?' Nathalie asked eagerly.

Clara nodded. 'The great house was sold. Papa asked me if I'd like to keep it, but I immediately said no. All that came to mind when I thought of that house was the dying lady in the dark, oppressive room. Besides, I had a better idea.'

'Tell me.' Nathalie sat up straight.

'I adored the house across the road from St Herbert's school. It was like a small child's hand-drawn picture: rectangular, with three windows upstairs and one either side of the front door. The lovely bonus was the large barn out the back and the sizeable garden. The For Sale sign had only appeared at the bottom of the drive before our trip to Austria. So I asked if we could swap the house in Austria for that one. I thought it would be the most perfect spot for us. Close to Papa's work and right beside the cottage we'd settled in. I didn't want to move anywhere else, you see. I'd done enough roaming to last me a lifetime.

'The builders were called upon to add more bedrooms and a large dining room. The following September, Hannah and Lukas took charge of ten boys. I adored all of them. We fought and played just like siblings, but only one made my heart flutter. From the moment I met Gus, I knew there was something different about him. He was steady and slightly serious without being stuffy.'

'Was he good-looking?' Nathalie asked, raising an eyebrow.

'I was just about to get to that part.' Clara winked. 'Even at the age of fourteen, he was tall and broad. He had chiselled features and the kindest eyes I've ever known.'

'He sounds divine,' Nathalie sighed.

'Gus and I were friends for several years before anything ever happened. As his graduation ball was looming, he shyly asked if I would accompany him.'

'So that was like his prom, right?' Nathalie asked.

'Yes. Exactly.'

'Oh Oma, that's so gorgeous that you guys were prom sweethearts!'

'I'm not sure Papa felt quite as enthralled,' Clara remembered. 'He was terrified of letting his little girl go. I overheard him saying to my mother that I would leave the house a girl and return a woman . . .' Clara shook her head and grinned. 'He was right, I knew that night as Gus held me in his arms and danced with me that I never wanted anything other than to be with him.'

Nathalie understood so much more. Slowly the pieces of the past were clicking into place.

Chapter 26

ACROSS TOWN, AVA'S PALMS WERE WET AS SHE SAT bolt upright in a chair at Dr Saul's office. There were no other people in the waiting room, which both delighted and unnerved her. She detested the idea of accidentally bumping into anyone here, yet at the same time it might be nice to know she wasn't the only one.

The door swung open and a very attractive woman similar in age to Ava appeared, holding her hand out.

'Hi, I'm Clare Saul, it's great to meet you, Ava. Come on through to my office.'

The office was nothing like Ava had imagined. She had thought it would be dark and sombre, with a brown leather chaise longue and a white-coated doctor sporting round wire glasses. Instead the room was light and airy, and Dr Saul was sophisticated and glamorous. Her long blond hair was pulled back off her face with a glittery clip and she wore a beautifully cut dress.

'I love your dress,' Ava said without thinking. 'I sell that label in my shop. They do amazing mix-and-match pieces, don't they?'

'Oh, I'm thrilled to hear that you sell it. I bought this in Barcelona last year and I live in it. Where's your shop?' she asked, beckoning for Ava to sit in the plush cream leather chair opposite her.

'It's on Lochlann Main Street.'

'Ah, you see, that's where I go wrong. In Ireland I tend to

shop in Dublin city centre. But the real gems are the boutiques run by their owners.'

'I put my heart and soul into my business,' Ava agreed. 'We also have a bespoke service where we design one-off pieces. My mother is an incredibly talented seamstress and taught me all she knows.'

'You've sold it to me. I'm there on my next day off!' Dr Saul quipped. 'So what brings you to my office today, Ava?'

'Yikes,' she said. 'This is the bit I've been dreading . . .' She attempted to smile, but her mouth wouldn't conform and she knew she was grimacing and looking terrified.

'Nobody likes coming here the first time,' Dr Saul said. 'But most of them come back, which I choose to take as a good sign. Coffee, tea or mineral water?' she asked, opening what looked like a normal cupboard.

'Wow, you've almost got a full working kitchen in there,' Ava said.

'Yup, this room's like a ship. I wanted clean lines so the place isn't cluttered. It's better feng shui, and I'm naturally incredibly messy, so I need to have a place for everything or else it'd be like a jumble sale in here.'

'I'd love a coffee, please,' Ava said, eyeballing the sleek machine.

'I'll join you.'

She wasn't sure if it was the familiarity of sharing a cup of coffee, or whether Dr Saul was simply a brilliant psychologist, but almost without noticing, Ava began to talk. Not just namby-pamby words that meant nothing, either. Instead she felt as if a bung had been removed so she could suddenly spill her inner thoughts without holding back.

'I hate to cut you off,' Dr Saul said, 'but I'll have to leave it there for today.'

'Already?'

'I'm afraid so,' she smiled. 'It's great that you weren't sitting uncomfortably, unable to speak. That can happen too.'

'I'm a little confused, though . . .' Ava hesitated. 'Don't *you* tell *me* stuff? Will the next session work differently? Will you summarise what I've just said and tell me what to do?'

'It doesn't quite happen that way, Ava. Most of the time counselling is about talking things through. Sure, I'm trained to deal with all sorts of issues, but problems can only be dealt with when a person can verbalise or illustrate what's bothering them.'

'So you work on the basis that a problem shared is a problem halved?'

'In simple terms, yes. I will give you guidance if and when I feel you need it. But you might have noticed you were doing very nicely today. You were telling me things and offering solutions. For example, you mentioned your brother briefly. You said you realise, now that you've met your niece, that the silence between you has gone on too long. That you'd love to reconcile things in some shape or form.'

Ava nodded. She hadn't known she felt that way previously. In fact none of it made any sense in her own head. Yet it seemed so much simpler and easier to fathom once it was out in the open.

As she bid Dr Saul farewell and made another appointment, she felt lighter in her heart than she had for years.

She wasn't in a hurry to return to the shop. Ruth was well able to manage. Although Ava guessed her assistant was reeling: in all the time she'd worked at the shop, Ava had never taken a single day off until recently.

She decided to drop out to Lochlann and visit her mum and Nathalie. She explained where she'd been. She was tentative at first, but she knew she needed to be more open with everyone, so she told them all about Dr Saul. She confessed what had happened the night she was mugged and how much of a mess her life had become.

'It was my rude awakening,' she said sheepishly. 'It's time I faced up to the future and let go of the ghosts from my past.'

'That's wonderful news, dear,' Clara said. 'Letting go of the past is good. I'm discovering that too. I'm very proud of you.'

The two younger women chatted about the power of talking and sharing.

'Mama, you're not saying much,' Ava said eventually.

'I'm just observing,' Clara said wisely. 'I'm very relieved you've had this revelation. I don't want to say a word in case I jeopardise the progress. I'm of the strong opinion that words aren't always necessary. This is one such occasion.'

Ava rolled her eyes and looked at Nathalie. 'Your *Oma* is such a wise old owl at times. She reminds me of Yoda from *Star Wars*.'

Nathalie giggled.

'Isn't he the little green fuzzy creature?' Clara asked. 'He's like the love child of a gooseberry and a gremlin.'

'That's the one,' Ava grinned.

'Oh yes, I like him,' Clara nodded. 'I could be called worse things.'

They sat and talked for a while longer until Ava announced that she needed to get going. She hadn't told Nathalie about Angelina, and she wanted to do that. But not until she'd seen Sean. She needed to be with him face to face and know that she had sorted out that relationship before she faced up to Nathalie. One thing at a time, she whispered to herself, slow and steady is the way to go.

Clara decided they should have a family dinner the following night.

'I couldn't imagine anything more delightful than having all of us around one table together. Will you help me prepare?' she asked Nathalie. 'Would you like to bake a cake? I'll give you the recipe and I'll be there if you need me.'

'From scratch?' Nathalie asked, wide-eyed.

'Well it's not going to be from a box,' Clara huffed. 'I know people often don't have the confidence to bake, but it's so simple once you know what to do.'

Nathalie grinned.

'If you get on with doing that, I'll start to coat the meat . It will keep perfectly in the fridge until tomorrow. It'll be a lot tastier too, I'll use plenty of garlic and I like it to have time to amalgamate with the veal to add extra flavour. Besides, that'll be one less job to do then. I'll need to go to the supermarket later on, but I have the basics to get us started. I'm making Wiener schnitzel.'

'What's that?'

'It's veal bashed flat to tenderise it, coated in crushed garlic, then flour, then egg, then breadcrumbs, and shallow-fried.'

'Sounds awesome!'

'Yes it is,' Clara said matter-of-factly. Nathalie laughed, loving her straight-up comment.

'Afterwards can we do some more sewing? I'd love to have more of my quilt done. Mom is gonna die when she sees it!'

'Of course,' Clara said as she found her mobile phone and texted Ava and Max, inviting them both to a family reunion dinner.

Nathalie switched the oven on and began to weigh her ingredients.

'Mackenzie would've loved you,' she said sadly. 'She was such a sweet girl. We talked about anything and everything, but most of all she had my back. All the time. No matter what.'

'That's what friends are for, *Liebling*. People who don't treat you that way aren't your true friends. Having said that, it's good to have lots of people in your life. You just need to learn who to trust, that's all.'

'That's easier said than done,' Nathalie said.

'I know. But the older I've got, the better my judgement has become.'

Clara crushed the garlic and bashed the pieces of veal with her little meat mallet before beginning the coating process. Leaving the schnitzel in the fridge overnight usually meant the crumb was nicely stuck on before cooking. No matter how many years had flown by, she was certain of one thing: a decent home-cooked meal would work wonders with Max. He'd always loved her cooking, and she was bargaining on that old wives' tale that a way to a man's heart was via his stomach.

Ava dialled Max's number. She didn't want to tell everyone that Sean was on the way. But she needed to talk to someone, to feel as if she wasn't alone, even if she couldn't divulge her innermost thoughts.

'Can we meet for coffee?'

'Can you make it to the hotel?' he asked.

'See you there in five minutes.'

Ava felt queasy as she waited in the hotel lobby for Max. He strode out of the elevator and smiled when he saw her waiting there.

'Still anal when it comes to timekeeping, I see?' he jibed.

Ava knew she was a stickler about many things, but she'd always seen it as a positive thing. Maybe she needed to try and take a chill pill from time to time.

She approached a hovering waiter and ordered two coffees, then perched on a sofa opposite Max.

'Listen, Max . . .' She hesitated. 'I haven't brought you here for a run-of-the-mill catch-up . . .' She looked at the floor and began to wring her hands. 'I need to tell you what happened after you left.'

He leaned forward and accepted his coffee from the waiter.

'You look seriously guilty,' he said with a half-smile. 'What have you done?'

The smile left his face rapidly as Ava began to relay the night-mare that had unfolded all those years before.

'Oh Ava,' he whispered sadly, getting up and crossing over to sit with her. 'I'm so sorry.'

Ava began to sob.

'It was the worst time of my life,' she said. 'Then I heard that Sean was hanging out with you over in America . . .'

'There's nothing I can say to you,' he said. 'Words aren't enough to show you how guilty I feel. I figured I was the only one with problems. I never stopped to think about the bigger picture.'

'Surely Sean told you what he'd done?'

'Yes, of course he did. But I was in such a dark place, I couldn't allow any feelings for other people to infiltrate my selfish head.'

'For years I thought your silence was yet another punishment for what happened to Angelina,' Ava said sadly. 'No matter what the doctors or anyone else said, deep down I believed it was all my fault. I never even went to the doctor for a check-up while I was pregnant . . .'

'Really?' Max stared at her. 'I know we do things a little differently Stateside, but not to go to a doctor at all . . .' He whistled. 'Weren't you terrified?'

'I was so miserable that nothing else sank in.'

'But you know it wasn't your fault now, right?'

'Yeah, I do,' she sighed.

They talked about all the reasons Ava had resented Max in the past.

'I needed someone to blame for Angelina's death, for the messed-up engagement and all the other things that happened. You were the perfect scapegoat now that I think about it . . . You weren't here to defend yourself, but more than that, I didn't even need to argue with you. I could simply hate you and you wouldn't ever know.'

'That was a handy number in many ways. You could seethe and absolve everyone else around you of blame.'

'I was content with making it all your fault, Max.'

'So what's changed your mind now?' he asked.

'Nathalie. She put a spanner in the works. She's the most wonderful girl. Sunny disposition, pretty, clever and adorable.'

Max nodded.

'How can she be all those things with an ogre of a father?' Ava sighed shakily.

'Because her mother is an angel,' Max said, looking at the ground. Ava didn't notice his pain.

'All these thoughts have been zooming around my mind since meeting Nathalie. I always knew that what happened to me had absolutely nothing to do with you, but I was so hurt by your silence. Then you accepted Sean into your life. It's like you took his side instead of mine . . .' Ava jigged her leg up and down in agitation.

'I know.' Max clenched his jaw. 'I guess I—'

'But recently,' Ava interrupted, 'I'm thinking that you needed Sean. You'd walked away from everything and everybody you knew.' She gazed up at her brother. 'Now, I'm actually glad you had one another all this time. I'm ready to forgive you, Max. I'm here to say I'm sorry for being so awful about you. Even if it was only in my own head. Can we try and become brother and sister again?'

He nodded and held his arms out.

It was the best hug either of them had had in years.

Chapter 27

CLARA LEFT FOR THE SUPERMARKET WHILE Nathalie put the finishing touches to her cake, complete with home-made butter icing. She was thrilled with her efforts.

'Mom and Dad will never believe I made this,' she said proudly. 'And I'm going to put my head down and try to get another big bunch of quilting done,' she vowed.

'They'll be delighted with you, my dear,' Clara agreed.

Nathalie went straight to the sewing room, resolute about getting lots of work done before the family reunion the following day.

Several hours later, Clara joined her.

'My goodness, look at how much you've done! Did you hire some elves to speed this up?'

'No, Oma!' Nathalie giggled. 'I'm determined this will look good for tomorrow. I want the others to see how much we've achieved.'

'I don't think they'll be in any doubt as to how wonderful you are, *Liebling*.'

By dinner time, both women were boggle-eyed, but the quilt looked stunning. There was a definite feeling of excitement in the air as they busily prepared the house for the following day.

'You know, the atmosphere in here isn't unlike the day before my wedding,' Clara said. 'This charged, tense excitement.'

'When did you get married?' Nathalie asked.

'December 1954. I was eighteen, and Mama and I were putting the finishing touches to my gown. Mama had bought the lace when we were in Austria for Oma Madeline's funeral. It was the most exquisite fabric I'd ever laid eyes on. If she'd told me it had been woven by elves using fairies' wings, I would've been inclined to believe her.'

Clara explained that her parents were understandably supportive when Gus asked for her hand in marriage. Having wasted such a long time searching and yearning for one another, they never wanted their daughter to go through similar heartache. So they readily agreed to allow them to marry.

Gus's parents, Lauren and Harry Conway, had a totally different view of the whole idea, however.

'Lauren was an insufferable snob,' Clara said. 'God bless her, she was a limited woman in many ways. She was convinced I was stealing her only son.'

'But you were in love! Gus wanted to marry you too. How could you have been stealing him?' Nathalie asked.

'The real crux of the matter was that I was foreign,' Clara said. 'Lauren wanted her son to go to college, become a doctor and marry a nice Irish girl. She didn't want a flighty young thing with a German accent tarnishing her son.'

'What a pile of horse shit!' Nathalie fumed. 'She sounds like a total loser.'

Clara laughed. 'I doubt she would have approved of your language either. But now that I'm older, I understand her a little better. We were like aliens to her. We spoke German amongst ourselves, my mother designed and sewed all my clothes, my father was a crazy musician and we lived in a house full of boys!'

'You were sooo cool!' Nathalie said. 'I'd say Gus *had* to marry you so nobody else could!'

Clara threw her head back and laughed.

'The day before I walked up the aisle in Lochlann church, Hannah and I sewed the last of the seed pearls on to my veil before icing the chocolate wedding cake.'

'It had to be chocolate, of course,' Nathalie grinned.

'Of course! The congregation at the church was small, and snow sparkled on the ground as I skipped up the aisle on my father's arm. I never knew love could feel so intense until he put my hand into Gus's that day. We promised to love and cherish one another until death parted us.'

'Do you miss him all the time?' Nathalie asked.

'Every single day.' Clara nodded. 'He was a darling man. His love for me never faltered. I was blessed to have him in my life.'

'You guys were so young. How did you manage with Gus at medical school?' she said.

'My parents gave us the barn beside their house.'

'Wasn't the house technically yours anyhow?' Nathalie asked.

'I never thought of it as mine. My parents had done all the work on it, and besides, it was their business too. They still housed boarders, of course.'

'Is the barn still there today?'

'Oh yes, the main house and barn were sold as a single lot to another family. But it was far from a barn by the time we finished decorating.'

Clara explained how she and Hannah made matching curtains and bedspreads and painted pretty stencils around the doors. With hard work and dedication and the remainder of the money from Oma Leibnitz, the place was transformed.

'I didn't want to stray far from my parents. So I never did. Some people have a wanderlust that never quite leaves them. They long to travel the globe and see different places,' Clara said. 'I was the opposite. I wanted to stay put and create roots for my family.'

'I can understand that for sure,' Nathalie said. 'But would you travel to LA and see us?' she asked coyly.

Clara looked at her and smiled. 'I'd travel to the ends of the earth for you, my sweet child.'

'Aw,' Nathalie said, hugging her. 'Tell me more about when you got married.'

Clara went on to explain that soon after her marriage she became pregnant with Ava. Gus continued with his studies, and by the time Ava was walking and talking, he had qualified as a doctor.

'An angel was watching over us at that time. The local GP, a true gentleman by the name of Dr O'Brien, took a shine to Gus. He invited him to work by his side at his surgery. Little did we know at the time that he was grooming him to take over. Dr O'Brien had nobody to succeed him. He'd watched Gus's progress as a young student and liked everything about him, from his manner to his hunger to be the best doctor possible. When Dr O'Brien passed away, Gus took over his practice.'

'Did Gus's parents like you any better when Gus qualified as a doctor and you had the children?' Nathalie wanted to know.

'They mellowed somewhat,' Clara said. 'But there were always barbed comments cast in my direction. They detested my accent and were highly suspicious of everything I did. They weren't familiar with the food I loved to cook, and my customs were very different. Ah, they meant no harm really. I learned to stop worrying about them and mind my own business.'

'I think they sound like fools,' Nathalie said, with wide eyes.

'Some people are just set in their ways,' Clara said. 'But I had enough to occupy my mind, and once I'd made my peace with the fact that Lauren and Harry were never going to welcome me with open arms, I simply got on with my life instead of waiting for approval that would never come.'

'Did they know about Jacob?' Nathalie asked.

'No,' Clara said. 'Gus didn't want anyone to know that Max wasn't his son. Not for his own sake, or mine for that matter. Purely because he didn't want anyone looking at Max differently. He wanted him to be wholly a part of our family.'

'Wow, he was amazing,' Nathalie said.

'He certainly was,' Clara agreed. 'My parents knew the full story, of course. They knew everything about me and never once judged me or made me feel I'd messed up in any way.'

'They were totally supportive?' Nathalie asked.

'Always. No matter what I did or how many times I made a mess of things, which was rather a lot as you can probably tell! They were unbending with their display of unconditional love.'

'What happened to your parents?' Nathalie asked gently.

'Oh,' Clara sighed. 'Mama passed away first. Her health began to fail just after Max was born. We all noticed her confusion. At first it was silly little things, like muddling the days of the week. But one day she called me Frau Schulz, who was the woman who ran the orphanage. That was when I knew there was something drastically wrong. She never mixed me up with anyone else. Gus diagnosed Alzheimer's disease, saying he had no idea how long she had left. It was utterly heartbreaking watching her decline. Her frustration was palpable, yet there was so little we could do to help.'

'Alzheimer's is such a vile disease,' Nathalie said. 'Mackenzie's grandma had it when we were kids. I remember it clearly. And it seems so grossly unfair that Hannah should end up with it after all she'd suffered already,' she added.

'As the months passed, she became almost childlike. She shadowed me and couldn't bear to be alone. Flashbacks from her time in Bergen-Belsen came back to haunt her.'

'It sounds as if she was suffering delayed shock,' Nathalie said.

'Yes, I agree,' Clara said sadly. 'One afternoon, I went out to hang clothes on the line. When I returned, Mama was crouched on the floor in the living room pretending to stir a large pot. Even though I called out to her and placed my hand on her shoulder, there was no rousing her from the scene. It was as if she'd been transported right back to that awful time. She was answering people in her imagination as if they were real, holding conversations with other prisoners.'

'Wow,' Nathalie said, aghast. 'What was she saying?'

'She was consoling someone called Georgia. Telling her that her baby was at rest now. That the Germans couldn't torture him any longer now he was with God.'

'How awful,' Nathalie whispered.

'She coaxed her imaginary friend to her side and pretended to take her in her arms. She made stroking gestures with her hand, as if she were smoothing this girl's hair, and tears began to cascade down her cheeks. She cried and begged Georgia not to leave her.'

'That's beyond awful,' Nathalie said sadly.

'For weeks she'd get caught up in that dreadful vision where she'd sob and beg Georgia to stay, telling her she didn't want to be alone with the soldiers.'

'Wowzers,' Nathalie managed. 'Hannah had so many ups and downs in her life, didn't she?'

'Yes, *Liebling*, she did. As the Alzheimer's took charge of her it became obvious that the only way she would find peace was when she passed away.'

'Oh Oma, you must've felt so cheated. You'd hardly forged your wonderful relationship with her and she was being taken away from you once again.'

'It was terribly cruel,' Clara conceded. 'I felt immeasurably angry about it all for a short time. As you rightly pointed out,

Nathalie, she had suffered enough, but I soon learned that hardship isn't doled out in rations that are evenly shared across the globe.'

'What happened to her?'

'I knew there was something different about her one particular morning. She called to my house at six o'clock. The air was freezing and I could see her breath as she spoke. There was a thick covering of frost on the ground outside, yet she was barefoot,' Clara said, shuddering. 'Luckily I was in the kitchen baking bread when she rapped on the door. I took her hand and she led me back to her house, to the bedroom where my father lay sleeping.'

'Didn't he know she was up and had gone from the house?'

Clara shook her head. 'She was a tiny little pixie of a thing and my father was a heavy sleeper. She gently stirred him and curled into his arms, beckoning for me to lie down with them. She was totally lucid for a few moments. As the three of us lay there entwined, she told us that we were her dreams come true and she would wait for us for ever.'

'She seemed to know that her time had come,' Nathalie said.

'More than that, she appeared to be happy to pass on. She thanked Lukas for believing in their love and for showing her that miracles can happen. She told me that I was her driving force when life seemed impossible and that she could never thank us enough for loving her. As she passed away, the broadest smile spread across her beautiful face.'

'Oh Oma,' Nathalie said, hugging her close. 'Poor you, and poor Lukas.'

Clara laced her fingers together.

'I've never been able to think of things in an angry way for long, Nathalie,' she mused. 'I don't feel there's any point. We can't change the past. It's over and done with. But we can certainly decide how we'd like to be in the future. I don't look back. I prefer to put my energy into moving forward.'

'That's easier said than done,' Nathalie scoffed. 'Especially when the people you love are being taken from you one by one.'

Clara tucked Nathalie's hair behind her ear and smiled.

'Isn't it better to know that there are people either down here or up there,' she looked skyward, 'who you love and cherish? Imagine living your whole life and never *feeling* love? How sad would that be? The way I look at it is this . . . We need to cherish the good times. They're what get us through the hard times. There's nothing more beautiful than sunshine after rain.'

'How did you get to be so wise?' Nathalie asked, shaking her head in wonder. 'I hope some day I can be as accepting and caring as you are.'

Clara stood up and hugged her, rocking her back and forth.

'Good things come to those who wait, *Liebling*.'

Chapter 28

THE FOLLOWING DAY WAS QUIET. AVA RETURNED to work and sorted out all the things she'd been neglecting at the shop.

Max and Amber walked around Dublin city, shopping and enjoying each other's company.

Clara and Nathalie had a leisurely breakfast before parting company for a while. Clara went to see Gus.

'I think you've been helping from up there,' she said as she arranged some flowers from the garden at his grave. 'Things are getting better by the day. I honestly feared that Nathalie was in terrible danger. Thank you for minding her, *Liebling*. Because I know you did.'

She sat and waited for the usual feeling of warmth this spot gave her. The wind wasn't exactly high, but she felt cold.

'I miss you, Gus. More than that, I feel so incredibly ashamed all over again. Having to tell people what I did to you brought it all back. It never gets any better. It never seems right.'

Nathalie rushed to the beach and jumped up and down waving her arms. As if by magic, Conor appeared.

'You're like one of those little wooden figures in a cuckoo clock,' she teased as he approached.

'You're like a raving lunatic jumping about by yourself,' he said, as he pulled her into his arms and kissed her.

They walked for a bit before Nathalie stopped and asked him what he did with his time.

'How come you're always looking out your window? What do you do to occupy yourself?'

'Want to see?' he asked with a grin.

They walked to Conor's house. As soon as he opened the door, Herbie came bounding up, wagging his tail and licking Nathalie's hand.

'Mum!' he called out. 'This,' he looked very pleased, 'is my Nathalie.'

'Hello there,' said a beautiful-looking woman with hair the same shade as her son's, the only difference being that hers cascaded down her back in glossy waves. Dressed in tight jeans, a glittery tank top and flip-flops, she looked more like Conor's sister than his mom.

'I'm Brea,' she said, holding her hand out. 'Conor has talked about you so much. I believe you're Max's daughter.'

'Yeah,' Nathalie said. 'He and my mom are actually here visiting right now.'

'Well I haven't set eyes on your father for over twenty years,' Brea said. 'Please tell him I was asking for him. If he and your mother would like a cup of tea, send them down. They'd be more than welcome.'

'Come on,' Conor said, taking Nathalie's hand. He led her to a beautiful room with a stunning bay window. Instead of being a living room as Nathalie had assumed, it was almost bare apart from an artist's easel and a messy paint-splashed table covered in art supplies.

'Welcome to my studio!' Conor announced.

'But I thought you said you played the Irish drum thingy,' she said.

'I do, and it's called a boudhrán,' he smiled. 'But that's only a bit of fun. This is what I really do.'

Nathalie walked around the room and gazed at some of the pictures. All oils, they were incredible. Most depicted the sea, and the movement of the water made it look almost real.

'Wow, these are amazing,' she breathed. 'How did you learn this stuff?'

'I went to art college, but I've always loved art. I wasn't book-clever at school, so I used my paintings to express myself.'

Nathalie nodded, knowing that she was literally falling in love with everything about Conor. What he showed her next left her speechless.

He turned the easel so she could view it. There on the canvas was an image of her face. He'd caught the exact way her hair curled and framed her face, but it was encompassed in a rolling wave.

'That's astonishingly beautiful,' she said. 'Totally awesome.'

'Just like you,' he said.

Nathalie placed her hands on his face and kissed him deeply. Nobody had ever moved her the way he had. All of a sudden she had a momentary flash of what it felt like to want to spend the rest of her life with one person. A person who wasn't her family.

Conor took her hands and sat her on a chair.

'Will you pose for a few minutes? I need to shade your eyes a bit better. I did it all from memory, but it's so much easier to have you here.'

At first she felt slightly embarrassed as Conor popped his head to the side and back again repeatedly. But she soon relaxed and began to feel very curious about the results.

What seemed like moments later, he called her over.

Masterfully he'd changed her expression to a half-smile and

added a twinkle to her eyes that only her closest confidantes would recognise.

'I love it,' she said.

'Good,' he smiled back.

She looked at her watch and reluctantly said she'd better get home to help Oma with the family reunion preparations.

'Come by whenever you feel like it,' he said, planting a kiss on her lips. 'You're delicious, my Nathalie.'

She grinned all the way home. Conor had no qualms about calling her his Nathalie. There was no tiptoeing around his feelings. She thought he was brilliant.

The afternoon flew. Once they began setting the table and putting the finishing touches to the food, Nathalie and Clara were totally engrossed in their duties.

Music flooded the room, with Clara often pausing to listen to a particular phrase or movement. For the second time that day, Nathalie witnessed a person being totally swept away by art.

Ava arrived with Max and Amber in tow. Clara promptly handed each of them a glass of mulled wine.

'I know it's summer, but this was what my mother always served her guests. It's sweet, potent and delicious.'

They clinked glasses and almost instantaneously conversation flowed. By the time they sat down to eat less than an hour later, they were all ravenous.

'The way we do it in this house is that everyone helps themselves,' Clara announced.

'And if you're too polite, you'll get nothing,' Ava added as she dug a large spoon into the dish of tiny rustic potatoes that Clara had tossed in oil and rosemary and shallow-fried.

'I didn't think I was even hungry,' Amber said. 'But this looks so delicious, I'm suddenly famished.'

Before long the conversation turned to past events. Clara told

Amber about her move to Ireland. They all listened in silence as she recalled the pain of leaving one family and forging a brand-new relationship with her biological parents.

'Life can be riddled with pain and angst,' she said. 'But I'd like to propose that from here on in, we try and come together again as a family.'

There was a brief silence until Nathalie spoke.

'I know I'm the youngest person here, but Mackenzie's death has taught me a pretty harsh lesson. Life is precious. It's short. We don't know the day or hour that it's all going to end. So why are we wasting time? Often we cannot choose who stays and who goes. So while we have a chance, let's do what Oma suggests and give this a go.'

'Good job,' Amber said. 'I'm very proud of you, darling. You've been braver than I could ever be. When Mackenzie died, I honestly thought you were going to die with her.'

'A part of me did,' Nathalie admitted.

'Sometimes it's not as easy as you're making out,' Max said. 'I hear what you're saying. I get the point. Life is precious. But it doesn't make the mistakes go away.'

'None of us is free of fault,' Ava conceded.

'Mistakes are easy to make,' Clara said. 'What isn't so easy is learning to forgive. In turn,' she looked at Max, 'you must decide to accept the forgiveness and move on. Otherwise life becomes nothing but a downward slope of bitterness and sorry regret.'

'Can you answer one question?' Max asked. 'How come Gus forgave you, just like that? Wasn't he hurt and betrayed by what you did?'

Clara sighed deeply.

'He was devastated,' she said. 'But there were a few factors involved in us managing to rebuild our marriage.'

'Which were?' Max said. 'I'm sorry, but I need you to help me out here. I don't get it . . .'

'Firstly, Gus had had the vasectomy without telling me. He took matters into his own hands because he thought I would be in medical danger should I become pregnant again.'

'OK, that's not totally honest, but he was still thinking of you,' Max said.

'I know that, lovey. Two wrongs don't make a right, but we came to the conclusion that we had both been at fault. He didn't decide to forgive me overnight either.'

'What happened?' Ava asked.

'Once Gus discovered I was carrying Jacob's baby. . . Well, I confessed as I couldn't bear to live a lie, he couldn't look at me, so we slept in separate rooms for the remainder of my pregnancy. He certainly didn't want to be intimate with me.'

'You moved into my room,' Ava said. 'I remember now.'

Clara nodded. 'I honestly didn't know what was going to happen once Jacob's baby came along. Oh, poor Gus was like a shell of his former self when news of my pregnancy became known. Staff at the hospital and patients in his surgery all congratulated him and wished him well.' Clara smiled sadly and a telltale tear trickled down her cheek.

'Where did he have the vasectomy done?' Amber asked.

'In England,' Clara said. 'He covered his tracks so nobody knew his business.'

'So he had to grin and bear it when people were wishing you well with your pregnancy,' Ava said.

'There were lots of innocent remarks from men especially, crossing their fingers and saying they hoped it was a son and heir this time,' Clara recalled. 'Gus would nod and thank people, all the while refusing to discuss the subject with me. We drifted further apart as my belly grew bigger. The day I went into labour, he was at the hospital with a patient. I'd lost a lot of blood while having Ava, so the staff were eager to ensure I wasn't in danger with Max.'

'Did history repeat itself?' Amber asked.

'As it turned out, yes, I began to haemorrhage once again. An emergency Caesarean was performed and I was sent to the intensive care unit. I needed blood transfusions and anti-biotics. I was so ill that I was completely unaware of all the commotion going on around me.' She stopped and took a mouthful of wine. Nathalie put her hand on her arm, encouraging her to continue.

'Gus was notified and told he had a son. As my health stabilized, Max's took a nosedive. He'd contracted an infection and became gravely ill. I wasn't compos mentis, so Gus had to take action. He signed the consent form for Max's treatment and stayed by his cot for a full twenty-four hours.'

'Wow,' Nathalie said, looking over at her father.

'He told me afterwards that he'd never been so afraid. He'd built up such anger and resentment during my pregnancy, but when he saw the tiny child struggling to survive, he said he had a moment of realisation. None of this was the baby's fault. More than that, he knew that he had the opportunity to be his father.'

'Had you told Dad that you didn't love Jacob the way you loved him?' Ava asked.

'Of course, *Liebling*. I told him ten times a day in the hope that he might believe me.'

'And eventually he did?' Amber asked.

'Well, by the time I was well enough to see the baby, Max was out of danger and slowly improving. Gus arrived at the ward with a wheelchair and took me to the baby care unit. Oh, I was devastated when I saw his tiny body covered in tubes and wires.

The little blue card at the end of his cot showed all his details, from his birth weight to the medicine he was on. It also said his name was Max.'

'So Gus named me?' Max said in awe. Clara nodded.

'I cried happy tears when I saw what he had done. He told me he wanted to call you Max because it was Latin for "the greatest". He admired your sense of determination and your will to live. But most of all he felt you deserved a strong and stoic name.'

'And Gus's name was on my birth certificate,' Max said proudly, his eyes moist with tears.

'Yes,' Clara nodded. 'We made the decision there and then that nobody would ever know the truth.'

'Isn't that illegal?' Ava asked.

'Only if you get found out,' Clara said with a wry smile.

'Ha!' Nathalie giggled in spite of the gravity of the story. 'That reminds me of Dad's advice when I used to get into hot water at school. He'd say that the worst offence was not the getting into trouble part, it was the getting caught!'

'Well I can hardly argue with that. Your father had that very concept branded on his soul from the day he was born,' Clara said.

'How about you and Gus? You obviously got back on track,' Amber said. 'How did you manage to do that?' Clara noted that the other woman was very keen to know the answer to this question.

'It took a long time, Amber. All the wasted time was my fault, I must add. Gus was astonishing. He was so protective of Max. I suppose they'd bonded in those first crucial hours. In turn, they ended up forging a wonderfully close relationship that nobody could touch.'

'You must've been so relieved that Dad was being so fantastic with Max,' Ava said.

'I was, *Liebling*, but I couldn't get past the crippling guilt that was threatening to ruin my life. I had nightmares about Jacob and felt utterly responsible for his broken heart. I blamed myself for ruining his life, not once but twice. I honestly felt I must be evil. I figured that Gus and Jacob would have been just fine had they not met me.'

'Oh Mama,' Ava said. 'That wasn't the case.'

'Ava, I broke Jacob's heart as a little boy and again when he was a grown man. I even attempted to convince myself that it was my fault that my mother and father had lived through such horror and heartache. After all, *I* was the common denominator in all of it.'

'Oh Oma, I can't believe you thought that. You didn't encourage Hitler's men to take Hannah!'

'I hit rock bottom, Nathalie. I had no energy or *joie de vivre* and I was aware that I had two children depending on me. I honestly didn't know what to do.'

'So what happened? What changed your mind?' Ava asked.

'I went to Mama. I told her everything and begged her to help me. I don't think I expected to find the answers – she was already slipping away from us into a dark and deep place – but I had nowhere else to turn.'

'I'm sure she was more than happy to help you, Mama,' Ava said.

'Yes, she was,' Clara said fondly. 'Mama had never been anything but meek and mild. To a stranger she appeared to be afraid of her own shadow. But when I went to her that day, that same strength and fire that had kept her going through Bergen-Belsen and the years of separation from her family reignited.'

'What did she do?' Nathalie asked.

'Mama wasn't a touchy-feely sort of woman. How could she be? Very few people had ever shown her affection . . . Also, I think she'd witnessed too much horror to end up that way inclined. But, my goodness, was she brave and practical! She did something that has always stayed with me. She told me some home truths. She laid it all on the line.'

'Did she tell you to cop on and stop wallowing?' Ava asked, looking slightly shocked.

'In a nutshell,' Clara grinned. 'I know it's certainly not the way of the world these days. Now it's all about finding your feelings and working through your inner thoughts . . . But she spoke about the concentration camp and the fear that she might never escape. She said I was the only thing that kept her alive during her detention. She'd given up all hope of ever seeing Lukas again. She filled me in on the fresh terror she'd endured when she took me from Alina and Frank, and how she had struggled to cope with guilt, terror and mind-blowing flashbacks that threatened to mar the future.'

'So how *did* she manage?' Amber asked.

'She said she had a defining moment,' Clara said. 'She was serving supper to Lukas and me in our kitchen when she had an out-of-body experience. She suddenly compared that homely scene to the ones at Bergen-Belsen, and understood how lucky she was to be alive. She knew that all the years of fighting to survive would be utterly in vain unless she grasped her new life with both hands.'

'And how did that help you?' Nathalie asked with interest.

'It made me realise that I was in danger of falling into the exact same trap. I'd made a mistake. A stupid and selfish one at that. But Gus was willing to stay with me and continue to love me.' She sighed. 'I was committing the worst crime of all by wallowing in the negative and refusing to embrace the positive.'

'That's kind of harsh, don't you think?' Nathalie said. 'I mean, most people don't experience half of what you did in a lifetime and they struggle with stuff. It's human nature, isn't it?'

'Of course, dear,' Clara agreed. 'But we always have a choice. We can either sit back and allow the bad things to win, or we can stand up and fight.'

'And you put on your boxing gloves that day,' Nathalie finished. Clara nodded emphatically.

'It wasn't easy. I had dark days where the guilt and sadness shadowed me like a cloud. But after a spell I got better at being happy. It takes practice, you know.'

'Some days I wake with a heaviness in my heart and it takes me a moment to figure out what's hanging over me. Then I remember Mackenzie's frozen face as she lay in the hospital. It's so hard to believe she's gone, and I get a tightening in my chest and fear I can't live without her.'

'I can appreciate how you feel,' Ava said. 'Grief can be so dreadful at times that I feel as if I'll choke.'

Clara tilted her head to the side. Nathalie's brow furrowed as she tried to work out who Ava might be referring to.

'It's good to remember loved ones who have passed away. You'll never forget them. Trust me. The people who make a mark on your heart never truly leave. You simply learn how to carry on without them.'

'We need to accept that life is different but not necessarily awful all the time,' Ava said. 'I'm sure you miss Dad terribly. I know I do.'

'Yes,' Clara agreed. 'I miss him all the time. But I promised him I wouldn't spend the rest of my life waiting to die. That'd be a shame.'

'That's pretty amazing,' Amber said. 'It makes my heart glad that you and Gus were able to rekindle your marriage. He sounds like a wonderful man.'

'He was,' Clara said. 'As I've said many times, he was the love of my life. It still terrifies me to think that I could have lost him.'

A silence descended upon the room. But it wasn't awkward. This was different. Each person was clearly lost in thought as they tried to process the events of the past.

Clara needed to be alone for a few moments. She had the perfect excuse to escape.

'You all stay put,' she announced. 'I insist. I have something tasty for dessert ready to go. I only need a few moments in the kitchen.'

'Please let me know if I can be of assistance,' Amber said.

Amber was being marvellous. Clara liked her a lot. She was certainly an all-American lady. From the way she spoke to her perfectly coiffed appearance. She was just what Max needed.

As she ladled the warm berry salad on to plates to accompany Nathalie's vanilla cake, her granddaughter padded into the kitchen and rubbed her back tenderly.

'Well done, Oma,' she said with genuine affection. 'You never cease to amaze me. Your courage and honesty is mind-blowing. You rock!'

'Even though you now know I'm a scarlet woman?' Clara asked seriously.

'People who play by the rules *all* the time make me nervous,' Nathalie said. 'Who wants to be related to people who never break out and do something left of centre?' She raised an eyebrow.

'We'll talk more when everybody leaves, OK?' Clara said.

'Don't you know it!' Nathalie said, hugging her again. 'But right now, this looks totally awesome.'

Grabbing the laden tray, Nathalie shuffled into the dining room.

'Just wait until you taste this, Mom,' she said. 'It's to die for!'

The atmosphere was certainly still strained, but Clara knew the worst was over. All that remained was for them to digest the information and decide whether or not they could come to terms with it.

With plates and glasses charged, she proposed a toast.

'To family,' she began. 'To forgiveness, and to knowing it's never too late to start again.'

They all clambered to their feet and joined the toast. There wasn't much said, but Clara was relieved that both her children clinked glasses.

'Tuck in, everyone,' Nathalie said. 'Mom, just wait until you try this cake. I baked it from scratch. Oma knows how to do some totally awesome stuff.'

Amber's eyes rolled as she tasted the dessert. The combination of the warm, rather sharp-tasting berries cooked in syrup and the fresh, light sponge was delectable.

'It's nice that you're learning some traditions. It's good to see it all being passed on,' Max said.

The rest of the evening was filled with pleasant, if slightly forced, conversation. The tension was hard to ignore.

By nine thirty, Amber was visibly wilting.

'I think I need some sleep,' she said apologetically.

'I'll drop you both at the hotel,' Ava said. 'I've an early start tomorrow.'

'You're welcome to stay here, of course,' Clara said.

'No, we'll be fine at the hotel, thanks,' Max said.

Clara showed them out and returned to the dining room, where Nathalie had made great headway clearing up.

'Leave it, dear. I'll do it in a while.'

'No way.' Nathalie was emphatic. 'You sit down and try to fathom what the hell just happened there.'

'It was a little crazy really,' Clara said. 'Crazy good, though, eh?'

'Oma, it was awesome. I know it's going to take plenty of time before everybody feels relaxed, but it was a good start. You gotta expect the awkwardness and kooky silences. It'd be pretty damn weird if we all slotted into place and started acting like the Brady Bunch.'

Clara laughed. 'You're right, dear. It was fine, I suppose, considering that it took twenty years to happen.'

'You're brave,' Nathalie said. 'It can't have been easy to talk to your own kids about an affair.'

Clara sighed and shook her head. She recalled the day Max found Jacob's letter.

'He was always a sensitive soul, your father. So he took it very badly. Not that I blame him, you understand? He was adamant that his sister never know the truth.'

It turned out that Max had gone to his university tutor and arranged to have his course transferred to LA. Within two weeks he was gone.

All Ava knew was that there'd been a dreadful row. At the time, Clara and Gus had reassured her that Max would return. As the months marched on and there was no sign of him, it became an unmentionable subject.

Sean and Ava's break-up and little Angelina's death took centre stage after that. As the years rolled by, they all had to come to terms with the fact that Max didn't want anything to do with them.

'The argument was mine and Max's, but his stubborn resistance and refusal to see or speak to Ava eventually had the desired effect. She pretty much wrote him off.'

'I know I'll toss and turn half the night if I try to sleep now,' Nathalie said. 'Would you mind if I pop into the sewing room for a spell?'

'I'll join you. It sounds like a lovely idea.'

Not for the first time, sewing and being creative was just the therapy the Conway women needed.

Chapter 29

NATHALIE AND CLARA WERE SEWING PEACEFULLY when Ava reappeared, having dropped Max and Amber at the hotel.

'Are you OK, lovey?' Clara asked in surprise.

Ava clenched and relaxed her fists as she paced. 'I was driving home and I knew I'd be awake all night if I didn't come back and talk this out with you.'

'OK, *Liebling*, what did you need to know?' Clara asked patiently.

Ava looked pained. 'I know you've said so much tonight, but would you mind telling me a little more about the time Oma and Opa came to collect you from Alina and Frank's?'

Clara looked exhausted and Ava felt a bit mean about asking for further details, but she wanted to strike while the iron was hot. Now that the seal had been broken on the silence, it was as if she couldn't get enough information.

Clara smiled and said she'd be happy to continue talking. She cast her mind back and tried to recall the scene as best she could, to help Ava understand.

'It became apparent that Lukas had managed to organise some forged papers to allow Hannah and me to leave Austria. But time was of the essence. If we didn't make it on to a certain ship at a set time, Hannah would be in danger.'

'Wasn't the war over?' Ava asked.

'Yes, but there was still ferocious anger amongst Austrians.

There were many ongoing feuds involving anti-Semitic groups. People weren't going to change their minds overnight. My father knew it would be years before it was entirely safe for Jews to live comfortably in Austria.'

'I suppose it would take a while for people to learn to stop the hate,' Nathalie said.

'Alina took me to my little bedroom and packed some clothes into a red leather suitcase. On top of the clothes she laid the pretty pastel patchwork quilt we had lovingly crafted together.'

'Is that the one you've always had on your bed?' Ava asked.

'Yes, *Liebling*, it is,' Clara said tenderly.

'Wow, it must bring you comfort to have it close to you after all these years. I know mine is going to do that for me,' Nathalie said.

'Oh yes. To me the pieces of fabric represent the love we will always share. Mama Lee-Lee was so brave. I still remember her exact words as she placed the quilt in my suitcase: "The patches are sewn together and will remain fastened and bonded for ever. No matter where you go in this world, you will never leave my heart, Clara."

'Of course I cried and begged to stay. But Mama Lee-Lee reiterated that I wasn't hers to keep. She took my hand and placed it on her heart. Just like this.' Clara took Ava's hand and placed it on her chest. Nathalie watched on in awe.

'Can you feel my heart beating?' she whispered.

Ava nodded.

'Alina instructed me to place my hand on my own heart any time I was lonely for her. She held my gaze just the way I'm holding yours right now. She told me we were like two synchronised cuckoo clocks and that a part of her heart would always beat with mine.'

'Wow,' Ava said. 'I'm blown away by that and I wasn't even there! How did you cope, Mama?'

'Mama Lee-Lee made me promise to make her proud. She told me that my mother was a wonderful woman who deserved to have me back. That my job was to help her smile and heal her poor sad heart. That Hannah had been subjected to years of cruelty and I could help save her.'

'That's too much to lay at the feet of a tiny child,' Ava said, looking cross.

'None of it was easy for any of us, lovey. But there wasn't time for stamping our feet and pouting. We had no choice but to deal with it as best we could.'

'I know all about not having a choice,' Ava whispered sadly.

'Mama Lee-Lee gave me some very sound advice as I left her. She told me to be a good girl, and above all she told me I needed to learn to be happy again. That we only had one life and one chance to live and I mustn't waste it crying.'

'She was a tough cookie, wasn't she?' said Nathalie.

'She was,' Clara said, smiling through her tears. 'But her words made me strong, Nathalie. I hugged her and stood tall, jutting out my little chin and squeezing my back teeth together to stop myself from sobbing. Then I walked down those wooden stairs to the people waiting in the kitchen and announced that I was ready to go.'

'Jeez, you were a little fireball,' Ava said. 'If anyone had tried to make me leave home when I was eight, I think I would've curled up into a ball and died.'

'Well, luckily you weren't faced with such a conundrum. People have a habit of stepping up to the plate when situations dictate it,' Clara said. 'If anyone had forewarned you that your beautiful Angelina was going to die, I'm guessing you'd have said you couldn't go on living.'

'Who was Angelina?' Nathalie asked in confusion.

Ava looked to Clara and she nodded. Taking Nathalie's hand

she began to tell her what had happened and how time had certainly helped to heal some of the hurt. But how she often struggled to carry on still. Nathalie sobbed as Ava held her tightly and rocked her.

'Oh Ava, I had no idea,' she said. 'But now it makes sense. I know how you've understood my feelings about losing Mackenzie. I get it now. I'm so proud of you for keeping going. You're even more amazing than I thought.'

'I have had moments where I feel I can't go on,' Ava admitted.

'But you're doing it, darling. You're surviving,' said Clara. 'It's called growing up. Some people never do, you know? That's not a good thing. We all need to stop and take our emotional temperature every now and again. I do it regularly. I give myself a moment to look around and check whether I'm doing my best to be happy.'

'It's odd that you mention this,' Ava said, dropping her gaze. 'Lately I've looked at myself and wondered where I'm going in life. I'm lonely, Mama. I wish I had someone to share my bed and my life with.'

Clara hugged her. 'You've just taken the most important step, *Liebling*. You've admitted you want somebody to love. For years I've witnessed you charging about like a headless chicken, running to the arms of anyone who'll have you and rushing away just as swiftly. Try to trust people. There are far more wonderful people than evil ones in this world. I firmly believe that.'

'I do too,' Nathalie said. 'I know I'm only a little skut and I've a lot to learn. But the feel of someone's arms holding you tight has got to be one of the best ones imaginable.' Ava smiled at Nathalie and over at her mother.

'I get it now, Mama. But I'm still in awe of you. You were some gutsy kid. I don't care what you say. You had grit.'

'I'll say,' Nathalie agreed widening her eyes.

Clara laughed. 'I suppose I did!'

'What happened with Jacob that day?' Ava suddenly asked.

'As Dr Schmitt's car was driving away, Jacob shot out of the house. Dr Schmitt had to slam on the brakes. Jacob yelled my name and lunged towards the back window where I was sitting. I wound the handle down and opened the window as fast as I could. He shoved a die-cast model of a red fire engine in through the window.'

'How sweet!'

'Well, it was his favourite toy. I told him I couldn't accept it. In my innocence I said, "I can't take that, it's your very best thing!" To which he answered, "No, Clara, *you* are."'

'Oh Mama,' Ava said. 'My heart is breaking even thinking about that. The poor boy must've felt as if his world was being torn apart too. How did you cope driving away with a group of total strangers like that?'

'The doctor was a lovely man. In retrospect, it must have been the strangest atmosphere. My parents and I were so shell-shocked I don't think we knew what we ought to say or do. Dr Schmitt kept the conversation going as we wound our way through the hills and towards the city.'

'I'd say it was totally surreal.'

'It probably sounds incredibly odd to you, but I was OK. I was massively excited about the prospect of going on a ship. We were also headed for the big city of Vienna, which I'd only ever heard about. Don't forget, children think differently to adults. I wasn't really looking that far ahead. I was caught up in the adventure and living for the moment.'

'It sounds like a movie . . . But I can't say I would've liked to be part of the cast like you were.'

'Once we arrived in Vienna, Hannah and Lukas rushed away while Dr Schmitt took me to a coffee shop.'

'No! Did you think you were being abandoned? Where did they go?'

'Well, I clearly recall sitting on a high stool with my legs swinging as I drank hot chocolate from a bowl and ate the most delicious almond croissant I'd ever tasted.'

'Weren't you frightened?'

'No, I wasn't actually. Dr Schmitt was wonderful, as I've already said. He had the most calming, easy manner. Instinctively I knew he wasn't going to allow me to come to any harm. Needless to say, since he'd bought me the hot chocolate and the croissant, as far as I was concerned we were pals. What do they call it? Ah, cupboard love!'

Ava laughed. 'I can get with that. When I was little, I loved anyone who'd bring me to the sweet shop!'

'There you go,' Clara said nodding. 'Well, Dr Schmitt and I were chatting quite happily when the door burst open and Hannah and Lukas rushed in with the happiest smiles I'd ever seen. Hannah was like a different person. She'd been meek and desperately sad-looking before that point. But now there was a pinkness to her cheeks and her eyes were dancing.'

'Where had they been?'

'To the registrar's office to get married,' Clara said.

'No way!'

'When I think about them now, it still brings me such joy. I know that was a major turning point for me. I knew by the looks on their faces that they loved one another totally. At the tender age of eight, I suddenly understood what true love actually *looked* like. I could see it beaming from their souls.'

'Amazing,' Ava said, shaking her head. 'And so romantic.'

'Lukas was ecstatic too. He scooped me up and swung me around, kissing my cheeks and telling me we were a real family now. I was truly happy for them, but I also felt so torn. Alina and Frank were obviously the only parents I'd ever known. Yet here were two wonderful people with such love in their eyes for me. I sat back on my high stool and watched them. Lukas couldn't keep his hands off Hannah. He was so protective. His hand was around her waist, on her shoulder, touching her hair or holding her hand.'

'Almost as if he was afraid to let her go?'

'Precisely, dear.' Clara nodded. 'It soon became clear to me that we were indeed meant to be together. There was a kind of magic beaming from both of them. By the time we left the patisserie, Lukas's excitement was contagious. He had so many plans for *mein Mädchen* – my girls – as he called us. I think Hannah and I were simply swept along on the wave of his enthusiasm.'

Clara told Ava how they'd rushed to make it to the train station so they could travel to Rotterdam in order to catch the ferry. They bid farewell to kind Dr Schmitt before Lukas bundled them on to a waiting train.

Clara longed to explore the train, but Lukas reiterated that they needed to stay together and wait until they reached the safety of Hull port in Rotterdam. Once they were safely on the port, over ten hours later, Clara noticed Lukas visibly relaxing. She remembered being impressed by the sheer size of the ship, and by the well-dressed folk on deck.

'It was so exciting, I think I quite forgot to be sad.'

Lukas did all the talking while she and Hannah remained mute. Mercifully the guard waved them on, the ship's horn sounded and within moments they were tugging away from Rotterdam and the life they'd known.

'I went up on deck and gripped the side of the ship, watching the shoreline disappear. As soon as land faded, I turned to look at the other passengers. Oh, the fashions were magnificent!'

'Were the ladies all in frock coats with bonnets and sassy lacy parasols?' Ava asked, caught up in the imagery.

'Oh no, at that time there was very little fabric available so it was all about nipped-in waists with accessories like gloves or if you were fortunate enough a hat with a feather was all in. I can still recall the sound of fine leather hitting the boards as the ladies walked on deck. It was like nothing I'd ever experienced before.'

'It sounds like a scene from *Titanic*,' Ava sighed.

'To me it was even better,' Clara said. 'I was never so proud of my own moss-green pea coat with matching hat. Mama Lee-Lee had always dressed me like a little doll, even though I was a dreadful tomboy. I was happiest up a tree or swinging from a rope. I could outrun Jacob by the time I was six!'

'I'd say you were pretty,' Ava said dreamily. 'You were always beautiful when we were younger, so I can only imagine how stunning you were then. It's only just struck me that there are no baby photos of you in the house. Wow, isn't it amazing how I grew up without knowing any of this stuff and never really noticed? What kind of a person does that make me?'

'Children go along with what they know, Ava. I never made a fuss of the circumstances in which I'd come to Ireland, so why would you have delved into them?'

'Hey, I'm worse than you,' Nathalie pointed out. 'I thought Oma was dead and never thought to question it ever.'

'I suppose Mama is right,' Ava said. 'We go along with whatever we are presented with in life. Plus, our relationship with Oma and Opa was always so positive too, so I never suspected they'd been through so much.'

'They idolised you and Max,' Clara said wistfully. 'I know Mama especially doted on you as a baby. I think she was making up for lost time. She used to just appear at the door. I often asked Gus if it bothered him, but he was terribly patient in that way. She loved to bathe and dress you and spent hours sitting and gazing at you.'

'It must've been quite hard for her in many ways.'

'Oh it was, dear. She used to cry and say how sorry she was that she hadn't had those times with me. But I always assured her I hadn't missed out on anything. Sadly, she was the only one who had been deprived during that awful time.'

'I know you said you simply adapted, but wasn't there even a small part of you that was terrified when you came to Ireland at first?' Nathalie asked.

'Of course,' Clara answered honestly. 'But I forced myself to focus on my innate sense that Hannah and Lukas were good, kind people. During the course of that long boat journey I got to know them a little. My mother was clearly damaged. She was timid and nervous and so unsure. I think that brought out an inner strength in me. I felt indescribably protective towards her.'

'How was Opa?' Ava asked.

'Oh, he was vibrant! He had mischievous eyes and a wonderfully wicked sense of humour. He was incredibly tactile and obviously adored us both. He told us every hour how blessed he felt that we'd been reunited.' Her expression darkened momentarily. 'The hardest part was how I was to address them. I didn't want to call them Mama and Papa.'

'No, of course not,' said Ava. 'Because you'd just left the people you thought fitted those names.'

'Precisely,' Clara said. 'Lukas and I had a lovely moment out on deck. It was evening time and as the journey was going to take almost two days it was a good opportunity to get acquainted. Hannah was resting, and we lay down on the wooden boards and gazed up at the inky sky. He told me how he'd wished upon those very stars each and every day that he would find us. He said I was worth more to him than any money or jewels. I picked up on the German word for jewel and nicknamed him Ju-Ju.'

'I never knew that was why you called him that. I figured it was just a meaningless endearment. I heard you using that name several times and I never thought to ask why.'

'He was my knight in shining armour, my golden star and most definitely more precious than any jewel. I still miss him each and every day. I hope you're watching over me and that you can see us sitting here, my darling Ju-Ju,' Clara said, turning her face upwards.

'I called Hannah by her first name for many years. You were the catalyst I needed to eventually call her Mama. She was with me when I had you. She held my hand and supported me every step of the way. Your father was a doctor, as you know. He worked at the hospital and I was meant to go there to give birth. But you had different plans! The labour and birth were swift and I ended up having you on the floor in the hallway at home!'

'I always like to make an entrance,' Ava grinned.

'Hannah handed you to me for the first time and stroked the hair back from my forehead. As she bent to kiss me, instinctively I said "Thank you, Mama."'

'Wow, that's powerful,' Ava said. Flapping her hands in front of her face, she tried to blow away her tears.

'It was also a turning point for us as I had complications following your birth. I began to bleed furiously and Mama needed to take control, which she duly did. She called an ambulance and managed to keep me calm until the medics arrived to help me.'

'That all sounds horrific,' Nathalie said, shuddering.

'Do you actually believe in heaven, Mama?'

'Oh yes,' Clara said. 'I think there's an amazing place waiting for us all. I think it's full of the things that make us happy. There's no suffering or hurt. People don't worry about whether they're fat, thin, blonde, brunette, rich or poor. And nobody is sick. There's no cancer, heart disease or strife.'

'That sounds wonderful,' Ava smiled.

'Yes, it does,' Clara agreed. 'Most of all, there's no brutality. It's serene. Like the very best day we can imagine, all the time.' She sat upright. 'But there's still time to have fun while we're roaming around this beautiful earth,' she added.

'I know, but it's not easy, is it?'

'No. I often have to scold myself. I've looked in the mirror on more than one occasion and told myself in no uncertain terms that I mustn't waste the time I have here. Life is precious. It's a gift.'

'I agree with you,' Ava said eventually. 'But I find the unfairness of Angelina's death seriously difficult to get my head around.'

'I appreciate that. She was such a beautiful and precious little girl. But unless you want to drive yourself insane, you're going to have to accept that she's gone.' Clara rubbed Ava's arm gently. 'I'm not saying that's going to stop the hurt, but sadly there's absolutely nothing we can do about death bar accept it. The best way for you to do her memory justice is to enjoy your own life.'

By the time Ava left, Clara was yawning.

'I can't believe it's three o'clock in the morning,' Nathalie said with a grin. 'When I've stayed up this late before it was either at a sleepover when Mackenzie and I were much younger, or a few months back when I was drinking lots.'

'It's a long time since I've done this for any reason,' Clara smiled. 'I enjoyed it, though, and I know I wouldn't have slept. So thank you for keeping me company.'

'Hey, the pleasure is all mine.'

'Tonight has been a long time coming. I had begun to lose hope of ever seeing Max again,' Clara admitted. 'You were great this evening, Nathalie. You've a wise head on young shoulders.'

As she lay in bed, Clara smoothed out her patchwork quilt and allowed it to transfix her just as it had done for decades. She never grew tired of admiring the multitude of patterns and pretty fabrics. Tracing her finger over the shapes, she thought of Gus. Was he looking down on them all this evening? Was he with Jacob? Did they talk up there in heaven? Had they made peace with one another?

It would probably sound crazy to anyone else, but one of the first thoughts Clara had had when her darling Gus passed away was of Jacob. She wondered if he was feeling sheepish in heaven. Had he apologised to Gus for the affair?

'I'm so sorry you never got to see Max again,' she whispered to Gus. 'He's such a fine man.' She teared up and addressed Jacob. '*You* missed him entirely. I hope you were both with me this evening. Even if you were sitting in separate parts of heaven.'

Clara didn't advocate the idea of keeping regret alive in her heart. But she still struggled to forgive herself for that night with Jacob. In spite of her speech this evening, at moments like this, when she was all alone with nothing but her conscience to keep her company, she still felt immense guilt for what she'd done.

She'd tried to reason that Jacob had died in tragic circumstances. But she knew in her heart of hearts that he had left this world feeling desperate and desolate because of her.

After Max's birth, she'd written to Alina and Frank. It was the most difficult letter she'd ever written. In it, she'd apologised for any part she might have unwittingly played in Jacob's demise. She said how sorry she was that he'd suffered after she'd left as a child. She thanked them for being so wonderful and explained that she'd never forgotten them.

Lastly, she'd explained about Max and asked if they would like to meet him

Ju-Ju and Hannah knew she was extending the invitation and said they'd welcome the couple with open arms.

They all waited with bated breath for the response. When six months passed with no reply, Clara sent another letter.

'The first one hasn't come back, so I'm assuming they received it,' she said to Ju-Ju. 'Surely if they've moved, the new occupiers would have the decency to return the letter . . .'

'Yes, I would have thought you'd have it back by now if they weren't there.'

The second letter was similar to the first, full of apologies and concern. She begged them to write back, but assured them she understood totally if they wanted nothing more to do with her.

Silence prevailed.

Clara took that as a sign that they weren't destined to be in contact, and left it there. She'd noticed the anxious look on Gus's face each morning as he checked the post.

'I don't think they're going to write,' she said one morning as he placed more bills on the kitchen counter. 'I've done what I can, so I feel we should try and move on. Get on with the rest of our lives.'

Gus smiled and she knew she'd said the right thing.

Clara went through phases of being almost choked by guilt over the next couple of years. But when Hannah passed away, a new feeling engulfed her. She realised that the past needed to be left where it was and that the present and the future were the most important.

Two days before her death, Hannah had a window of lucidity where she asked Clara to fulfil a promise.

'There are so many things we cannot control in this life,' she said. 'So often we are thrust into situations we don't wish for. There's no right or wrong way to deal with our mistakes, but I would urge you to leave the past behind. Move on with your life. Gus is a good man. You made a mistake but you've apologised. He forgives you. Be happy. Accept his forgiveness before he changes his mind.'

Clara drew on her mother's words often. But every now and again, the awful niggling at the back of her mind won over.

The fact that she'd never heard from Alina and Frank hurt dreadfully, and to this day she wondered what had become of them.

Chapter 30

IT WAS SIX O'CLOCK IN THE MORNING AND AVA WAS wired. She knew she'd probably want to sleep later, but right at this moment she wanted to talk about Sean. The only person she could think of telling was Max. She knew she could have told him last time they'd met, but she didn't feel quite ready to have a heart-to-heart with him after so many years of estrangement. Now seemed like the right time. She dialled his cell number.

'Hi,' she said. 'Were you sleeping?'

'I wish I was,' he said. 'Clearly you're wide awake too.'

They arranged to meet for breakfast in twenty minutes.

At the hotel, she explained about her conversation with Sean and how he was winging his way over to see her.

'That's great,' Max said, looking genuinely pleased for her. 'It's about time you guys had a proper talk. You have so much to share with him.'

'Even if we never see one another again after this, it's going to put my mind at ease. I'm so happy that I'll be able to show him all the mementos I have of Angelina. I have a shoebox with some memories inside.'

'Seeing as we're having a let's-bare-our-souls session . . .' Max flicked his hair in agitation. 'Can I tell you something?'

'Go for it,' she said, sitting up and crossing her legs.

'There was another reason I stayed away for so long,' Max said. 'I had a letter from Alina and Frank.'

'Jacob's parents?'

'Yes, my grandparents,' Max pointed out.

'Duh, of course. Sorry, I wasn't thinking.'

'They wrote to me just after I moved to America. It turns out they'd been keeping tabs on me via a private detective for years.'

'Did you feel creeped out when you realised they'd been stalking you?' Ava asked.

He laughed. 'Well, it was hardly that. They simply hired a man to give them quarterly updates along with some photographs over the years.'

'Jeepers, I'm sorry but I think that's total stalker territory.' Ava shuddered. Max paused and closed his eyes. 'Sorry,' she said. 'Continue.'

'So about eighteen years ago they got in touch. In the letter, Alina told me all about Jacob as a tiny baby and their joy when Mama came into their lives.'

Max explained how Alina had felt that Clara had completed their family. She was the most precious gift they could have hoped to receive. When news came that Hannah and Lukas were on their way to take her back, they were understandably devastated.

Once Clara left, a shadow descended over their home. Jacob retreated to a place where neither of his parents could reach him. Their previously sunny-natured boy was withdrawn and sullen.

When he announced his desire to become a doctor, they were overjoyed. Money they'd carefully put aside over the years was proudly handed over. His brilliance paid off, and he was offered a once-in-a-lifetime opportunity to travel the world teaching fellow surgeons a new technique in brain surgery. They had no idea he was heading for Ireland.

They heard nothing from him for several months, until a most bizarre call came. Jacob told them that he and Clara were a couple. He said the situation was a little complicated as Clara was married to a man called Dr Gus Conway. When Alina tried to question him, he became irrational and angry, yelling at her to mind her own business and to stop trying to ruin his life. He said she would only hear from him when he was ready to bring Clara home.

They waited and waited for Jacob to contact them again. Days turned to weeks before Walter Brandt called them and their worst fears were realised.

'It was so tragic,' Ava said. 'That car crash . . .'

'You haven't heard it all yet,' Max said. 'Alina asked me to respond to her letter. To an address in Vienna.'

'So that's why they never replied to Mama's letters.'

'Yes, clearly the new owners didn't pass them on.'

'What did you say when you wrote back?'

'I was so angry back then,' Max admitted. 'I told them they were a part of my life that I wasn't proud of and that I wanted to start afresh with my pregnant wife. I asked them in no uncertain terms to stay away from me.'

'Oh Max,' Ava whispered. 'You really cut yourself off from everyone, didn't you?'

He sighed. 'I felt utterly trapped and boxed in by the weight of the past. At that time I was convinced that the best way out would be to reinvent a whole new life with Amber and Nathalie. To me they were pure and free of the shackles of my sordid past. I honestly thought I'd be happier with the slate wiped clean.'

'And were you?' Ava asked. 'Because you stayed away for a bloody long time.'

'I know,' he said. 'I'm not proud of how I acted, but I couldn't see a way out.'

'So if Nathalie hadn't had the accident, would you have come back?'

'It was a decent excuse,' he said sheepishly. 'I guess Mackenzie's death reminded me of the fragility of life. I heard Papa had died too. That rocked me to the core. Also I knew Nathalie was going to love you all. I guessed you'd love her too. But most of all, I'm tired of running and hiding.'

'I know what you mean,' Ava said. 'It gets kind of wearing after twenty years, doesn't it?' She smiled wryly.

'Alina wrote me another letter just before she passed away,' Max said. 'I received it shortly after Nathalie was born. She would have been on all sorts of drugs at that point, so she didn't hold back when it came to describing her emotions.'

'What did she say?' Ava asked.

'That Jacob had ripped her soul out. That she'd known there was something not quite right with him for years, but his brilliance and excellence in his field had sidetracked her and led her to question her suspicions.'

'Did they ever find out what happened the day he crashed?' Ava asked, shuddering.

'He didn't crash, Ava,' Max said gravely.

'But Mama said—'

'She doesn't know the truth,' Max interrupted. 'Jacob took a lethal overdose and left a separate note blaming Mama for everything bad that had happened in his life. He said his depression and sadness was brought on by post-traumatic stress disorder following her original departure.'

'Oh my God,' Ava said, aghast. She shook her head. 'But Mama had no choice but to leave with her parents . . .'

'Well any reasonable person can work that out,' Max said. 'Alina and Frank travelled to America to recover Jacob's body and managed to fit together the pieces of jigsaw that made up his sad life.'

'What did they find out?'

'Jacob was self-medicating for schizophrenia.'

'What?' Ava said. 'But how could he practise as a surgeon if he was on that stuff?'

'He was taking it in secret,' Max confirmed. 'The evidence was only found after his death. Alina uncovered a diary that he'd kept meticulously each day.'

'So he was a total nut job?' Ava said.

'You have such a gorgeous way with words, Ava,' Max said drily. 'He was extremely ill, and sadly, once he met up with Mama again, it seems he stopped taking his medication, firmly believing that her love would cure the desolation and sadness caused by his illness. It was all there in black and white for his poor parents to read.'

'That's so distressing,' Ava whispered. 'Do you reckon Mama knew he was so ill?'

'Gosh, no,' Max said, shaking his head. There was silence as both were caught up in thought.

'Alina finished her letter by saying that she would leave it up to me whether to tell Mama why and how Jacob died. I was so eaten up by anger that I kept it all from her.' Max looked utterly shattered. 'I did an awful thing, Ava,' he said. 'I wish I'd been braver. Alina and Frank have both passed away and I never gave Mama the opportunity to speak with them. I should have told her they'd sold the house in Brixental and moved to Vienna. If I'd been just a tiny bit less pig-headed, she would've been able to contact them before they died.'

'Oh Max.' Ava looked stricken. 'I'm sure Mama will forgive you. You've got to tell her immediately, though. The time for hiding and burying secrets has come to an end. If we want to progress and move forward as a family, all these secrets must be shared.'

'I know,' Max said. 'But I'm terrified Mama won't find it in her heart to forgive me.'

'All you can do is try,' Ava said. 'I'm not a betting woman, but if I were, I'd say she'll come up trumps. Of all the people I know, our mother is the wisest and most open-minded. You'll be doing her a favour, I reckon. She's always wondered what became of Alina and Frank. Set her mind at rest, Max, please.'

'I don't feel as bad about it all now that I've shared it with you.'

'A problem shared is a problem halved,' Ava grinned. 'Promise me you'll tell her before you return to America. I think she has a right to know. Awful and tragic as it was, she should be told the truth.'

'I know,' Max said, nodding.

'We're not exactly the perfect family, are we?' Ava said with a wry smile.

'No, we're pretty darn messed up,' he agreed with a grin. 'But on the up side, there's plenty of potential for improvement.'

'Do you think?'

'Yup, we can only go in one direction, and that's from rock bottom upwards!'

Ava looked at her watch and reluctantly realised she had to leave. She had some work to do and she needed to get some sleep before Sean arrived tonight.

She said she'd call Max later on once she'd met up with Sean. They hugged for the longest time before going their separate ways.

Chapter 31

CLARA COULDN'T GET USED TO THE FACT THAT Max was back in her life. It was a dream come true. As she lolled in bed, memories of Jacob and their time together came flooding back.

She remembered his face when she'd left Austria as a child. He'd looked as if his entire world was ending. It had plagued her dreams for years. She wished she could have seen him when they attended Oma Madeline's funeral, but it wasn't to be.

And the day she'd answered the door to him when he arrived in Ireland had been incredible. She'd recognised him instantly. His face had matured but his stance and his eyes were exactly the same. It was as if the world had stopped turning. The air became thick and she could barely contain herself. She'd thrown her arms around his neck and hugged him for the longest time. His expression emanated such raw and honest emotion, she'd been overwhelmed to see him. So much had happened in both their lives, yet it was as if they'd never been apart.

They'd whiled away the afternoon talking about days both had thought they'd forgotten. They recalled birthdays, Christmases and wonderful summer picnics. Clara knew it was the comfort of those shared memories and the knowledge that this man knew her better than anyone else at that time that had seduced her. She found it beguiling that he remembered her with such detail. She'd had to tuck it all into the far recesses of her mind for so long, that she often wondered if her early childhood had actually happened at all.

She had no photographs or mementos bar her patchwork quilt, her tiny red leather suitcase and of course Jacob's fire engine to remind her of the first part of her life.

So seeing him again, rebuilding a relationship and hearing all about Mama Lee-Lee and Papa Frank was like a reawakening from a partial coma.

But nothing would ever ease the aching guilt she still felt to this day as she recalled the night they'd spent together. Her feelings for Jacob were ones of deep and pure love, but never with a trace of lust. In her heart he was her brother, not her lover. But she'd allowed herself to be swept away on a road that she'd never have considered in the cold light of day. She hadn't many regrets in life. But she deeply regretted making love to Jacob.

The morning she began to vomit, she knew she was pregnant. She'd never felt worse than the day she told Gus her news. As he sat staring at her across the kitchen table, he looked as though the light had been extinguished in his soul.

She never intended to hurt people, but it always seemed to happen just the same.

They got through the trauma of the pregnancy and the dangerous birth and were still together. But they might as well have been living a thousand miles apart. Clara was so numbed by shame she could barely look Gus in the eye.

Gus was so hurt he struggled to smile.

Clara went to fetch Hannah late one afternoon. Max was in his playpen and Ava was busy with play dough. She explained that she needed to talk. Knowing the children were occupied, Clara hesitated.

'Come and sit with me,' Hannah instructed, producing a lemon drizzle cake. 'We'll have some coffee if you please, dear.'

Clara had brewed the coffee and joined her mother. Once Ava had been given a slice of cake, with a few bite-sized pieces for Max, Hannah spoke.

'I've been watching Gus. He is at his wits' end with you,' she stated. 'And so am I. You made a mistake, Clara. You've paid dearly. You are truly sorry. We know it and so do you. So now you're at a crossroads. Either you continue down the road of self-loathing you've placed yourself on and destroy your marriage and all you hold dear, or you take a new road with hope and positivity in your heart.'

'It's not as easy as all that, Mama,' Clara had said crossly.

'Actually,' Hannah paused, 'it is. You have the love of a good man. He's willing to forgive and forget but he can't do it alone. He needs you to join him.'

'I've tried,' Clara said, grinding tears away with her fists.

'With all due respect, Clara, you haven't tried one bit. You've wallowed and dragged yourself around looking as if you're expecting to be flogged. Hold your head up, my girl, and find that wonderful spirit we all know and love. Nobody wants to be shackled to a misery-guts.'

Clara spluttered and burst out laughing, almost choking on her tears.

'Mama! You're the most blunt and direct person I've ever met.'

'Yes, well . . .' Hannah tutted. 'Some matters require a gentle suggestion, while other times people need a straight shooter who will leave them in no doubt as to where they stand.'

'Well consider your shot a bullseye,' Clara giggled.

'*Liebling*,' Hannah said, grabbing her shoulders and holding her gaze. 'You are in danger of turning your back on a wonderful life. Open your eyes, ears and heart and move on. Move onwards and upwards. Don't question happiness when it's gently coaxing you towards its warmth. You need to separate your night with

Jacob from the existence of your son. One lasted a short time; the other will stay with you for as long as you live.'

'I'll try, Mama, but Max is a product of that one night.'

'That is a fact. But you need to put the two into different compartments in your brain. Pack the night with Jacob away and push Max and his need for his mother to the forefront. Otherwise you're headed for ruin, my child.'

'I want to be happy again, Mama,' she said sadly.

'There's enough cruelty going on in this world. Don't invite more of it to your door. Take a deep breath and release the guilt. It's possible, dear. I should know.'

'What do you have to feel guilty about, Mama?' Clara said. 'You've survived against the odds and built an amazing life for us all.'

'I'm glad you think that,' Hannah said. 'So stop trying to ruin what I've worked so hard to create.' She winked, then stared into the middle distance. 'I was racked with guilt for years, Clara. All I wanted was for Lukas to live the life he was destined for. He was born to be a leader, a gentleman.' She looked into Clara's eyes and stroked her cheek. 'For so long I feared I'd deprived him of his wealth. But now I know that no amount of money could ever have bought the love we share or the treasure that is you. I felt guilty for leaving you and dreaded the thought that you knew and felt abandoned. Believe me, *Liebling*, I understand how it feels to shoulder guilt. It's a heavy burden. But I carried on and in the end I realised that Lukas loved me, and I hope I am right in thinking that you have forgiven me for leaving you and then snatching you back again?'

'Of course I forgive you, Mama. Dear Lord, there's nothing to forgive in the first place. I love and admire you, and I thank God for every day we've had together.'

'Thank you, darling girl,' she smiled. 'You have filled my heart with more joy than you will ever know. So now, please, Clara, don't destroy the happiness thread. Preserve the joy. Allow it to flourish for generations to come.'

That was the moment Clara changed. She realised for certain that she was jeopardising her own future without respecting her past. She had the power to change things. All that was required was a bit of gumption.

Now, all these years later, the only question that remained unanswered lay with Alina and Frank. She longed to know what had become of them. She knew that the world worked in mysterious ways and that many of the issues her family faced had taken decades to resolve. But she was growing tired. She wanted things resolved.

Nathalie appeared at her bedroom door.

'May I come in?'

'Of course,' she said, smiling. 'How are you, *Liebling*?'

'OK. I've been doing a bit of soul-searching.'

'I see,' Clara said, moving over so Nathalie could get in beside her.

'I think I'd like to stay in Ireland for a bit. Defer my college course for a year and hang out. Would you consider allowing me to stay with you?'

'Well now,' Clara said, putting an arm around her. 'I should tell you to discuss this with your parents, which I know you will. I should tell you to think about it deeply, which I know you have. I should tell you to look into your heart to see if this is indeed the right thing for you . . .' She looked at her beautiful bronze-skinned granddaughter and grinned. 'You are welcome here whenever you wish, for as long as you see fit.'

'Thanks, Oma,' she said, wrapping her arms around her. 'That's all I wanted to hear. There's a part of me that knows I'm avoiding LA because Mackenzie is gone. But more than that, I feel as if

I belong here. It feels like I've come home. Does that sound crazy to you?'

'Not at all,' Clara said. 'Lochlann seemed like my home from the first moment I arrived. Why do you think I never left? Austria held too many harrowing memories for me. As a family we would never have been comfortable there. So this is the place where I know I was destined to stay.'

'I think I feel that way too.'

'I don't suppose your decision has anything to do with a certain red-haired strapping young man who resides at the beach, does it?' Clara asked with a grin.

'He's part of it,' Nathalie admitted as she told Oma all about his paintings.

'He's won many awards for his work, you know. He's been pictured in the papers and everything.'

'Really? Well I'm not surprised. He's the sweetest guy. He's so . . . comfortable in his own skin and why wouldn't he be . . . He's so darn gorgeous and funny and kind. He doesn't seem to think it's necessary to act like a jerk or carry on with annoying bravado the way some guys do . . . It's incredibly refreshing.'

'You need to speak to your parents, though. See what they think. Talk to them and try to listen. Let's not allow any more wedges to be driven between us as a family.'

'I know,' Nathalie said, sighing. 'I was thinking of asking Ava if I could help out at the shop for a bit. I'd love to learn more about design too.'

'I think you'd be fantastic at that, *Liebling*.'

'Tell me about your shop. How did it all begin?'

'At first I think it was a wonderful way for Mama to avoid having panic attacks. She suffered with post-traumatic stress disorder after Bergen–Belsen. Most of the time she could control it, but I knew it was an ongoing struggle. When I left school,

Mama made my prom dress. I had a matching velvet coat with the most incredible sequin detailing down the front and on the cuffs. I'd never had so much attention!'

Clara went on to explain that Hannah was usually immersed in looking after her boarders, but any time she was idle, the sweating would begin and her stricken look returned.

'If I suggested we sew for a bit, her shoulders would relax and the terrified look I'd become used to detecting would soften. The light came back into her eyes and I knew she was back with me again.

'Orders came in thick and fast from other girls and even their mothers. There were very few high street fashion stores catering for women, and the only shops that sold evening gowns and wedding dresses were extortionately expensive.

'We were making good money on the designs, but the house became a little crowded. Mama took matters into her own hands and approached Mr Wigfield, a property owner in Lochlann who had a small premises on the main street that had just become vacant. He had three young daughters, and Mama said she would make each girl a dress for Christmas, one for Easter and another on her birthday in exchange for the first two years of rent.'

'What a brilliant idea! Bartering at its best,' Nathalie said.

'As I've said so many times, Mama was astonishingly practical. She didn't look at conundrums feeling she couldn't solve them; she knew there was usually a straightforward way of getting things done. In fact, she was often far too direct for comfort. She had no problem with telling a woman, young or old, that something didn't suit them.

'"You'd be prettier in a grain sack . . . That makes you look as wide as a ship . . . That colour enhances one thing, the broken veins in your cheeks . . ." I used to laugh out loud at some of the things she came out with. The most hilarious part was that she was utterly unaware of the offence some women took. She'd tut and tell them to dash back into the changing room and put on something else. Then she'd wave her arms and exclaim how much better they looked in a different dress.'

'Honesty is the best policy in a boutique,' Nathalie said. 'There's nothing worse than some insincere person oozing all over you and saying you look fabulous when you know you look a fright.'

'You and Mama would've been a force to be reckoned with.'

'How did she cope with the bookkeeping and the business end of things?'

'Ah, she had a great plan for that too. She approached Mr White, the maths teacher at St Herbert's, and made a dress for his wife for the annual Christmas ball in exchange for his doing our bookkeeping.'

'Brilliant!' Nathalie grinned.

'She was fantastic at making money stretch, so she always kept back enough of the profit to buy fabric.'

'It sounds as if you had a constant stream of eager customers, mind you.'

'Yes, we did. In fact women used to travel from all over the country to order gowns. I remember sitting at the kitchen table with a hugely pregnant belly sewing lace appliqué on to a wedding dress while Mama chopped up a fur jacket.'

'Chopped up a fur jacket? A real one?' Nathalie asked.

'She started a restyling service for fur coats. Wealthy women who had full-length mink coats they didn't like any more came to us, and for a small fee Mama would cut them to the newly fashionable short length and add a large sparkly button or a new double cuff. We'd be paid and would usually end up with wonderful fur trimmings, which she turned into stoles or luxurious collars for winter gowns.'

'Wow, she was some businesswoman!'

'Most of her acumen came from necessity and living with so little for so long, rather than a conscious desire to become rich. She wasted nothing, took nothing for granted and saw potential in even the cheapest and most lacklustre fabrics.'

'So when did Ava get involved?' Nathalie wanted to know.

'From the time she was a couple of weeks old! We were so busy that I couldn't leave Mama to do it all alone. Ava was popped into her pram and brought to the shop as soon as I recovered from the birth.'

'No such thing as maternity leave back then!'

'Well not in our shop, I can tell you! I don't think I ever consciously planned to stay at the shop all my working life. But it felt right and I thoroughly enjoyed it. More than that, Mama and I became so much closer. We built a business and a relationship all at once. We were rich beyond our wildest dreams, in every sense of the word. The shop made a tidy profit and we rarely spent much. It was a little gold mine in a way.'

She described how Ava had displayed a talent for colour and design from a young age and was happy to join them in the business. She bought the adjoining units and expanded the boutique, making it into the thriving emporium it was today.

'Do you think she'd consider allowing me to help out?' Nathalie asked.

'I'm sure she'd be honoured and delighted. It makes my heart glad to know that you'll spend a bit of time there. You'll be the fourth generation to walk those floorboards. There's no pressure for you to stay, either. If your heart is set on medicine, that too is a tradition in the Conway family.'

Nathalie lay there thinking. Would her parents have a complete meltdown if she said she wanted to defer medical school? She didn't want to cause them any further distress, but she was certain this was the right thing for her to do. As she knew only too well, life wasn't a dress rehearsal; she only had one shot at it and she knew this move would make her happy. Conor's beaming face and cheerful laugh wasn't far from her mind either.

Chapter 32

MAX HAD TALKED IT THROUGH WITH AMBER ONCE Ava left that morning and both of them agreed that Clara had a right to know the truth about Jacob and Alina and Frank.

Feeling nervous, he hailed a cab and asked the driver to take him to his mother's house.

As soon as Clara spotted him through the window, she rushed to open the door.

'Hello there,' she said sunnily. 'Nathalie is taking a bath. She's pumping out that fun pop music she loves. It's a hoot having someone booming music again,' she said. 'I'm a bit florid in the face, I'd say. I was dancing!'

Max smiled in spite of his heavy heart. His mother really was completely bats. They ventured to the kitchen-cum-diner, where he perched on a chair.

'So, spit it out,' Clara said. 'Say what you need to say.'

Max smiled and shook his head.

'I haven't seen you for two decades and you can still read me like a book,' he said.

'I'm your mother, Max. Even if I didn't see you for thirty years, I'd still know you.'

He nodded silently. Closing his eyes for a moment, he took a deep breath.

'It's about Jacob,' he said.

'Oh?'

'Mama, he didn't die in a car crash. He committed suicide.'

Clara's hand shot to her mouth as she gasped.

'Tell me what you know,' she said.

Once Max started talking, he couldn't stop. The whole sorry story of Jacob's illness and Frank and Alina's discovery poured forth.

'So you knew all this time . . .' Clara looked over at him and tilted her head to the side.

'I'm so terribly sorry, Mama,' he said as tears trickled slowly down his unshaven face.

Standing up from her chair, Clara walked to him and held her arms out.

'You poor darling boy,' she said as she pulled him into her arms. 'You've held that terrible secret in your heart all this time.'

'But I thought you'd hate me,' he said. 'I was certain you'd never want to speak to me again once you knew I'd deprived you of the chance to get back in touch with Alina and Frank.'

'All I feel right now is desperate sadness for Jacob's poor tortured soul. I hope he's at peace. But most of all I am exceptionally pleased to know that Alina and Frank didn't detest me.'

'I should have told you long ago,' Max said. 'I had no right to leave you in the dark. I could have saved you years of torment.'

'Let's not look back, Max,' she said, sighing deeply. 'There's no point. We can't change any of it. The future is more important.'

Clara's usual answer to major problems, coffee and cake, was produced. They savoured the combination of sweet soft sponge and bitter strong coffee.

'There's something else bothering you,' Clara stated, looking into his eyes. 'What is it?'

He smiled wryly. 'I've been an idiot with Amber . . .'

He explained about the mix-up with Amy and how he'd been so emotionally absent with his girls over the years.

'You were doing your best, Max. Sometimes when you concentrate so hard on making work a success, home life slips. I know you would do anything for your girls. Any fool can see how much you love them. You've been sucked into the pressures of helping your colleagues and building your career. You have lots of time to put things right with Nathalie and Amber.'

'I'm a horrible person,' he stated.

'No, *Liebling*, you're not. You're only a man. Human nature is a complex thing and none of us is perfect.'

'I've been very good at blaming other people for things over the years. Everyone else was at fault in some way or another. Everyone except me.' He shook his head and wiped his tears with the back of his hand. 'How did I get to be such an arrogant shit?'

'If you hadn't a dash of arrogance, you wouldn't have made it as a surgeon. But we all have traits that mightn't be lovely. Becoming aware of them is the key. Being a shit is your own addition,' she said with a poker face. 'I can't help you with that.' He laughed.

'So what do you think I should do about Amber? I know she's feeling neglected and I want to show her how much I love her.'

'I think you should spend the rest of your life cherishing her and reminding her just how you feel about her. It won't be difficult. I did it with Gus and the pleasure was all mine. My affair with Jacob made us stronger in the long run. Our marriage was rock solid and so was our friendship. It can be done. You need to be prepared to work hard, though.'

He nodded. 'I need to forge a better relationship with Nathalie too. She needs to know how much I adore her.'

Clara smiled.

Max looked at his watch and realised the morning had run away with him. He promised to see Clara and Nathalie later that evening.

'Why don't you both come to the hotel for dinner tonight?'

'Phone and let me know,' Clara said. 'You and Amber may need a bit of breathing space.'

As soon as Max had gone, Nathalie walked into the room.

'There you are,' said Clara. 'What have you been up to? The music went off so I thought you might have gone out to see Conor.'

'I was in the sewing room. I need to get my head straight before I talk to my folks. I didn't want to tell Dad about my idea of staying without Mom being here.'

Clara explained that they had a loose arrangement to meet for dinner that evening.

'Cool, that'd be perfect. Is Aunt Ava coming?'

'Not that I know of. I'm not sure what she's up to,' Clara said absent-mindedly.

Nathalie tugged her *Oma*'s hand and they went into the sewing room. The quilt was almost complete.

'I'd like everyone in the family to sew on a patch. That would make it really special.'

'What a lovely idea,' Clara said. 'I've helped so I don't need to add to it.'

'Oh no!' Nathalie joked. 'You don't get away with it that

easily. I want you to do a special one that has meaning for you.'

Pondering for a moment, Clara walked to her shelves and picked out a plastic bag with dark green fabric inside.

'This is the remnants of the material Mama used to make the beautiful velvet coat for my prom. This very fabric started off the idea for our shop. I think it will be an apt reminder of all the generations of women who have been involved. My mama because she bought and sewed it, Ava because she grew up in the shop and has taken it over, and the two of us because we are doing this together.'

Nathalie stroked the kitten-soft fabric in awe.

'That's really special, Oma, thank you.'

Nathalie had a great feeling inside. She knew she was making the right decision to remain in Ireland. She hoped her parents would understand.

'Would you mind if I go for a quick walk? I won't be long,' she said.

'I think you could do with some fresh air,' Clara agreed. 'Besides,' she looked intently at what she was doing, 'I doubt you put on all that make-up and that belly top for my benefit.'

Nathalie bounded down to the beach. She didn't even need to wave. Herbie and Conor were already there.

'Nathalie, I'm delighted to lay eyes upon you,' Conor said, bowing dramatically.

'Guess what?' she said, wrapping her arms around his waist.

'Er, you've won the lottery?' he guessed.

'Sort of,' she grinned. 'Life's lottery, that is. I think I'm gonna stay here in Ireland for a bit.'

'Seriously?' he said, looking thrilled. 'So you'll be my Nathalie for a lot longer? Herbie,' he called. 'It worked, we've beguiled her!'

As Conor kissed her and swung her around, Nathalie giggled.

'Oh no you don't,' she screeched as he plucked her off the ground and headed at full tilt towards the ocean.

Chapter 33

AVA HAD TRIED ON ALMOST ALL THE DRESSES IN her wardrobe. Her bed looked as if a clothing recycling bank had exploded all over it. No matter what she put on, she didn't feel good enough to meet Sean.

She had no idea what sort of man Sean had turned out to be. But she desperately wanted to impress him. At the very worst she wanted to be sure she didn't disappoint him. She pulled her hair back off her face and scrutinised her wrinkles. She'd never thought of having Botox, but right at this moment she'd administer it herself with a sewing needle if she could get her hands on some.

She'd applied her make-up but was sweating so badly it was beginning to slide down her face. Opening the bedroom window, she stuck her head out and took some deep breaths.

Conscious that she could be spotted in her bra and knickers from the car park below, she retreated and found a plain black shift dress. She knew it would complement her figure while looking sophisticated. She paired it with black peep-toes and a simple clutch bag; her trusty string of Chanel pearls added class without being too over the top.

Her hand hovered over the three bottles of perfume on her dressing table. She still owned a bottle of Chanel No. 5. That was the scent she'd worn way back in the day. That was the one Sean would recall. Her heart thumping, she dabbed it on her pulse points and left the apartment.

She was a few minutes early and figured she'd have plenty of time for a glass of white wine to steady her nerves. She planned to be sitting on a high stool by the bar when he arrived, legs crossed, back straight, tummy pulled in and hair over one shoulder.

As she slammed the taxi door at the hotel entrance and stood back, her foot clipped the wheelie suitcase of a passing tourist and she lunged sideways.

'Oops-a-daisy,' she said, luckily finding her footing.

'That's the first time in twenty years I've heard anybody use that phrase.' She looked up and locked eyes with Sean.

'Oh!' she gasped. 'I wasn't expecting you just yet.'

'No, me neither. I was hoping to go for a sneaky pint to give me some Dutch courage,' he admitted.

She straightened her dress and attempted to arrange herself a little better. As if rooted to the spot, he stared at her.

'Hi,' she said, and an involuntary smile spread across her face. Automatically he leaned down and kissed her gently on the lips. She'd forgotten how tall he was. He looked almost exactly the same. His hair was slightly thinner and a lot greyer, but his expression hadn't changed. He inhaled deeply.

'Chanel Number Five.'

She nodded.

'Let's get inside and order some drinks,' he suggested. 'I think we both need one.'

It felt easy to slip her hand into the crook of his offered arm. She was more secure that way. It wouldn't have felt right to totter behind or ahead of him. The porter opened the door and offered to take Sean's bag.

'I haven't checked in yet, but I need to meet with this lady first,' he said.

'Of course, sir. I'll leave it at reception and let them know you've arrived.'

Ava perched on a high stool as planned, and Sean stood beside her, leaning against the bar.

'You look incredible,' he said.

'I do?' She looked doubtful.

'I'd forgotten how stunning you are . . . I knew there was a good reason why I've never been able to find anyone who even comes close to you over the years.'

She wanted to swat him and tell him he was being a corny silver-tongued chancer, but instead she had to fight back tears.

'You look great too,' she managed. 'Better than I thought I'd find you . . .'

'Cheers,' he said, and nudged her with his shoulder.

'That didn't come out the way I intended,' she said. 'I'm overwhelmed to see you, Sean.'

Their drinks arrived and they had no difficulty chatting. His openness astonished her. He didn't try to big himself up or show off. There wasn't a hint of anger or bitterness in his tone and he made it plain that he was thrilled to be home and to see her.

They ordered bar food and she was surprised to realise she was ravenously hungry.

He asked her to tell him more about Angelina, which she did with great joy, finding it liberating rather than traumatic.

'She was so beautiful,' she finished.

'Of course she was.'

Ava found Sean intoxicating. She waited until her bladder was at bursting point to even excuse herself to go to the ladies'. When she returned, he was standing waiting.

'I've checked in. But I'd like to see your shoebox of treasures,' he said. 'Will you take me to your apartment?'

She knew there was no need to act coy or play games. Too many years had been wasted and too much silence had passed between them. She took his hand, which felt natural, and led him to a taxi. The ten-minute journey seemed to take an eternity, but at last they arrived at her apartment.

'What happened in here?' he asked, looking around her bedroom in amused astonishment.

'Oh, sorry,' she said sheepishly. 'I was kind of hassled earlier trying to find something that made me look good.'

'You have to be the messiest broad I've ever met,' he said, laughing, as she swiped her arm across the bed to clear a space for them to sit.

She pulled the precious box from the wardrobe. Kicking off her shoes, she sat up on her hunkers and shared the memories of their daughter. Sean sobbed as he looked at the photo and held the tiny hospital bracelets.

'My hands are like shovels compared to these. She was so tiny.'

Ava stared at him as he drank in every detail of Angelina. The raw emotion on his face, the incredible love, blew her away.

'I'm more sorry than you will ever know,' she said finally. 'I should have told you.'

'Hey,' he said tenderly. 'I should have tried harder too.' He held up his little finger and indicated for her to link it with hers. 'Pinky promise that there's no blame game from here on in.' She nodded, tears peppering her eyes again.

When he leaned forward and kissed her, Ava was ready. As his lips touched hers, she realised that this was what she'd been waiting for the best part of twenty years.

Max closed his eyes and held Amber close.

'I've never loved you more than I do right at this moment,' he said, stroking her face. 'You've been so amazing to me over the years. You never pushed the point about my family. You allowed me to talk when I needed and left me alone when I didn't.'

'Er, honey,' Amber said, 'you *never* talked about your family. Just for the record, in case you go off into some dream land and think you didn't shun them for almost two decades.'

He grinned. 'I'm so lucky to have you here with me.'

They had met for lunch, just the two of them, and spent the afternoon talking. Amber had conceded that she'd been trying to punish him and make him aware that she wasn't a pushover.

'You're not a pushover, Amber. I'd built a wall so high around myself . . . I'd no intention of ever knocking it down. I'm my own worst enemy and so bloody stubborn.'

'It can be really hard to back down when you make up your mind about someone or something,' Amber accepted. 'But if we're to stay together and move forward with our lives, we need to communicate better.'

'I know,' he said. 'I get it, honestly I do. I'm lucky to have a second chance with you. I promise I won't mess up. I won't kiss anyone but you in the canteen again either.'

'You'd better not,' she said firmly. They'd ordered a bottle of champagne and spent the early evening making plans.

'I want us to spend more time in Ireland,' Amber said. 'If I know our daughter, and I reckon I do, she's going to want to stay here for a while. She's settled. More than she is at home.'

'Huh?' Max looked astonished. 'Ah no. Nathalie is a real LA kid. She'll be home well before medical school starts.'

'We'll see,' Amber said calmly.

A message had come through from Clara asking if they still wanted to have dinner, so a couple of hours later they met for a late one-plate meal.

As soon as Max excused himself to go to the bathroom, Clara winked at Amber and smiled.

'All OK, dear?' she asked.

'Yes,' Amber said, looking shifty. 'Did Max talk to you earlier on?'

'Yes, only briefly. But I knew,' Clara admitted. 'We know our own children. You understand that. It's a mother thing.'

'Yes, it is,' Amber agreed.

When Max returned, Nathalie said she had an announcement to make.

'I'm gonna stay here with Oma for a bit.'

'You are?' Amber said, raising one eyebrow and looking smugly at her husband.

Max stared at Nathalie. 'Did you talk to your mother behind my back?' He wasn't saying it crossly, just suspiciously.

'No, why?' Nathalie said, biting her lip nervously.

'Your mom guessed,' Max said.

'Of course she did,' Clara tutted. 'I've told you, Max. Mothers always know.'

He nodded and looked slightly bewildered.

'So?' Nathalie was on the edge of her seat. 'What do you guys think? Can I stay for a while? I'll defer my place at college.'

'You do whatever makes you happy,' Max said.

'Really?' Nathalie screeched. 'Wow, thanks, Dad. I thought you'd totally freak out and give me a massive lecture about becoming a doctor like you!'

'Nathalie,' he said, looking suddenly serious, 'I only want you to become a doctor if that's what you truly want. And as for being like me? I think I'd rather become more like you. Stay the way you are, darling girl.'

Nathalie stood and held her arms out to Max. They hugged for the longest time. After a while, Amber stood and joined in.

'I agree with Dad,' she said into Nathalie's hair. 'You just carry on being you, honey.'

'Group hug,' Nathalie said, lunging her head back to look at Clara. 'Come on, Oma!'

Before they had time to sit down again, Ava's throaty laugh interrupted them from behind.

'Is this a private party, or can two strays join in?'

'Ava!' Clara said, releasing herself from Nathalie's arms. She stopped dead when she recognised the man beside her. 'Well look who's here,' she said, smiling. 'Hello, Sean. It's good to see you, dear.'

'Hi, Mrs C,' he said sheepishly. He turned to Max. 'Sorry I didn't warn you I was coming. It's all been a bit of a whirlwind.'

'That's cool, buddy. Ava gave me the heads-up on the quiet! Seeing as you've interrupted our group hug, which is all the rage in this hotel, you may as well join in!'

To any of the other diners in the restaurant that night, it seemed like a perfectly fun and jovial scene. But all six of the people involved knew that what was taking place was of monumental importance.

The past had finally been laid to rest. As a result, the future would be wide open for all of them to embrace together.

Chapter 34

AS AMBER STIRRED IN HIS ARMS, MAX SIGHED happily.

'I hope you're hungry,' he said as she opened her eyes. 'If I know Mama, she's been up since dawn baking.' It was their last day in Ireland, and Clara had invited them all over for breakfast.

'It's fine for Nathalie. She has the build of a greyhound, not to mention a metabolism that runs at a rate of knots. But I'm going to turn into a blob if I stay here much longer!'

'Would you mind if I went on ahead?' Max asked. 'I'd love to have a few moments on my own with Mama.'

'Of course. I'll go shower and wash my hair and I'll follow in a while.'

Max dressed swiftly and made his way to Clara's. Sure enough, she was in the kitchen putting the fresh muffins and pancakes she'd made on a plate.

'Hello, dear,' she said calmly.

'I wanted to spend some quality time with you. Amber is on her way.'

'How lovely,' she said, leading the way to the dining room. 'Coffee?'

Max nodded, and watched in delight as she went through a routine he'd been so familiar with once upon a time. She took her tiny saucepan and filled it with milk. Whisking non-stop, she brought it to a quivering heat. Meanwhile, the cafetière she'd filled with ground beans was drawing.

'That smells awesome,' said Max.

'Awesome.' Clara smiled. 'Nathalie sounds just like you when she says that word.'

Reaching for two mugs, she poured the coffee and topped it with the heated milk. Then without another word she opened the oven and removed two freshly baked pains au chocolat, arranged them in a pretty basket lined with a floral linen napkin and handed it to Max.

That first sip of coffee along with the flaky, buttery pastry made his eyes roll.

'It's been a long time since I've tasted anything this good first thing in the morning,' he said.

'What would you have on an ordinary day? I need a little picture of you in my head. I've done nothing but wonder for so many years now.'

'Coffee from a paper mug,' he said.

'With nothing to eat?'

'No.' He shrugged. 'I'm usually at the hospital trying to get my head around the patient list.'

'All the more reason to eat something,' she said. 'I couldn't live without my home-made food. There are many awful things we cannot control in this life, but thankfully I've never been in a position where I can't afford decent ingredients.'

'I can afford them, I just don't bother,' Max said.

Clara pondered. 'Your *Oma* would be terribly cross if she heard you say that.'

'I know,' he said quietly, looking ashamed. 'She had little or no food for so long. It's a travesty to ignore nourishment, I guess.'

Clara nodded.

'Gus's funeral was terribly sad,' she said, quite out of the blue. 'Though he managed to get some people into the church who'd vowed they'd never go there again,' she chuckled. 'Lots of our friends have turned away from organised religion since the dreadful stories of abuse emerged. But Gus wanted to be buried beside his parents, so it meant rolling with the Catholic Church.'

'I'm so very sorry I wasn't there,' Max said, taking her hands.

'So am I, dear,' she said. 'He never gave up hope that you'd come home some day. He told me a short time before he passed away that he would do his best to guide you back to me. I believed him.' She looked up at Max with shiny eyes. 'You know, I held on to that promise and tucked it away in a pocket of my heart and nurtured it. I knew that if I believed it strongly enough, my wish would eventually come true.'

Max blinked. He wanted to say about a million things, but nothing came out.

'I'm sorry I didn't tell you about Jacob and Alina and Frank,' he managed eventually.

'I know you are,' she smiled. 'I'm a lucky person. Alina was an angel on earth. I can safely say I had two mamas growing up. Some children are neglected and treated with disdain. I had two couples who loved me totally.'

'Anyone listening to that last sentence would be forgiven for thinking your life was a bed of roses,' Max said.

'I've had a good life, lovey,' she said. 'Parts of it were tough, but I've been blessed with people who've filled my heart.' She pondered for a spell, lost in her own thoughts. 'You know, it actually makes sense that poor Jacob was schizophrenic. He had an intensity that I've never seen in anyone else. I was so wrong to spend the night with him.' She gazed at Max. 'But I firmly believe things happen for a reason. If Jacob and I had never come together, you wouldn't exist. That would be the biggest tragedy of all.'

'Even though I've caused untold trouble?'

'We all make mistakes, Max. But thank goodness we have enough time to mend the broken parts of our lives.'

'Mama, do you forgive me for holding out on you?'

'Yes, *Liebling*, I do,' she sighed. 'Do you forgive me for hiding your biological father's identity?'

He nodded and wrapped his arms around her.

'Hey, I hate to break up the party,' Nathalie said, bursting through the door. 'But what kind of time do you call this?' She tapped her watch. 'It's like totally crack of dawn!'

'Good morning, Nathalie,' Max said. 'Nice hair! Did you spin on your head during your sleep?'

Nathalie grinned. 'You're just used to seeing me looking perfect,' she teased. 'I could smell the chocolate and had to come see.'

Mumbling through a mouthful of pain au chocolat, Nathalie scolded her father that he still hadn't added his patch to her quilt. Max held his hands up in defeat and walked to the sewing room to complete his task.

'Watch this,' Clara said. 'He'll sew as accurately as the machine, but he'll do it by hand.'

'Dad!' Nathalie said as he finished. 'I can't believe your work. If you ever get bored with sewing people, you could go into quilting!'

'I'd say he makes far more money sewing people,' Clara said with a wicked grin.

Amber arrived next and was duly ushered into the sewing room.

'Do your work first and then you can eat,' Nathalie said bossily. 'Time is running out. I know the way conversations go in this house. We'll get into some crazy story from the past and it'll be time for you guys to leave.'

'Wow!' Amber breathed. 'I've never seen anything like it. I can't believe you gals made this.'

'Isn't it beautiful?' Nathalie said. Her smile faded as she realised that Mackenzie would never see it. Reading her mind, Clara hugged her.

'Mackenzie *can* see it. I know she can.'

'Thanks, Oma.'

'Hello?' Ava's voice came from the hallway. 'Where are you all?'

'In here,' Clara said. 'Nathalie is being very bossy. You've to do your patch and then you're allowed to have breakfast.'

'I've done mine,' Ava said, pulling something from her pocket. 'I just need to attach it now.' She crouched over the quilt and sewed it in place. 'Ta-dah!' she said with delight.

'No way!' Nathalie screamed. Ava had sewn a Chanel label to her black lacy patch.

'This officially means you've designed a one-off Chanel piece, sweetie!'

'I love it!' Nathalie said, jiggling up and down laughing. 'Where's Uncle Sean?' she asked suddenly. 'Don't tell me you've gotten rid of him already?'

'Nah,' Ava said nonchalantly. 'He's gone back to the States to pick up his stuff.'

'What do you mean?' Max asked, appearing with a mug of coffee from the kitchen.

'We've talked so much over the last couple of days,' Ava said. 'We've wasted too much time and we're not kids any more. He's coming home and we're going to give it a go together.'

They all hugged her, but it was Clara who noticed the ring on Ava's finger.

'Are you two engaged again?' she asked incredulously.

'Please don't tell me I'm being ridiculous, Mama,' Ava begged. 'I know this all seems unbelievably rushed, but I love him. I've never stopped loving him and I know it's right.'

'Hey,' Clara said. 'Who am I to tell anyone who to love? If you feel it in here,' she patted her heart, 'then I wish you the very best.'

'Can I be bridesmaid?' Nathalie said.

'I'll fully expect it,' Ava said, hugging her. 'Will you two come home for the wedding?' she asked Max and Amber.

'Of course,' Amber said instantly. 'Besides, we'll want to see our daughter, so it'll be a pleasure.'

Once Max and Amber had departed for the airport and Nathalie had gone with Ava to start her apprenticeship at the shop, Clara sat at her desk to write.

She hadn't the energy to walk to Gus's grave today. So she'd tell him her news in a way that had worked in her family for generations.

My darling Gus

Now that Nathalie has moved in, my days have become so much brighter. Our house is no longer quiet and lonesome. I still keep waiting for you to walk through the door, though. You are all that is missing now.

I still put on my lipstick and dress as if you were with me, Gus. I believe that if God wanted us to look plain, he would never have invented Coco Chanel.

I always knew there would be a right time to tell my story. For so many years I held my silence. I didn't think the details were required. In fact I knew they would've caused irreparable damage. Even though you knew it all, we never discussed it. Should we have been more open? Should we have harboured so much inside? Did it do us any service in the end? I'm not so sure now.

When Max left and refused to have anything to do with us, it shook me to the core. I questioned my previously certain mind. You kept reminding me that he was entitled to be angry, and that he would return in his own good time. You were so certain that time would heal all the wounds. You were adamant that we should respect Max's wishes and that some day he would be ready to forgive and forget.

As your health faded, I wanted to jump on a plane and find him. But I knew it wasn't what you wanted. I hoped with all my heart that a miracle would send him back, so he could say goodbye to the only man he'd ever called Dad.

After you left this world, I wavered for the first time. I felt disillusioned and utterly bewildered. I didn't think I had the energy to carry on.

You and I know that the cancer diagnosis prompted me to write to Nathalie. Of course I didn't tell her I was ill. I didn't want to put pressure on her to visit because she felt sorry for me.

I believe we are all put on this earth with a job to do. For some it's to be a mother or father, a teacher or entrepreneur. I know I was meant to come to Ireland and leave a legacy of fresh minds and souls in my wake. As I sit here and ponder, I can see that I've also sent positivity to America.

I am inexplicably proud of our children, Gus. Ava is stoic and belligerently strong, with a twist of creativity to soften her edges. I am certain she and Sean will be happy now. I could lament the fact that they have wasted so many years by being apart. But this isn't the first time two sweethearts have been reunited after a long absence, and I doubt it will be the last.

Max is a gentleman and a scholar. His wife is a dear and wonderful lady. She is sugar and spice and all things nice, with a little bit of steel thrown in for good measure. They are a wonderful couple and perfectly balanced.

And as for Nathalie . . . Well, using her own word, she is simply awesome.

I suppose it was a feat in itself that I arrived on this earth at all. Ju-Ju and Hannah's love should never have grown. From the very moment I was conceived, all the rules were broken. So that is how I know I was sent for a reason.

For the longest time I believed I had broken Alina and Frank's hearts. But age and new knowledge have afforded me hindsight. I was a child and my departure from their lives needed to happen. I belonged with my birth parents. They paid dearly for the right to bring me to Ireland.

Finally knowing that Alina and Frank didn't hate me or blame me for Jacob's demise has lifted a shadow from my soul. They showered me with love during the years we shared, but the greatest gift they ever bestowed upon me was the ability to forgive.

I have a close connection with my angels and they have whispered to me that Nathalie is a heart and soul mender. That is her purpose on earth.

Amber mentioned at one point that she and Max longed for more children. I didn't want to sound facetious so I simply nodded in apparent understanding. But inside I know the reason why they only ever had Nathalie. It's because she was all they required. She has enough energy, light and love to fill their hearts.

I'm certain she has many minders in the spirit world. People who watch over her and guide her. When my time comes, I will join that parade.

I'm getting tired now, Gus. As autumn draws in and the pinks, mauves and yellows of my garden begin to shrivel, I know how they feel. I am at one with nature at last. The niggling voices have stopped. I no longer feel as if I have one last job to do.

The Secrets We Share

My housekeeping is done, Gus.

Perhaps my subconscious ear has heard a little whisper as my angels from above begin to beckon me to them. I have a palpable sense that Mother Nature has begun the countdown to my eternal rest.

When I saw them six months ago, the doctors urged me to have chemotherapy. They said there was an outside chance that the medicine could prolong my life.

But I'm not willing to put myself or my family through the gruelling journey the medics have described. If I were young, with my life ahead of me, I'd be the first to don my armour and fight the good fight. But I'm certain there is a time for each of us to die. My time is nigh.

I'm not sad and I'm not afraid. Why would I be? I know that Ju-Ju and Mama, Alina, Frank, Jacob, Angelina and you, my darling Gus, are waiting.

We'll have coffee and chocolate cake and sit at close quarters, watching over the people we love. It will be like viewing a wonderful movie with the ability to blow a little magic into their days from time to time. I'll never leave my family. I'll mind them and guard them and if there's any way of nudging them in the right direction, I'll happily do that too.

I'm now a pill popper. I take so many tablets I'm surprised I don't rattle when I walk! Apparently there's a multitude of tumours on my liver. The oncologist told me he's astonished at how well I've endured the pain so far.

I tried to explain that physical pain is nothing compared to the pain imparted by the anguish of longing for people who make your heart sing. Joy can override physical pain too. I know because that's what Nathalie, Max and Amber have done for me. Holding a person you love in your arms after years of yearning is an indescribable balm.

I know Nathalie will tell my story to others. In fact she told me a little secret only the other day. She wants to write a book. She begged me to give her permission to write my story. I think it's a wonderful idea. Not because I want to become immortal or anything like that. But because I believe that the story of the little Jewish housemaid and the handsome son of an Austrian cavalry officer finding love in the most unthinkable circumstances will stand the test of time. Love knows no boundaries, Gus. No matter what obstacles stand in the way, hearts that are destined to be together will always unite in the end.

My head feels heavy now. I need to rest. I'm ready to curl up with my quilt and trace my gnarled fingers across the pretty little edelweiss flowers depicted there. I can see so many wonderful memories rushing past my vision. I can smell the polish of the Leibnitz home . . . breathe the air of the Brixental mountains . . . hear Jacob's childish laughter . . . taste our first kiss, Gus . . . I can hear the sound of our firstborn child's cries . . . see the smiles of my family united in my garden . . .

A force is drawing me near to you, my Liebling. The old images are fading. New ones are becoming clear. I feel your arms are open wide. So many smiles are welcoming me in. It's time for a new beginning. It's time for new gifts. I am ready to receive them.

I know I was right to finally reveal the secrets we once shared.

It's time for us to be reunited.

I love you.

Clara x

Acknowledgements

This book was inspired by my Austrian grandmother's story. Her name was Melanie Fuchs but to me she was Oma, the German for grandmother.

On the day of my twenty-first birthday, Oma asked me to visit her. Upon arrival she told me my gift was not one I could unwrap. It was something far more precious – her story. She told me things she had never told anyone else before.

While *The Secrets We Share* doesn't exactly mirror my *Oma*'s story, what she told me that day sparked an idea in my head and many years later inspired this novel. For people who knew and loved Melanie Fuchs, this is not her actual story but my fictional interpretation of the events she outlined to me all those years ago. I want to be clear when I say that I have used poetic licence and changed *many* of the personality traits and events of my *Oma*'s real life while writing this book.

For the record and, without wanting to spoil the plot, the storyline involving Jacob in the later years is completely fictional. So too is Clara's marriage as it appears in this book. What I can assure you is that the basic love story between a powerful man and a Jewish girl was true. The notion of forbidden love surviving in a war-torn place where Hitler and the Nazis promoted relentless hatred has always fascinated me. I am a sucker for an old-fashioned romance and a story where love conquers all.

In a modern world where technology seems to develop at a faster pace with every passing year, sometimes it's comforting to know that matters of the heart always have and always will prevail. Thankfully my *Oma* never went to a concentration camp. But I came to know an incredible, courageous and wonderful man by the name of Tomi Reichental while writing this story. Tomi is a long-standing friend and business associate of my father's. He is also one of the remaining survivors of Bergen-Belsen concentration camp. For over fifty-five years Tomi held his silence. Nobody had any idea that he had been incarcerated during World War Two. Now, he shares his story openly and frankly so that nobody ever forgets what happened during the Holocaust. Tomi has given me his blessing to incorporate part of his journey in this book, in my own words. I cannot thank him enough for the courage, hope and inspiration he has bestowed upon me during our chats together. Tomi, you are a remarkable, serene and astonishingly brave man.

I hope I have captured some of the emotion I absorbed from both Oma and Tomi and that my novel meets with their approval. Long before I ever even dreamed I would become an author I asked Oma's permission to write my own version of her story. She threw her head back and laughed, wondering who on earth would have any interest in her journey. When I pushed her for permission she jokingly agreed I could write it after she was gone. She left this world on New Year's Day in 2009. I believe the time is now right to share my version of Oma's gift.

If you are familiar with my writing you will know that I carry a cancer gene. The gene I carry is called BrCa 1 and the specific mutation I have is called the Ashkenazi Jewish Gene. As I wrote this book, I felt the emotion as if it were emanating from a long-forgotten chamber of my soul. Each and every word of this book came from my heart.

As always I have so many incredible people to thank for helping me along the way. My agent and confidante Sheila Crowley and her able assistant Becky Ritchie of Curtis Brown UK run my affairs like clockwork. Thank you both for always being there. I am applauding and blowing kisses to my remarkable and gorgeous editor Sherise Hobbs. She began editing this book while still on maternity leave before seamlessly slipping back into work and carrying on like a true Mama swan. I cannot imagine how you've juggled a toddler, new baba and the workload you fly through. Thank you for your kindness, enthusiasm and gentle encouragement. Thanks also to Mari Evans who is always in the shadows keeping an eye on me. I appreciate that so much. To Fran Gough and all the wonderful team at Headline UK, thank you kindly too.

It's my first time working with Jane Selley and all I can say is that you have made the copyedit seamless! Thank you so much for all your hard work.

To all the Hachette Ireland gang – Breda, Jim, Joanna, Bernard, Siobhan and my book-signing buddy Ruth – thank you for helping me fly the home flag. Thank you to Susie Cronin for all your hard work and help with publicity. Congratulations to Ciara Doorley on the birth of her darling daughter Elsie.

My husband Cian along with my children Sacha and Kim are my world. Thank you all for making our house a noisy and often crazy home. To my furry pets Tom the cat and Herbie the dog – meow and woof. You two are always happy to see me and treat me like a long lost lover.

Thanks to Mum and Dad who continue to support me and keep me sane. I couldn't do what I do without you both.

Congratulations to my darling cousin Robyn on her marriage

to Joe Copage. Joe, we're delighted you're now officially Uncle Joe even though we've all called you that since the first day we met you! Thanks to my in-laws and extended family especially my wide circle of cousins for being fabulous.

To my friends, you all know who you are, thank you for listening, laughing and looking out for me. I am the luckiest girl to have so many special people in my life.

Thanks to Mark Bourke at Slap Bang Wallop for doing my website.

Thanks to Amy Stephenson for bidding and paying money towards cancer research to have her name used as a character in this novel.

For those who follow my story, I am happily through cancer treatment for the ninth time. I am still having three-weekly chemotherapy sessions but it's all good. The message is clear – cancer is becoming more treatable all the time. If you have just been diagnosed, please have hope.

Lastly, please allow me to roll out the red carpet, open a case of champagne and herd in the stilt walkers and fire-eaters in celebration of my dear and loyal readers. Your continued letters, messages and emails make me smile like a goon. I sincerely hope you enjoy *The Secrets We Share*. If you would like to get in touch you'll find me on Twitter @MsEmmaHannigan, Facebook at /AuthorEmmaHannigan or via my website www.emmahannigan. com. For now, I hope that you are being showered in positivity and that your world is filled with sparkles and smiles. Thank you for reading my books. You are all fantastic!

Love and light

Emma x

Emma Hannigan

The Secrets We Share

A Recipe to Share . . .

This is a really old-fashioned lemon cake, that Oma used to make. It's delicious with strong coffee or lemon tea. I've heard it keeps well in a tin for a few days, but it's never lasted long enough in our house to find that out for sure!

Lemon Curd Sandwich Cake

Ingredients

For the cake
225g butter
225g caster sugar
4 eggs
225g self-raising flour
Grated zest of 1 lemon
Juice of ½ lemon

For the glacé icing on top
275g icing sugar
Juice of ½ lemon

For the lemon curd filling
Grated zest and juice of 6 lemons
225g butter
275g caster sugar
10 eggs

Method

Preheat the oven to 170°/gas mark 3.
Grease and line a 23cm tin with baking paper.

Cream the butter and sugar until pale and fluffy.
Add the eggs and flour alternatively until combined.
Add the lemon zest and juice.
Bake for an hour or until a skewer comes out cleanly.
Remove from the tin and leave to cool on a wire rack.

To make the icing simply put all the ingredients in a bowl and beat until smooth. An electric whisk makes this so much easier.

To make the curd put the caster sugar, lemon juice and zest and the butter into a glass bowl over simmering water. Once the butter has melted beat in the eggs. Leave to thicken (this can take 40 minutes) but don't forget to stir the mixture occasionally. Once the mixture is thick enough to coat the back of a spoon it's done. Remove from the heat and put in a Kilner jar. It'll keep for about ten days in the fridge if you don't use it all at once.

Cut the cooled cake into three discs. Sandwich back together with the cooled lemon curd. Finally, ice the top and sides with the lemon icing.

Enjoy!

Memories to Share . . .

As a very small child, I always had a quilt on my bed. It was made lovingly by Mum, using pieces of memorable fabrics along with scraps that were left over from other projects. It wasn't until I was a lot older that I truly appreciated the thought and effort that went into those labours of love, because that's what home-made quilts really are.

In fact, I look back with slight regret at how much I wanted to get rid of my quilt and replace it with something that 'matched' my room. Mum was always philosophical when I flexed my teenage muscles like that and allowed me to redesign my own décor. I can't believe I removed my patchwork quilt in place of a gaudy, cheap mass-produced throw! But I suppose 'that old thing' wasn't cool at the time. Oh, the shame of it!

Many old-fashioned crafts are making a massive comeback today and I think it's a wonderful thing. There are lots of crafters online now offering to make memory quilts, especially for people who have lost a loved one. What a wonderful way of remembering someone, by keeping them close to your heart at night.

As I wrote *The Secrets We Share* quilting seemed to work its way through the story organically. It wasn't a conscious effort on my part. So I guess in a way I have created my own quilt in a slightly different manner.

How to Make a Memory Quilt

What you will need

Old baby clothes or some items of clothing from a
  loved one
Scraps of various coloured fabric
Scissors
Sewing machine
Ruler

Method

Measure the squares (4 ½ inches) using the ruler. Cut
them out remembering to use parts of the clothes that
have interesting patterns included e.g. embroidery or
ribbon details.

Iron a small fold around each patch on the reverse side.
This gives you the seam.

Pin the squares together into a row. 12 rows of 18
patches makes a nice size.

Sew the pinned patches together.

Attach the rows together to form the front of the quilt.

Cut a layer of padding to fit the entire quilt and attach it to the reverse side of the fabric. Trim any excess padding.

Attach the backing and finish off by edging the whole way around with bias tape.

While the directions here are obviously very basic, it should give you an idea of what's involved. There are some wonderful step-by-step methods online.

I would love to see any quilts that my readers may have created. You can find me on Facebook at /AuthorEmmaHannigan or on Twitter @MsEmmaHannigan. Do send me a picture when you've finished. I would truly love to see your work.

My Favourite Things

Favourite place to grab a coffee with a friend?
It would have to be somewhere buzzy like a Butlers café because their coffee is very strong and they give a free chocolate! What's not to love?

Favourite beauty tip?
Wear sun block on your face all the time. I use a tinted moisturiser with factor 45 built in for my face and Tan Organic tanning oil on my body. There's nothing more harmful or damaging for the skin than sun (sadly!).

Favourite holiday destination?
At home it's Connemara on the rugged west coast of Ireland. If I'm going abroad as long as I don't have to cook and my children are happy, I'm happy!

Favourite piece of advice you've been given?
'Be yourself; everyone else has already been taken' Oscar Wilde (and reiterated by my parents!)

Favourite novel of all time?
Me Before You by Jojo Moyes. It made me laugh and cry and I

still remember the characters even though it's years since I read it.

Favourite item of clothing?
I'm a shopaholic and I have far too many clothes but I love them all! If I had to choose one thing it would probably be my wedding dress. The last time I tried it on, I was eight months pregnant with my son. I cried because it didn't fit. I'm blaming the hormones!

Favourite quote from literature?
'I am not afraid of storms, for I am learning how to sail my ship' Louisa May Alcott, *Little Women*.

Favourite age so far?
With every passing year I feel more comfortable in my own skin. I'm also incredibly grateful to still be alive, nine cancer diagnoses later. So I'll go with the present rather than the past! I also hope to add many more digits to my age . . .

Favourite inspirational person?
Katie Taylor – World, European and Olympic champion boxer. She has paved a way for her sport and broken records and boundaries. Her spirit, faith and determination are awesome. I think she's an incredible role model for all, especially women. She had a dream and put her heart and soul into making it come true.

Favourite way to spend a Sunday afternoon?
Shopping. I know that's utterly shameful and I should say going for a lovely walk (which I do enjoy too), but looking at fashion never bores me! If I'm tired or I've had a tough week, I also

adore baking. There's nothing quite like the aroma of freshly baked cakes or bread. It also makes people (even my teenaged children) gravitate toward me. It's a good way of coaxing them into being in the same room as me!

Read on for an extract of Emma Hannigan's latest glorious novel, *The Heart of Winter* . . .

Huntersbrook House

PIPPA SHOT THROUGH the main gate of her childhood home, Huntersbrook. Almost instantly she passed the gate lodge to her right. The two-bed bungalow with its painted wooden-framed windows and immaculate hanging baskets reminded her of the cottage from *Hansel and Gretel*, minus the cauldron witch and cruelty, of course. It blended in so well, she found it hard to remember it hadn't always been there. Grandma had built it a few years ago as her own oasis, away from the hustle and bustle of the main house. Sadly, she'd passed away before she could really make it her own. Still, Pippa mused, as it had transpired it was a good thing. Her parents Holly and Paddy had taken up residence there a couple of years ago and seemed to have found it quite easy to mould it into their permanent home.

It was still weird to Pippa that none of them actually lived in Huntersbrook House any longer. The stunning Georgian residence had been in the Craig family for generations. But the downturn in the economy had forced them to rethink things. Rather than letting it go, they'd come together as a family to save it.

As she zoomed up the drive she remembered her mother's finger-wagging the last time she'd come home. 'Do you absolutely *have* to drive that fast, Pippa? What difference will it make to your journey from the gate to the front door? Seconds? You need to slow down, my girl. Just look at the wonderful scenery that's on offer if you choose to glide down the driveway toward the house.'

Pippa grinned triumphantly as she glanced back at the dust cloud she'd created. She knew she was being a bit of a brat, but she'd always had a problem with doing as she was told. Her mother was right about one thing though, Huntersbrook and the surrounding land was pretty spectacular. After the muggy, traffic-jammed chaos of Dublin city, this really was like a slice of heaven on Earth. Not many houses boasted such an expanse of unspoilt land, bereft of freshly constructed housing estates or even purpose-built shopping centres. The rolling fields as far as the eye could see were a joy.

Grinding to a halt at the back of the main house, Pippa jumped out of her car and stood onto the side, leaning on the door. Craning her neck, she tried to squint across to the right and into next door. Her sister, Lainey, had married Matt from next door and was now living in the farmhouse with her baby son, Ely, and father-in-law, Jacob. Their houses were very much separate, but close enough for Lainey to feel as if she hadn't really left home. That was one of the many differences between the sisters. Pippa would get on a plane, train or jet-ski at the drop of a hat if she thought it would lead to an adventure of any kind. While Lainey had always been a home-bird and was perfectly content living a stone's throw from Huntersbrook.

As she walked in the side door to the kitchen Pippa was greeted by a happy screech from Ely.

'Hello baby nephew!' she said scooping him into her arms. 'Hi Lainey,' she said rushing to kiss her sister on the cheek. 'I thought you might still be across the path in your lair.'

'Joey said to be here for ten,' she said. 'It's almost ten fifteen now. I've made scones and the coffee and tea are waiting for boiling water.'

'Organised to within an inch of your life as usual,' Pippa teased. 'Where are Mum and Dad? I didn't notice any sign of life at the gate lodge just now.'

'Might that have been because you careered by at a thousand miles an hour?' Lainey asked.

'Who, me? Drive too fast? Nah,' she said. 'Have you seen them this morning?'

'Last I spotted, Mum was wrestling with an apple tree she bought. Dad is pottering in a shed, I'm guessing. Do you know what Joey's up to?'

'Not a breeze,' Pippa said, picking a tasty sugary bit from a scone.

'Hey, get away,' Lainey said slapping her hand. 'I'm putting them in a basket and we'll all sit and have them nicely once Joey arrives. I can't bear the way you pick like that.'

'I get it from Mum,' Pippa said shrugging her shoulders. She put a wriggling Ely down so he could continue playing with his wooden bricks on the kitchen floor.

'That's not a good thing,' Lainey said crossly. 'It's so rude to pick food like that. Besides, remember the saying Grandma used to recite? "Little pickers wear big knickers",' said Lainey smugly.

'Well my knickers haven't changed size since I was sixteen,' Pippa said slapping her own backside.

'Don't I know it,' Lainey sighed. She looked down at her own figure. Instead of losing the post-baby weight after Ely's birth last year, she'd kind of filled in around her saggy tummy. Even though her mother and Pippa shared that annoying picking habit, neither of them ever put on weight. She, on the other hand, seemed to put on half a stone by even being in the same room as a calorie.

'I wish I had your metabolism,' Lainey said wistfully. 'I try so hard. I'm good for a week and then I seem to lose the run of myself and eat my way back to square one.'

'Don't be too hard on yourself,' Pippa said. 'You grew a person inside you. That has to have a totally nasty effect on your body, right?'

Lainey stopped short and stared at her sister. With her dark sleek ponytail trailing down her slender back and her stick thin legs in her painted-on-tight jeggings, she could easily pass as a model.

'We can't all look like you,' Lainey snapped.

Pippa threw her head back and whistled before bursting out

laughing. 'Touchy touchy! Jaysus, someone got out the wrong side of the bed this morning. How about I go into the pantry and pull a black sack over my head and sit in the corner rustling?'

In spite of herself, Lainey's scowl turned into a grin. 'Shut up, Pip,' she said swatting her arm playfully. 'I suppose I'm a bit over-sensitive. Mum didn't help by telling me yesterday that I look "good and solid".'

Sadie, who'd been their housekeeper for over forty years, came through to the kitchen from the hallway.

'Ah now Lainey,' she said gently. 'I couldn't help overhearing you just now. Your mum didn't mean any harm with that remark. I was there. She was trying to say that you're toning up with all that walking you've been doing.'

Lainey sighed. It was typical that everyone would take Holly's side. Nobody seemed to recognise that she treated *her* differently from the others. She'd never dare make a remark like that about Pippa. Even if she did, Pippa would probably drop-kick her, Lainey mused. Maybe that was what she needed. To be more forceful with her mother. Maybe then she'd treat her with a little more respect and a little less disregard.

'Your mother loves the bones of you three,' Sadie continued. 'Even though you girls and Joey are grown-ups now, she still sees you as her babies.'

'Huh,' Lainey said unable to let the comment slide. 'When I was a baby she handed me over to Grandma. She was too delicate to cope with me and yet now she expects me to be unfathomably capable in everything I do.'

'Your mother would walk over hot coals for each one of you,' Sadie said firmly. 'I remember the time you had chicken pox, Lainey. You weren't more than four or five. You had the worst dose I've ever seen. You scratched and cried and your mother stayed awake for four nights on the trot bathing you in bread soda baths.'

Lainey busied herself with setting the table. Not for the first time, she felt Sadie had a rose-tinted image of what had gone on during her childhood. Lainey and Holly had been like sandpaper rubbing off one another from as far back as she could remember. No matter what Sadie or anyone else recalled, Lainey knew the truth. Holly had been there physically while Lainey was small, but mentally she'd been in a dark and clouded place where nobody, least of all her daughter, could reach her.

The sound of a car pulling up on the gravel outside made Lainey sigh with relief. She was uncomfortable with this conversation and didn't want to get into anything negative with darling Sadie.

'Here's Joey,' Pippa confirmed. 'This better be good. I don't appreciate being hauled out of bed at the crack of dawn at the weekend.'

'It's half ten, Pippa!' Sadie said with a giggle. 'Although knowing you it was dawn before that pretty little head of yours hit the pillow.'

Joey arrived in looking very smug.

'What's happening?' Pippa asked, attempting to grab the A4 envelope he was carrying.

'Ah-ah, all in good time,' he said slapping her hand away. 'Mum and Dad are on the way. They're having a healthy discussion about an apple tree,' he said. 'They're getting battier by the minute, you know?'

'We know,' Pippa said. 'They were never exactly "normal" but the passing of time is certainly taking them to a whole new level of insanity,' she grinned.

'I'm getting out of here before I swat one of you with a tea towel,' Sadie said. 'Anyone would think this place is flanked by dotty geriatrics. I'd challenge any of you to a game of Scrabble and beat you. My mind is as sharp as a razor and your parents are babies in comparison to me. So be careful who you're labelling as past it.'

Sadie disappeared, tutting and muttering about the youth of today.

Lainey laughed. 'That'll tell you, Pippa. Jeez, I have to hand it to Sadie, there are no flies on her!'

'Quick one before the folks arrive,' Joey interjected, glancing back to make sure there was no sign of them. 'I need a bit of girly advice here.'

'Ooh excellent,' Pippa said leaning in.

'Turns out I'm ninety-nine per cent sure I'm about to be promoted at work.'

'Hey that's amazing, Joey,' Lainey said rubbing his arm. 'Good for you.'

'Yeah, thanks. I'm stoked. But it's kind of a bit awkward. It's going to mean a fair bit of social stuff. Skye isn't really wired for sound when it comes to fancy-schmancy outings. Would you two be a little bit mindful of her over the next while?'

'In what way?' Lainey asked.

'Well, help her out with stuff to wear and all that kind of malarkey.'

'I'll do that,' Pippa said instantly. 'Oh I'd love to give her a makeover. I tried a few times when we shared the flat, but she never seemed that interested.'

'Hold up a second,' Lainey said looking concerned. 'Skye is beautiful just the way she is. She's admittedly quite bohemian in style, but that's part of who she is. I'm not sure she'd be too happy with either of us barging in and telling her what to look like.'

'No, and I don't expect you to do that,' Joey said attempting to backtrack. 'It's just that our social calendar is going to fill up quite a bit and these corporate do's are a different kettle of fish from what she might be used to. Just keep an eye, that's all I ask.'

'Sure,' Pippa said looking as if it was a perfectly reasonable request. Lainey wasn't so sure. She was probably overthinking things as usual, but she couldn't help feeling slightly protective of Skye.

'Joey,' she ventured, 'Mum and Dad are about to walk in, but being the elder lemon here, don't forget the reason you fell in love with Skye to start with. You love her because she's different. Am I right?'

'Yeah. Sure,' he said. 'Forget I said anything. It was literally just a thought and I only suggested it so she wouldn't feel ill at ease. Maybe I'm on the wrong page. I'm only a man after all,' he said bumping her shoulder and smiling.

Holly and Paddy arrived in amidst hugs and kisses. By the time they were all seated at the table with a cuppa and a fresh warm scone, they were all begging Joey to put them out of their misery and tell them why he had called them all to a family meeting.

'It's really good news,' he announced. 'We've been granted a commercial licence! We're good to go as far as the authorities are concerned. Huntersbrook House, the venue, can officially open!'

Joey raised his coffee cup high in the air. 'A toast to Huntersbrook House and her bright future.'

'To Huntersbrook,' they all chimed, grinning widely at each other.

Lainey smiled as she clinked cups with each of her family members. None of the gripes and cribs really mattered once they could all pull together when necessary. She glanced over at Pippa and Holly. Her mother had her arm around her sister and was kissing the side of her head affectionately as she smiled in delight. Lainey adored Pippa, but she couldn't help noticing that her mother had never been that affectionate with her. As if to bridge that painful gap, she scooped Ely from his high chair and spun him around in the air, making him giggle loudly.

'Whee!' she said. 'Huntersbrook is going to be a destination to be reckoned with, baby boy!'

They all clapped as Ely joined in, bashing his chubby hands together, lapping up the good humour.

**Don't miss *The Heart of Winter*,
coming in paperback October 2015.**

*What makes a house a home?
And what happens when your home must
become a house again?*

Holly Craig's family have lived happily in Huntersbrook for
generations but when times grow hard, even she must admit
defeat and sell off their once-successful stables.

The three Craig children, Lainey, Joey and Pippa, find
themselves locked in a fight to keep their beloved
Huntersbrook; dare they transform it into one of Ireland's
most sought after countryside venues?

Renovation work is well underway when life rears its ugly
head and everything stops in its tracks. The Craig family is
forced to reassess what matters and although they no longer
live at Huntersbrook, can the house work its magic even so . . .
and lead them into the light once more?

(2)

Uncover the secrets of Caracove in Emma Hannigan's enchanting novel.

A little magic is about to come to sleepy Caracove Bay . . .

Lexie and her husband Sam have spent years lovingly restoring No. 3 Cashel Square to its former glory. So imagine Lexie's delight when a stranger knocks on the door, asking to see the house she was born in over sixty years ago.

Kathleen is visiting from America, longing to see her childhood home . . . and longing for distraction from the grief of losing her husband.

And as Lexie and Sam battle over whether or not to have a baby and Kathleen struggles with her loss, the two women realise their unexpected friendship will touch them in ways neither could have imagined.

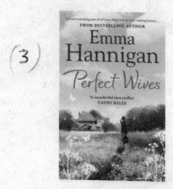

(3)

A heartwarming novel of love, friendship and coming home from this bestselling author . . .

When actress Jodi Ludlum returns to the Dublin village of Bakers Valley to raise her young son, she's determined to shield him from the media glare that follows her in LA. But coming home means leaving her husband behind – and waking old ghosts.

Francine Hennessy was born and raised in Bakers Valley. To all appearances, she is the model wife, mother, home-maker and career woman. But, behind closed doors, Francine's life is crumbling around her.

As Jodi struggles to conceal her secrets and Francine faces some shocking news, the two become unlikely confidantes. Suddenly having the perfect life seems less important than finding friendship, and the perfect place to belong . . .

A delightful, irresistibly romantic e-short featuring much-loved characters from Emma Hannigan's novels *The Summer Guest* and *Driving Home for Christmas*.

Tess can't quite believe her luck – she's marrying Marco, the man of her dreams, in an exquisite traditional Italian wedding, surrounded by her adoring family.

But when an ex puts in an unexpected appearance in Rome, Tess is instantly taken back to glorious Huntersbrook House and the warmth and joy of the Craig family. Memories she thought she had long buried and left behind in Ireland suddenly resurface at the worst possible moment.

Forced to face both her past and future on the evening of the rehearsal dinner, Tess is thrown into turmoil. Which man – and moment – will win out?

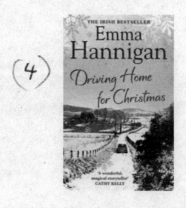

(4)

**The perfect magical read from
Emma Hannigan . . .**

Christmas at Huntersbrook House has always been a family tradition – log fires, long walks through the snowy fields and evenings spent in the local pub. And this year the three grown-up Craig children are looking forward to the holidays more than ever. Pippa to escape her partying lifestyle and mounting debts in Dublin; Joey the demands of his gorgeous girlfriend who seems intent on coming between him and his family; and Lainey to forget about her controlling ex and his recent engagement to another woman.

But with the family livery yard in financial trouble, this Christmas could be the Craig family's last at Huntersbrook as they face the prospect of selling the ancestral house.

As the holiday season gets underway, the family need to come up with a way to save their home, and face the problems they've been running away from in Dublin. And what better place to figure things out than around the fire at Huntersbrook House?